The Hawk Laird

Celtic Hearts, Book 1

Susan King

ARE YOU SIGNED UP FOR DRAGONBLADE'S BLOG?

You'll get the latest news and information on exclusive giveaways, exclusive excerpts, coming releases, sales, free books, cover reveals and more.

Check out our complete list of authors, too!

No spam, no junk. That's a promise!

Sign Up Here

www.dragonbladepublishing.com

Dearest Reader;

Thank you for your support of a small press. At Dragonblade Publishing, we strive to bring you the highest quality Historical Romance from some of the best authors in the business. Without your support, there is no 'us', so we sincerely hope you adore these stories and find some new favorite authors along the way.

Happy Reading!

CEO, Dragonblade Publishing

Additional Dragonblade books by
Author Susan King

Celtic Hearts Series
The Hawk Laird (Book 1)
The Falcon Laird (Book 2)

For Josh, the first one out of the nest

Acknowledgements

To George Bittroff, for sharing his knowledge of falconry, and for inviting me to watch him work with Sammy, his beautiful goshawk.

To Julie Booth, now and always, for support and some late hours, and to the Jachowskis for leading me to the hawks.

To Mary Furgol, Ph.D., Scottish historian, and Ed Furgol, Ph.D., for help in sorting through some historical complexities and conundrums.

And to my cousin, Jolie Chamberlain, who bravely stayed with three boys so my husband and I could go to Scotland and explore one of the most wonderful places on earth.

"Though her jesses were my dear heart-strings,
I'd whistle her off and let her down the wind
To prey at fortune."

—Shakespeare, *Othello*

Preface

Every book is a learning curve for its writer. This novel has had more than one arc, and I have learned a lot in the process. *The Hawk Laird* is a new edition of one of my earlier books, *Laird of the Wind,* an award-winning, *USAToday* best-selling Scottish historical romance. To freshen it up for Dragonblade, I sat down to read through, pen in hand (I love erasable pens in pretty colors!)—and realized that I am a better writer now, twenty-plus years and twenty-plus books later, than I was then. When I started, I enthusiastically loved words, visual descriptions, tons of interior thought, and angst; I also relished digging in the weeds of whatever was going on with my characters. I've gained experience, wisdom—and restraint—since then.

Since the book needed trimming but the story and characters were strong, I have tightened the language and pacing throughout for a more accessible read. If you first discovered *Laird of the Wind* in its original Penguin/NAL edition, I think you will enjoy revisiting the characters and story in this freshly minted version. If you are new to *The Hawk Laird*—I hope you enjoy it!

As a historical fiction writer and a postgraduate historian, I care about historical detail, accuracy, and creating a sense of authenticity. I try not to overload a story with that stuff, though, leaning toward the value and virtue of authenticity in fiction. Years ago, my research for this book led me to a local falconer training a goshawk—and also to Scotland, where I learned some unique historical facts that I wove into the story. You can read more about the historical aspects in the Author's Note at the end of the book.

Among my books, this tale of a forest outlaw, a prophetess,

and a badly behaved goshawk holds a special place in my heart for many reasons. This story of freedom, forgiveness, and love reaches beyond the romantic, and I am grateful I had the chance to edit and improve it.

I love this story even more now. I hope you do too.

Prologue

Scotland, the Lowlands
February 1305

A FLASH OF light, then darkness as the vision began. Isobel, through closed eyes, saw a man emerge from the shadows. Tall, wide-shouldered, cloaked like a pilgrim, he moved with the easy grace of a warrior. On his gloved fist, he supported a hawk. Mist whirled, and he was gone. She frowned at the haunting image; she did not know the man.

"Isobel?" Her father's voice was hushed. John Seton's only child, the heiress to his castle at Aberlady, waited silently for another vision to appear. "Tell me what you see."

She shook her head. Had she opened her eyes, she would not have seen the bowl on the table and the gleaming water surface that sparked visions for her. Nor would she have seen the stone walls of the chamber, the fire in the hearth, or the three men watching her intently. She was blind.

The prophetic visions usually took her earthly sight for a little while, hours or a day, sometimes more. She relied on sheer faith for her sight to return. So far, it had.

More images formed, faces and scenes, and the words came. "Treachery. Murder."

The men whispered to each other—her father, her priest, her betrothed. "What sort of treachery, Isobel?" her father asked.

"What do you see, Isobel?" Sir Ralph Leslie—her father's choice for her husband, and her father's friend—had a pleasant voice. He moved heavily, short but powerfully built. She could hear the hawk that he had brought with him chirring on a perch in a corner of the room.

"Stay back, Ralph," John Seton murmured. "Let Father Hugh and I question her. And keep your hawk quiet. That bird has a poor temper."

Isobel listened, eyes closed. She had been betrothed to Leslie at Whitsunday; this was the first time Sir Ralph had witnessed her speaking prophecy. She vaguely realized he was not sure how to behave during the session. Truly, she had not wanted him present—had wanted the betrothal even less—but her father and the priest had decided, as they often did, for her.

Her eyes rolled under closed lids as she let her own thoughts go and focused on the rapid images crossing the dark field of her inner vision. "I see an eagle flying over Scottish hills," she said. "Hawks pursue the eagle," she continued. Her visions often blended real and symbolic, and a sudden understanding came to her.

"The eagle represents a man," she said. "And the hawks are men—hawk of the tower, hawk of the forest, and others. English and Scots both, come to take the eagle, that man, in treachery. He is a leader they fear and would stop." She heard a hawk call out— *kee, kee, kee-eer*—in the vision.

"Gray goshawk on a gloved fist," she described. "Its master led other men here. Hawk of the tower, hawk of the forest. The eagle is trapped in the dark of night. He struggles, though strong in body and heart."

She watched as a huge man resisted while others dragged him away. "They accuse him of crimes. They will kill him. Sacrifice. Murder. They take him away." She saw the man hauled off on horseback. "An arrow. Hawk of the forest loses a white feather. He flees into the greenwood."

"What of the eagle?" her father asked.

Isobel sucked in a breath against images of cruelty. "His great heart is torn from his breast." She gasped against the disturbing vision. "The English lion claims triumph. The hawk betrayed the eagle, though they were friends. The hawk vanishes into the forest."

"The English lion—King Edward," Father Hugh murmured, his quill scratching over parchment. "Who are the eagle, the hawk of the tower, the hawk of the forest?"

She did not know. She felt sad, a terrible sense of betrayal. The strong, brave man—the eagle—would die before autumn.

And suddenly she knew who he was. *Dear Lord,* she thought, *let me warn him. For once, let me help, not just foretell. Let me remember. Please let me remember this one.*

Usually she forgot her visions, and her father and the priest did not often tell her all that she said. They told her not to worry, they would take care of everything. But she wanted to know what she prophesied. She had begun to foretell events as a young girl, and it had frightened her so that her father had become protective of her. But now she was a woman and no longer content to let others have control over her visions.

A few years ago, the priest had talked of her predictions, and word had spread in the parish and beyond. He then wrote to the exiled king of Scotland, John Balliol, and to the men who acted as the Guardians of the Realm of Scotland. The English had heard of her prophecies, too.

Her father and the priest told her she could help the cause of Scotland, and she was glad of that. The visions, and the price she paid for them, seemed worthwhile if the Scots benefitted.

"Isobel, who is the eagle, the man taken?" Father Hugh brought her back to the moment.

"The rebel leader William Wallace." She felt sure of it. "The English king will butcher the freedom fighter to appease his anger," she continued. "He will call it righteous justice. Wallace is an eagle among hawks, and he will be betrayed by a hawk."

She heard Sir Ralph murmur to her father. "Go on, Isobel,"

John Seton urged.

Eyes closed, she saw a lovely scene, a goshawk flying above a dense forest. "Hawk of the forest. He is laird of the wind. Laird of hawks. Laird of freedom," she said spontaneously. She loved the bird's freedom in the vision.

"Who is he?" her father and the priest asked together.

"He has no home, lives in the forest, flies free." She saw the hawk soar, then frowned at what came to her next. "Others hunt him. He flees for his life." She twisted her fingers together. "He betrayed. Not willing—now he is betrayed. Oh, treachery!" She gasped in anguish.

"Who betrayed whom?" Father Hugh asked. "Tell us what you know."

She fought tears. The visions did not often pull her into their vortex like this. She felt grief and loneliness as the images flickered in her mind. Mist, and the man in the cloak again, holding a hawk on his gloved fist.

"I see a pilgrim," she said. "He has a penance of the heart. He longs for peace. He is the laird of the wind. Laird of hawks. Hawk of the forest."

"But who is he?" This from Leslie. "Lady Isobel, make sense. This is nonsense," he said aside to the others.

The man in the cloak was tall and strong. He stood alone in the rain, gloved hand supporting a gray hawk. Under the shadow of his hood was a handsome face. Somber. Firm features, sad blue eyes. She felt his sadness and pain, felt bitterness, even rage within him. How could she know the heart of this stranger so well? She wanted to soothe him. Help him.

He strode through the rain to a hawthorn tree. The bird fluttered to a branch. "A secret," she said. "A hawthorn tree. A hawk," she said.

"What is she blathering about?" Sir Ralph demanded.

"Keep quiet," her father growled to the knight.

"She often speaks in symbol and metaphor," Father Hugh said. "I will study her words later. Look, she sees more. Isobel, what is it?"

She was silent. For the first time, she saw herself in a vision.

A woman glided through mist toward the hawthorn tree. She was tall, slender, wearing a blue gown, black hair streaming like midnight down her back. Stunned, Isobel watched herself move toward the man in the cloak. He turned, beckoned to her. But she stopped.

She yearned to go to him. The desire was overwhelming, yet something equally strong held her back. Then the scene faded and she saw stone walls in sunshine. Her home, Aberlady Castle. Arrows whined over the battlements. Men shouted. She smelled smoke and felt cold and hungry. She was shivering. An arrow struck her—

"Siege," she whispered. *"Siege!"*

The vision disappeared. *Dear Lord, let me remember the man, the hawk...the siege.*

When she opened her eyes, she was blind. Her father handed her a cup of wine, easing its cool metal shape into her fingers.

August 3, 1305

HE RAN SILENTLY through the moonlit forest. Breath, step, pounding heart blended with the sound of the wind. Onward, never slowing, he slipped between the trees, leaping easily through the bracken with his long-legged, swift stride. Pray God he was not too late.

He ran until his breaths heaved in his chest and the air burned his throat until his legs ached, but he would not stop. Finally, a light gleamed through the trees. He saw blazing yellow torch-light, a house—then horses and armored men. He heard shouts.

They had reached the house before him.

He stopped behind an oak, heart slamming, tunic damp with sweat. Men in chain mail, some on horseback, on foot, filled the moonlit yard. Twenty—no, thirty, he decided.

A dead man lay on the ground. Someone kicked the body

aside. Others brought forward a horse, its rider bound and gagged: a giant of a man. Blood streamed from a head wound. A guard struck the man again.

Silent and stealthy, the watcher in the forest pulled out the bow slung behind his back and strung it. Quickly nocking an arrow from the quiver at his belt, he aimed. The guard, about to strike the captured man again, fell from his saddle, an arrow in his chest. The archer released a second arrow. Another soldier went down like a felled oak.

Men now shouted, wheeled, drew swords, loaded crossbows. Watching from his place behind the tree, the renegade archer saw the prisoner turn and look toward the trees, nodding as if he knew his ally and was grateful for the attempt to help him.

The renegade saw something pale and small flutter to the ground, dropped by the prisoner, unseen by anyone else. Later the archer meant to fetch that thing. For now, he was busy. A quarrel from a crossbow slammed into a tree trunk. He slipped forward, closer, and loosed another shaft, hit his target.

Three guards less, now; nock, draw, aim, release. Four less. Still too many to take alone. But he had several arrows left, and each one would count for a life before the night was done. Even so, without a horse or men at his back, he had little hope of saving his friend, taken in treachery.

A treachery he had aided. The knowledge cut like a razor. He drew the bowstring again.

Five on the ground now, silent. The other men mounted and led the prisoner hastily out of the yard. Bolts from their crossbows hammered into the trees as they rode away, but none of them caught the unseen archer in the night.

That one lunged forward like a wildcat and ran, bow gripped in his fist. The horses were English-bred, powerful beasts, and soon pulled far ahead of the runner.

He paused, drew, sighted, let loose another arrow and another, and yet more. He shot so fast that he did not think about his aim. Each bolt was an extension of his will and his rage. Each one found its mark.

He ran forward again. The horses were nearly out of range now. He climbed a slope rapidly to overlook the earthen road. Eyes narrowed, even in the moonlight, he saw—with the pristine clarity of vision that had helped to earn him the name of the Hawk Laird—the glimmer of armor ahead in the moonlight. Barely within range they were, now.

He had two arrows left. The distance would lessen his accuracy, but he aimed, drew back, letting one fly. The bolt hit one of the men, but he rode on with the others.

These men would escort their captive to a trial, and a horrible death. The archer was sure of that. His friend was a leader and a rebel who had driven the English king to mad obsession. Neither justice nor mercy would be shown.

One arrow left. He nocked, drew, sighted. And lowered the bow.

For one fervent moment, he wanted to take his friend's life with a sure, swift arrow before the English could do it with torture and humiliation. He raised the bow again, eyes steady, jaw locked. His heart sank within him like a stone, and he shot.

The arrow fell short.

Chapter One

September, 1305

RAIN PATTERED ON stone as the pilgrim mounted the low steps to the abbey church. He pulled open the oak door and stepped inside. Shafts of light, silvered by rain, pierced the dimness in the vaulted nave. Plainsong drifted toward him, chanted by monks in the choir space past the altar.

Danger shadowed him like a demon, even here. He could not linger, but he paused, closed his eyes. Peace enveloped him like mist veiled the hills. But serenity, for him, was fleeting. He was glad for the simple blessing of shelter from the rain. The forest was his home now, and he was not as accustomed to enclosing walls or stone underfoot as he used to be.

He drew his cloak closer over his wide shoulders and dipped his fingers in holy water, crossing himself with a swift, practiced gesture. Cautiously he moved along the right aisle through shadows toward the nave. He was hunted daily now by English and Scots alike, but the summons of a friend brought him here to Dunfermline Abbey, out of the sanctuary of the forest. If he was discovered, his capture—or his escape—would disturb the hard-won peace of the abbey.

Last year, the English king had stayed here, summoning Scots nobles to pay him submission, and dispensing what he called justice. As he departed, King Edward had ordered the place burned, even though his sister was buried beneath the abbey stones. The blackened ruins of the refectory and dormitory were a stone's throw from the church, which had survived.

He genuflected by the altar and moved past. In several years as a fugitive, he had never submitted to King Edward, unlike most Scottish nobles by now. He had taken a pledge of freedom for himself and Scotland.

Months ago, he had been wounded in battle, captured with two of his cousins, and thrown in an English dungeon. One cousin had died beside him and the other—a young woman—had been taken away. And still, James had refused to promise fealty to King Edward.

What he had promised, ultimately, had been far worse.

As he walked, his tall warrior's build and gait naturally attracted glances, but he bowed his head and moved on. The scallop shell and brass saint's badge pinned to his cloak identified him as a penitent man. Dunfermline Abbey was a frequent stop along the pilgrimage route, so the disguise served him well.

He looked about for the one he was to meet after vespers. A few worshippers knelt or sat on benches, absorbed in prayer. The smell of incense lingered, and plainsong swelled in the church. He knew the melody—a kyrie he had sung countless times in what seemed another life.

Now his soul had rough edges. He had changed much.

He entered the chapel of Saint Margaret at the east end of the church and moved toward the massive carved marble tomb of the long-ago Scottish queen. Kneeling in candlelight beside the plinth, he lit a new candle in homage to Margaret, a holy friend to pilgrims and those in need. He folded his hands and waited.

Footsteps, then a monk wearing the black robe of the Benedictine order entered the chapel and knelt beside him. The monk whispered a prayer, then glanced at James. He had a tonsure, brown hair, and a long and familiar face.

"Brother, I have traveled far on a poor day, and hope for good news," James said.

"And I wish I had that for you, Jamie."

James glanced sharply at his friend, heart sinking. "He is dead?"

"Wallace is gone," the monk whispered.

James nodded, steeling himself against grief and anger.

"William Wallace was taken by foul treachery, Christ have mercy on his soul." The Benedictine shook his head. "We heard just days ago. Captured by treachery, brought to trial in London, found guilty of treason…and executed."

"Treason! He never declared fealty to King Edward," James murmured. "He was not an English subject. He was condemned on false grounds."

"Aye. They accused him of deeds he never committed—well, some he did, but naught to merit his fate. He was dragged to the gallows and hung until he scarcely lived. They took him down and—" Blair stopped. "I cannot say the rest, not here in this holy place."

"Tell me," James growled.

Blair murmured low, detailing cruelty and courage, while James listened in silence. His blood surged with sorrow and rage. A single arrow could have saved his friend untold suffering, had he only had the courage to—he clenched his hands, felt his spirit harden within him as if the last tender feeling turned to stone.

"Martyr," John was saying. "His death will spark the Scottish cause, just when King Edward thought to extinguish the flame forever."

"True. John, join us again in the Ettrick Forest."

"An outlaw's life does not suit me now. I came here for peace, and to write an account of a great man's life. The truth of Wallace's deeds must be known. You belong in the forest, James, not I. You left our holy order years ago to join a cause you believed in. You were knighted on a bloody Scottish field, while I remained behind and took priestly vows."

"Yet we both ended up forest rogues. We need your weapon hand and your good sense once again. There are only a few who support me now. You must have heard the rumors."

"I know that you are hunted. I know Wallace was betrayed by Scotsmen—the lord of Menteith, for one. I hear he fled into England to be rewarded by Edward."

"Another rumor is that Wallace was betrayed by Sir James Lindsay of Wildshaw."

"Jesu," he muttered. "That I had not heard."

"So those who once gave me their support now turn their backs on me."

"You would never betray Will."

For a moment James wanted to confess what he had done while in English captivity, and the tragic result. But he could not say it aloud. Not yet.

"I mean to find the man who arranged Wallace's capture," was all he said.

"Menteith?"

"He is one of them. I seek another. Sir Ralph Leslie. He caused the death of one of my cousins and has my cousin Janet in his keeping. He commands a garrisoned castle. I cannot get to him, or free her, with just a few men."

"Once there were fifty and more following your command."

"Most have lost faith in me."

"I have faith in your purpose, but true, you need more men for the task. Where is Leslie?"

"King Edward made him constable of Wildshaw Castle. My home."

"So you do have a quarrel with the man."

"Aye," James ground out. "He has my castle and my cousin. If I cannot get the castle—yet—I mean to trade for Janet, at least."

"What does he want so badly that he might agree?"

"The prophetess of Aberlady," James said.

"You have her?" John asked in surprise. "Black Isobel of Aberlady?"

"I mean to get her," James answered smoothly.

"The English king will be furious if she is harmed. He values her."

"I will not harm her, just take her. Edward hates me already. I do not fear him."

"He wants her brought to him so that she can divine for the English."

"Exactly. A valuable hostage. She predicts good tidings for the English, and bad fortune for the Scots. And she set a noose round my neck with her pretty tunes. But Leslie would trade Janet for this so-called prophetess."

"Why would he want her?"

"She is his betrothed."

"This is a risky scheme, even foolhardy. Let your head rule, not your anger, Jamie."

"I am a pilgrim and I seek wisdom from the prophetess of Aberlady. I doubt she speaks the truth since she is paid for her words by the English, or so they say."

John Blair frowned. "Sir John Seton, baron of Aberlady, is a rebel knight in English custody now, I believe. Be careful. There could be English guards with her."

"I simply require her counsel," James drawled. "And I want a hostage."

"If you keep her half so well as the hawks you train, she will be safe."

"Once trained. Most are gone. I have no castle or mews to keep them. But I have learned from hawking that patience achieves goals."

"Honor and revenge are at cross purposes in you just now, I fear."

James stood. "Black Isobel condemned me along with Wallace with her rantings about hawks and eagles. She is a Scotswoman, but her false prophecies favor the English."

"Jamie, what if she is a true seeress?"

"Then she had better divine what I need to know. Farewell, John."

He left the chapel, pulling his hood up against the rain, walking quickly away from the abbey. The prophetess had caused him much trouble with that cursed hawk prediction, which many had heard of by now. He would like the truth behind that—but the damage was done.

Passing the hawthorn tree near the cemetery, he paused. Wallace's mother's remains lay beneath that tree; he remembered the morning that he and John Blair and Wallace had buried her there in a private, unmarked grave. Will had wanted it that way, had asked James to keep the secret forever, or the English might disturb her rest.

It was the least he could do for a friend. And he owed him far more.

He took a footpath down into the greenwood below the abbey hill, and within moments, ran into the forest.

Chapter Two

THE SANDSTONE WALLS of Aberlady Castle glowed in the sunset as Isobel Seton climbed the steps to the battlement. She walked resolutely, head high and proud, her gaze trained on the crenelated wall ahead. Reaching up, she pulled off her white silk veil and undid her black braid, still walking forward steadily. But beneath her gray gown and surcoat, her knees trembled.

Hunger weakened her, she told herself firmly. Not fear. She would not show that. Every day at set of sun through ten weeks of besiegement, she had come up here to show the English that she was still here, still defiant.

The breeze lifted her hair as she went toward the crenellations above the foregate. She looked down through an embrasure. Sunset light poured over the incline that led up to the castle: a rocky slope pitted with ditches. Below, a hundred English soldiers gathered near cookfires and tents near wooden palisades set up for protection. Their weapons would be close at hand, she knew, although the day's fighting had quieted.

Her father's men—hers now, she reminded herself, for Sir John Seton had been captured by the English months ago— watched from positions along the wall walk. Eleven Scotsmen remained of Aberlady's garrison; sixty had manned the battlements ten weeks past.

She glanced behind her. The bailey, with its massive stone keep in the center, was deserted, its thatched-roof outbuildings empty of workers, supplies, and animals. They had let the horses go during the one truce day they had been allowed. A few of the hawks had been released; the rest had been eaten by now.

And one corner of the bailey had become a graveyard for those who had died from injury, illness, or starvation. Soon they might all be buried in that bleak corner.

Her men nodded as she passed, their bows held ready. They did not object to their mistress walking the battlements, knowing she was safe from the English camped below. The Southron enemies did not dare harm Black Isobel, the prophetess of Aberlady. Her value protected her. Now and then, the English would shout up to her that King Edward wanted her brought to him, whole and unharmed.

The English king approved of Black Isobel's predictions of the defeat of the Scots at Falkirk, the recent fall of Stirling Castle to the English, and the capture and execution of the freedom fighter William Wallace. King Edward was eager to hear the Scottish prophetess foretell more triumphs for the English. He wanted her to do that in his presence.

She had tried to prevent Wallace's death by sending a warning, so the news of his execution had made her feel ill. She had stood on the battlements and listened as the siege commander had shouted that she would be well rewarded for helping the English king.

But she had wrapped her note of refusal around an arrow shaft. One of her men had delivered by shooting it quite accurately into the commander's thigh while he sat his horse. After that, the siege had tightened. The English had brought in engines to batter the outer gate, and their archers had sent flaming arrows over the walls of Aberlady.

Now a cool breeze stirred past as she stood on the high battlement, spreading her hair like a glossy black banner. She welcomed the effect, raising her chin, standing proud. In the encampment below, English soldiers gazed up at her, while others practiced with weapons or packed the ditches leading to the castle gates with rubble and branches. A few men repaired the wooden framework of one of the two siege engines used to batter the thick walls.

The delicious smell of meats roasting over English cookfires made her stomach rumble miserably. Chain mail glimmered in the sunset as the English ate and talked and settled for the night. In the morning they would begin another battle, she knew. But Aberlady's few defenders were weak from hunger and could not withstand another onslaught.

Isobel looked around. The castle rested upon a high dark crag with cliffs on three sides, set on a vast moor, the place was said to be impenetrable, unbreachable. But they were not impervious to starvation.

Isobel sighed, her fingers on gritty sandstone. She had been born here, and she might die here. But not so soon, please God, not so soon.

"Come away from the wall, Isobel." Sir Eustace Gibson, knight and castle baillie, stepped out of the shadows, stretching out his hand toward her.

"Stay back," she warned. "They will shoot if they see you."

He smiled grimly. "They have tried, and I am still here. Come inside the keep." He guided her toward the steps, and Isobel heard the familiar whine and thwack of an arrow bolt hitting the outer wall where they had stood moments earlier.

Isobel turned back, determined, returning to the wall walk. She pulled her white silk veil from inside her sleeve and leaned deep into the embrasure opening. With an exaggerated motion, she wiped at the fresh scar on the outer stone wall, shook the stone dust from the cloth, and stood back. The breeze caught the black length of her hair again.

Cheers and shouts rose from the English troops. Isobel lifted her head regally and turned to descend the steps. Eustace smiled.

"Och, Sir John would be proud to see such wit in his daughter!"

"My father would not have surrendered, and neither shall I."

She walked down the steps calmly, but inside she trembled. The wit might be there, but she had learned to hide her fear.

"Eustace, last night I dreamed that we walked out of here into freedom."

"Is that a prophecy?"

"Just a hope." She looked up at the sky, where the sunset faded into indigo. The dream was not prophetic. The blinding burden of prophecy had not come over her, nor had that come over her for a long while. Yet a small, strange shiver rippled through her.

She frowned, sensing a compelling new presence somewhere nearby. Fatigue was overtaking her, she told herself. She set a hand to the wall and paused.

"There is soup left," Eustace said. "Come eat."

"I will." She had eaten little for three days; the thin soup of barley had to feed all of them. When the last of the grain was gone, they would face an enemy stronger than any. She could already feel the effects of starvation in lingering dizziness and a dull headache.

"Isobel." Eustace sounded grim. "You must give the final order to surrender."

"My father would not want that."

"He would not want us to die."

She glanced at him. Eustace Gibson had been part of Aberlady's garrison since Isobel had been a small girl. She had come to rely on his skills and his steadfast nature. She sighed.

"Sir Ralph will be here soon—before the siege, he went to find my father. He will return soon with Sir John." She heard the brittle note of doubt in her voice.

"We will not see that one soon," Eustace muttered. "Surrender, girl. The English will not harm you."

"But they will harm you, and take all of us prisoner as soon as we set foot out of the gate. Aberlady will be made into a Southron stronghold."

Eustace sighed. "We must put the torch to Aberlady as we

leave. Then the Southrons cannot take it."

"Torch Aberlady!" She stared at him.

"Isobel, we cannot stay. We cannot defend this place."

Silent, she stared at the darkening sky, unsure what to say—or what to do.

"Look there!" Eustace grabbed the hilt of his sword. "In the far corner of the yard."

She gasped. A group of men—four or five, she counted hastily—emerged from the shadows beneath the back wall of the enclosure. They walked boldly into the bailey and came toward the steps where Isobel and Eustace stood. On the battlement, the few men of the garrison lifted their bows and held them ready. Eustace lifted a hand to hold their attack.

"Who are they?" Isobel whispered.

Unkempt and wild in appearance, the approaching men wore simple tunics, leather hauberks and cloaks, but carried good broadswords and bows. One man moved ahead and dropped back the hood of his long brown cloak.

He was taller than his companions, shoulders wide, legs long and lean. His clothing was shabby at the edges and his tangled brown hair and beard needed trimming. His features were handsomely shaped despite grime. His strong, agile stride and his very presence seemed to charge the air like lightning.

Then Isobel realized that she had sensed his arrival moments ago.

He gripped his unstrung bow like a staff and halted near where she stood. A broadsword was slung across his back. Nodding to Eustace, he looked at Isobel.

"Are you the prophetess of Aberlady?" His quiet voice had a richness that carried.

"I am Isobel Seton. Who are you? How did you get in here?"

He inclined his head. "We came to rescue you."

She stared. The stranger possessed a wild beauty and an aura of power. His eyes were deep blue, like indigo twilight, his hand on the bow graceful and strong. He seemed beyond the ordinary realm, a man out of the mist and legends of an ancient race.

Isobel felt almost bespelled. His steady gaze held hers, assessed her from the top of her head to the roots of her soul.

In turn, she saw the spark of purpose in his eyes and sensed a current of danger. She pulled in a breath and lifted her chin. "You know my name, but I do not know yours," she said calmly, though raw excitement thundered through her. "How did you get inside our walls?"

"Through the postern gate in the north wall," he said.

"But that small door is hidden by scrub and rocks and overlooks a cliff more than a hundred feet high. How did you reach it?"

He shrugged. "It took some time."

"Who are you?" Eustace asked abruptly.

"James Lindsay," he replied. "Sometimes I am called the Hawk Laird."

"Jesu," Eustace breathed out. "I thought as much."

Isobel gasped. She knew the name—the Hawk Laird was a renegade Scotsman who hid from English and Scots alike in the vast lands of the Ettrick Forest. His arrival inside Aberlady could mean salvation—or defeat. His loyalties were known only to himself.

She had even heard that the Hawk Laird was a sorcerer who changed his form at will; that the man was immortal, born of the fair race, the Fey. And it was also rumored that he had committed some heinous deed against Scotland.

She had mentioned him in one of her prophecies, or at least had said something about hawks and lairds, men and eagles, and such. But she did not recall much of the prediction. Now she wished she knew the whole of it, although Father Hugh had once dismissed it.

"James Lindsay," Eustace said, "I hope your purpose is fairminded. We still outnumber you by a few." He indicated the parapet, where men trained bows on the newcomers.

"Why would you climb up here to rescue us?" Isobel asked.

"I came here on another matter," Lindsay said. "We did not know about the siege until we approached the castle. We bring assistance and some food." He beckoned, and one of his men stepped forward, pulling three limp rabbits from a sack. "I think these may be needed."

"Aye!" Eustace said. Lindsay's young comrade turned to run toward the stone-walled keep that towered over the center of the bailey yard, where the meat could be prepared.

"Did you bring an army ready to attack the English?" Isobel asked then.

"We are but five."

"A hundred English outside, and you bring five men?" She was incredulous.

He frowned. "We will bring you to safety, lady."

"They say the best knights fly with the Hawk Laird," Eustace said.

"'Twas once said." Lindsay shrugged. "We must leave here soon."

"How?" Isobel asked, astonished.

"By the north cliff. After you have eaten and we have more darkness."

"The English will take the castle if we abandon it," she said.

"'Tis Scottish practice to render castles unavailable for Southron use. Either a castle is held by force of arms, or destroyed."

"But—" she began.

James Lindsay brushed past her to climb the steps, and Eustace turned to follow him. Isobel lifted her skirts and ran up the steps behind them both.

Eustace turned. "Go to the keep, Lady Isobel."

"He means to ruin Aberlady!" she hissed.

"This is necessary."

"We cannot trust this man to help us! You know what they say about him now!"

Eustace sighed. "He brings hope, where we had none."

"Aberlady will be destroyed!"

"I would have set fire to these walls myself when we left. It is our chance."

She stared at him, stunned. He hurried away to join Lindsay, who stood behind a merlon stone, scanning the English garrison. Isobel hesitated, then ran after them, pausing by an embrasure in full view of the English soldiers below.

Lindsay grabbed her arm, pulling her behind the merlon. "Are you a dimwit, to stand there?" he asked.

"The English will not harm me," she said with certainty.

"If you believe that, you are not much of a prophetess," he snapped, as he held her fast.

"Watch this," Eustace said to Lindsay. "Each day, the English fill their ditches with bracken to smooth the incline for their siege engines. Each night, we set them afire, see."

Just then, two men on the wall walk lit arrows wrapped in cloth and pine pitch, touching them to a torch. They loosed the flaming arrows to sail toward the lower ditches, setting them ablaze.

Held fast in the iron curve of Lindsay's arm, Isobel watched the fires spark and blossom. She saw Lindsay's men mount the steps and arrange themselves along the battlements.

"When I let go of you," Lindsay murmured in her ear, "I want you to crawl along the wall-walk to that corner tower over there."

"When you let go of me," she said between her teeth, "I will go where I please."

"Do as he says," Eustace pleaded, as he loaded a crossbow. An English arrow whined overhead and slammed into the wallwalk. Two more clattered on stone and fell aside.

Lindsay released her. "Go! Keep down!"

Isobel rose boldly to face the embrasure gap, sure that the English would stop when they saw her there. But an arrow slammed into her upper arm with tremendous force, and she spun with the blow.

Lindsay grabbed her, pulling her down. Isobel curled forward in searing pain, and he supported her with one arm.

"Lady Isobel!" Eustace called. "Dear God, she stood too quick."

"It is not serious." Deftly, Lindsay cracked the long shaft protruding from her arm, leaving the broadhead arrow embedded in the muscle. "Can you bear it for a while?"

She nodded, wincing. Arrows fell around them in a cruel rain, smacking against stone and wood. Within seconds, an arrow whooshed through the crenel and glanced past the back of Lindsay's leather hauberk.

Another broadhead bit hard into her left ankle. The shaft fell aside. Isobel flinched, grabbing her leg. Lindsay pulled her to him roughly, shielding her.

"You will be killed out here," he growled, holding her. As arrows whined and clattered around them, he carried her toward a corner tower, kicked the narrow door open, and brought her inside.

Setting her down on the stone floor of the tiny room, he hunkered down beside her. In the dusky light that came through the arrowslit window, he bent to examine her wound.

Without asking her leave, he lifted the hem of her skirt—she gasped at that—and tore a wide strip of linen from the embroidered hem of her chemise, wadding the cloth around the seeping, throbbing wound in her right arm. Isobel drew the silk veil from inside her sleeve with a shaking hand and pressed it to the bleeding cut above her ankle.

"Arrow wounds are painful," Lindsay said. "I have had several. Wounds like that heal." Then he shook his head. "Foolish to stand up on a battlement like that."

"They will not fire when I am on the wall. They must not have seen me then."

He took the cloth from her to wrap it around her ankle. "Do you have some agreement with them?" He glanced at her sharply.

She sucked in a breath at his implication. "Their king wants me brought to him. That has helped us in this siege. I stood up because I hoped to halt a battle."

"Heroic," he muttered, then rose to his feet to gaze down at her as if that angered him.

"Why are you here?" she asked. "What do you want?"

"I came," he said softly, "to find the prophetess of Aberlady." Something in his tone sent a shiver along her spine. "We have matters between us, you and I."

"I do not know you, though you seem to know me."

He shrugged. "You are widely known. Let me make a prediction, Black Isobel," he said in a low voice. "You will come to know me well. And you will come to regret what you and yours have done to me and mine."

She gasped. "I do not understand."

He turned toward the door. "I will come back to look after your wounds. You will be safe here." He stepped through the doorway into a clatter of falling arrows.

Staring after him, Isobel wondered just how safe she was.

— ◆···• •···◆ —

Chapter Three

"T HOSE SOUTHRONS ARE overfond of fire arrows," Henry said, as another burning shaft traced an arc overhead, smacking into the wall walk. He glanced at James.

"Aye. Let them fire the castle—we will not have to bother." He nocked an arrow and drew back the string. The point found its mark over a hundred yards away, for he saw an English archer clutch his shoulder and fall to the ground.

"That," James announced grimly, "is for the lass."

"This morn you were not so fond of her."

"I did not know she was besieged, or starving—or quite so young." James drew another arrow from the quiver at his belt and set it to the bow.

"Or so lovely, hey." Henry grinned.

James released the arrow. "She needs our help, regardless."

"True. Hah! Look there! I'll wager that soldier would like to know he was just caught in the leg by the Hawk Laird!"

"I am sure he would," James drawled, and shot again.

The full moon rose quickly in the indigo sky, and English fire arrows flew like a host of comets. James shot steadily, one arrow after another, and beside him, Henry Rose did the same. Beyond them, James saw Aberlady's garrison, and his men—Quentin Fraser, Patrick Boyd, and Geordie Shaw—raining a steady volley of arrows down on English heads.

Henry looked around then. "Sir Eustace, is it?" he asked the man who approached.

"Aye, baillie and captain of Aberlady Castle."

"I am Sir Henry Rose." Henry held out a hand.

Eustace put a hand to his sword hilt. "That's a Southron name," he growled. "And you use a longbow with Southron skill."

"I'm English," Henry said. "Would you have me use a short bow like a Scot? Scotsmen are a sorry lot of archers. But for Jamie here, I'd think none of them had any worth with a bow. With a broadsword, now, 'tis a different matter."

Eustace scowled. "If you be Southron by fealty, then leave this castle the way you came into it, or bid the world farewell."

"Peace, man." James held up a hand. "Henry is Southron by birth and a master of the longbow. But he fights for the Scottish cause."

"My wife is a Scotswoman," Henry said. "Her people are mine now. And I've seen King Edward's chivalry toward the Scots. I'll take no share in that."

Eustace nodded and glanced at James. "Your loyalty is questioned of late."

"So I hear." James returned an even stare.

"Shall I doubt your fealty too?"

"If you like."

Eustace frowned. "We have to trust you for now. So far you have proved helpful. But if you think to lead us into Southron hands by treachery—" He touched his hilt again.

"I mean to help you," James said flatly.

"Judge him by what you know of him yourself, rather than by rumors," Henry said. An English arrow whistled overhead then, and Henry pulled another shaft from his quiver, preparing to shoot.

James looked down. Far below, under the light of torches, a group of men shoved a massive wooden framework into position close to the castle walls.

"That mangonel will be ready for use come dawn," he said.

"'Tis stout enough to damage these walls. They mean to finish you off within a few days."

"You came at our neediest moment," Eustace said. "Lady Isobel welcomes your help, too. But she fears you will destroy her castle."

"I will," James said bluntly. "But we will all be free of here first."

"Climbing down that cliff is a dangerous venture," Eustace said.

"But it offers less risk than giving up to the enemy," Henry Rose pointed out.

"Aye then." Eustace nodded. "You should know that Lady Isobel loves this place dearly."

James looked away. Years ago, the English had burned his castle. He knew the devastation of such a loss and more. In that terrible blaze, he had lost someone precious to him. He had no desire to fire Aberlady. But he had no choice.

"War brings sacrifice," he said harshly. He glanced at Eustace. "When everyone has eaten, and the hour is late, we can make our escape. Go down to the kitchens with the garrison. My men will guard the walls, and I will fetch the lady and bring her to the keep."

Eustace nodded. "We have ropes to help us scale the cliff. What else can we do?"

"Pray to God, sir," James said.

MOONLIGHT SLICED THROUGH the narrow window opening as James opened the tower door. He stepped into the dark, bare little room, leaned his bow and his broadsword against the wall, and crossed the tiny space in two long strides.

Isobel Seton sat on the floor, her head bowed low, her black hair streaming over her shoulders. Blood darkened the sleeve of her gown. She curled forward, clearly suffering.

He dropped to one knee beside her. "How do you fare?"

"Well enough." The words were soft and husky. She looked

at him, her face pale in the moonlight, and he saw the keen burden of pain in her taut features. Sympathy whispered through him, and he touched her left, uninjured arm gently.

"The wounds are painful, I know, but you will recover quickly," he said.

She watched him uncertainly. He noticed that her eyes were wide, large, and extraordinarily beautiful in the moonlight. In sunshine, James thought, they might be pale blue. Now they seemed opalescent, like captured moonlight. When she swept her dark, thick lashes down, a light seemed to extinguish.

"The noise of the arrow volleys has stopped," she said.

"Aye, 'tis nearly full dark."

"They often send random shots at our walls through the night." She drew in a shaky breath. "Were any men hurt?"

"No men," he said. "Just one woman. Let me look at your arm." When he touched her right shoulder, she started and winced. "I am sorry," he murmured.

She frowned, watching him with those great, pale, jewel-like eyes. He slit open the sleeves of her gown and chemise and bared her arm.

When he brushed the silken mass of her hair away, its cool luxury spilled over his hand. The skin of her neck and shoulder was smooth silk beneath his roughened fingertips. A soft, warm scent, womanly and sweet, tinted with roses, drifted up from her. James felt his gut spin and his loins contract impulsively with a swift, intense desire. He focused his thoughts and his gaze on the wound, forcing all else from his concentration.

The broken arrow shaft thrust viciously out of her upper arm. He took the base of the arrow shaft between two fingers and tugged gently. Isobel sucked in a sharp breath and bit her lip to stifle a cry. James murmured a quiet assurance and narrowed his eyes to judge the angle of the arrow.

A few probing touches, another tug on the base of the shaft, told him what he most dreaded: the removal would be difficult, and excruciating for her. He sighed and sat back on his haunches.

"The broadhead is wide and barbed," he told her. "I cannot pull it out without doing grave damage to the muscle." He paused. "I will have to push it through."

She swallowed hard. Her lustrous, stricken gaze tugged at him oddly. "Have you ever done this before?"

"Nay. But I have seen it done, and I have had it done to me. A field surgeon once pushed a barbed arrow through my leg." Even with the benefit of a few drams of _aqua vitae_, the pain had been considerable, he recalled. "We should go down to the kitchen for the task. And we need water and wine—a good deal of the last if you have any left in your stores."

She shook her head. "The wine is gone, but our well water is still clear, if low. We can cleanse the wound, at least."

"Have you herb simples?" he asked. "Willow, or valerian? Is there salt left? A saltwater poultice would be helpful if there is naught else to use."

"After ten weeks of siege, we are fortunate to have water and a few grains of barley left." She touched the back of his hand, her gaze entreating. "Take it out now. Here."

He frowned, puzzled. "'Twill be easier in the kitchen. I will need to cauterize the wound since there are no medicines."

"Can you do it here?" She looked down. "I do not want the others to see. My men think me strong. You will be the only one to see the truth...I do not have the courage for this."

He turned his hand to take her fingers. "You are stronger than you think, I suspect," he murmured. "But so be it. We will do it here if that is what you want." He peeled down her sleeve. She glanced at him while he examined the wound. "'Tis so dark. How can you see?"

"Well enough. I am called after a hawk," he said lightly, "not a mole."

"I do not like darkness much. Can we sit closer to the moon-light?" A tremor in her voice made him glance at her sharply. His fingers, upon her arm, sensed the quiver that ran through her body; he felt a cold, strong stream of fear in her.

"Aye," he said softly, wondering if the daunting prospect of the arrow removal had made her so fretful. He helped her to shift more directly beneath the arrow slit. The moon cast a bright, cool light through the window.

He frowned as he returned his attention to the wound. He would have preferred her to be deep in her cups when he took out the arrow tip, for the thing was wickedly made. The broadhead, which he had felt through her thin flesh, was wider than his thumb and barbed like a double thorn. The removal would not be easy no matter how he did it.

He encircled her arm with his hand and felt tension thrum through her like a plucked harp string. He murmured a few words of reassurance and felt her begin to relax under his touch. She glanced at him, a quick look of innocence and pleading, and closed her eyes, leaning back against the wall.

Touching her, watching her, he felt her courage, fragile but definite. She did not know its existence, but he did. And he saw something more, too: she placed her trust in him. He was humbled by that. So few trusted him now.

Ironic, he thought. He had come to Aberlady to use the prophetess to regain the trust he had lost. Yet all he saw in her eyes was trust; he felt suddenly ashamed of his purpose here.

Isobel gave James a tremulous smile. A feeling flared inside of him, brighter than the moonlight, then faded before he could grasp its enticing warmth.

"Do it," she whispered. "Now, James Lindsay."

He watched her hard, thin collarbones rise and fall with her rapid breaths, and looked at the broken arrow shaft jutting cruelly out of her slender arm. He unlaced the wide leather arrow guard that he wore around his left forearm and handed it to her.

"You might want to bite on that," he said.

She nodded stiffly and slipped the leather piece between her teeth. He angled her torso in preparation for his task. As he moved her, she whimpered and squeezed her eyes shut.

He knelt beside her and took her right arm above the elbow.

With his other hand, he gripped the broken arrow shaft.

"Easy, now, Isobel," he murmured.

Eyes closed, teeth pressed to the folded leather, she waited with gentle, shining courage. He admired her bravery and wondered why she did not see it in herself. She glowed with it, like a flame inside a horn lantern.

He drew a breath and sighted the angle carefully, wary of hitting bone. Then he shoved the arrow through, fast and hard. The bladed iron tip burst through her flesh. Isobel cried out once, a low, guttural sound that ripped through his heart.

Biting his lip, aware that he hurt her dreadfully, James pushed the rest of the broken, bloody shaft through her arm and pulled it free.

The leather piece dropped from her lips and her head sagged forward against his chest. Her head rolled in a drunken sort of agony, her breathing ragged and fierce. But she neither screamed nor swooned.

"Soft, you," he whispered. "Soft, now. 'Tis done. You did well, lass." He touched her head, smoothing his fingers over the silkiness of her hair, and pressed the folded cloth to the fresh wound. She uttered a raw gasp and grew silent.

No matter what else he thought of her, he could not forget the way she had endured the ordeal. He encircled her back with one arm and held the wadded cloth against the wound.

Isobel leaned against him so heavily that he feared she had passed out. She turned her head, reassuring him. Her small, tremulous sob stirred a rush of compassion through him.

He murmured as he held her, soft phrases that he had used while training his hawks, or while loving a woman. He had not uttered such phrases in years, for he had not kept a hawk in a long time—and the last few women he had loved with his body had heard no such tender words from him.

Nearly forgotten, endlessly gentle, the words streamed from his lips. He spoke to Isobel as if he held his beloved, not a woman who had conspired against him. The warm embrace felt like a fit of glove to hand, bringing him comfort even as he gave that to her.

Startled by his reaction, he released her and helped her to sit up.

"Thank you." Her voice was faint and hoarse as she leaned against the wall, eyes closed.

James pressed the cloth to her wound and watched her carefully. Her breathing gradually calmed, and color came back into her lips and cheeks.

Even ravaged by pain and distress, she was elegant and delicate, wrapped in cool light and shadow. Her brows and lashes were black against her pale, creamy skin. The thin moonlight revealed the square shape of her face, wide at cheekbones and jaw, curved at the chin, with a full, gentle mouth. Her face combined strength and fragility in exquisite balance, enhanced by her extraordinary eyes.

Her bare shoulder and throat were thin, revealing the bony grace beneath the skin. The long limbs beneath the drape of her gown, and the well-defined frame of her shoulders and hips, told him that she was a tall, strong woman.

She reminded him, suddenly, of a female goshawk he had captured and trained years ago. Strong-willed, powerful, and beautiful, the bird had remained partly wild, and yet had given him her exclusive loyalty. He had mourned her when she was gone. He frowned; he had not thought of her in a long while.

He tore a second strip of cloth from the first and wrapped it around Isobel's arm, tying it in place. "That should do for now," he said as he pulled the neck of her gown higher. "Let me see your ankle."

She sat forward. "'Tis not so bad," she said. She pulled the skirt of her gown higher to reveal her left foot, bandaged in white silk over her bloodied woolen stocking. Awkwardly, using her left hand, she undid the silk and peeled down the hose, biting her lip to smother a wince.

James took over the task from her and carefully pushed the

stocking past her long, slender ankle, shoving down the collar of her low boot. Just above the outer ankle, an ugly slash marked where a passing arrow had sliced through the skin.

"This was done by a crossbow bolt," he said. "I saw the shot. You were fortunate it did not shatter the bone." As he spoke, he pressed the torn linen against the wound. She drew in a sharp, whistling breath.

James tied the cloth in place and pulled up her hose, tucking the top under the braided silk garter above her knee. Her leg and ankle, he noted, were lean and hard as a lad's, the bones elegantly shaped.

He stood and held out his hands in an offer to lift her. "I'll take you down to the keep now. I will cauterize the wounds, and I want you to eat and rest. You are weak from this ordeal, and you have fasted too long."

"I have not fasted by choice," she grumbled, and refused his hands, rising slowly to her feet, one hand on the wall, swaying when she stood upright. She stepped forward, and her cry of pain tore through James. He growled and swept her up into the cradle of his arms, though she protested hoarsely.

He carried her down the tower steps and out into the bailey and strode across the shadowed yard. A few English-sprung arrows sailed over the wall and whacked into the earth not far from them. James stopped to make sure the way was clear, and glanced up at his men, who stood sentry on the moonlit battlement.

Isobel looked up as he did. "The English shoot at us almost every night," she said. "We ignore the attacks as much as we can since we lack the men to return each shot."

"The siege commander has a relentless sense of duty."

Isobel tipped her head and watched him. "James Lindsay," she said. "Did the English send you here to capture us and bring us out of here into custody?"

He stopped, holding her in his arms, and stared down at her. "I do not take orders from Southrons," he snapped.

"Did Sir Ralph Leslie send you here, then?"

"No one sent me. I came here of my own accord."

"Now why would the so-called Hawk Laird do that?" she asked softly.

"To rescue the prophetess," he said irritably.

Isobel's gaze was wary. "I do not believe you. There is more on your mind than rescue."

He walked on through the bailey without replying. He knew that her trust in him faded as her suspicions grew. Some needy part of him regretted the loss, but he could not blame her.

Apart from the rescue, she should not trust him at all.

When he reached the tower in the center of the bailey, he looked up. Like many castles, the upper level, where the great hall and living quarters would be located, had no direct access; the upper door stood bolted, its stout ladder removed. He went toward the back wall of the keep, where he saw a narrow door hidden in the shadows.

The door swung open. Sir Eustace Gibson motioned them forward. "This way. My lady?" he inquired softly.

"I am fine," she answered.

James followed Eustace through a wide, dark storage chamber. The room was bare except for empty grain sacks, upturned wooden crates, and a pile of sturdy rope. Torchlight illuminated some steps in an alcove.

James crossed the room behind Eustace, aware of the warm, easy pressure of Isobel's weight in his arms. Her hand was soft at his neck, her torso close and curving, her slender legs draped easily over his forearm. When he shifted her for balance, she laid her head lightly upon his shoulder.

He sucked in a breath, wishing she was strong enough to walk. He was too aware of her soft, satiny textures, her flowery scent, her luxurious warmth. She rode like an angel in his arms.

He would have preferred a hell-hag. When he had set out to find the prophetess of Aberlady, he had expected a shrewish, manipulative woman, a perfect mate for Leslie. Instead, he found a gentle, brave girl and her garrison, all in need of help.

But he could not let this sway his original plan. He must hold Isobel Seton hostage long enough to free his cousin, and in the process bring revenge upon Leslie's head.

James claimed to be her champion, but he intended to be her captor. He felt a keen twinge of guilt. However briefly, she had given him her full trust. The sensation had been sweet and refreshing, unlike the heavy, raw taste of revenge.

He set his jaw and hardened his gaze as he followed Eustace up the stairs, holding Isobel in his arms. Guilt be damned. A long while had passed since he had allowed his sins to bother him. He would not begin now.

Chapter Four

THE FAINT RUMBLE that woke her was not the low growl of thunder, as she thought at first, but the sound of men's voices. Isobel opened her eyes, blinked away a fog of sleep, and looked around.

She was alone in the huge, stone-vaulted kitchen, lying on a pallet in a corner near the warm hearth. Voices floated up the stairwell from the storage chamber, and although she could not distinguish the words, she recognized the tones of a few of Aberlady's men.

An hour or two—perhaps more—had surely passed since Isobel had fallen asleep on the pallet of blankets and straw in the corner of the kitchen. The hearth fire blazed at a low fever, but the iron kettle, suspended inside the arched fireplace, was empty. The men had devoured the soup that they had prepared themselves from the barley broth and the rabbit meat.

James Lindsay and Eustace had insisted that Isobel have some as well. The soup strengthened her, although she had no appetite after James had treated her wounds.

She winced sharply at the vivid memory. He had touched the red-hot tip of his dirk to her wounds to burn out the bad humors and seal the flesh. The agony had caused her to black out for a few moments. She had come to awareness with his arms around her, and his soothing voice in her ear.

"Forgive me," he had said softly. She had, silently, for she knew that serious wounds had to be cauterized if no medicines were available.

Now, as she sat awake and alone, his warm embrace seemed like a deeply comforting dream that could not be recaptured.

Moving slowly, she sat up and leaned against the wall, wincing at the ache in her arm and foot. Long strips of linen cloth bound her bent arm securely against her side and waist; her ankle, too, was more firmly bound. James had added the outer bandaging before she had fallen asleep. Now she found that the support lessened the discomfort when she moved.

Looking around, Isobel noticed a yellow flash sail past the window on the other side of the room. Fire arrows, she thought with a heavy sigh. She pushed herself to her knees and stood, her movements stiff and awkward. Biting her lip as her injured foot took the weight of a step, she limped to the window.

As she moved, she felt lightheaded. Likely that was caused by hunger and the strain of her situation, she thought. She breathed slowly, and when she felt steadier, she leaned forward to look out through the open window.

The bailey yard was a vast, dark field, surrounded by the vague moonlit shapes of the high curtain wall and outbuildings. Isobel narrowed her eyes and looked around. In the far corner of the curtain wall, near the postern door that opened on the edge of the cliff, she saw a few men from Aberlady's garrison with one or two of the renegades. The men seemed intently occupied with several ropes, although she could not tell what they did there.

Two more blazing arrows sailed through the night, trailing flames and smoke, and landed in the bare earth of the bailey, quickly burning out. Isobel glanced toward the battlement, but the angle made it difficult to see if the garrison returned the shots. The bailey seemed empty but for smoking arrows.

"My lady? Excuse me, my lady."

Startled, Isobel turned. A young man entered the kitchen from the stairwell and came toward her with long, loping steps. His russet tunic sagged on his thin, gangly frame, and the firelight made a dark halo of his curling, tangled brown hair.

He stopped, his cheeks flushing. "Jamie Lindsay sent me here to see to your welfare, my lady, and if you are ill, I am to fetch him straight away."

"I am fine," she said.

"Then I am to watch you close and wait for his signal." He peered at her. "Are you truly Black Isobel the prophetess?"

"You need not stare so," she said, amused. "I will not vanish in fire and brimstone."

The boy's cheeks, faintly whiskered, blushed deeply. "Pardon, my lady." He cleared his throat as if embarrassed. "I did not mean to offend."

"No pardon needed. What is your name?"

"Geordie Shaw. I'm cousin to the hero Wallace," he added proudly.

"You are with the brigands? How old are you?"

"Fifteen summers," he said. "I've been with Jamie for more than a year. My father was with him too. We ran with him and with Wallace. Da died," he said gruffly, looking down. "Six months ago. 'Twas a braw fight that day. He died well fighting Southrons."

"He must have been a brave man, like his son," she said quietly. "My father was taken in a battle last spring. He's in an English prison still."

Geordie seemed intrigued. "Jamie was in an English dungeon for months. He finally escaped. Will you ransom your Da?"

She shook her head. "We lack the coin for that and have naught to offer in trade. I do not even know where he is held. But a friend has promised to find him," she added. "But for the siege, I would have heard word of my father by now."

"You will find your father." Geordie straightened his bony shoulders proudly. "We have come to rescue you. And I will help you find him, my lady," he added sincerely.

"Thank you, Geordie Shaw. I appreciate it." She frowned. "James Lindsay was in prison?"

"Aye, taken last spring. He escaped just before Wallace was taken." He looked away, and Isobel saw a glaze of tears in his eyes. "You may not have heard about Wallace."

"We heard," she murmured.

"How could you know of it, under siege these weeks?"

"The English took delight in shouting the report to us. Once, they allowed us to declare a truce for a holy day and let our priest come inside to give us communion. Father Hugh told us much news before he left. That was the day he took our horses and animals out with him so the animals would not starve," she said. "And the day we let my father's hawks and falcons fly free. So 'tis true, then," she added. "Wallace is dead."

"Aye," Geordie said hoarsely.

"We heard that the Hawk Laird betrayed Wallace. I hope it is not true," she added.

He shook his head. "Evil rumors. Jamie will not speak of it, but I would never believe it of him. We few stayed with him, but the rest have gone, for he is a hunted man. He came here to seek you out," Geordie said suddenly. "But he did not say why. Will you make a prophecy for him? Can you help him?"

She blinked at his blunt, eager questions. "I do not know." Had Lindsay come to ask a prophecy of her? Perhaps he had questions about whatever she had said of him, but she did not even know what that was and so she could not help him.

"Do you trust him, Lady Isobel?" Geordie asked quietly.

"Trust?" She looked away. "I do not know him," she said carefully. "I cannot say."

"He will save you from this siege," he said confidently. "Then you will place your faith in him just as we have. If only folk would trust him again, all would be well for him."

Isobel sensed that the lad adored this forest rogue, his hero, so much that he was willingly blind to his faults. James Lindsay was said to be a traitor to Wallace and Scotland. If that was true, she feared that Geordie Shaw would be deeply hurt.

"I will try to trust him," she said, gazing out the window.

Isobel had placed her faith utterly in James Lindsay when he had pulled the arrow from her arm. She remembered the warm comfort of his arms afterward, and his soft, deep voice as he soothed her. Exquisite shivers rippled through her at the memory.

Had she known only his compassion instead of ill rumors, she would have trusted him completely. She would have felt safe. Loved, she thought oddly, quickly.

Foolish yearning born of loneliness, she told herself sternly. She was betrothed to a man who had no compassion in his nature. But, she reminded herself, Lindsay had only comforted her because she was in pain. Not because he cared about her, and she must remember that.

She sighed and leaned against the windowsill. "Geordie, those men over there in the corner. What are they doing?"

"Jamie told them to knot the ropes and make ladders and harnesses so that we can go down the cliff side. Jamie says the full moon will give us muckle light to climb down. He says we will leave as soon as—" He stopped, coloring deeply. "When he gives the word."

She narrowed her eyes. "When the castle is put to the torch? I know what he intends."

The lad looked uncomfortable. He peered out the window. "I am to watch for his signal."

"What signal? He is not even down there."

"Aye, he is, see. Straight below us." Geordie indicated the area near the base of the keep. "He is talking with your bailie."

Looking straight down, she saw Lindsay's wide shoulders and the glint of his dark, gold-streaked hair. He walked beside Eustace past the base of the keep. Cool moonlight cascaded over his face and commanding form.

The two men strode into the center of the yard. Lindsay paused, standing with a bold, relaxed power, one hand on his upright bow, the other pointing toward the battlement. Eustace nodded in response to something the outlaw said.

Isobel leaned against the windowsill, watching. Though her legs trembled with fatigue, she stayed there, fascinated, as if the forest rogue who had entered her castle exerted some mysterious power over her. She could not look away.

But, she asked herself as Geordie had, did she trust him? She did not know. Even her perceptive inner senses gave her no hint. She only knew that his appearance here had thrown her into a turmoil of fear and hope, of suspicion and faith. She was not certain whether to accept or refuse what he offered.

Why had he come here? She recalled the bitterness in his voice when she had asked him that question earlier. *We have matters between us, you and I,* he had said. The ominous words still echoed in her mind.

But she could not forget, regardless of what mission brought him here, that Lindsay had brought food when they were starving, had helped her when she was hurt, and now intended to get them out of the castle.

He brought hope, as Eustace had told her. Isobel was grateful for that. But she would do well to be wary of him.

Beside her, Geordie waved, and James Lindsay glanced up toward the window that framed them both. Sensing his gaze on her, she returned it steadily. Then James Lindsay motioned toward Geordie.

"He needs me," the lad said. "I will be back." He turned and ran, descending the turning stair with pounding, rapid steps. She looked out the window again, seeing Geordie reach Lindsay within moments. Then another of the outlaws joined them, holding a longbow. As they gestured at the walls, Isobel knew they discussed destroying the castle.

As much as she dreaded it, she could not stop such a thing and knew it was necessary to prevent the English from entering and taking it. Like the outlaws, she did not want Southrons to hold the castle. Aberlady was her home, the refuge she needed.

She sighed, watching the men who gathered in the moonlit bailey. James Lindsay was about to destroy the haven that surrounded the prophetess of Aberlady, where she and her gift had always been protected.

Only a few men, including Eustace, knew about the fits of blindness that assailed her when the visions came. No women remained near her now; her mother had died the same year the gift showed itself, and now her nurse and maidservants were gone too, some lost to illness and death, others to lives with families away from Aberlady. The last woman to serve Isobel personally had died early in the siege, a victim of age and worry.

The cocoon that her father had spun around her was snug, but now it would be gone. Her father and the priest had decided Sir Ralph could protect her in marriage. None of them had ever thought Isobel would be forced into the situation she was in now.

James Lindsay turned then, distracting her. He looked up at the window where she stood. A soft shiver rippled through her. Even in the darkness, she felt his steady, penetrating gaze. She drew back.

She had never thought she would leave Aberlady. Her prophetic gift, which most often appeared at her urging, sometimes burst upon her without warning, bringing glorious or disturbing visions of the future. Aberlady was the safe place where that occurred.

She had learned to depend on a very few who understood her singular world, and she had been raised to depend on her father. But he was gone, and she did not know when or if she would see him again.

She was sure Eustace would take her to find Father Hugh as soon as they escaped the castle. The priest would give her refuge in his home near the parish church, and he would send word to Sir Ralph, who had gone in search of John Seton.

She longed to know that her father was safe, but she balked at the thought of relying on Sir Ralph, let alone marrying him. Beneath the rough manners common to many men, she felt he had real harshness. Sometimes he frightened her, though he had never deliberately offended her. But her father and the priest trusted and admired him, even when Sir Ralph had changed his fealty. Leslie was a practical man who watched the weather of the war, her father had said.

"He loves you well," her father had said. "He has promised me to keep you safe no matter who wins this struggle over Scottish lands and rule."

Safe! She nearly laughed. Aberlady had been besieged for weeks, but Sir Ralph had not come to her aid. His search for her father must have taken him deep into England. If he had known, surely he would have come to Aberlady quickly.

She had spent these weeks learning new lessons. Now she could lead where she had only followed, could defy where she had only obeyed. She was stronger in spirit than she had been.

Still, the thought of leaving Aberlady terrified her. Inside the walls of her home, she had learned independence; inside her cocoon, she could be brave, but she was not a winged butterfly yet. She was not ready for the real freedom of leaving her home.

From the window, she watched a rogue contemplate the best method of torching her home and ripping her away from its protection.

Aberlady Castle would be sacrificed, but its inhabitants would be safe. Homes could be made anywhere, she knew. She sighed and tried to accept what she realized was inevitable.

Another English fire arrow whistled through the dark like a comet, trailing bright flame. The arrow landed, like the others had done, in the earthen yard, flaming and smoking. James Lindsay strode forward and plucked it out of the ground. Then he raised his bow, nocked the flaming arrow, drew the string taut, and released it.

The arrow shot upward, its glowing tail tracing a new arc through the darkness. Then it smacked into the thatched roof of the empty stable and burst into flame.

Isobel gasped.

Another English arrow flamed through the darkness. Lindsay tore that one out of the ground too and shot it forth. The flaming bolt landed on the roof of a storage hut, which began to burn within seconds.

Isobel put a shaking hand to her mouth, unable to move, unable to tear her gaze from the bailey. Golden sparks flew about in the brisk night wind. One by one, the dry thatch and wood in the outbuildings caught flame as if they were kindling.

James Lindsay stood amid the brilliant, growing light, his bow propped upright, and watched the fire grow. Other men gathered near him. No one made an effort to stop the fire from spreading.

Eustace ran toward the burning stable, snatching up a long stick and lighting it like a taper on the low, flaming roof of the storage building. Then he flung the brand toward another thatched roof. More flames erupted.

Isobel felt as if her heart shattered within her breast.

"'Tis to prevent the English from taking Aberlady," Geordie said quietly. He was beside her; she had not heard him return. "The policy of scorched earth is based on an old custom of war."

"I know," she whispered. But she did not want to watch her home burn before her eyes.

"You can return later," Geordie said. "Repairs can be made. The stone will not burn, just the thatch and the wood, enough to keep the Southrons from taking the castle."

"I know." Tears stung her eyes.

Fiery patches blazed on the thatched roofs of several buildings now. An apple tree in the orchard near the small stone chapel began to burn, its branches bedecked in glowing necklaces. When flames ran along the gate to the garden, Isobel caught back a sob.

"We must leave, my lady." Geordie put an arm around her shoulders and tugged. "Come, Lady Isobel. Jamie wants you down in the bailey. He means for us to escape now."

She allowed Geordie to lead her to the stairs. Searing pain shot through her arm and her ankle, and she put an arm around his waist as he helped her down the steps.

As they emerged from the keep and stepped into the bailey, Isobel stood still, staring at the awful beauty of the raging fire.

Sparks flew around her like stars. The bailey was full of hot, brilliant light. She moved toward the garden, pausing some distance from the blazing gate.

She felt a hand on her arm. "Lady Isobel. Come away."

That quiet voice was already familiar, like the voice of a friend. But he could not be a friend to do this so thoroughly, denying her the chance to bid her home farewell.

"Leave me be." She shook off his hand.

James Lindsay's face was lean and hard in the golden light. "Come away," he said firmly, reaching out again.

"Nay." She limped forward, despite the pain in her foot, despite the danger. The garden had been the heart of Aberlady; her mother had designed it years ago. Memories and need drew her there. She moved toward the gate that now gaped wide, its wooden struts flaming.

Chapter Five

T HE GIRL GLIDED through the blazing gate like an angel
crossing the threshold of hell. James strode after her. "Are
you mad?" he called. "Come away from there!"

She ignored him, limping along the path, her head and shoulders held proud. James knew that it must cost her considerable
pain to advance like that. He followed her.

Flames lingered on the gate, and a few vines blazed nearby,
but so far, the fire had touched a small part of the garden. Striding
along the path after Isobel, James saw the careful arrangement of
paths and plant beds—but he also noticed the garden had been
ravaged even before the fire reached it. Stalks and vines were
plucked clean; beds had been dug up and not replanted.

Isobel Seton went toward a side wall, where a wooden trellis
sagged against the stone. Bare vines clung to it, empty of flowers
but for a few ragged blossoms. James was close enough to
overtake her in one or two strides, but he paused, ready to snatch
her away from there if need be. Behind them, the gate and some
dry vines crackled as they burned, and smoke and sparks drifted
overhead. But the fire had not yet reached this corner.

A white rose clung to the highest part of the vine, a swirl of
pale petals in the light of the fire and the moon. The girl stretched
her hand upward to reach it.

James stepped forward and plucked the rose for her, laying it
in her open hand. Despite the heavy odor of burning wood, he

caught a drift of the rose's delicate fragrance.

Isobel lifted the bloom to her face to breathe in its scent. "My mother treasured these roses," she said. Her voice was soft and hoarse, and tears glistened in her eyes. James waited, expecting angry accusations from her. But she seemed calm as she ran a fingertip along the edge of the rose. "The garden was all that we had left of her," she said.

"I am sorry," he murmured. "I did not know."

She gave a hollow, hoarse little laugh, surprising him. "The siege destroyed this garden before you set your fire." She glanced around. "We stripped everything edible, even the flowers. This rose bloomed days ago. Eustace wanted me to add it to the soup, but I refused." She gazed at the pale blossom, and her lower lip trembled.

She puzzled him, so gentle and sad when he had expected anger from her. But they did not have time to pluck roses, with a fire raging beyond, and a hundred English at the gates.

"Isobel, we must go," he said, quiet but firm.

"You did not give me time to say farewell," she murmured, "before you loosed that fire arrow. Let me have the chance now."

James sighed and shoved his fingers through his hair in a gesture of regret. He had been quick to act on his decision to fire the castle; perhaps too quick, but they had little time to spare. He had not meant to cause her this sort of grief.

He remembered his own mother's garden, a haven of scent and color that had provided hiding places for James and his older brother, and created pleasant memories. But it was gone now, burned, as this garden would be soon.

"When I was small, my father brought back the first of these rose bushes from a Crusade," Isobel said. "He said my mother had sweet magic in her fingers for making roses." She smiled. "The garden was always full of roses—white, pink, and red— from spring until fall. When she died, he buried her in our chapel, so that she could be near her roses, and us, always." She pointed beyond the garden wall, where a small chapel roof jutted up, its clay tiles bright in the firelight. "Dear God, if the fire reaches the chapel—" she said.

"I have already told my men to soak the chapel roof with water to protect it," he said. "I do not burn churches."

She nodded. A tear pooled in her eye and hovered there.

James felt a compelling urge to touch her—a hand to her shoulder, a finger to that shining tear, some gesture of comfort. But he held back, fisting his hand against the craving.

And he waited, silent and still, while a slender, ebony-haired girl cradled a pale rose amid destruction.

In some detached, philosophical part of his mind, long ago trained by scholarly monks to see the symbolism in all things, he realized that heaven and hell existed in perfect duality here in this ravaged garden, in the gentle, lovely girl, in the pure rose, and in the darkness and the inferno that surrounded them.

A blaze that he had caused.

"Isobel," he said. He felt emotion constrict his throat but went on. "Years ago, I lost my own castle when the English set it afire. Those—those who were inside were killed—my kin, my men, my—" He stopped.

She glanced at him. "You know how I feel," she said softly. "You suffered even worse. And yet you set Aberlady afire."

"Aye," he said gruffly.

"I know you had no choice," she whispered.

He nodded silently. He had felt hollow, black inside when he shot that fire arrow toward the thatch. Devastating memories, six years past, had sparked again with that burst of flame. But he had locked them away. He had no time, no strength inside to let them out.

Watching Isobel, he would have preferred her to shout at him, to call him vile names, to echo his anger and tap the darkness that he carried inside himself.

But her poignant sadness tugged at him, challenged him, unsettled him. She stood there holding that sooty, bedraggled white rose, and he suddenly wanted—something, and could not name it. He had not felt this raw, this open, in years.

Then she glanced up at him, and he saw in her translucent eyes that she bore no grudge toward him for setting the torch to Aberlady. He saw, God help him, forgiveness.

He turned away.

For one long, dreadful instant, he felt as if the hard casing around his heart began to crack. With the next breath, he willed the gap sealed again.

He reminded himself why he had come in search of the prophetess of Aberlady, and why he had found it expedient to fire her castle. Isobel Seton might be distressed, in need, and impossibly lovely. But he reminded himself that she was the only pawn he had, and he must use her as he had already schemed.

"The policy of scorched earth is sanctioned by the Guardians of the Realm of Scotland," he said coldly. "'Tis a necessary action to prevent the English from taking Scottish properties."

He turned back toward her.

She blinked at him; those sad, magnificent eyes nearly undid him.

"I know," she said. "But I—I hoped my castle would be spared."

"The Southrons ready their engines to knock down your gates in the morn. You were willing to defend these walls for weeks to keep them out. I have ensured that they will stay out, for now at least, for the good of Scotland, and your welfare." His tone was sharp.

She frowned. He saw her temper blossom then, a hard blue spark in her limpid eyes. "I thought the Hawk Laird had only his own good in mind," she snapped.

He felt the jab keenly, startled that her words could wound him so easily. But he felt on more certain ground with anger and conflict than with her sadness, her softness.

Many shared the opinion of him that she had just voiced. After all, his new reputation as a traitor had begun with this girl's own words, months ago. His temper surged.

"Come ahead," he said abruptly, taking her uninjured arm to pull her toward the gate.

She stood her ground. "Why would my welfare matter to you? 'Tis said the Hawk Laird is loyal only to himself. They say—"

"I know what they say," he barked. He glanced through the burning frame of the gate. The fire in the bailey, which lit up the dark sky, had consumed the outbuildings and now encroached on the tower. In the shadows by the back wall, he saw his men, and Aberlady's garrison, waiting.

"Come," he said firmly, taking her right wrist. "We have to get out of here. Now."

She resisted his tug. Fiery light gleamed on her fine-boned cheeks and in her glossy dark hair as she looked up at him. "Why did you come here, James Lindsay?" she asked.

"I came to rescue you, whether or not you believe that," he snapped impatiently.

"I do not believe it," she said. "There is more. Tell me what 'tis."

He leaned forward. "Are you blind, lass? There is fire all around you! We do not have time for a wee chat."

She gaped at him. He could not think why.

"For now, I am your champion," he muttered sourly. "Later you may call me something else, if you like."

He bent down and scooped her into his arms. Then he strode through the smoldering, fire-spitting gate and headed across the bailey amid a shower of bright sparks.

SHE MIGHT HAVE done him the courtesy of passing out, James thought, as he climbed hand over hand down a sturdy knotted rope ladder. Then he could have carted her down the cliff as he had wanted to do, slung over his shoulder, head down. Both he and Henry Rose had argued with her that she should let James carry her draped over his shoulder; a little time like that would not harm her, they had said. But Isobel had protested the idea stubbornly, and James had relented.

He had also given in to her insistence that she needed spare clothing and other items. Their escape had been further delayed while Isobel and Eustace had gone off to collect her things in a cloth bundle, which Eustace now carried down the cliffside.

Although she had not complained, James saw the traces of fatigue and starvation on her face. He was keenly aware of her physical weakness as she rode in his arms. She was a well-made girl, but hunger and injury had left her scant strength. And he heard every groan of pain that she tried to suppress.

He glanced to either side and saw the other men, lowering along lengths of rope nearby, moving silent and steady over the jagged rockface. All of those who had come out of Aberlady were weakened by the strain of the siege. James had reminded his men, who were fit and rested, to usher Aberlady's survivors down the cliffside with care.

He glanced back at Isobel. "How do you fare?" he asked.

"I do not envy birds," she said wryly, her pale face inches from his own. She was face to face with him, her legs circling his hips and her uninjured left arm around his neck. James had fastened her to him with a rope harness, like a bear cub to its mother, leaving his arms and legs free to manage the rope ladder.

"Ah, then, I promise we will not fly," he said with a half laugh. Isobel grimaced and glanced down, and the grip of her arm became choking strong. "Do not look down," he said quickly. "Be at ease. You are safe." She loosened her hold around his neck and tucked her face against his shoulder.

The cliffside was high, raw rock, plunging straight down in some places. The northern face, where they descended, was steep and jagged. Mossy ledges and crevices provided hand and foot holds, some large enough to stand upon. Each man proceeded carefully; in the moonlight, a loose bit of turf or rock could be mistaken for a secure hold. Mist drifted over the cliff face in torn, gauzy veils, making the descent even more dangerous.

James and his men had climbed upward in fading daylight, using ropes fastened to scaling forks, which they tossed up as they went. The downward climb was a greater challenge than James had anticipated. During the hours in the castle, he and the men had created two long rope ladders, and had added sturdy knots along the lengths of the other ropes to aid climbing. But the going was slow and dangerous, for the ropes were not long enough to reach the ground. The lines, secured to the iron forks, had to be loosened and reattached in different places, while the climbers waited on narrow ledges.

James glanced toward the ground and saw its dark expanse beneath the mist. He looked upward at the castle, perched high overhead, its blazing walls casting a reddish glow into the night sky. Moonlight both helped and hindered them. If they could see their way, then the enemy could see them as well. Only the treacherous mists and darkness protected them.

James knew that the English could discover their escape at any moment, and attack them on the cliffside, where they would be most vulnerable. He hoped that the blaze would so distract the enemy that they would neglect to send a patrol around the area until the cliff face was again deserted.

Cold wind whipped his hair into his eyes, and he turned his head to clear his vision. He went down another rung, easing his weight onto the bouncing brace of the rope. The girl's weight was not a burden, though her long legs and her injured arm, strapped tightly, proved awkward to balance. His quiver and bow thumped against his back in the wind, and he paused on the ladder, gripping it firmly with one hand. He rested his other arm and hand around her hips while he caught his breath.

Another strong breeze blew past, and he heard Isobel gasp softly. Her hair unfurled like a banner, weaving a dark curtain with his own. The next gust of wind knocked them roughly against the cliff side. Isobel cried out as her arm slammed against the rock. She buried her face in his shoulder with a ragged whimper. He turned to shield her from the driving force of the wind, and held still to allow her a moment to recover. She sucked in a breath and raised her head, nodding to him to go on.

"Bonny lass," he said with approval. He glanced down to find the next rung. "'Twill not be long now. We're nearly there."

He was amazed to hear Isobel laugh, a frightened, doubtful little squeak, but a laugh nonetheless. He half smiled as he resumed his descent.

ISOBEL KNEW THAT she should feel terrified, but she felt strangely secure, wrapped in a cocoon of rope and cloaks, held firm against the outlaw's hard, solid body. She laid her head in the hollow of his shoulder and studied his clean profile, silhouetted against the moon.

She had already discovered that she could not look down at the dark expanse of ground below the cliff. Nor could she look up at the castle, where a hot red light spread into the dark sky; the sight of her burning home hurt far too much. And any glance to right or left, at the others who made their way down ropes, sent chills of fear through her.

Nor could she close her eyes completely—never that, for then the world became an uncertain, frightening place, full of darkness and sharp, unending pain.

So she looked at the outlaw and discovered an odd sort of safety in danger. His strength held their combined weights with ease, and his long reach and powerful muscles made the awful descent seem effortless.

Isobel was utterly dependent upon his strength, his ability, and his goodwill. She had no choice but to trust him—for now. She rested her cheek against his shoulder and felt his muscled body shift, solid and reliable and warm, against hers.

James paused on the rope, breathing hard as he summoned the strength to continue. Isobel looked at him.

"How do you fare?" she asked, as he had so often asked her.

He nodded brusquely. "Well enough. We're nearly there." He sank to the next rung.

She felt a stirring, profound excitement. They hovered between heaven and earth, between night and dawn. Tied to him in a strange intimacy—cheeks touching, breaths mingling, abdomens pressed together, hearts thumping in tandem—Isobel felt protected, and more. Lindsay held her life in his hands and risked his own life and safety to help her.

His legs worked beneath her, thighs pushing gently, rhythmically, into her hips. His arms stretched around her to grip the rope as he moved steadily downward.

Finally his feet struck flat on the ground. James released the ladder and stepped away from the massive curtain of rock that towered over them. He supported her in his arms, and stood for a moment, his cheek against hers, his breath ragged as he gathered his strength.

She smiled and tightened her arm around his neck—an impulsive embrace rather than the fearful grip of before. He held her and murmured something that the wind took away.

Then Geordie Shaw leaped to the ground, and ran toward them, helping to undo the knots that bound Isobel to James. Within moments, she was lifted away from him to stand on her own. James steadied her with an arm about her waist while he spoke with Geordie. But she was keenly aware of the chill of the wind that separated them.

James gave her a small, private smile. "Brave lass," he murmured, and walked away.

Isobel waited while each man silently reached the ground. But her gaze rested most often on James Lindsay as he and his men helped the others, and then gathered the ropes to hide them, coiled, behind a large boulder.

He came back to her side and drew an arrow from his quiver. Nocking the great bow, he shot a single shaft high into the cliffside. The feathered end, pale in the moonlight, trembled in the wind.

"There," he said. "Now they will know who was here."

He turned to Isobel and held out his arms and she stepped forward willingly as he lifted her. With exhaustion settling bone-deep in her body, she rode again in his arms and did not want to remind herself that she might be leaving Aberlady forever.

"Where are we going?" she asked.

"Into the forest," he said.

She was too weary to ask more. On the morrow, truths would be faced, questions would be asked. But the blessing of the earth was beneath her at last, and the warmth of his arms was still around her. She wanted to trust James Lindsay for a little while longer, whatever the future would bring.

She closed her eyes as he carried her toward the trees.

Chapter Six

MORNING LIGHT DISPELLED the mist as the group advanced through the forest on horseback and foot. Isobel rode a feather-footed white stallion, its broad back covered with a blanket. Geordie sat behind her, his arms around her waist while he held the reins. As they rode, she looked overhead at the tall, swaying trees, and then glanced at the cluster of men and horses moving along the earthen track.

At dawn, James had led them to the place where the horses had been hidden previously, remarking that he and his men had borrowed the warhorses from English soldiers. Isobel did not care if the horses belonged to King Edward himself. In her exhaustion, she was deeply grateful for the chance to ride.

Since several of the garrison had already departed the group to seek out nearby kin, there were mounts enough for all, with some sharing. James rode a huge black stallion, and Eustace a bay; Isobel saw them side by side, ahead of the group, deep in conversation.

For Isobel, most of the morning was a blur of fatigue, pain, and the tedium of riding, all of which she endured in silence. The men all showed concern for her, but she noticed that James Lindsay kept his distance from her once the journey began.

She saw him glance toward her often and heard his brisk order whenever she was thirsty or wanted to stop and rest, as if he somehow knew what she needed. Willing hands were always available to fetch food or water for her, to lift her down, or help her remount. But those hands never belonged to James.

The men kept a watchful patrol as they rode, with their weapons held ready. They stopped just after dawn to catch fish from a burn and cook them. Isobel, however, had so little appetite that she ate only berries and drank cool, fresh water.

Whether riding or resting, the men amiably discussed the lay of the land and the confusing map of the political situation. Isobel noticed that the Hawk Laird's outlaws and the survivors of the siege quickly became a band of comrades, united by their bold escape and a shared dislike for the enemy.

But the tentative bond that had formed between Isobel and James seemed to dissolve as they rode deeper into the forest. Isobel became certain, as the day wore on, that James avoided her deliberately. He rarely spoke to her at all, and his quick, frequent glances toward her were cryptic.

He seemed remote and somber. Even his deep blue eyes had hardened to the color of steel. He rode apart from the rest, or beside Eustace or the outlaw Henry Rose, his watchful gaze grim.

She reminded herself that he was a rogue and an outlaw, said to be treacherous. Now that she had entered his world, she told herself, she would probably find out that the rumors were true.

But she missed the feel of his arms around her and longed for his quiet voice in her ear. She desperately needed the comfort he had shown her earlier. His distant mood, after the easiness that had existed between them, hurt her unexpectedly.

On the cliff, suspended with him between earth and heaven, she had known an exhilarating balance of danger and safekeeping. Now, whenever she heard his voice or caught one of his glances, her heartbeat quickened. He was a brigand and untrustworthy, but he fascinated her.

Isobel sighed, impatient with her thoughts, and turned her head to ease the stiffness in her neck. Her arm ached fiercely, as did her ankle, and she had leaned against Geordie for the last hour or so of the journey.

Even more uncomfortable was her growing hunger, a sensation difficult to ignore now that food was available. Her stomach had been uncertain earlier, but now she felt ravenous.

The sun climbed higher over the treetops while the group traveled, and translucent beams poured through the leaves. Several yards ahead, James set a steady pace along the forest track. A turn of his head brought a glint of gold to his hair, stirring that odd feeling in her midsection.

After a while, he held up his hand and halted. The others stopped behind him, leather creaking and weaponry jingling softly. James circled his black stallion about and rode toward Eustace, who had halted beside Isobel and Geordie.

"By God's grace, we have not been followed," James told Eustace, his low voice carrying easily in the forest hush. "We can risk a short rest near here if the lady wishes it." He glanced at Isobel, a flash of intense, dark blue.

"I am tired," she said gratefully.

He nodded brusquely. "Remind your men, Sir Eustace, that if any more of them wish to seek friends or kin, now is the time to depart. We will turn south from here and cross the Tweed, and then enter the heart of the Ettrick Forest. Tell them that any man who rides with me may be branded a broken man and a traitor by Scots as well as Southrons."

"Those who wanted to leave have already gone," Eustace said. "The rest will stay."

James nodded. "The grove over there, where the birches are thick, will provide safe cover."

"Good. Lady Isobel needs the respite," Eustace said.

James looked at her again, blue lightning beneath straight brown brows. Without a word, he circled his horse and rode toward the grove.

Quietly and quickly, they followed him into the cover of the birches and dismounted. Geordie helped Isobel settle in a shaded spot beneath the trees, and turned away to help Henry Rose and another outlaw, a young Highland man in a wrapped and belted plaid, make a small fire. Then James, Geordie, and a burly outlaw called Patrick went off to hunt small game for the meal, while Aberlady's men established a guard around the grove.

Eustace fetched cold water from a burn in his steel helmet and brought it to Isobel. She thanked him and drank, and then he walked away to stand watch among the trees.

Only the Highlander stayed in the clearing with her, a tall, slender young man, bare-legged but for low, shabby boots, and wearing a worn plaid of brown and purple. Isobel relaxed against the tree trunk and watched him as he bent over the fire, cooking flat cakes on a small iron plate that he balanced on two rocks.

He glanced at her and flashed a quick, shy smile. A dimpled smile transformed his lean, serious, young face, and Isobel smiled in return. He blushed and shoved at his blond hair, which slid continually over his eyes despite the sloppy braids he wore to restrain it.

He used his dagger to flip a cake jauntily from the griddle and came toward her, holding the hot cake with a corner of his plaid. He sat down beside her.

"An oatcake for you, Isobel Seton, if you be hungry," he said. He used her full name in the Highland way, rather than her title as Lowlanders tended to do. And the Northern English he spoke had the soft, resonant lilt of a speaker of Gaelic. "Take care, now, 'tis hot," he warned.

"Thank you." She took the thick, hot cake using a fold of her gown to protect her fingers. "I am surprised to see a Highland man among outlaws of the Ettrick Forest."

He shrugged. "I am a Fraser—Quentin Fraser, from near Inverness. My kinsman is Sir Simon Fraser, whose name you may know. I came south to fight with him for Scotland."

She nodded. "I have heard that Sir Simon is one of the rebel leaders. How is it you are with James Lindsay now?"

"I met Jamie when he came north with some of Wallace's men to help Simon around Stirling. I joined him then. Simon asked me to study the lay of the southern lands and to learn the moves of the English armies. Now and again, I travel to wherever Simon is and report to him." He looked intently at her, his eyes bright azure. "I trust you, Isobel Seton of Aberlady, or I would not tell you that." He smiled again, and winked, with such charm that Isobel felt immediately befriended.

"My thanks. But how do you know you can trust me?"

Quentin grinned, fleeting and delighted, as if he knew a secret. "Ah, I have the Sight," he said. "I have always had it, and it tells me you're a fine lass and a true seeress."

She smiled, liking him even more. "I have it, too."

"I know. The visions and prophecies of Black Isobel are well known in the Lowlands."

She blushed. "But my visions only tell me about war and kings, about strange events in the future that I do not truly understand. 'Twould be pleasant to know things about people and help them. Can you do that?"

He nodded. "Sometimes. It just comes to me, like a knowing. I think you could do that easily, for your gift is great, and mine but a wee talent beside it. I have had visions, too, a few. I've seen death for those I love," he said, looking down, brushing dried leaves from his plaid. "And I do not want to ever see that again."

Isobel sighed. "I've seen death, too. Usually I forget what I see, though. Do you remember?"

"Always," Quentin said grimly. "What would you want to see, if you could, Isobel Seton?"

She broke off a piece of the oatcake to nibble on it. "If I could," she said, swallowing, "I would use my Sight to learn why James Lindsay came to Aberlady to find me, and why he is so discontent with me now." She slid him a wry glance. "I trust you, Quentin Fraser, or I would not tell you that."

He smiled wanly. "Ah, well, I cannot tell you why myself. Jamie has a burden to carry, and he has good reason for whatever he does. But he keeps his thoughts close. No seer could penetrate them. To be truthful, he hasna told any of us why he came to find you. But he was furious that the English would besiege a castle held by a woman, and I know he meant to get you out of there. If there is another reason, I do not know it." He shrugged. "When he is ready to speak his mind, he will do it."

Isobel watched his fine-cut, youthful profile while she savored the nutty taste of the thick, warm cake. "You follow him when so many have left him," she said after a while.

"I do." Quentin nodded firmly. "I will never believe that he betrayed Wallace. He's a changed man since he returned from English captivity. But he will always have my faith."

"Does your Sight tell you aught about his betrayal?"

He shook his head. "I believe he did not do it. Jamie would trade his own life for a friend. He did that for me, once, and so I owe him loyalty, no matter what is said of him." He rose to his feet. "Another cake, Isobel Seton?"

She refused with soft thanks. Quentin gave her another appealing smile and walked away, stepping between the trees to leave her alone in the little clearing. She watched him go, glad to have found a friend among the outlaws; his smile and easy manner had left a warm glow inside of her.

She sighed, looking toward the fire crackling inside a circle of stones, and she thought about James Lindsay, and what Quentin had said. Geordie, too, had stubbornly insisted on his hero's innocence, but she had attributed that to his youth. Now the Highlander, a man of about her own age, shared the opinion.

But surely the few followers of the Hawk Laird all believed him innocent of treachery. Outside that circle, disturbing tales persisted about him. She had heard the rumors from Father Hugh, a Scotsman and a priest, who would not spread lies.

Unable to make sense of the matter and too exhausted to try, she settled her back against the tree, eased her hand over her aching shoulder, and closed her eyes to rest.

THE TANTALIZING SMELL of roasting fowl stirred her out of her doze, and she opened her eyes. A few feet away from her, she saw James Lindsay's broad back as he sat by the fire, clothed in the leather hauberk and green tunic. He listened to Henry Rose and laughed softly at something the man said.

James turned to glance over his shoulder and saw that she was awake. He nodded briefly to her, then leaned forward to slice off a portion of meat. This he placed on a bit of bark and handed to the outlaw Patrick, who sat at his other side.

Patrick came toward her. "Here, my lady," he said in a deep, graveled voice, kneeling to offer the steaming white meat. "Jamie said you would be hungry."

"Thank you," she said, glancing at Lindsay's back. He did not turn. Patrick returned to his place by the fire, and Isobel ate hungrily. The meat was charred outside, but inside was moist and delicious. When she finished and licked her fingers, Patrick glanced at her, and quickly brought her another portion of meat.

"My thanks," she said. "I have only eaten berries and an oatcake until now. I did not realize I was so hungry."

He nodded. "Your belly was not ready earlier for heavy food, lass. But now that your hunger has returned, we know you'll recover well."

"We?" She glanced at him while she ate.

"Jamie and us," he answered. He sniffed and wiped his nose on his grimy sleeve. "Jamie watches over you like a hawk watches its fledgling. He says you have not eaten much."

"He does not care," she muttered, pulling off a bit of steaming flesh. "He lets you and the others do the caring. And I thank you for it," she added.

Patrick leaned forward and lowered his voice. "Och, he will not admit it, since he was not too pleased with the prophetess of Aberlady."

Isobel cast him a quick frown. He pulled off his helmet to scratch his unkempt brown hair. He spit into the helmet and buffed it with his sleeve. "I know ladies like fine courtesy," he said. "So I'll fetch you some water in a clean helmet, see." He held it out to show her.

"My thanks, Patrick," Isobel said. "But I will go to the burn myself, to wash in privacy."

"Let me show you the way." Patrick helped her to her feet and supported her with a huge hand at her waist as she limped forward.

Isobel saw James look up as they passed. Quentin glanced up too, and gave her a dazzling smile, lifting his eyebrows jauntily. James saw him and frowned sharply.

Isobel smiled at Quentin, smiled at Patrick, and slid a scowl toward James. He glanced away as if he had not seen her, and rubbed his fingers over his whiskered jaw in silence.

LATER IN THE day, as she rode the white stallion in front of Geordie, Isobel felt so tired, so filled with aches and plagued by dizziness, that she sometimes thought she could not go on. Yet she said nothing to Geordie of her discomfort, nor did she mention it to anyone else who asked after her welfare.

She had found a moment to tell Eustace that she wanted to part company with the outlaws when they neared Stobo, where Father Hugh had a parish church. Sir Eustace had agreed reluctantly. Isobel decided that he liked the freedom of running with outlaws after weeks trapped in a besieged castle. Isobel, however, wanted rest and peace.

But some part of her wanted to stay with the Hawk Laird in the forest, too. However foolishly, she wanted to be with the compassionate man he had been while tending her wounds—but that man had disappeared from her life.

If she had possessed greater strength, clearer thoughts, and better boldness, she would have challenged him to tell her what his intent was concerning her, and why he had grown so cool toward her. But, exhausted and drained, she said nothing to him, and let the stallion carry her deeper into the forest.

She remembered Lindsay's ominous statement that he had come to Aberlady to find her, as if he had some business with her. She felt his intentions hovering over her like storm clouds. The prophetess could not tell if he was her champion or her enemy.

She did not seem to have Quentin's easy gift for simply "knowing" something, and wished she did.

Devastated by her ordeal at Aberlady, and scattered in her thoughts without rest, she could answer none of the questions that plagued her. All she truly wanted was a place to lie down and sleep.

The dense forest canopy admitted only a little light so that the forest path was dim and green. Isobel heard the steady footfalls of the horses, the trills of birds overhead, and the wind soughing through the branches. The sounds were so peaceful, soft, and monotonous that she nearly fell asleep as she rode.

She stirred herself as she leaned against Geordie, and looked around. A long wooded slope rose to one side of the path, covered with trees. Over her shoulder, she saw a bright, silvery flash among the trunks. Dazed and tired, her reactions slow, she did not realize until too late that she had seen the gleam of metal armor.

An instant later, she heard the rapid whoosh of an arrow and felt its hard thud as it struck Geordie. He jerked against her, cried out, and fell, suddenly, and heavily, to the ground.

Isobel screamed and turned, instinctively reaching out, but Geordie was gone, fallen beneath the hooves of the horse. So fast that she hardly knew what was happening, the men around her began to shout and turn their mounts. She saw Eustace's grim face as he flashed by, saw Henry Rose draw his great bow, saw James turn and ride back, his face furious, his hand reaching behind him for the broadsword at his back.

Another arrow sped through the trees and nicked her horse in its flank. Isobel tried to grab the reins and turn him, but he whinnied and reared up, nearly dumping her to the ground. She clung desperately to the mane with both hands as the horse landed hard, jarring her.

With a surge of muscle and power, the warhorse bolted ahead.

Chapter Seven

FIERCE SHOUTS, THE thwack of arrows finding targets, and the ringing clash of steel echoed behind her through the trees. Isobel found the reins with her left hand and yanked desperately. The horse ignored the command and galloped along the track, carrying her toward another part of the forest. Isobel curled forward to shield herself from whipping branches as the stallion swerved left and propelled through the trees.

Finally the horse slowed and came to a halt among leafy oak trees. His fetlocks were immersed in green ferns, his sides heaving and slick. Isobel leaned against his neck, shaking all over, her heart slamming in her chest. Her wounded arm hurt savagely as she tried to turn the horse, pulling hard. The stallion refused to move, though she tugged, cajoled, pressed with her knees, and even begged tearfully.

She bowed wearily over his neck in sheer frustration. In the stillness, she heard the wind shove through the trees and birds chitter. But she heard no sounds of a skirmish.

Lost and in pain, she sat uncertainly on a horse who possessed a stronger will than she did. Unable to command him, she felt too weak to dismount and tend to him properly.

She patted the horse's broad neck, spoke calmly to him, and attempted to turn him again. The stallion moved in a stubborn circle and began to crop a patch of grass beneath a tree.

Isobel sighed and looked around. They were on a long slope

thick with trees and bracken, the forest track was out of sight somewhere, and the light had begun to fail. Increasingly alarmed, Isobel tugged on the reins again. The horse whickered, bowed his head, and simply would not move. She yanked at the reins, rocked on his back, and grew close to losing her temper as she strained to turn him.

"Och, now, lass." She heard a deep, quiet voice, so familiar that she felt a surge of relief. "He's as tired as you are. Give him time, and he'll do what you wish."

She whipped around and saw James Lindsay leaning against a tree, watching her, a bemused look on his face. In the thickening shadows, he seemed to blend into the forest that surrounded him, a long, lean figure in leather and muted green, strong and straight as an oak.

"James! Oh, James!" she burst out. She was so relieved to see him here, and unharmed, that tears welled in her eyes. She dashed her hand over her face as he strode forward. "Where are the others?" she asked. "What happened? Did English attack us?"

"Aye. Our men fought well and chased them off." He reached up to pat the horse's neck, murmuring to him. Then he walked back to examine the horse's flank, where the small cut from the arrow tip bled slightly. "Are you hurt?" he asked her.

"Nay. The horse ran off. I could not stop him, and then I could not find the path. I thought I was well and truly lost."

"You're safe now." He went back to the horse's head and patted its wide nose gently, murmuring low.

"How is Geordie?" she asked.

He paused. "He's badly hurt. The arrow went into his back. Eustace offered to take him to Stobo—he says the priest there will help the lad. Henry Rose went with them."

"Good. Where are the others?"

"Patrick and Quentin followed the Southrons to learn which patrol they were. I do not think they were Clifford's men, come from Aberlady, but 'tis possible. Most of your men went with them." He came closer, resting a hand on the horse's neck.

"Isobel," he murmured. "Two of Aberlady's garrison were killed. I am sorry. Eustace said they were his cousins."

Isobel gasped. "Thomas and Richard Gibson?"

"Aye." His hand was gentle on the horse, and his gaze was steady on hers. She saw keen regret in his eyes. "Eustace and Henry are taking their bodies to Stobo with Geordie."

She nodded. Tears stung her eyes and she looked away, feeling a piercing sadness. "Thomas and Richard fought well at Aberlady, only to lose their lives after—after escaping."

James's long fingers traced through the horse's mane. "Sometimes life is bitter, lass," he murmured. "We must have faith that the sweetness will return someday."

"Aye," she whispered. His fingers grazed over hers, warm and dry and strong, pressing her hand briefly.

"Eustace said you know this priest in Stobo," he said.

She nodded. "Father Hugh has been the priest serving Aberlady all my life. He will see that Thomas and Richard are honored, and he'll see to Geordie too."

"Good." James stepped sideways and leaped up behind her in one quick, lithe movement. His torso was warm and solid against her back, his arms encircled her, and his long thighs pressed hers. When he reached past her to lift the reins, she allowed herself to lean back against his strength.

He tightened the reins and directed the horse to turn. The animal responded easily to his command and carried them down the slope and along the path.

"We'll go back where I left my horse," he said. "Are you well enough to ride on? 'Twill be dark soon, and the going will be hard after that."

"I can continue." In truth, she felt dizzy and weak and wondered if she could ride another ten feet. His nearness was reassuring, as was his gentle manner toward her. She could not have borne more coolness from him just now. "Stobo is not far."

"Stobo? We will not go there." His voice vibrated low and mellow at her ear, sending an odd echo deep into her body. "You and I go elsewhere, lass."

"But—you arranged to meet Eustace at Stobo," Isobel stammered.

He shook his head. "Southrons could be patrolling the entire area. 'Tis dangerous enough to go back for my horse. I will not risk another attack by riding to Stobo. We will go south into the Ettrick Forest, the way we headed before we were ambushed. I will take you to my aunt's house. She lives across the river, in the forest."

Isobel looked at him in alarm. "But I must go to Stobo. Eustace promised to take me there. Now I must ask you to do that. I have nowhere else to go, no home, no kin nearby."

"Have you no family at all to take you in?" He spoke brusquely. She half turned, puzzled by his demand, and decided that he, too, tried to think of somewhere suitable to take her.

"My father is in prison, and my mother is dead," she said quietly. "I do not have brothers or sisters. But I have Seton kinsmen, including my cousin Sir Christopher Seton, married to one of Robert Bruce's sisters. Another cousin, Sir William Seton, holds Dalrinnie Castle near Ettrick Forest. But I have not seen him since before the siege. You could take me to meet one of them."

"Those places are too far from here," he said bluntly. "I know Sir Christopher Seton, and your cousin Sir William—Liam—as well. I suppose you did not know that Dalrinnie was taken by the English."

"I had not. Where is Liam Seton now?"

"Doing what many of us have done for the cause of Scotland. So he is not a man who is easy to find—even if he would rescue his cousin. You will stay with me."

She blinked, stunned by his brusque tone, his hard manner. "Then the town of Stobo is closest. Father Hugh will take me in."

"I will not go to Stobo." He had turned to stone again in moments.

She sighed. "Then take me to Castle Wildshaw. The constable there will help me, even if you will not."

Tension gathered in the strong hand that circled her waist. "That place is west, beyond the forest, a few hours' ride from here." His tone was flat.

"Sir Ralph Leslie is constable there. He will help me. If you will not take me to Stobo, then please escort me to Wildshaw."

"Leslie? Your betrothed."

"Aye," she admitted. "How do you know?"

"I have heard of him. Another Scottish knight who has changed his allegiance."

She heard the edge in his voice. "Many Scotsmen have pledged to King Edward. Sir Ralph is a worthy knight who has ties through kin to both England and Scotland. He says this is a complex war, and he tries to remain neutral."

Lindsay laughed, short and curt. Though she had no real love for Ralph Leslie, Isobel's temper flared. "'Tis said that you yourself changed—" she began.

"You know naught of my fealty," he snapped. "When do you plan to wed this paragon?"

"Sir Ralph and my father wanted the marriage done a few weeks ago."

"And you? When do you want it?"

Never, she thought. "The marriage has not happened yet because my father was captured, Sir Ralph went off to search for him, and Aberlady fell under siege."

"Good reasons to cancel glad nuptials," James drawled.

She did not like this cold, dark side of him or the bitterness she heard in his voice. "I do not understand why you will not help me in this," she said carefully. "It might have to do with the wars and with your loyalty—whatever that may be. But I, too, have loyalties and desires."

"And what are those?" he asked in a low, even tone.

"I want to see my father again. He may be at Wildshaw now—Sir Ralph promised before the siege began that he would retrieve him from an English dungeon."

"I see. And your loyalty?"

"I am loyal to my father. And I am a Scotswoman." She lifted her chin in answer to any doubt of her loyalty.

"Betrothed to a Scotsman with English fealties."

"You saw the stand I took at Aberlady, I hope." But she looked away. The matter of her betrothal had troubled her from its outset. "But I will do what my father asks of me. And I want to find him. Surely you understand that."

"I do. I imagine that you want to be with your betrothed as well."

"I need to be welcome somewhere. I may find that at Wildshaw. Please take me there."

"I would sooner take you to your grave," he growled.

A shiver ran down her spine. She glanced at him, seeing a gaze hard and cold as steel.

"Why do you bear such vehemence toward Sir Ralph?"

"Wildshaw," he said, "belongs to me."

She stared in surprise. "But the English king made Sir Ralph its captain. My betrothed did not take it from you."

"I inherited it upon my brother's death. The English took it."

"Then I will not trouble you to go there, but if you take me near it, I will find it myself. I have no other refuge."

"I will not do that."

She turned to frown at him, but he did not look at her. Puzzled, she turned back. Within moments she saw a black horse tied to a hazel tree. James slid down, mounted the black, and drew up beside her. The leather satchel with her spare clothing, which Sir Eustace had carried, was tied to the back of his saddle. Wordlessly, he took the reins of her horse to guide it alongside the black.

"Father Hugh and Sir Eustace will help me. Once in their safekeeping, I will be off your hands," she said.

"You are in safekeeping now. Mine."

"Am I? It seems as if you are holding me hostage."

"In a way I am." Bold words, spoken quietly. His grip pulled her reins taut.

Her heart thudded, but she lifted her chin to disguise her panic. "What do you mean? You cannot think to ransom me. I have scant value now, with my castle destroyed."

"You have value outside of Aberlady."

"What? Oh! Does King Edward want me brought to him? Is that why you came to Aberlady? You mean to escort me to the English king and make a profit for yourself!"

"If I intended that, I would have walked you out the gate of Aberlady and handed you over to the English, and saved myself the bother of descending a cliff in the dark."

"Then what do you want?" Anger and fear struck through her with hot, quick force. She yanked on the reins. "You cannot take me where I do not want to go!"

He did not loosen his hold. "Lady Isobel," he said, not unkindly. "Just now, I want to take you where your wounds can be looked after properly."

"And then you will barter me for coin to the English!"

"If you prove a wearisome guest, I will give you to them for naught."

"Ah, so you do mean to barter me!" She yanked back.

"Possibly." His grip was firm on the leather.

Panic struck her. "Why? I have done naught to you! You treated me with kindness at first. I do not understand you!"

"Must you?" he asked, sounding exasperated.

"Aye," she said. Suddenly she wanted to know him, very much; his thoughts, his past, his feelings. Her heart pounded with a heady combination of fear and fascination. "Aye! Why do you do this? What do you want of me?"

He sighed. "We cannot stay here, Lady Isobel. Come ahead." He pulled on the reins. She held on to them stubbornly.

"You helped me with a gentle hand when I was injured," she said, the words spilling forth as her temper boiled. "You gave me time in my mother's garden for my farewells. And I was sure that you regretted setting Aberlady afire."

"I did. Let go of the reins."

She would not let go, though it took all of her weight and strength to hang on to it. "This is unchivalrous. I thought you felt some kindness toward me!"

"And I thought you were a gentle, well-bred lass," he muttered in irritation. He pulled on the taut leather straps that linked them in a silent struggle. "Unhand the reins. I do not want to topple you off. *That* would be unchivalrous."

She held her end of the reins though her arm ached to do it. The horse shifted uneasily beneath her. "You would not topple me."

"I would." He yanked, and she jerked forward. He relaxed his hold and sighed. "I would not," he admitted, but did not release his grip. "You are as stubborn as that warhorse. Surely you realize the danger in lingering here for a wee chat."

She rushed on, ignoring his logical point; she felt no need to obey logic just now. Her temper, rarely stirred to this degree, was in full flare. "I wanted to think kindly of you," she said through clenched teeth, as she tugged on the rein. "Even though the Hawk Laird is said to be a wretched traitor. But all this day, you have treated me coldly. And now you take me hostage and will not say why. When we came down the cliff side together, I thought that the rumors were wrong about you. But now I think they may be right!"

"You do a good deal of thinking," he said, slinging her a grim look. "Come ahead."

"Nay." She glared at him. "What will you gain from keeping me? Tell me why, or I will not budge from this spot. I would rather go with Southron soldiers than go with you. I would rather be lost in this forest than go with you!"

She knew that outburst sounded spoiled and petulant, but it was the best she could do. Confrontation was not her strength. And she had never met a man with his powerful force of presence. She had scant experience with resisting another's will through the strength of her own—until the siege.

She did not lack determination, and weeks of siege had taught her skills she had hitherto not possessed. She called on those now. She mustered a look of stony fury and held on to the reins out of pure stubbornness, though her arm ached and her body trembled. "What will you gain from this?" she repeated.

His gaze filled with an inner storm, deep and dark. "You, Black Isobel," he said, "are the only hope I have for gaining someone's freedom. I intend to barter you for a life."

"Barter me?" She gaped at him, barely taking in what he told her. "To whom, and why?"

"Ralph Leslie holds my cousin at Wildshaw," he said.

She blinked in astonishment. "He holds no one there!"

"He does. I want her back unharmed. I trust that Ralph will trade one woman for another."

"A woman?" she squeaked. "He would not hold a woman prisoner. Unlike you!"

James slid her a long look. "He has her. And I will shortly let him know that I have you. You see, then, Lady Isobel," he said smoothly, "we will both get what we want from this. You want to go to Sir Ralph. But it must be on my terms."

"You lack honor," she snapped.

"So they say of me. Come ahead." He pulled on the reins.

She pulled back so hard she thought the stretched leather would break between them, thought her arm would come out of its socket. "Why do you do this to me?" she asked, panting. "I have done naught to you! If you have a quarrel with Ralph Leslie, 'tis not my doing. Let go!" she burst out in frustration.

He did not. "I do not bear you a grudge. But you know well what you have done to me."

"Have I burned your castle or stolen your freedom, as you have done to me?" Her voice rose to a shout.

He held up a hand, palm out, a swift, silencing gesture. "Your words took away what small chance for peace I had in my life. Your words ruined my name, and set all this in motion."

She stared at him. "Do you mean one of my—my visions?"

He nodded. "You know what you said of me."

She blinked in astonishment. "I know naught."

"You know more than naught," he snapped.

"I do not recall what I said. If you heard the prophecy, you know it better than I."

He huffed. "Who told you to say what you did of Wallace

and me?"

"Wallace—" She paused, her heart beating fiercely. She had strived to remember one prediction out of all of them; she knew, now, what he meant. "No one told me what to say. The words just come to me."

"Do you know the damage your words have caused?"

She saw thunder in his eyes. "I meant no harm through my visions. I forget the prophecies as soon as I say them. I am sorry if whatever came from me harmed you and yours. I want my prophecies to help people." She looked up at him with true regret. "Mayhap that will bring you some sense of peace."

"Hardly," he muttered. He yanked firmly on the leather and she let go. Her horse stepped forward to follow his and she rode in the wake of his silence like a boat in a storm.

"If Ralph does house your lover at Wildshaw," she said, after a while, "then let me go there and I will ask him to release her. Then we will both have what we want, without all this fuss of ransom and anger."

"We will not talk more of this now," he said over his shoulder. "We will wait until you are rested and less irritable."

"Irritable! You are the ill-willed one here."

He said nothing, his back to her. The steady footfalls of the horses filled the silence. She watched him for a long time, seeing the wide strength of his back, the power in his arms and thighs, the beautiful strands of gold that threaded his hair—and the invisible iron rod that seemed to form the core of his being.

She remembered his gentle words, his warm touch. All that was irretrievably lost between them. She felt the disappointment of that like a betrayal.

"I thought I could trust you," she said. "I was wrong."

"You will not be the first to say that of me," he replied.

He kneed his horse to a canter, drawing her along behind him. Isobel gripped the horse's mane and glared at the man's back, even as she tried to keep her balance at the pace he set.

Profound weariness, made heavier by fear and anger, settled like a lead cope over her shoulders. As they rode on, she grew too exhausted to even think about arguing with him. She rode in a daze, her body aching with fatigue, her wounds burning, her thoughts and emotions in a thick muddle.

When James slowed to silently hand her an oatcake that he took from a pouch at his waist, she said no word of thanks. She ate woodenly, hardly tasting it.

The sky was almost fully dark as they reached a narrow wooden bridge over a river. The moist air and the loud, white-capped rush of the water below them revived her senses, and she guided her mount across the bridge. They left the riverbank and rode across a moor, entering the rim of the forest.

The trees seemed to swallow them in rich darkness. James slowed their pace, for only silvery strands of moonlight lit the earthen path. But he went steadily forward, as if he saw through the night, as if he knew this track blinded.

Isobel frowned at the thought. Her misery—physical, mental, and emotional—increased as the horses' hooves thudded onward. She did not want to ride any farther; she did not want to be held hostage by this infuriating outlaw; she did not want to feel the deep aches of pain and fatigue any longer.

She did not even care to gain her freedom in this moment. All she wanted was to rest, and oddly, she longed to be held like a child. Her thoughts could barely go beyond simple yearning for someone who cared about her, soothed her, as her parents had done; both were gone. James Lindsay did not seem willing to offer her comfort.

Tears pooled in her eyes and she dashed them away, then she let them slide down her cheeks, too tired to hold them back. A hiccoughing sob escaped from her, and James glanced at her. He opened his mouth as if to speak, then turned away, his jaw set tight.

As they reached a fork in the path and turned left, Isobel uttered a small, involuntary cry and slumped forward, collapsing in raw exhaustion. She hardly knew, or cared, if she fell or was lifted down. All she wanted was sleep.

She heard him say her name as she melted into a black void.

Chapter Eight

KEE-KEE-KEE-ER.

Pearled light filtered through the overhead leaves as James opened his eyes. Certain he had heard the cry of a hawk, he scanned the clearing in which they had spent the night, but saw no hawks overhead or in the trees. He glanced down.

Lady Isobel lay stretched out beside him, wrapped in his cloak, still asleep. He had dozed with his back against the wide trunk of an oak tree, while a sturdy root, covered by his cloak, served as her pillow and his armrest. She slept deeply, curled warm against his thigh, serene and lovely. But her snores created an earthy contrast that made him smile.

He remembered how his older brother had snored like that in the bed they had shared as boys. James had pinched and pushed at him to gain quiet, and his brother often returned a solid, sleepy punch before rolling over. At the thought of his brother, killed on the bloody, tragic field at Falkirk seven years earlier, James lost the smile.

Kee-kee-kee-keer.

Again he heard the unmistakable cry of a hawk. But it was an agitated kakking rather than the long, clear cry of a hawk in flight. To his practiced falconer's ear, the bird sounded distressed. James sat straighter, careful not to wake the girl. He looked around the glade but saw no hawks.

Beside him, Lady Isobel blew out a long, loud breath. James

patted her shoulder gently. She inhaled and sighed out another noisy snore. He touched her jaw, petal-soft yet firm beneath his fingertips, and she turned her head. The shift quieted her breathing. He rested his hand on her shoulder and continued to look around for a hawk.

He had only dozed, yet felt alert. Years of living as a forest renegade had taught him to rest warily, his weapons close at hand. In the weeks since Wallace had been taken and his own name had become an anathema, that ability had served him well.

He leaned back his head to look at the dense texture of the trees, pierced by shafts of light. The forest at dawn had a sleepy silence where sounds carried clearly. He heard the soft, steady rush of a burn close by, the rustle of ferns as small creatures slipped past, and the whirr of wings among the leaves.

Odd, that. He frowned and glanced about again, his eyes, sharper than most, as keenly attuned to the forest as was his hearing. A handful of larks scattered into the early sky, a sure sign that a predator, perhaps a hawk, was nearby, even without the kakking he had heard.

If the hawk was a trained bird rather than a wild one, hunters would be nearby. Concerned, he touched the girl's shoulder to wake her, though she needed sleep. She whimpered and turned. Her body was firm and warm against his leg, and her cheek, soft as a sun-warmed rose, rubbed against his hand.

The sensation plunged through him and whirled in his groin. He withdrew his hand, but several pulsing moments passed before the honest reaction of his body calmed.

The hawk kakked again, somewhere close to the glade. He frowned and shoved his hair back in exasperation. He and Lady Isobel should take to their horses again. Hunters could be Scots or English, and willing to take a forest outlaw and a prophetess as a good day's quarry.

He must be certain before waking her. As he began to ease away, she moaned and turned further, resting her hand on his thigh.

His body throbbed with the sudden contact. He picked up her hand—delicate and fine-boned in his large fingers—and set it aside. She snuggled against him. He sighed heavily.

Total exhaustion had caused her to collapse last night, he knew. James regretted pushing her stamina and stubbornness so far. He should have made camp long before she fell from her horse. Fortunately, he had caught her before she injured herself further, and he had discovered the little glade where they and the horses could rest safely.

Time had slipped inexorably toward dawn. Now they would be lucky to arrive at his aunt's house before the sun was high. He sighed again, aware that every plan he had made concerning Isobel Seton had unexpectedly altered since the first moment he had sighted Aberlady Castle and found it besieged.

He had expected the prophetess to be a malicious, hard woman. To his dismay, her courage and grace made it difficult to coldly remember who she was and what she had done.

Subtle but certain, his body hardened and his heart softened whenever he was near her. He could not easily ignore the charm of her eyes or the graceful sway of her supple body.

He had never met a truly irresistible woman. The one girl who had caught his young heart had been sweet and good and had died horribly. In the years to follow, willing village girls interested him, but his fascination was easily sated, and his heart remained safe in his keeping.

The young prophetess enchanted him, distracted him, confused him, and touched off his temper like a flint. And her dazzling smiles, given easily to Quentin and even to rough-edged Patrick, but not to James, had made him simmer with unaccustomed jealousy.

Last night, her exhausted, lonely sobs had sliced through him. He was not proud of himself for turning away, for she had collapsed soon after.

He shook his head, wondering suddenly if he had met a woman he could not resist. What if together they sparked one of those rare alchemical integrations of the male and female natures? He had read about such things in long, postulating theories years ago.

God knew what else it could be. He made a sour grimace at the irony of feeling an extraordinary pull to the prophetess of Aberlady, of all women.

But if he succumbed to the effect she had on him, he would risk his sole chance to save Janet and avenge what had happened to his comrade, his kin, and his reputation. But to accomplish that, he must keep his reason cold and his emotions colder.

Isobel of Aberlady sighed, and her hair slipped over her pale cheek like a fold of black silk. He brushed her hair back, resting his hand on her head. She was finely wrought, delicate yet strong. Thoughts of pleasure and peace slipped across his mind.

He lifted his hand from her satiny head and fisted it against the tree root.

Kee-kee-kee.

The hawk sounded closer now. He eased away from the girl and stood, then stepped through the undergrowth to walk between the trees and look around.

The hawk's cry sounded again. Overhead, the upper branches of a large oak tree swayed, and he heard the frenzied thrash of wings. He circled the gnarled base, gazing up.

He saw the hawk high up through the leafy cover. Wings flapping, crying intermittently, the bird struggled on its perch. James glimpsed brown leather straps, the bird's jesses, wrapped around the branch.

Quickly he grabbed hold of a tree limb and hoisted himself up, climbing cautiously, watching the bird. The gray and cream feathers, delicately barred, and the distinctive white slashes over each blazing red-gold eye told him that the bird was a goshawk, probably male, and not yet fully adult.

"There, now," he said quietly as he came closer. "Hush you bird, hush." Knowing that the steady sound of a male voice could calm a trained hawk, he glided upward, keeping his pace slow and careful.

The bird's jesses—two straps, each several inches long and knotted to slitted leather anklets looped around the legs—had tangled around a branch, probably snagging when the bird perched. James noted with surprise that the hawk wore no bells on its legs. Perhaps the falconer had removed the customary bells to fly the bird silently after waterfowl, and the bird had flown off then. Had the bells been attached, the owner might have found his lost bird already.

As he drew closer, the goshawk bated, violently flinging itself backward off the branch to hang upside down, wings thrashing. Helplessly caught by its jesses, the bird could damage its feathers, injure itself, even die.

James straddled a thick tree limb and took off his waist and sword belts, dropping them to the ground. Then he unlaced his padded leather tunic, stripped it off, and removed his woolen tunic after that, letting them fall as well.

He was careful to make each movement slow while he slipped off his linen shirt and draped it over his bare shoulder. He did not want to approach the bird bare-skinned, for the talons could be vicious, but his shirt would serve as a trap.

Clad in breeches, hose, and boots, he rose higher in the tree, murmuring softly and soothingly. Years of raising hawks like this one had taught him to develop a falconer's patient tone and a relaxed, alert way of moving, as necessary for falconry as for forest rogues. When he was close enough, he cautiously extended his hand toward the goshawk.

The quickest way to retrieve a bird from a tree, he knew, was to distract and dazzle it with a bright lantern light. Lacking that, a slow approach would have to do. The bird was trapped and could not fly away, and James was aware he might scare it literally to death.

As he drew nearer, the goshawk squawked, helpless where it hung, and beat its wings furiously. Green leaves spit down to the ground, and the treetop shook. James paused and waited for the bird to exhaust itself. Having seen such outbursts in many trained birds, he knew it would not last long.

He narrowed his eyes to examine the bird while it spent its frenzy. One wing moved unevenly; James hoped that indicated a sprain rather than a more serious injury, or one of a variety of illnesses that affected hawks.

"Easy, you bird," he said as the flurrying wings quieted. "Hush, you bonny gos." Quick and sure, he slipped his hand behind the bird, scooping under the tail to grasp the body firmly between the legs. The surprise contact sent the goshawk into a limp state of shock, as James expected.

Goshawks taken in the wild had a nervous tendency to fall into a faint when grabbed by a human. Trained birds who no longer feared humans did not fall over so readily. This bird had been free long enough to revert to wildness, he realized.

Slipping his dagger from his belt, he cut the jesses. The leather was dry, cracked, and filthy; the goshawk must have flown away from its owner weeks ago. And the goshawk had fallen into shock immediately, another clue that it had been free for a few days, probably longer.

He gently righted the bird's head, ready to restrain the goshawk, not wanting to contend with an awake, angry, powerful bird. He held the limp goshawk in one hand and tugged a shirtsleeve over the finely shaped head, deftly trapping the wings and compact body inside. He wound the rest of the shirt around the body and padded the talons as best he could.

With the goshawk cradled in one arm, he looked down. Isobel stood at the base of the tree, staring up at him with her mouth open. She held his tunic in one hand.

"What are you doing?" she called.

"Rescuing a hawk," he answered. He began to make his way down the tree carefully, using the strength of his free arm. The bird stirred, squealed, and began an awkward struggle.

James leaned his weight against a sturdy branch and murmured soothing nonsense, stroking the bird's head and breast as if he held a babe in his arms. All the while, he avoided the vicious, powerful feet. When the exhausted bird quieted, James climbed down, dropped to the ground, and straightened.

Isobel clutched his tunic to her chest, her eyes wide as she stared at James, then at the curious bundle. He noticed that her eyes were the fine blue of a clear morning sky.

"You found a hawk?" She blinked at it in disbelief.

"A goshawk. Its jesses were tangled in the tree."

She nodded and bent to retrieve his leather hauberk, wincing when she jarred her injured arm, still bound to her side. James took the leather garment and belts from her. "How is your wound?"

"It hurts some."

"It must hurt a good deal for you to admit that much. We should change the bandaging before we travel on."

"'Tis fine," she said.

He shot her a doubtful glance and walked toward the glade.

"What will you do with the hawk?" she asked, following.

"I do not know. But I could not leave him there to die." He dropped the garments he carried, and sat on a fallen tree trunk, his feet deep in ferns. He held the squawking, trembling hawk firmly in his lap and studied it.

Lady Isobel sat on the trunk with him and leaned toward the bird. "My father had goshawks in his mews. They were gray like that, with the white band over the eye, but much larger."

"Females," he said.

"We released them during the siege. Eustace was for eating them, but I told him to let them go."

"Was there a male gos in your mews? This could be one of Aberlady's birds."

She shook her head. "I do not remember a smaller goshawk."

"Well, he came from someone's mews. Settle down, you bird. Let's look at you." Wary of the talons, he began to probe the body gently. "His crop is full enough—his breastbone is well padded—so he's had good hunting while he's been free."

"I know little about hawks, though my father kept them. I did not go in the mews often, and I have never been hunting." She leaned closer.

"Watch the talons," he warned. She pulled back. "Size is the best way to tell a male from a female," he explained. "This bird is much smaller than a female goshawk would be at this age. So the males are called tiercels, a third smaller." He stroked the delicate feathering over the head, the only exposed part of the bird. "His feathers have begun to change from the brown of an immature bird to gray, but he's not a full adult yet."

"He's beautiful," she murmured. "His eyes are bright as red gold. Can you unwrap him?"

"Not yet. The swaddling helps calm him," James answered. "That orange-gold color in his eyes means he's under two years old. Next spring those irises will be colored red as blood." He held the hawk upright, and the tiercel squawked at him. "Och, lad. He has a stubborn spirit," he added with a chuckle. "He does not like being tucked in my shirt."

"Will you keep him or release him?"

"I cannot let him go yet. His left wing moves awkwardly, and it feels swollen at the joint. I hope 'tis but a sprain. When he can fly well, I may let him go." He tipped his head and looked at the bird. "Then again, I may keep him. Goshawks are fine hunting birds."

"But he belongs to someone."

He shrugged. "He could have flown a very long way. I think he's been free for a while. His owner will have given him up for dead or lost."

"'Tis against the law to keep a found trained hawk or falcon," she said, frowning. "Men have been hanged for that."

He met her gaze evenly. "If I am caught, my girl, they will hang me for more than this hawk, and you know it."

She lowered her eyelids and did not reply.

James stroked the bird's breast, watching her. "Besides, that is an English hawking law. Scotland does not have such a rule.

Think you English law should prevail in Scotland?"

She shook her head, an unconsciously graceful motion. He wished he could believe her.

James rose and walked over to lay the bird breast down on the rumpled nest of his cloak. "Well, it hardly matters if I keep him," he said, squatting beside the bird, scratching its head while it chittered unhappily. "We'll never find the owner. And I do not intend to look. I have other matters on my mind."

He picked up his bow as he spoke, and carried it to the middle of the glade. Kneeling, he bent the bow in an arch and thrust the ends into the earth.

"What are you doing?" Isobel asked.

"Making a perch. I cannot leave the poor thing cast like that for long. He does not like me overmuch as 'tis." He went back to the bird, who rocked and struggled on the cloak. "Lady Isobel, help me, if you will," he said as he knelt.

"Aye." Kneeling beside him, she reached out her left hand to touch the bird's trembling back, her right arm snug against her body. "What should I do?"

"Can you keep the hawk still with just one hand?"

"I think so." She held the bird down.

James reached down to his ankle and began to unwind one of the leather thongs that bound his thick woolen hose to his leg. When he had freed one long strap and readjusted the stocking, he cut the thong with his dagger, producing two pieces, each less than a foot long.

"Hold him fast," he said. "I'll tie these on as new jesses, and take him out of the shirt."

While she held the goshawk's back, James tied the thongs to the bird's leather anklets. He snatched his fingers away a few times to avoid the clenching talons.

"Be careful," he told her as he worked. "He'll foot you quick. And he could crack your fingers with hardly an effort."

She eyed the bird nervously but did not move her hand. James noted her courage with approval as he unwound the linen shirt. Then he took her hand to guide it beneath the cloth.

"Hold him here, behind the shoulders. Firmly, now."

While she did, he unlaced the thick leather guard that he wore over his forearm for protection while shooting his bow and shifted it to cover the back of his hand. Then he picked up one of his discarded belts and wrapped it around his hand to protect his thumb and fingers.

"Lacking a leather gauntlet," he remarked, "'tis the best I can do. Let go, lass. We'll see if he remembers how to come to the fist."

He wound the makeshift jesses around his fingers. Then he slipped the shirt off the bird.

Isobel leaped back. The goshawk, freed from the restraining cloth, flapped its wings and rose upward, shrieking furiously.

Chapter Nine

"THE FIRST RULE of hawking," James said, "is to hold fast."

He extended his arm, feeling the tension in his shoulder and chest muscles as he resisted the bird's considerable upward force. The goshawk thrashed and flapped at the limit of the tightened jesses.

James tilted his head to avoid another fierce pass of a wingtip. "There is some cooked meat in my pouch over there. Can you get it, and tear it into bits?"

She did so, and came forward cautiously, glancing up at the furious, struggling hawk. She handed the meat to James, who took it in his free hand while she stepped away quickly. Her gaze, like his, centered on the frenzied bird and its wide, sweeping wings, its flexing talons. Though James held his arm out patiently, his muscles ached from the effort of resisting the hawk's strength.

With the other hand, he held the food. He would not exert force over the bird. He knew the tiercel was hungry and tired, and he hoped that the appeal of easy food, and the discipline of previous training, would assert itself.

Finally, the goshawk raked its wings more slowly and settled on James's offered fist with a decisive flapping. The bird cocked a resentful golden eye toward him.

"Ah," James said, smiling. "Here, you stubborn, bonny bird." He transferred the meat to his leather-covered hand. The bird tore at the food immediately. "'Tis cooked, but 'tis all there is.

Take it, aye, and the rest." He watched the bird eat. "Ah, look at him, Isobel," he said impulsively, grinning at her. "He's on the fist faster than I thought."

"He's quiet. Is he tamed?"

"Hardly. He's just tired and hurting, and only reluctantly willing to accept me."

"Ah," she said. "Like me."

He flashed a glance at her and gave a grudging laugh. Then the goshawk bated again, flinging himself off the fist to dangle head down, flapping his wings.

"What is it?" Isobel asked, sounding alarmed.

"A bate. Just temper. He wants us to know he does not like this. Hawks, particularly gosses, can throw fits like a spoiled infant. A falconer needs a good deal of patience to deal with a goshawk." He cocked a brow. "This one looks as if he will need a lot of patience."

The tiercel beat his wings in a fury, then hung motionless. James placed a hand on the breast and gently lifted him back to his fist. The narrow-toed feet clenched fiercely through the unpadded protection of the bowguard, and James bit back a wince. The bird roused his chest feathers and hissed.

"Soft, you," James murmured. He went to the bow that he had stuck in the ground and lowered his arm. The tiercel took to the perch with scarce urging, and James quickly secured the leather thongs to the bow to keep him there.

"He is quite temperamental," Isobel noted, watching.

"Short-winged hawks are of high temper by nature, and more of a challenge to train than long-winged falcons." James shook his head. "Poor bird. He was manned and lost and has gone feral again, and now he's had the shock of being trapped and taken. Temperamental and likely to stay that way."

"Mayhap you should let him go," Isobel said. "You should not keep a creature who wants to be free." Her eyes sparked with meaning.

He raked his fingers through his tangled hair and suddenly

felt the chill air over his bare chest and back. He retrieved his woolen tunic from the ground—his linen shirt was soiled with the bird's mutes—and pulled it over his head. While he laced his leather hauberk over the tunic and relatched his belt, he frowned in thought.

The unexpected responsibility of the goshawk would throw his plans into chaos. So far, nothing had gone the way he wanted. The sun would be high before they left the glade, and each daylight hour along the forest path brought the risk of being seen. He had no men to fight at his back if they met soldiers. He sighed and looked at Isobel.

"Are you hungry?" She nodded. "We must leave soon," he went on. "But first I want to look after your wounds and find you some food. The gos ate the meat I had saved for breakfast."

"I saw some blackberries beyond that elm tree."

He nodded. "I'll gather some, and bring the horses to the stream." He moved away, then looked back at her. "Guard the hawk, if you will, until I get back. If he bates, lift him gently to the perch. Be wary of his feet."

"Will he try to escape?" she asked.

"He is well and truly caught, though he does not like it." He tipped a brow at her. "And what of you, Lady Isobel?"

"Do you wonder if I am well and truly caught?" she asked in a spicy tone, head high.

He nearly chuckled at the unconscious charm in her defiance. "I just wonder if I should leave you here unguarded."

"I will not leave. I do not know this forest, and I can barely control that surly English stallion. And I am hungry." She fisted a hand on her slender hip. "For now, you have two captives."

James returned a frank stare. "And I'll keep you both. Be certain of it." He walked away.

ISOBEL SAVORED THE last few blackberries and sucked the ripe juice from her fingertips. The taste and satisfaction of fresh food were wondrous after the hardship of the siege. She sighed.

"Shall I fetch more?" James Lindsay asked, seated beside her on the fallen tree trunk. Amusement crinkled his eyes. She noticed tiny creases there, and the golden tips on his dark, thick eyelashes. His eyes were a vibrant, deep blue in the sunlight, like lapis lazuli shot with gold.

She shook her head and felt a blush touch her cheeks. "I am full," she murmured.

"Let me look after your arm."

"My arm is fine." The wound ached fiercely, but she was loath to admit it. Her behavior embarrassed her a little. Exhaustion had made her sob like a child and collapse on the horse, and she had likely snored like a soldier after a feast; that, she knew, was a fault of hers. Just now, she had eaten with a ravenous appetite, while James watched with an indulgent look on his face.

She did not want to appear needy or weak to him, and she did not want him to think that she trusted him. At Aberlady, she had put her faith in him, but his rescue had no honor in it. Her anger sparked each time she thought of it.

"I'm fine," she repeated stubbornly.

"Fine enough to make your cheeks paler than they should be, and so fine that you bite your lip and wince whenever you move. Do not be a fool. Let me see it."

She sighed. The arm did need attention. She began to loosen the cloth strips that bound her arm to her side. James leaned forward, the morning sun glinting over his hair. He gently pushed down the strap of her dark gray surcoat, and peeled back the torn sleeve of the pale gray gown beneath it. When he opened the bandages on her upper arm, Isobel winced sharply.

As he removed the cloth, she peered at her wound and gasped. The large punctures in the front and back of her upper arm had clotted, but the surrounding flesh was pink and swollen. The pale flesh of her arm was a mass of purple bruises. James turned her arm in his hand, the fierce ache nearly taking her breath. After a moment, he nodded.

"This looks bonny," he said.

"Bonny?" she squeaked in dismay.

"There are no streaks of infection. You are fortunate to have only swelling and tenderness. You will have some deep scars, but certain ointments can help the scarring. Let me see your foot." He bent to lift her ankle and peel back the bandage, the wound stinging when exposed. She decided not to look.

"'Tis healing well also," he said. "And you seem able to walk more easily, though you still limp. I will clean these and rebandage them, and my aunt can apply ointments and remedies to help the wounds heal cleanly."

"Is she a healer, your aunt? Where does she live?"

"She understands healing, if more for animals than humans. Her house is a morning's journey to the south."

"Will you tell your aunt that you intend to hold me for ransom?"

He picked up a cloth he had soaked in cool water from the nearby stream and folded it. His eyes flashed to hers. "I never said ransom, lass," he said softly. "Just a simple trade, one woman for another."

She sucked in a breath in answer, for he pressed the cold, wet cloth to her arm.

"The cold will help the swelling and ease the pain," he said. "Hold it there for a while."

He went to the hawk, who puffed out his feathers as the man drew near. James held out his arm patiently, nudging the goshawk's taloned feet with his leather-covered arm. After several moments, the goshawk stepped onto his arm with a flutter of wings. James stood, praising him in a calm, low tone. He offered a strip of meat, which he laid on the leather.

"I thought the rabbit meat was gone," Isobel said.

"It is. This is part of a mouse I caught when I got the berries and the water."

Isobel grimaced. A sparkle of amusement lit James's eyes. "He needs to eat too, and he would not care for nuts and berries, even as we would not care for his food."

"You fed him not long ago."

"I will overfeed him now so that when we travel he will be fat and full, and less eager to try to fly his own meals down."

The bird finished the food and clenched his feet, but did not bate. He stayed where he perched, as if he had begun to trust the man who had taken him.

Isobel watched, wishing she could have such faith in the man. But he had taken her prisoner. "If I were a hawk," she said, "I would bate and bite and foot you until you let me go."

"How fortunate for me that you are a woman," James drawled, glancing at her. She blushed.

The tiercel flattened his feathers and squawked. James began to pass his hand in slow, graceful arcs over the bird's head, again and again, while he uttered affectionate phrases in a soft, soothing tone. The hawk watched the moving hand in fascination, and seemed to relax, his feathers flattening.

"What are you doing?" Isobel asked.

"He will fall into a lazy trance watching my hand," he explained. "There, you bird, easy," he murmured. "He will forget that I am his natural enemy, and become comfortable perched on my hand, listening to my voice. Eventually he'll learn that I will not harm him. He will trust me."

"That is not so easy."

"So I understand." He slid her a quick look.

She let it pass. "Do you mean to train him?"

"I mean to reclaim him. Soft, you gos. There." He swirled his hand in graceful, long loops. The hawk watched, intrigued. Isobel watched, too, feeling drawn in by the peaceful, sweeping gestures.

"But he belongs to someone," she said after a while.

"He did." He emphasized the last word.

"A goshawk is a yeoman's bird," Isobel said. "But knights and barons, even earls and kings, favor goshawks, too. That tiercel could belong to anyone. If his owner is a man of rank, you could suffer for it. You must return him."

"I am an outlaw, my lass. I do what I please." He watched the hawk. She watched his hand, strong and supple and beautifully made. The bird stared at it too.

Isobel sighed. "Well, he might be from Aberlady's mews," she admitted. "Eustace would know." She came closer, drawn by the hand, the hawk, the man. "If you ever let me see Eustace again, that is."

James slid her a look. "Come here beside me, where the gos can see you. If you stand behind him 'twill make him nervous. And do not stare at a hawk," he added. "It means danger to them. Wildcats stare before they pounce."

"Ah." She moved to stand at James's right side, still holding the cool, damp cloth to her arm. "My father owned a beautiful goshawk once, a sister to one that King Alexander called his favorite hunting hawk."

James lifted a brow. "My uncle was a royal falconer to King Alexander. Mayhap he raised your father's hawk." He spoke to her in the same voice he used with the bird—low and mellow, almost musical. Shivers cascaded down her back.

"Did you learn hawking from your uncle?"

"Aye. I fostered with my uncle and aunt in Dunfermline when I was a lad, before I went to a seminary school in Dundee. My uncle taught me much about his art."

"You are a falconer, then." She looked at him in surprise.

"I am but a brigand who knows hawks." He leaned forward and set the tiercel on the bow perch, then turned to Isobel. He took the cloth from her hand to wipe his fingers, crammed it in his belt, and leaned forward to refasten the bandages on her arm.

She felt the ache ease as he touched her. Shivers rippled from head to foot as he pulled her sleeve up over her shoulder and wrapped the bandages that bound her arm close to her side. The simple sensations roused by his hands on her were relaxing, even compelling.

She did not want his hands to stop. She felt like the hawk, caught and enthralled. Perhaps she even had the same blithe, silly look on her face.

She cleared her throat. "Let me do that," she said, when he knelt to lift the heavy hems of her gown and surcoat.

"Just quickly," he said, slipping his fingers beneath to find her ankle. She felt a tender melting sense at his touch, and shifted her weight to her right leg to lift her foot, laying her hand on his head to keep her balance. His sun-warmed hair had a soft, fine texture. Her cheeks flamed suddenly.

"Why do they call you the Hawk Laird?" she asked, groping for something to say. She felt oddly breathless.

"Oh, because I strike with swift skill in the forest, taking English prey," he said in a mocking tone. "Or because I can see distances clear as crystal. Or mayhap"—he glanced up at her—"I earned the name for my nasty temper."

She pinched back a smile. "Tell me truly."

He shrugged as he wrapped the cloth strips firmly around her foot. "I had another hawk, years back, when I first came to the forest," he said. "She was a goshawk too, large and beautiful, a fierce hunter. She hunted grouse with a passion, just as my men and I hunted Southrons. Quarry never escaped us." He set her foot down. Isobel removed her hand from his head. "She was a fine bird."

"You kept her with you in the forest?"

"I made a mews for her in a cave." He turned to crouch beside the tiercel. "She would come out with me nearly every day. If we came across prey for her, Astolat would fly to it. If we came across my prey—Southrons—she would perch in a tree or soar overhead, or even fly off for a few hours. But she always came back." He smiled faintly, but Isobel saw a bitter sadness in his eyes.

James began to move his hand once again in languid passes over the bird's head. Isobel watched, standing behind him.

An easy peace existed in the little clearing, apart from conflicts of will and temper, of prize and captor. She wanted to preserve that, even if she had to stand here unmoving, just watching the man and the hawk until the sun sank.

"Astolat sounds a remarkable bird," she said. "You must be a gifted falconer to have trained her so well."

"Hawks differ in mood and nature, like people. Astolat was a perfect hawk, intelligent, with an almost human loyalty. I have never known a better-tempered bird." He waved his hand, and the goshawk stared upward, looking enraptured and slightly dimwitted.

"What happened to her?" Watching his fingers glide, Isobel felt as beguiled as the tiercel.

"She caught a Southron arrow meant for me," he said quietly.

"I am sorry," she whispered.

He nodded, his hand tipping and spiraling like a hawk in flight. Isobel watched as his hand moved in endless, gentle loops over the tiercel's head. All else began to fade from her awareness. Somewhere a bird trilled and a soft wind rushed through the trees. The restrained grace and power of his hand swept her along in its flight. He murmured the same low phrases over and over to the bird.

Suddenly she understood what the goshawk knew of the man: a soothing presence, a safe presence, a presence to be trusted.

She wanted to feel that for James Lindsay again, but could not. Then a remembered image came to her suddenly like a dream recalled—a man holding a goshawk on his gloved fist, standing beside a hawthorn tree in the rain.

This man.

Her heart began to thump. Months ago, in a vision forgotten until this moment, she had seen James Lindsay with a goshawk. She drew in a breath and wanted to tell him, yet could not. She wanted to take her gaze from his sweeping, gliding hand in the air, and could not.

The sunlit clearing around her began to fade. His hand was all she saw. Lights sparkled and glistened at the newborn edges of the field. Isobel felt the darkness slide in, filling her head, replacing the world her eyes saw with another world.

She wanted to cry out, but could not. She wanted him to pull her back, but she could not reach out. Darkness and light mingled and swept in like an ocean wave. She fell to her knees. Then light swirled into her, brighter and finer than glowing fire or sun, shimmering and dancing in her mind, brilliant, enthralling, loving, magical.

The images began.

She saw swirling clouds of mist. The veils parted to reveal a green mound and a hawthorn tree. Beyond it rose the soaring walls of a church, its stones dark with rain.

James Lindsay stood beside the tree, cloaked and hooded, a goshawk on his gloved fist. Isobel felt herself there, too, gliding over the damp grass to stand beside him. He turned to look at her, and she felt his sorrow, deep and dark and endless. He stepped away and she moved after him, floating on the misted air. But he walked into the mist.

She wanted to follow but felt trapped somehow, as if chained. Swirling away, she saw another man standing beside the tree. A large man, an armored knight, handsome in a bold way, broad in bone and muscle, taller than any man she knew. His body was powerful beneath a chain mail hauberk and a green cloak. He held a long broadsword upright, his hands folded on the high hilt, as he watched her. His eyes were gray and somehow filled with light.

"Jamie seeks peace," he told her. His voice was deep, rough, but kind. "And he seeks forgiveness. But he must grant them to himself and resists it."

"Who are you?" she asked.

"A friend. Be patient with him, Lady Isobel. He will find what he seeks."

She looked in the direction that James had gone. But the mist swirled, empty, lonely. She turned back. The huge, handsome knight had vanished.

The mist shifted into darkness again. This time it was a

brown murk, cold and filthy, with a vile odor. In the dank shadows, she saw stone walls, and a man crouched in a corner.

Her father. His hair was long and straggling, gray and filthy; his beard hid his face, his flesh sagged on the jutting bones of his large frame, but she knew him. She recognized his blue eyes, dulled to a slate color. He covered his head in his shaking hands and curled forward.

She cried out and he looked up, hope lighting his features. Then the image was gone.

"Father!" she screamed, reaching out. "Papa!"

The darkness flooded into her, sparkling with colored stars, sweeping her away. As it faded to a velvet black depth, she fell forward.

THE GROUND WAS firm and cool beneath her cheek. She felt the dewy grass between her fingers, smelled its fresh scent and the pungency of wild onion somewhere nearby. The wind and the sun were soft on her face and hands. She heard a lark singing overhead and heard the soft chirr of the jessed goshawk, a few feet in front of her. She pushed up to prop herself on her hands and knees.

"Isobel?" His voice was gentle with concern. She turned toward it. "Lady Isobel, what is it? Are you ill?" James crouched beside her. She felt warmth radiate from him. His hand rested on her shoulder, grip strong and firm.

"I am fine," she said, a little breathless. "I am fine." She began to stand, rising slowly. His hands supported her as she came up. The breeze pushed her skirt against her legs and the sunlight felt warm and gentle on her face.

"Can you walk?" he asked. She nodded. "Come over here and sit down." His fingers gripped hers, warm, caring, strong. She felt the weight of his other hand at her waist.

She stepped forward and stumbled as her toe caught something, a root, a stone. His hands steadied her. "Isobel, what is it?"

"I am blind," she said.

$$\text{—} \blacklozenge\cdots\bullet \quad \bullet\cdots\blacklozenge \text{—}$$

Chapter Ten

"**B**LIND?" HE WHISPERED.

"Aye." Isobel gave a trembling nod.

James stared at her. Bright sunlight lent her irises a pristine delicacy, but her gaze was flat and unfocused. He lifted a hand and waved it slowly, letting the shadow of his fingers pass over her face. She did not blink.

"Isobel," he said, his voice hushed. "What happened?" He wondered if she had been injured when the horse ran off. Head wounds could cause odd effects. "Did you hit your head yesterday?"

She tilted her head slightly as she listened to him. Her eyes stared, their dull gaze aimed somewhere beyond his shoulder. "Nay. The blindess comes over me whenever I have a vision. 'Twill pass."

"When you fell to your knees and cried out, and spoke aloud, you saw a vision?" he asked.

She nodded. "And the blindness always follows."

He raked his fingers through his hair, trying to piece together cogent understanding amid his alarm and astonishment. "Blind?" he repeated.

"The blindness will pass," she said calmly. She reached out and found his arm, rested her hand there. He gripped her elbow. "I have learned to expect this," she said.

"How long does it last?"

She shrugged. "An hour, an afternoon, sometimes through a full day. It passes each time. I pray 'twill always be so."

"Is there aught wrong with your vision otherwise?"

"Only a little blurring of distances, but that is common enough. My father once had a physician examine my eyes, and he said they looked healthy. This only happens during and after the prophecies, and then goes away. Father Hugh says 'tis my burden to bear for the gift of the prophecies."

"Mother of God," James said softly. "I did not know."

"Few do," she answered.

He watched her, thinking. "What vision did you see?"

Her brow furrowed. "I saw you."

"Me." He felt wary.

"And a goshawk, beside a hawthorn tree. I am trying to remember. I forget them so quickly. There was another man—a knight—who spoke to me." She shook her head as if confused. "The rest is gone. 'Tis like forgetting a dream upon waking." She bit her lip, looking intensely frustrated. "I am sorry. I try to recall them." She shrugged, shook her head, her blue eyes blank and innocent.

He felt a curious softening of his heart. Logic told him to doubt this, but he could not, watching her. He was greatly concerned and wholly shocked.

"You remember only a little?"

"Aye. After a vision, I barely remember anything of it. My father or the priest would sit with me to write down what I say, and question me about what I see and hear, and I answer them. Father Hugh has recorded my prophecies. He understands them better than I do. I remember little and they are often puzzles to me, full of symbols." She sighed. "I try to make myself recall, but—" She shook her head.

"Perhaps the shock of the blindness drives all else away," James said.

"That could be. The blindness used to frighten me, but I am used to it now. It will pass."

She did not look used to it, James thought. She looked like a frightened child pretending to be brave. Her fingers flexed on his arm. He pressed her elbow to reassure her with touch.

"How long has this been happening?"

"Since I was thirteen winters. I have learned to call the prophecies forth by gazing into a bowl of water or into fire. But just now, it came upon me strangely—suddenly. That has not happened since I was young. Do you recall what I said? Sometimes it comes back to me if I hear what I said."

He rubbed his brow. "You said 'peace and forgiveness,' and something about a friend."

"Ah. I saw a knight. He said he was a friend."

"Who was he?"

"I do not know. A large man, tall. What else?"

"You called out 'Father!' and I thought you were calling for a priest."

She gasped. "I saw my father!" Her fingers tightened on his forearm. "He was in a dungeon. He was...ill, weakened." She bowed her head. "What if he is hurt, or dead?"

"He is alive," James said quickly. "You saw him alive. Remember that, Isobel."

She nodded. Her face was pale cream in the strong sunlight, and her eyes were transparent blue glass, perfect yet sightless.

"Dear God," he murmured. He felt stunned, dizzy, whirled about in an unknown direction. "Tell me what you need."

She paused. "Safekeeping from you."

"Aye," he said gruffly, willing to grant her anything. He touched the curve of her cheek and she tipped her face into the cup of his palm. Her eyes drifted shut. "I promise."

"Thank you. Then, James Lindsay, let me go." Her tone was light, a mock scold.

For a moment, he did not think he could ever let her go. The force and certainty of it astonished him. Sympathy, he told himself; pity, perhaps. Just that, and no more.

"Come with me," he said gently and led her, step by careful

step, toward the horses.

Isobel tilted her head as they rode along the forest track. Sounds seemed louder to her in the blinded state, scents and tastes stronger, and her fingers told her more of texture and shape. The effort needed to sort through so many sensations, without sight to tell her what she heard or felt or tasted, could be overwhelming. But sometimes she exhilarated in her awareness of the commonplace.

She knew James held the goshawk on his leather-wrapped fist, for she could hear the creak of the leather and the scritch-scratch of the bird's talons. She heard James murmur often to the bird. His deep, soft voice had a comfortable texture, like warm wool on a cold night.

She knew he held the reins of her horse firmly, for she could feel the tension in the strap. His leg occasionally brushed hers as they rode, sending quick leaps of pleasure through her.

James rode close beside her, sharing what he knew of the Ettrick Forest. He told her he had lived in caves in the Ettrick for almost ten years, and she could sense his respect and love for the place. He was a natural storyteller, spinning entertaining tales about life as an outlaw and a Scottish rebel.

He spoke of his years running with Wallace and his men, engaging in skirmishes and trickery, weighing strategies and risks. He told of acts of cruelty, courage, and cleverness. With deft words and mellow tones, he painted images for her of intelligent, spirited men who believed freedom should exist in Scotland and sacrificed much for their beliefs.

But he told her nothing of how he had come to this life, nor did she ask. She listened and was glad that the earlier conflicts between them had entered a truce.

"My uncle was partly blind," he said after a while. "I fostered with him as a lad."

She tilted her head in interest. "Your uncle the falconer?"

"Aye. Blinded in the left eye by a trained eagle."

"An eagle! I did not know they could be trained."

"If the falconer is skillful enough, they can. Years ago, Uncle Nigel caught one in the mountains, an eyas—a young bird of prey—straight from the nest. He raised and trained it. A magnificent bird, though nearly impossible to manage. The bird was feeding on Nigel's fist one day. Birds of prey have a habit of swiping their beaks to clean them, and the eagle swiped against Nigel's head, taking the eye."

"God in heaven! And he still trained birds after that?"

"Aye, continued as royal falconer for years afterward," James said. She heard a note of pride, even amusement. "He was proud of his eye patch. A falconer missing his left eye is most likely to have trained an eagle, so he had even more respect from others."

"Does he still keep birds?"

"He died a few years ago," he said quietly. "After King Alexander died, he retired from the work to live in Dunfermline and make hawking equipment. He kept an old peregrine that had belonged to King Alexander. That bird was over thirty years old when she died."

"Ancient," Isobel said impulsively. She heard his snort of laughter. "For a falcon or a hawk."

"Aye well, I'm even more ancient," he said wryly. "Though I suppose you are scarce twenty."

She lifted her head. "Twenty-six come winter. Most women my age would be wed with bairns of their own."

"And you have not done that. Why?"

She shrugged. "I am a poor bargain. Few men would want a blind prophetess for a wife."

He was silent for so long that she tilted her head toward him as if to seek his reply.

"I think you would be a fine bargain," he murmured.

"To win you back what you want?" she asked sourly. He wanted a certain woman; she marveled at how strong his love must be. A ripple of jealousy went through her.

"The man who gains such a bargain will be fortunate," he

said. Her insides swirled, and she felt her cheeks grow hot with a furious blush. His voice, a rich blend of soft and rough, felt as intimate as if he touched her bare skin. "You have a suitor?"

"Sir Ralph Leslie is my father's choice for me. Not mine," she said. "He has little interest in me, but great interest in what I possess."

"Aberlady?"

"Prophecy." She tilted her head, though could not give him the direct stare she wished.

"Ah, is that the way of it." Then he was silent.

Riding beside him, she listened to the muted rhythm of the horses' hooves, the tiercel's faint squawks, and the steady murmur of the forest—rustling leaves, wind, and birdsong. After a while, she wanted to hear his voice more than the tapestry of sounds around her. "You said you fostered in Dunfermline with your uncle?"

"From the time I was ten until I was fifteen," he said.

"I know the place. 'Tis where Saint Margaret is buried, and other Scottish royalty," Isobel said. "I have not been to the abbey myself, but I have heard 'tis beautiful."

"A great abbey, a holy place. The pilgrimage route goes through there," James said. "But King Edward declared it a den of robbers since Scottish nobles met there to make plans against the English. So he burned the place down last year. An atrocious deed. His sister was buried there, yet he burned it."

Isobel gasped. "Was the abbey ruined?"

"The church was spared by grace of God. I have a friend among the monks there. Most of the monks last year had no quarters after the great fire."

"And your uncle's house? Was it safe?"

"Burned. He and his wife retired to a small house in the forest. She lives alone there now."

"Your Aunt Alice?"

"Aye. Lass, lean left. Low branch." He touched her arm. She ducked as branches swept over her.

"I am causing you a good deal of bother. I am sorry."

"I do not mind." His tone was gentle, the same one he used with the hawk.

As the horses began to descend a slope, she leaned back, gripping her mount's mane, until the ground leveled again. She felt the wind blow through her hair, felt the heat of the sun on her face, and heard fainter, higher birdsong. The blindness was lingering this time.

"We have left the forest," she remarked.

"Only to cross a moor. We will enter cover soon and follow another forest track. The Ettrick Forest is a good deal more than forestland, with moors, hills, lochs and burns in its boundaries as well."

The hawk kakked loudly and Isobel heard the wild thrashing of wings. "What is it?" she asked.

"Just a bate," James said. Isobel felt the horses stop, while the frenzied whirr of the goshawk's wings continued, slowed, and ceased. "Calm down, lad," James soothed. "Back to the fist, then." After a few moments, the horses stepped forward. "He saw a pair of deer run past. They startled him." Isobel nodded, and they rode on. "He needs to be hooded."

"And he needs a name," she said.

"I usually call my hawks and horses after knights and ladies from the tales of King Arthur."

She tipped her head curiously. "Why so?"

"When I was a lad, my parents gave me a painted manuscript in French containing many of the Arthur tales. I read them again and again. I suppose the names stayed in my mind."

"I read them, too, and loved them. My mother owned a copy in English, with beautiful pictures. You called your other hawk after Elaine, Lady of Astolat, who died for love of Lancelot?"

"Aye. 'Twas a prophetic name." His grim tone reminded her of his earlier remark: the bird had been killed by an English arrow. She waited in the blind darkness, waiting to hear more. He was quiet.

She heard leaves rustle, smelled the tang of greenery, and felt the cool and the quiet in the air as they entered the forest again. The pace of the horses slowed. The hawk kakked.

"He does need a name," James said. "What shall it be?"

"Arthurian, you said. Hmm." She frowned. "Ah. Gawain!"

"Gawain the goshawk?" He sounded doubtful.

"It means hawk of May, I think. Hey, Gawain," she said to the hawk, hearing the soft stir of his wings. "There. He likes it. I feel—it is important for him to have that name."

"More than you know. Alice keeps a female red-tailed hawk called Ragnell."

Isobel smiled. "Ah, Gawain and Ragnell were paired in one of the legends. Sir Gawain promised to wed Lady Ragnell, though she was a hideous old hag."

"And believe me, it suits Alice's hawk," James said wryly. "She wants all her will, that one."

"I am eager to meet her." But she sobered. Regardless of kindness and patience, the outlaw had taken her captive. If he took her to his aunt's house, surely he meant to secure her there as his prisoner.

Sighing, enveloped in the frustrating blackness, she rode forward into an uncertain future.

— ◆··• •··◆ —

Chapter Eleven

S UNLIGHT STREAMED DOWN over the forest path. Isobel felt the warmth as the horses stepped into sunny pools and back into cool shadows. She arched her lower back wearily and pushed a hand through her bedraggled hair. Her woolen gown and surcoat had become uncomfortably warm, and she was growing more irritable due to pain, hunger, and fatigue.

And the darkness in her eyes lingered, making her feel as if she balanced precariously on a razored edge, hovering between fear and faith, waiting for her sight to return.

She heard the tiercel bate again and the horses stopped as James spoke soothingly to the bird. She felt sure the outlaw was tired and irritable, just as she was, for he had said little, but his patience with the bird and his kindness to her continued to impress her. Finally the goshawk quieted and they continued. Each time she heard the rustle of his wings, Isobel expected to hear the tiresome fury of another bate.

"Do you regret taking on the hawk?" she asked. "He seems a difficult bird."

"I could not leave him there. He needed help. And he cannot fly well as yet."

"Do you regret taking me?" she asked. "I cannot fend for myself just now, either."

"At least you do not throw tantrums."

She laughed softly. "Is your aunt's house close now?" she

104

asked after a while.

"Aye," he said. "We will walk around the base of a slope, and the house is just past that."

Soon they left the earthen track to ride between the trees. Isobel cried out as a branch brushed her unexpectedly. She felt the touch of his hand on her knee.

"I will ride ahead and bend the branches out of your way." He moved forward, Isobel's stallion following. "It is just at the edge of the clearing. It is a peaceful and welcome sight, this."

"Oh." Disappointment plunged through her. "It must be lovely."

"Aye. Sorry, lass." His horse was beside her again, and she felt him lean, felt the solid press of his shoulder and the warmth of his closeness. "Just ahead now," he said quietly. "The forest opens suddenly, like a green frame around a painting. The clearing beyond is filled with golden sunlight. The grass is sprinkled with dandelions, and a small stone house sits at the center."

She listened, entranced, seeing the images in her mind.

"Smoke curls up from a hole in the thatched roof," he went on. "Two tiny windows are open to the air and light, and the door is open, welcoming, with a white cat asleep on the low slate step. A goat wanders through the yard, and under his feet are a few chickens. He ignores them as he nibbles at the flowered turf bench tucked against the side of the house. There is a small garden at the corner, with some vegetables and herbs. The lavender is bright purple, the raspberry canes are green and tangled, and golden honeysuckle grows thick over the fence."

"Ah," she breathed. "How beautiful."

"I come here for the peace, and to see Alice. You will like her." His shoulder pressed hers, giving her a pleasant sense of ease and security. She let herself lean into him.

"Thank you," she said.

"My uncle used to ask me to describe things for him as the sight in his good eye began to dim with age. I thought you might like it too."

"Is Alice there waiting for us?" For the moment, she did not care that she was a captive. She wanted to enjoy the serenity, craved the comfort of what he described.

Then he tensed, straightening away from her, and swore under his breath. A familiar thumping rhythm sounded in the distance; she recognized the sound of horses.

"Who is it?" she asked in alarm. "Are they coming this way?"

"Listen." His voice was hard. "I am going to lead the horses into a stand of birches, and I want you to stay here, hidden away. It will cover the sight of you."

"But what—"

"Hush," he hissed. He tightened his grip on the reins of her horse and pulled. Branches clawed at her, and a limb snapped her in the jaw. She waved her arm, panicked, unsure where she was.

Then she felt his hands like iron around her waist as he hauled her swiftly from her horse. Then he brought her through deep ferns and shoved her down into the bracken, a hand on her head.

"Stay down. Be quiet," he whispered. Then he was gone, slipping away.

She lay in the bracken, face muffled in the crook of her arm. The smells of earth and green were strong and her injured arm throbbed, but she made no sound, listening with all her awareness.

Horses snorted through the cover of trees and the goshawk squealed nearby; James must have tied him to a perch in a tree, she realized. Then, as the cantering horses stilled, she heard male voices. She turned her head among the ferns, their soft fingers combing her skin, scent filling her nostrils.

Time stretched. Wildly, suddenly, she feared that James had left her in the forest. But soon she heard the soft, stealthy thud of footfalls and felt him drop down beside her in the ferns. With relief, she turned toward him and began to speak.

"Hush!" His finger touched her lips. Then he lay beside her, pulling her against his chest, her back to him, so that they lay spooned together. The length of his body pressed to hers, his arms firm around her. He placed the palm of his hand over her mouth.

"Shh," he whispered, his grip steel-hard, his heart thumping against her back. Unable to see, prevented from moving or speaking, she panicked, struggling, kicking out. James locked a leg over hers to still her legs, and as she gathered breath to scream, he tightened his hand over her mouth. She bit the finger touching her lips.

He uttered a soft oath. "Be still and silent," he growled. "Promise, or I will not let go."

She nodded and he lifted his hand from her mouth, keeping his arms tightly about her. Isobel felt like a wild thing caught in a trap—she was so wrong about him. She never should have trusted him. She twisted again and he yanked tighter until she stilled, breath heaving.

"Soft, you," he whispered. "I will not harm you." His embrace relaxed. "Make no sound."

She elbowed him heartily in the breastbone and he grunted, giving her but small satisfaction. Nothing short of a miracle could appease her anger toward him now. She could never trust him, and clearly he did not trust her either.

The thought sobered her, and she went slack in his arms. After a moment, she felt him lift his head to look around. "The riders are coming close to the clearing," he whispered.

The cadence of hooves vibrated the earth beneath her and she heard the muffled thuds of a single horse moving forward. "How many are there?" she whispered.

"Four," he said softly. "Just one crossing the sward."

"Scots?"

"I do not think so. Their armor is too fine. Few Scots could afford such trappings. But the Scots do not think too kindly of me either, so we will hide." His voice was nearly as silent as a breath.

"Tell me what the leader looks like," she whispered.

"Dappled horse. I cannot see the man. Hush."

A deep, smooth male voice gave a polite greeting, and Isobel heard a woman's voice in reply. Held nearly trapped in James's arms, she tried to listen to the knight and Alice, the woman.

But she was distracted by the hard wrap of James's arms around her, by the firm length of his body against hers, the rhythm of his breath at her ear. Feeling shivers go through her, she scowled and concentrated on what she could hear.

"Tell me where he is, madame." The knight's voice was angry and familiar. Isobel frowned.

"I have not seen the lad in months," Alice replied, her voice earthy, full, bold. "I live alone here, and no one bothers me, but for you. Begone."

"Surely he came to you for help. Tell me where he is!" he said, loud and demanding.

Isobel lay enclosed in James's arms, no longer tempted to struggle to get away from the forest brigand who held her, for if she was seen, she could not flee to safety now.

She waited for Sir Ralph Leslie to speak again.

DRAWING ISOBEL CLOSER, James pressed the palm of his hand over her soft lips. A moment ago, she had gasped in alarm, her blue eyes wide, startled, yet staring at nothing.

Her blindness alarmed him, but the only help he could offer her was to keep her safely hidden from Sir Ralph Leslie. Her expression told him she recognized the voice of her betrothed. James held her firmly and looked through the leafy cover to see Alice Crawford step forward.

His aunt fisted her hands on wide hips beneath her brown kirtle, and stared boldly at Leslie. Taller than most men, Alice Crawford was not easily intimidated. "What do you want with James Lindsay?"

"He's wanted for crimes against King Edward."

"I know that," Alice snapped.

"Then you know that William Wallace was taken last month and executed for treason."

"I heard. God rest his soul. The Southrons are heartless bastards," she added bluntly. "William Wallace never committed treason in his life. What do you want with Jamie Lindsay?"

"He betrayed Wallace."

"Never," Alice said.

"I have proof."

"I do not believe it. Why spread such a foul tale, you, a Scotsman?"

"If the Scots find him they will cut him down for betrayal. If the English find him, they will hang him, and worse." Leslie leaned closer. "I can help your nephew, Dame Crawford. The charges against him can be remanded by King Edward, who may see fit to offer him a reward."

James felt Isobel grow still as a stone in his arms as she listened. He glanced back to his aunt, facing the knight in the clearing.

"Are you one of those who turns his loyalty with the wind?" Alice asked.

"I am a practical man, Dame."

"Then show your good sense and get out of my yard!"

"Peace, woman. I came here for another reason as well."

"Speak of it," she snapped.

He lifted his left arm to display the black armband wrapped around his chainmail sleeve. "I am in mourning. I lost my betrothed two days past, in a fire at a castle in Midlothian. My beloved Lady Isobel Seton was inside with her garrison."

With a gasp, Isobel twisted in his arms as if desperate to go to her lover. James dragged her close, more roughly than he meant to do. Her hip pressed against his groin, her breast was soft under his arm, and her lips were moist and warm against his palm.

Sudden, unexpected lust flared. He drew a ragged breath, heart hammering. Stop, he thought. He had spent a few years in a monastery, and even more as a renegade; he had learned to master his body and emotions. Yet desire surged through him like fire at this most inconvenient moment.

But he felt her sob under his hand, felt her hands tremble as she touched his hands. Her distress was like a dousing of cold water. He lessened his hold.

"I will not hurt you," he murmured. "But do not think to call out to your lover." The word tasted bitter on his tongue. He held her and tilted his head to listen once again.

"I tried to save Lady Isobel from the fire, but I was too late," Leslie was saying. "I ran into the flames without fear for my life, so great was my urge to find her. Love makes a courageous heart."

James felt a chill of disgust run through him at Leslie's audacious lie. Even more, the words stirred old nightmares, so that James closed his eyes against the hollow pain of remorse.

Glancing through the leaves again, he saw his aunt clasp her hands over her wide bosom, caught by Leslie's story. Tough as she looked, Alice's sentimental heart could melt like butter over flame.

"But my precious Isobel died in the inferno." Leslie lowered his head.

"Oh, the poor lady!" Alice cried.

Isobel squirmed in his arms and James heard a muffled wince—a smothered cry for help?

"She was a beauty, and a gifted prophetess."

"Black Isobel? Do you speak of the prophetess?"

"Aye, the same. But someone escaped the fire, madam. An arrow protruded from the cliff side, white-feathered like those used by the fellow they call the Hawk Laird. If he killed my Isobel, I will kill him with my own hands."

"A white-tipped arrow is no proof Jamie was there. Others use such arrows. Goose feathers, duck feathers. And your beloved might have escaped the fire."

"That would gladden my heart. But if you see your nephew, give him a message from me."

"He does not come here."

"Best find him, then, and tell him that I have Janet Crawford in my keeping."

"Janet!" Alice burst out. "My niece! Is she safe? If you harm her—"

"She is my guest. Do not fret. But be sure to tell Lindsay where she is. He will want to know. And tell him," he continued, "if he wants to see her again, he must come to Wildshaw Castle, where I am constable, to escort her home."

James fisted his hand, white-knuckled, against Isobel's waist as he listened to Leslie's mild words that couched strong threats. As Isobel stirred in his arms, he tightened his hold again.

"You hold Wildshaw now?"

"King Edward put it in my command," Leslie said. "Deliver my message, Dame Alice. I am sure you have some way of contacting this outlaw. I will return in a few days and I hope you will have news for me by then." He circled his horse. "Good day."

He and his men rode out of the yard. Alice watched them, her hands clapped over her mouth, her cheeks flaming red. Then she turned and ran into her house.

James waited, the girl snug in his arms. Then he felt heavy pulsing in the earth beneath him.

"Riders," he hissed. Flattening belly down in the bracken, he pushed Isobel onto her back to flatten her, too, shielding her body with his, his torso half over hers, his hand over her mouth. High thick ferns enclosed them in a verdant cave, giving off a rich green tang. James waited, his cheek against the softness of Isobel's hair, her body a curving, warm cushion beneath his.

They lay still for endless moments, her breath in tandem with his. Closing his eyes, James listened with his entire being, feeling hoofbeats in the earth, hearing the jingle of armor and weapons. The riders came so close this time that the ferns quivered as the horses passed through.

Suddenly she twisted, nearly slipping away. A small cry escaped her mouth. Sudden and sure, James brought her back, scooping his hand along her jaw, turning her head, covering her lips with his own to silence her in a hard and swift kiss—all he could think to do in the moment.

She went still beneath him, mouths pressed tightly together, breathing together, while the thunder of hoofbeats surrounded them. Her lips moved beneath his, and a deep thrill spiraled through his body. He lay motionless, but his mouth softened over hers and his blood rushed. *Stop,* he told himself.

He lifted his mouth away, stunned by the force that had taken him, but the wild pounding of his heart, thumping with desire, with desperation, but an intense need that he could hardly explain. He pulled back. Her eyes, jewel-like in the green glow of the ferny cave, were filled with tears.

"Oh, God, Isobel, I am sorry." Gently he slipped his fingers into the tousled silk of her hair. But when she sobbed out a little and touched her lips to his, he stilled, and felt a true kiss. Her lips were sun-warmed honey beneath his, warm and allowing. The slow, exquisite kiss stole his breath and his reason.

Then he realized that the riders were gone. Drawing back, he lifted his head to listen.

Silence.

He glanced at Isobel. She stared at him, eyes glistening, keen on his, filled with awareness. Filled with sight. He touched her cheek with a finger.

"You can see," he whispered.

"Aye. Just now." She laughed. "Just when you kissed me."

He let out a stunned breath. "Does it always need a—a kiss?" He sounded like a halfwit.

"I have never tried kissing as a remedy." She laughed again, soft, clear. "But it helped. So I kissed you back, just to be sure."

He blinked in disbelief. "I do not understand any of this," he said. Then he rose to his knees in the ferns, nearly bolting upright as the meaning of what had just happened hit him like a blow.

Only in a collection of saint's tales or a *roman d'aventure* could a chaste kiss heal miraculously. But that had not felt chaste; his body throbbed, his blood surged.

By the Rood, he thought. This was not some epic tale. He

was a brigand, not a hero. But he could not shake the effects of that stunning, impulsive kiss. He wanted to feel its sweeping power again.

Isobel watched him calmly, almost sweetly. He was glad of it. The lass could see, thank all the saints. But the look of adoration in her eyes made him distinctly uncomfortable.

He preferred the safer ground of enemies, of distrust, of practical matters like hostages and strategies. He did not know what to do with visions, magic, or miracles. Or love and kisses, of all things.

Not love, he told himself, and surely not with the prophetess, of all women. He shoved a hand through his hair. Once again, Black Isobel brought something unexpected into his life. He did not know what to think of her. He did not know what to feel about her.

But he knew he wanted to touch her, kiss her, immerse his hardened heart in her gentle nature. He even wanted that adoration from her, but he knew he did not deserve any of it.

Scowling, he looked away. "Safe to leave now." Oh aye, safer than staying here and yearning after a lass, he thought sourly. "I'll fetch the goshawk and the horses. Stay here." He stood.

She rolled to her side and sat up. "James Lindsay."

He looked down. She rose out of the ferns like a faerie queen, with the green fronds clinging to her gown and her hair. He felt an odd sensation in the region of his heart, like a brightness somehow.

"Aye?"

"Thank you," she whispered. "For the kiss."

"Your sight would have returned soon or late, as you said. But I am glad to have been of help."

She tilted her head, watching him. He thought how innocent she was, yet how mysterious, with her strange wisdom, with her beautiful eyes and her sweet mouth. And he wished he were free to love her. Sometimes he wondered what it would be like to live a peaceful life. But he would never know. Danger lurked around him. He could not yearn after peace, or love, or black-haired prophetesses.

She brushed at her gown and began to move away. Reaching out, he stopped, steeling himself against touching her. He stepped back.

"James," she said. "Ralph has Janet."

"Aye. He means to trap me."

"But he said you murdered men. He said you promised to betray Wallace for a reward. But—but that cannot be true."

James looked at her. He understood what she wanted to hear, and knew his words would hurt her. "Aye," he said. "'Tis true."

He turned away. He did not want to see the disappointment in her eyes.

Chapter Twelve

I SOBEL LOOKED AROUND as she and James rode forward. The clearing was a sunlit jewel, green and bright, with a stone cottage at its center, cozy and welcoming, just as James had described it.

The blindness, when it cleared, often left her with a sort of visual hunger. She looked around avidly, then glanced at James. He rode ahead of her, holding the reins of her horse in the same hand he used to guide his horse.

His posture was agile, his back powerful as he swayed with the black stallion's steps. The goshawk on his fist was calm, his feathers delicately barred, his head unhooded as yet, eye blazing red-gold as he turned his head.

James glanced at her over his shoulder, then looked away.

A rising blush heated her throat and cheeks as she remembered, suddenly, that stunning kiss that had robbed her of breath. When the kiss turned tender, profound, the darkness had vanished.

She had felt such relief and gratitude in the moment that she had wanted to kiss him again, had simply, suddenly, adored him. But he had turned away, remote once again. And then he had admitted to committing treachery.

Isobel felt struck through the heart. The arrow that had slammed into her arm was a thorn compared to the stabbing force of his words.

Now, she watched the proud lift of his head, the strong carriage of his wide shoulders, and thought of his gentleness with her, with the hawk. And she could not believe him capable of betrayal.

Confusion flooded her. She knew now that Sir Ralph Leslie was not the staunch knight her father believed him to be. He had lied about his attempt to rescue Isobel just to gain Alice's sympathy, and he held this Janet Crawford hostage. And even if he believed Isobel dead, his grief did not seem genuine.

She scowled. She could not trust Sir Ralph any more than she could trust James Lindsay.

The tiercel fluttered his wings suddenly and squawked. James hushed the bird, and halted both horses. Ahead, Isobel saw a woman step out of the doorway of the house. Wearing a brown dress and a pale head-kerchief, she ducked her head slightly to clear the lintel. She was tall and large, with a broad frame and a cumbersome bosom. She fisted her hands on her broad hips and stared.

"Greetings, Aunt." James swung down from his horse and set the hawk on the saddle for a perch.

His aunt came toward him and grabbed him in a fierce hug, then stepped back. "Come inside. Hurry. They are searching for you." She looked at Isobel. "Lord save us! Is that the prophetess?"

"Aye. And quite alive, despite what Sir Ralph Leslie told you."

"You heard what the knight said?" Alice stared at him.

"Some. We were hiding in the fern brake." James went to Isobel's horse and helped her dismount, lifting her down quickly. She turned to face his formidable aunt.

"A weary pair of travelers," Alice said. "Where did you find that gos?"

"A long tale, Alice," James said.

"And I shall hear all of it," she said briskly, then turned toward Isobel. "*Tcha,* look at you, poor lass. Pale as a dove, and just as bonny." She gathered her into the warm circle of her arms and then ushered her toward the door while James fetched the hawk.

"Is your arm wounded, lass? And you're limping." Alice turned toward James. "How did that happen?"

"Arrowshot," James said.

"Lord save us! An arrowshot lady, a raggedy hawk, and Scots and Southrons searching for you both." Alice shook her head. "This lass is so weary she can hardly stand."

"And so I brought her here. I knew you would take us in without too many questions."

"Oh, you ought to be questioned, you great brigand!" Alice burst out. "How could you allow a lady to be so mistreated?" She scowled at the goshawk. "Is that gos trained? He has a wild look to him."

"He's part wild," James said.

"Then be wary of Ragnell if you bring him inside. You'd best put him in the mews when you look to those stolen horses. I know English horseflesh when I see it," she added crisply.

James hid a smile. "Aye, Alice."

"And do not smile at me. I lied for you this day, laddie, said I never saw you and pretended I knew nothing about Janet. The only sins I commit are wee lies for you. Pray heavenly forgiveness for me, will you."

"I will," he said. Isobel saw his affectionate smile.

Alice grunted in answer and escorted Isobel inside the cottage, where the dimness was relieved only by the glow of a fire in a floor hearth. Alice led Isobel to a flat-topped wooden chest, where she sat.

The moment James crossed the threshold, Isobel heard a shriek and the rapid flutter of wings. In a dark corner of the room, a hawk on a tall perch fell backward in a resounding bate.

On James's fist, the tiercel did the same, as if the other hawk had frightened the wits out of him. James extended his arm to give the goshawk space for his tantrum.

"*Benedicite,*" Alice said. "That gos has startled her, and I just got her calmed down from the last visitors." She bustled toward the perch and spoke soothingly to the agitated bird.

Isobel sat and watched, blinking from one hawk to the other, from one owner to the other. Alice's hawk was a large female red-tailed hawk, brown with a bright russet tail. The tiercel was smaller, but his fit was equally tempestuous. Both Alice and James waited with supreme patience until their bating hawks slowed.

When the tiercel calmed, James lifted him back to his fist. Isobel glanced at the female, who still hung upside down from her jesses, gradually slowing her wings to an occasional twitch.

"Ragnell's making this into a ceremony," James remarked.

"She should have been a mummer, much as she loves to perform." Alice heaved the hawk onto the perch. "Wee spoiled bird," she murmured, stroking the puffed breast feathers. "Useless bonny bird."

Ragnell chirred to her mistress and clenched the wooden perch with her feet, or what she had of them. Isobel saw with surprise that part of the bird's left leg was made of silver. The false foot, strapped around her leg, was shaped into a set of talons that slid over the perch.

"She's missing a foot?" she asked in surprise.

"Since she was a brancher," Alice said. "'Tis why she is so spoiled, see. We coddled her, and now she rules us."

James came closer, cautiously balancing the goshawk. "Hush, Lady Ragnell. I brought a friend."

"Be polite, you silly bird," Alice told her hawk. "I do not want to hood you, though 'twill calm you. Gentle, now." She turned to fix James with an intent stare.

"Ho," James said, holding up his hand. "I know that look."

"Aye, I want the truth," Alice said. "Why is Sir Ralph Leslie looking for you? Does he hold Janet for ransom now? And that gos needs a hood. He keeps staring at Ragnell."

"I was hoping you had a hood and a proper glove to spare. As for the rest—" James shrugged. "The English want me, and so does Leslie. They know I attacked the party that took Wallace. And you know Leslie was with those who took Janet and me to Carlisle in March." He glanced at Isobel as if explaining this to her as well. "When I escaped the English guard weeks ago, he took the lass into his custody."

"Enough that they killed my Tom," Alice said quietly. "I cannot bear to lose my niece as well. She insisted on joining her kinfolk in the forest, and this madness came of it. Will you go after her, Jamie? Naught would please me more." She peered at him. "Now tell me how it is you have the lady prophetess when Leslie thinks her dead?"

"The Southrons besieged her castle, but I took her out of there," James said. "We went down the cliffside."

"After setting the castle on fire," Isobel said.

Alice gasped. "An adventure indeed, but a grim tale!"

"Alice, we need your help. The lass needs care and rest."

"Sir Ralph will want to know that she is alive."

"Oh, he will find out," James said.

"He cares for the lass, it seems to me."

"He does want the lady," he said in a low, quiet voice that sent shivers through Isobel. A swift, intense memory of kisses among the ferns rushed through her. She drew in a breath, silent, listening.

"But he will not have her," James continued, "until we have the other lass back."

"You mean to barter her for Janet?" Alice asked.

"I had that in mind."

"If Leslie wants the lady and she wants him, and we want Janet, we all win in the trade."

"Who loses indeed?" James murmured, his gaze returning to Isobel.

Isobel sighed. "I will go to Wildshaw and ask Leslie to release your lass," she offered. "I must see my father. He may be there too. I have to know."

"Not on your own," James said in a flat voice.

"I will go there," she said, summoning boldness.

"Is that a prediction?" he inquired softly.

"Later for this. Your lady is exhausted. You look weary too,

Jamie," Alice said.

Your lady. The words sank through Isobel. She sighed and pushed her fingers through her tangled hair, then covered her face in her hands. "I am tired. Very tired," she admitted.

Alice went to a cupboard and took out a small red hood, which she handed to James. He slid it over the bird's head, and the goshawk seemed to relax. He went to the door. "I will take the gos to the cave, and tend to the horses."

"Good. Ragnell cannot tolerate that gos in the house," Alice said. "She will bate again." As if she understood, Ragnell uttered a squawk and lifted her wings. "I wonder what has gotten into her."

"Lady Isobel named the gos Gawain," James said. "Mayhap she knows she's met her match."

"Ragnell will never meet her equal," Alice said.

"We all do, Alice," James said. "Soon or late, we meet the one who will do our heart in." Without looking back, he turned and left the house. Isobel stared after him, her heart pounding.

"*Benedicite,*" Alice said softly. "Will you look at that."

"She snores, your prophetess," Alice observed much later of Lady Isobel, who rested in Alice's own box bed behind a curtain wall while James sat with his aunt by the hearth fire. "Near as loud as Nigel did. He could shake the bedcurtains with his snores, that man."

James laughed and swallowed ale from a wooden cup. After he had returned to the house, having tended to the hawk and horses, Isobel was already asleep in Alice's box bed. His aunt said she had treated the girl's wounds with herbal ointments, had prepared a bath for her, and had given her some hot porridge. He had not realized he had been out of the house so long, but was glad that the girl had time with his aunt to tend to her needs.

Now he watched his aunt's strong, thick fingers wield a needle as she repaired a rent in Lady Isobel's gown. The firelight flickered over her face, which creased in a frown.

"You and Janet are all I have left in this world," Alice said. "Nigel has been gone four years and our two oldest sons died at Stirling seven years back. And then young Tom, last spring." She stopped and bit her lower lip as it quivered.

"It has been hard for you," James said softly.

"You must get Janet back, Jamie."

"I will."

The needle flashed. "I hoped you might marry our Janet someday. You are cousins by marriage only. She is a good lass."

"Janet," James said, "has a will like an ox. She would do me in."

Alice chuckled. "Tom said that of her once," she said. "'The will of an ox and a rump to match, and I do not want to play with her.' I beat him about his own rump with my broom when I heard that!" Chuckling, she stitched the cloth while James finished his ale.

Hearing a sniff, then another, he saw his aunt blinking back tears. "Alice?"

"I am fine, lad. So long as I have you and Janet." A shadow passed over her eyes.

James nodded, knowing how deeply his aunt mourned the loss of her husband and her sons to the cause of Scotland. But she had James, her sister's son, and Janet, her husband's niece, and loved them as if they were her own.

Something warm shoved against James's leg. He reached down to pet the large, white cat. "Ho, Cosmo. Where have you been?" he asked, stroking the long back. "Out catching mice for Lady Ragnell? You must find a few extra for Gawain."

"He only brings mice to Ragnell because he is terrified of her," Alice said. "You will have to catch mice yourself for that gos of yours. Sparrows, too. Gosses love sparrows." She glanced up. "Cosmo, come away from the bed. You will wake the lass. Shoo!" She waved until the cat turned and settled by the hearthstones.

His aunt fixed him a bowl of porridge, the quickest meal she had for him, and as he ate he glanced again toward the curtained box bed where Isobel slept. Perhaps by morning she would be rested enough that he could question her further. When he set down his bowl, he helped Alice refresh the remaining bathwater with a hot bucketful.

As Alice went outside to tend to her garden, James stripped down and stepped into the luxury of a warm bath. The water was still scented with lavender and foamed with the herbal soap Isobel had used. He scrubbed his hair and shaved his unkempt beard, ignoring thoughts of Isobel's cream-skinned body, slick and nude, sharing the same water. Instead, he thought about other, simpler matters. He was used to bathing in a cold pool near his forest home, though the warmth and fragrance of the heated water eased his weariness as little else could.

Changing into a clean tunic and trews of brown serge—clothing that had belonged to his tall, large-boned cousin Tom—he settled by the fire to explain to Alice what had happened since he had escaped English custody several weeks before. His aunt listened quietly and offered steadfast praise for his attempt to save Wallace, even knowing he viewed it as a failure, and listened to his account of rescuing the besieged inhabitants of Aberlady Castle.

No matter what he did or did not do, his aunt believed in his integrity.

As the night deepened to true darkness, they sat quietly together. He always found peace beside Alice's hearth, here in the forest house as well as years ago in the Crawford home in Dunfermline.

"She truly does snore, that one," Alice commented then, looking around.

James hid a smile. He found the soft snores emanating from the box bed scarcely audible. But Alice lived in near isolation now with only animals for company; she had grown unused to human noise.

"If you tilt her head, she'll quiet," he said.

Alice gave him a sharp glance. "And how do you know that?"

"We slept in the forest last night. I learned it then."

"Ah, I noticed how gently you speak to her, and how careful you are of her comfort." Her brown eyes twinkled. "What about our Janet, eh?"

"Och, it is not the way of it," James said sternly. "Isobel is in my safekeeping."

"If you want to call it that. How long do you intend to keep her?"

"I will send word to Leslie soon."

"I wonder if you are reluctant to let her go," Alice said softly.

He pressed his lips. "She is more trouble than you can know. But she is injured and needs time to recover," he finished lamely. He could not explain to his aunt the tangle of his feelings toward the prophetess. He could hardly sort through the threads himself.

"Black Isobel is younger than I thought. So young, such a gentle girl, to make such predictions."

"Aye." James leaned forward, fingers spread toward the warmth of the hearth. "She foretold Will's betrayal and his execution, and her prediction laid the blame on me. The hawk of the forest. The Hawk Laird—that was the implication. Why, Alice? Why say that about Will, and about me?"

"Could be she is a genuine prophet," Alice suggested.

"Could be," he murmured, remembering what he had witnessed in the forest. "But there are some who would have done anything to stop Wallace, and stop those who fight for Scotland's independence."

"You think Isobel knows who these men might be?"

"I wonder if she can name them. Sir Ralph Leslie, for one. She might know of others who were after Wallace as well."

"Sir Ralph wears a black armband for Isobel. He loves her."

"I doubt his sincerity," James said. "He can love someone and still commit murderous deeds. Many do. But I have been blamed for Will's betrayal deliberately. If there is a scheme, I want the truth."

"Alice nodded. "You must vindicate your name."

He shook his head. "It may be too late for that. I owe this to Will. That is all."

"Leslie said he has proof you betrayed Will. What did he mean? It has to be a lie."

He sighed. He ought to tell Alice the truth, but he hesitated, fearing that she would no longer revere him—love him—once she knew what he had done. He said nothing.

"Jamie," Alice said quietly. "I would never believe treachery of you. Ever."

He nodded and let the silence linger. "'Tis late," he finally said. "I must see to the goshawk. He has been too long without me, hooded to keep quiet. With luck, he has been sleeping."

"I hope you get some sleep too. Do not stay up the night watching that hawk to train him."

"I will sleep. We will begin training in the morn."

"You swore never to take on another hawk."

"I found this one hanging in a tree by his jesses. I could hardly leave him. I will keep him only until he recovers."

"Aye, well," Alice said philosophically, "he might be a wee gift from the angels just for you."

"Or a wee trial," James answered.

"You have had too many trials, Jamie. 'Tis time the Lord gave you a gift."

"The Lord does not seem to agree," he said wryly, and opened the door to step out into the night.

Chapter Thirteen

T HE GOSHAWK'S GAZE was captured by the bright candle flame as James crossed the dark cave. Years ago, he had used the tiny, wedge-shaped cave as a mews for Astolat and Ragnell. Now he set the candle on a natural alcove in the stone wall where the hawk could see it. Then he bent to check the fire in the small iron brazier set in a corner; he had left the peat coals glowing earlier and the low flames were steady now. The hawk would benefit from the warmth and dryness here.

He opened a wooden chest tucked in the farthest angle of the cave and sifted through an assortment of hawking gear—leather gloves, pouches, straps, brass fastenings, ankle bells, tiny hoods.

Choosing a glove, he slipped it over his left hand. The fit was still perfect, though he had not worn it for years. He flexed his fingers inside the padded lining and adjusted the long gauntlet over his forearm. The leather needed oiling, but otherwise it was in good condition.

He had never intended to wear this glove again, much less handle a hawk of his own. The glove felt heavy and stiff at first, but soon the leather warmed and molded to his hand as if only days had passed and not years since he last pulled it on.

He looked at the old stain that darkened the palm of the glove, the scrubbed spot still faintly visible, left by Astolat's blood as she had died in his hand. The glove stirred other memories of that cursed day when tragedy had struck him again and again before the setting of the sun. James felt the dense weight of that old, congealed sadness again, like a burden he could never quite release.

But he shoved the thoughts away, gathered jesses and a pouch, and turned to approach the goshawk, who blinked past him, still entranced by the golden flame. James smiled ruefully.

The half wild tiercel was handsome but none too bright. The bird was not likely to enthrall his new master as Astolat had done. She had been a brilliant hunter and a rare, loyal creature. James felt sure he would never see her ilk again.

He would keep Gawain until the tiercel recovered, and then let him go without regret. James did not want a hawk to hand. The beautiful, difficult creatures complicated life too much, requiring time and attention he could no longer spare.

"Ho, you gos," he said softly, removing the hood. The goshawk's lids moved like lightning as he looked at the flame as if in fascination. James reached out his gloved hand, murmuring to the bird.

As he spoke, he detached the thongs from the tiercel's bracelets and reattached a pair of jesses that had belonged to Astolat. He wrapped the leather straps around his smallest gloved fingers, and nudged his covered fist against the backs of the thin, muscular golden legs.

Gawain must have been thoroughly trained once, James thought. With scarcely a hesitation, the goshawk stepped back and perched on James's fist, his talons flexing firmly on the glove just over the wrist and base of the thumb.

"Good lad," James said. He offered the bird some raw, sliced meat that he had brought with him from the cottage. "You do remember your training. Or else you are just too tired to bate. I do not have need of a hawk, lad, but I will keep you so long as you need care."

He stroked the back feathers softly, knowing that gentle contact would soothe the bird. Yet he was aware that too much human touch would flatten the feathers and make them heavy.

Then he gave the bird more of the meat and put the rest in the pouch at his belt. Gawain ate quickly and eagerly.

When the hawk finished his meal, James carried him toward the candle and blew it out. The goshawk stirred on his fist, then quieted, lulled by darkness relieved only by the glow of the peat in the brazier. James knew the young hawk was tired, perhaps in pain from what might be a sprained wing.

"So, Sir Gawain, the manning begins," James said, the words floating low and gentle in the darkness. "I am your source of food now. I am your captor, and I am your freedom. You will learn to know my voice like the beat of your own heart." He smoothed his fingers over the breast feathers.

Isobel drifted into his thoughts like a summer mist, softening his mood. He was her captor as well. Though she might expect him to try, he was not interested in bringing either woman or hawk under his will. With the bird, he worked toward the exchange of wary trust between master and hawk. That was all he could ask for with such a wild, elemental creature.

The woman was already gentled, with a fine and delicate character, but he craved the gift of her trust. Still, he thought he would never have it of her; the tension between them was too much. And he would keep the hawk longer than he would keep Isobel.

He drew breath, watching the hawk, and began to sing softly, repeating the notes in a haunting, airy pattern.

"*Ky-ri-e e-le-i-son. Ky-ri-e e-le-i-son.*"

Threads of moonlight slipped through the entrance, which was shielded by tree branches and vines. In the thin light, James saw the goshawk tip his head curiously to listen. He sang the phrase again.

"*Ky-ri-e e-le-i-son. Ky-ri-e e-le-i-son.*"

He had thought about the call he would use for this bird during the hours he had ridden beside Isobel in the forest. Somehow this one fit the bird, fit the master. The melody had an elusive serenity, the notes rising and vanishing like the graceful, soaring flight of a hawk.

He sang it again, soft and low. Steady repetition would teach the hawk to recognize the phrase as his master's call. He talked to the bird, his tone patient, quiet.

The hours slipped past. James sang, and murmured, and walked the bird around the dark mews. His intent was to keep the bird awake, and keep himself awake, and in the process, achieve taming as fast as possible.

He would give the exhausted tiercel no choice but to focus on his voice and the gentle touch of his fingertips. In the hawk's bleary, fatigued mind, the only reality would be the one his master provided for him. Gawain would never be tame, but he would learn.

Through touch and voice and endless patience, James would teach the bird that food and security came from one reliable source. The bird would grant him a certain amount of trust.

He was exhausted himself, but he forced himself to stay awake. Manning the bird quickly was paramount just now. Deep into the small, dark hours of the night, James walked, murmured, stroked, and sang.

And all the while, he thought about faith. He wanted faith and trust from the goshawk. He had it freely of Alice, no matter what he did. And he had sensed it, fleetingly, from Isobel, and tasted it like honey on her lips.

He craved more from her, but knew she had changed her mind about him again. He had seen trust flicker within her like a flame, sometimes bright, sometimes fading.

But when he had admitted to her that, indeed, he had taken part in Wallace's betrayal, he had watched the spark of faith disappear utterly in her eyes.

He could not blame her. He had lost faith in himself.

IN THE DARKNESS of the curtained bed, Isobel awoke to quiet, comfortable sounds: Alice hummed at some task, the fire crackled, Ragnell chirred, and rain pattered on the roof. She pulled the covers high and peered out through the curtains.

"There you are!" Alice stood by the table, kneading a large mound of pale dough.

"Greetings, Dame Crawford," Isobel said hoarsely.

"Just Alice," the woman corrected. "You slept yesterday and into today, nearly two days! Good rest heals, though."

Isobel blinked in amazement. "Two days? I remember waking a few times."

"But you could scarcely speak or move, you were so tired." Alice smiled. "You did get up once or twice, but went back to bed. If you are ready to rise now, you need some food." Alice worked as she talked, sleeves pushed up, hands capable as she punched and folded the dough.

Isobel glanced around the room. "Where is—"

"Jamie's with his gos. Gawain, he calls it." Alice laughed. "He asked me to bake bread for the tiercel, so I have been at that task this afternoon."

"It smells wonderful. But bread for a hawk? I did not think they ate bread."

"They do not. 'Tis for something else. Jamie knows I have the way of making bread, though few Scots do. Milled wheat is hard to find, with the Southrons harrassing all Scotland and denying us their goods in trade." She worked the dough while she spoke. "'Tis muckle hard to buy wheat from them, and Scottish wheat is a sparse crop. Jamie brings me milled wheat when he can. He brought me some a while ago, so I can bake bread today. If he stole this flour from the English, I do not want to know."

"Stole it?"

"Well, he is an outlaw who doesna care for Southrons." Alice shrugged. "Sometimes he and his men took supplies from Southron packhorses being led through the forest and gave the wheat and other goods round the countryside. You see," she continued, "there are many Scots with empty larders and fields, and even homeless, because of the Southrons who come through the Lowlands, stealing and burning. Jamie says we are owed goods back in trade."

"He is probably correct."

Alice nodded, shaping fat, round bread loaves. "I make a good, chewy bread with wheat, barley, and oats, and hops to rise it. Eat your fill of it, lass, with good churned butter. You are all bones."

Isobel blushed, and glanced at her thin forearms and the ribbed shadows along her breastbone. "I am hungry," she admitted.

"And I will feed you well. First you will want to dress. Your gown and surcoat are mended and freshened, and folded there." Alice set the loaves aside and covered them with a cloth. "Let me help you, since you have but one arm to use."

Within a short time, Isobel was washed, dressed, and seated by the table with her right arm snug in a sling, and her left hand cradling a cup of warm spiced wine. Alice set a bowl of hot porridge on the table and stuck a wooden spoon in it.

"More porridge. It is most of what I have. When the bread is done we will take some to Jamie. Now eat."

Isobel ate while Alice carried the loaves outside to a stone bread oven behind the house. When she returned, she refilled the porridge bowl, adding honey. Isobel finished nearly all that helping, too.

"Good lass! You are tall, but too slim. Jamie said you hardly ate for weeks during the siege."

Isobel nodded, and began to answer Alice's curious questions about the siege of Aberlady. Hearing thunder, she glanced toward the windows, two tiny openings covered in oiled parchment that let in faint grayish light. Rain battered the roof and the door.

"A soft rain," Alice said. "We will get wet when we take the bread to Jamie."

"Where is he?"

"A cave, not far from here, a walk through the greenwood and up a slope. He set it up for a mews long ago, and took the goshawk there. Can you walk on that ankle?"

Isobel stretched her foot. "It feels better. I can walk." Hearing a flutter of wings, she glanced up.

Ragnell left her perch and flew across the room, landing on the back of a chair. Her silver leg and claw foot thumped down as she found her balance. The bird fixed Isobel with a gleaming red eye.

"She is not leashed to the perch?" Isobel asked.

"Ragnell flies where she pleases," Alice said. "She is free to come and go, even outside." She smiled. "She will not go far. She cannot live on her own out there, one-legged and spoiled to the fist as she is, and she knows it."

"What happened to her leg?" Isobel asked.

"Ragnell was given to my husband as a wounded eyas—an infant bird taken from the nest to be trained. Nigel was a royal falconer, you see," Alice said proudly, as she poured steaming, spice-scented wine into Isobel's cup, and filled a second cup for herself.

Isobel nodded. "I know. Jamie told me about him."

Alice picked up a leather glove and slipped it on, raising her hand. With a rapid fluttering, Ragnell crossed the room, wings spread, to land on her mistress's fist. "Ragnell had been attacked by a jealous merlin in another man's mews. Nigel thought she would die, but she was a fierce wee hawk."

Alice produced a bit of raw meat from a dish by the hearth, and fed the bird a morsel, wiping her fingers on a cloth. "Her wounded foot turned black and fell off. Nigel made her a false one, then others as she grew. She learned to fly and perch wearing the silver foot. She even learned to fly at quarry, though she does not prefer it. She's spoiled to the fist and only feeds there. Lazy, silly bird," she cooed.

Ragnell kakked and stretched down to clean her beak sideways on the glove. She opened her tail wide, shot a wet mute across the floor, and blinked at Isobel.

Alice made a disparaging sound. "She wants you to know she's queen here. Nay, do not—I will clean it up. Lady Ragnell has trained me for her handmaiden, the price I pay for such noble company, I suppose. We are alone here, Ragnell and I, but for the cat, the goat, and the chickens. Ragnell has made a mewling servant of the cat, but so far the goat ignores her."

"It must be pleasant to live alone with no one to answer to but yourself," Isobel said.

"Pleasant some days. Lonely others."

"Sometimes I think living alone would be like paradise. I have always obeyed someone—my father, our priest. Now my betrothed wants obeisance from me too. Mayhap I should go into the forest and live as an anchoress."

"You would not be content as an anchoress, I think. Too young. Too full of curiosity for life, is my guess."

"You found contentment alone."

Alice shrugged. "Some. Not by choice." She stroked the bird. "My sons and my husband are dead now, all gone fighting for Scotland." Isobel saw Alice's eyes pinken with unshed tears. She sighed, shook her head. "All I have is Jamie and Janet, this arrogant bird and an uncaring cat." She cooed at Ragnell. "I thought one day James might wed Janet. They are cousins, but only by marriage, see."

"Jamie would do anything for you," Isobel said softly, feeling a deep tug at the thought that James loved this Janet so well that he was willing to risk all to gain her back.

Alice smiled. "He is like one of my own sons, though a brigand and a rogue."

"Alice, is he a traitor?" Isobel asked. The question had been troubling her.

"Nay." Alice shook her head. "He does not have that in him."

"Sir Ralph claims there is proof of it."

"There cannot be." She frowned. "But Jamie looks haunted. He keeps some secret to himself. But then, he has carried a heavy burden ever since Wildshaw was taken by the English."

"What do you mean?" Isobel asked.

"He has many deaths on his conscience."

Isobel frowned. "Do you mean those he killed in battle?"

"Such deeds bother him, but he is a warrior, and nae the priest his father wanted him to be. Battle deaths are deemed righteous deaths by the Church, and I am sure he confesses those and is absolved. But what sits upon Jamie's shoulders like a yoke are the deaths of…those he loved, though he did not cause their deaths." Alice got to her feet to set the bird on a perch. She took off her glove and turned. "That bread will be done now," she said crisply. "Come outside, lass, and help me fetch it."

She lifted a cloak from a wall peg and threw it around her shoulders, then held out Isobel's own cloak and helped her put it on.

"We will find Jamie and his gos," Alice said. "And hope the rain keeps Sir Ralph away."

Isobel followed Alice out into the rain, helping gather the heated loaves and wrap them in cloths. As Alice left some in the house and came back with one for Jamie, Isobel felt her heart thumping wildly at the thought of seeing James. What would happen later? Would he insist on keeping her captive, or would he let her go? She wondered for a moment if she should try to escape.

But for now, she thought, as she walked with Alice through the wet grass, she had no choice but to stay. Her arm would heal, her limp was already improving, and soon her foot would be strong enough for the long trek through the forest to Wildshaw Castle to find Sir Ralph, if he did not find her first.

As she passed between the trees, cool raindrops sprinkled over her cheeks and hair, and the damp breeze filled each breath. She inhaled deeply and sensed the freedom, somehow, in the scent.

Most of her life had been spent inside castle walls, effectively imprisoned by the will of those who would protect her. Now, tasting freedom and independence, she craved more.

Even so, she was still a captive.

Chapter Fourteen

ISOBEL CLUTCHED A loaf of hot bread wrapped in coarse cloth, savoring its warmth as she followed Alice through the murky rain. They climbed up a long, rocky slope, and halted near the top. A massive rockface soared beyond the earthen crest of the hill, a bleak stone surface covered with scrub and vines.

Alice walked toward the craggy rock. At first glance, Isobel saw several deep crevices as she followed Alice, who edged along between the rock and huge clumps of prickly gorse. One deep shadow was a narrow opening, obscured by thick green growth. Alice put a finger to her lips as they approached the cave.

From out of the rock came an unexpected sound. Mellifluous and deep, a singer created a resonant, low harmony with the silvery patter of the rain. Isobel looked at Alice in amazement.

"Jamie sang with the Benedictines at Dunfermline, in a choir the angels themselves would have praised," Alice murmured proudly. "When he was a lad, he sang alone for King Alexander. Now he sings to his hawk." She called his name.

The chanting stopped. "Come in, Aunt."

Alice turned sideways to squeeze through the small opening. Isobel followed her into darkness. The cave was a narrow, widening toward the back, with light filtering from the opening and a glowing brazier that gave out dry heat. A tall wooden perch stood on a floor covered in sand and earth to absorb the bird's mutes. James sat on a bench, back against the stone wall, goshawk perched on his gloved fist.

"Alice!" James and the goshawk both fixed bright gazes on Isobel. "My lady," he said.

"We brought bread," Alice said.

"Fresh baked, still hot?" James sat up. Isobel noticed he kept his voice soft and low for the bird's benefit. She perceived, too, the undercurrent of fatigue in his slumped shoulders and the shadows beneath his eyes. The goshawk stirred restively, and James shushed him.

"Certes, hot, or 'twould be of little use to the bird," Alice said. "And here's a loaf for yourself." She came close to James to set a wrapped loaf on the bench.

The goshawk bated, throwing himself from James's fist, flapping his wings and kakking. James extended his arm with a resigned expression while the bird beat the air furiously.

"'Twill not last long," he told them. "He is exhausted."

"As are you," Alice said sternly. "Have you slept at all these two days?"

He shrugged. The goshawk stilled, and James lifted him back to the fist. "Some."

"Hmph. You will kill yourself for that bird. I thought Ragnell was the queen of the ruined birds, but that tiercel is worse. But Nigel taught you well. If anyone can reclaim a ruined gos, 'tis you."

Gawain flapped his wings in agitation, opening his beak repeatedly to squawk. Isobel thought he might bate again.

"What is bothering him?" she asked.

"Alice makes him nervous," James said.

"He sees me and remembers the great fright Ragnell gave him yesterday," Alice said. "Gosses do learn quick, but they can be stupid just the same. There, Gawain, go easy, the rude lady redtail is not with me," she told the hawk. "Och, there he goes again." Gawain batted his wings, and James held him out patiently. "I will not stay and ruffle him further. Do you need anything more, Jamie? We'll be back to bring food later."

"I need Lady Isobel to stay here," James said.

"Stay?" Isobel asked. "Here?"

"I need help tending the bird, and Alice cannot come near him." He gave his attention to the hawk. Isobel and Alice watched until the bird settled down and James put him on the fist to feed him a strip of raw meat. "There, that is for going back to the fist, laddie," he said. He looked at Isobel. "Are you stronger? You walked up here, so your foot must be better. Can you help me with Gawain?"

His voice, as quiet and compelling as his gaze, sent curious shivers through her. A hot blush rose in her cheeks and her heart beat quickened as if in anticipation. "Well enough," she said.

"The lady slept all this time, so she's rested," Alice said. "If you have any wit left, Jamie—which I doubt after so long without sleep—you will let her watch that gos while you nap. I will be back." She went to the cave opening, squeezed out with a mutter and a grunt, and was gone.

Isobel lifted the wrapped, warm loaf that she held in her hands. "Shall we feed the bread to him?"

"He is not going to eat it. Come here." He patted the bench. "Sit beside me. The bird will have another fit if he cannot see you clear."

She sat where he indicated. Her left shoulder brushed against his arm. With his free hand, James withdrew his dirk from the sheath at his belt and handed it to her. "Cut the loaf in two," he directed.

She did so, a bit awkwardly, with her left hand. Hot steam rose into the air between them, and she closed her eyes briefly, smiling as she inhaled the comforting smell of fresh bread.

"Are you hungry?" James sounded amused. "We'll share my loaf later. Cut one half, slicing partway through. Aye, good. Now slide the split bread over his left wing."

Isobel hesitated. "You want me to put the bread on his wing?" she asked, incredulous.

"Aye. He has a sprained wing. See the way it droops at the

top? When he spreads his wings, he does not lift that one quite so high. His bates are making the sprain worse. The damp heat from hot bread is a good, simple treatment."

"Ah." Isobel lifted the cut loaf toward the bird. Gawain screeched, striking out with his talons. Isobel snatched her hand away and nearly dropped the bread. "I make him nervous, too. Should I go?"

"'Twas not you that alarmed him. He is used to your voice and face. But he does not know if the bread is friend or foe."

Isobel chuckled. James smiled, a quick dazzle that set her heart to thumping. He murmured gently to the hawk, then rose to his feet, carrying the hawk, and took an object from among a tangle of leather things on top of a small wooden chest. He returned to sit beside her.

"Hush, you bird," James said. With deft fingers, he dropped a small hood over the hawk's head.

Gawain fluttered his wings, stretched his neck as if to protest, then went utterly still and silent.

Isobel gasped. "Nay," she whispered. "You blind him with the hood!" She reached out.

"Careful." James took her fingers. She lowered her hand. James sighed. "Pardon. I did not think about the hood. Look, he is not troubled by it at all."

The goshawk seemed content, and Isobel felt foolish reacting with alarm over such a thing. She had not been so troubled by the bird's quick hooding in the house yesterday, too fatigued to notice much.

"He does not fight it," she said, watching the tiercel.

"Hawks are quieted by darkness. Hoods help to calm them," James explained. "Falcons tolerate them more easily, but they can be used sparingly with short-winged hawks. Some hawks resist hooding, but Gawain has obviously been hooded before." He glanced at her. "'Tis not cruel."

"I know," she murmured. "'Tis necessary sometimes."

"We cannot tend to his shoulder unless he's calm. I would

not mistreat a bird. They only accept gentleness and patience. They cannot be forced."

She felt her cheeks warm under his gaze. "Other creatures cannot be forced either."

"Och, I expected you might say so." She wondered if his affectionate tone was meant for the bird's benefit or directed at her. "I have not shown you cruelty or forced you to my will," he pointed out.

"You have been kind. For a brigand," she added.

His eyes twinkled. "I have learned well from hawks."

"Aye." She smothered a smile. James watchd the goshawk, scratching the bird's puffed-out breast with a fingertip.

True, she thought. His calm, patient manner, his low, soothing voice, even the agile way he moved had all been influenced by years of caring for hawks. Her father's falconers, and her father, too, had that same way about them of purposeful, gentled strength. She watched as James adjusted the tiny strap of the hawk's hood with nimble fingers. All the while, he murmured soothing phrases.

"My father sometimes said that falconers would make excellent mothers," she said.

He huffed low. "'Tis like mothering in a way. We must care for a young thing with endless patience, and we must put its needs before our own."

He began to hum again. The notes of the chant rose and fell in mellow, creamy nuances. Isobel leaned her head against the rock wall and listened, succumbing to his deliberate magic. Yesterday, he had waved his hand in languid patterns over the hawk's head, seducing Isobel, too, into a dream-like state. Now he wove the spell with his beautiful voice. As the hawk surrendered, so did she.

"Ah," James whispered. "He is calm. Place the bread over the top of his wing, if you will."

If he had asked her to set the loaf on her own head, she might have done it without question. She stirred out of her reverie and raised the bread toward the bird.

James lifted his free hand to guide her, long fingers warm over hers. Together they eased the warm bread over the joint of the wing and shoulder. Gawain shifted beneath their combined touch.

"Easy, bonny gos," James said softly. Isobel kept her hand on the bread and James let his hand rest over hers. Steamy heat gathered between their fingers.

He sang the *kyrie* again. The melodic drone thrummed through her body, as soothing as the heat and gentle pressure of his fingers over hers.

She closed her eyes. When he stopped, she looked at him in the silence. He leaned against the wall, flexed his fingers over hers, and lifted his hand away. She missed its comfort as she held the warm compress on the bird's wing.

"You have a beautiful voice," she said. "Like spiced wine, warm and cozy somehow. Your aunt said you sang for a king."

"I did, as a lad. I was in the choir at Dunfermline. I sang hymns when King Alexander came to mass. No terror could quite compare to that," he said wryly. "Knees knocking, hands shaking, a ten-year-old lad standing alone before a king and his court, singing. Later, when I went to the seminary school in Dundee, I sang in the monks' choir there. My singing voice survived the journey into manhood, as it happened." He smiled.

"Seminary? Did you study to be a priest?"

"My father wanted that. But I met William Wallace at Dundee and John Blair too, who became a Benedictine, though he fought at Wallace's side and acted as his confessor. When Wallace left Dundee and became a rebel, I stayed at the school, hearing more and more stories of his deeds. I stole away one night and went to join him. I was sixteen."

"Was your father angry?"

"My father," he said, "was a rebel himself, hiding out from the English because he refused to sign an oath of fealty to the English king. They killed him." He watched the bird, and murmured to it. Then he glanced at Isobel. "My older brother inherited our father's castle, but died at Falkirk. Shortly after that, the English took Wildshaw by treachery and fire."

"And they kept it ever since?"

"Ever since."

"You could not win it back?"

"I could not," he said, so quietly she hardly heard. He reached up to adjust the bread on the bird's wing, his fingers dry and warm as they glided over hers. As he took over balancing the bread, she lifted her hand away.

She wanted to hear more about his life as a rebel and how he lost Wildshaw, but she sensed he did not want to talk about it. "You have spent half your life fighting and hiding," she observed.

He smiled ruefully. "I suppose I have." He began to sing again, low and mellifluous, sending wondrous shivers through her.

"Why do you sing that phrase, over and over?" she asked. "Does it remind you of the past?"

"I'm teaching Gawain to recognize it as the call I will use for him. Later I'll whistle it, so he will know it in different ways. Then I will add food to the routine, feeding him each time he hears the phrase. When he learns to trust me, he'll come quickly, without fear of threat."

"Ah. I thought you sang it because you still longed for the peace of the monkish life."

"Sometimes I do."

They sat watching the hawk, James humming softly. Gawain tipped his hooded head as if trying to work out a puzzle. The goshawk looked so comical with the small leather hood over his head, like a hat fallen down over his eyes, the loaf of bread perched absurdly on his wing, that Isobel giggled.

"He looks like a king's jester or a mummer in a Yuletide play," she said.

"He does look silly." James shook his head. "But I never thought to be sitting here again, going without sleep and nursing another hawk."

"You have stayed awake these two days?"

"I dozed some." He yawned, jiggling the goshawk, whose head had begun to droop. "But whenever Sir Gawain starts to sleep, I need to wake him."

Isobel studied the man's face in the flickering light of the glowing brazier. His eyes were weary in the shadows and he was pale with fatigue. She noticed the soft shape of his lower lip, full and moist, the fine creases beside his mouth, the dark sand of his beard softening the lean jaw.

"Why do you force yourself to do this?" she asked.

"It is the quickest way to tame a hawk, lass."

"But hardest on the falconer and the bird. When I was small, my father would carry new hawks or falcons throughout the day and set them in darkness at night, keeping them close to him for a week or two. My mother objected to the birds sitting on his fist at mealtimes, and did not like having them sleep on a perch in their bedchamber. But he insisted it took time to train each one properly."

"Time is what I do not have. I did not plan on taming a hawk now."

She scowled. "You only planned to abduct a prophetess."

"True." He looked at her then, and lifted the bread. "'Tis still warm. We will keep it there until it cools."

"Can we eat the other half?" she asked plaintively.

James chuckled. "Aye." She tore the remainder of the loaf apart and handed James the larger portion. They ate in silence.

"I am glad you are here," James murmured when they were done.

"Aye?" She felt shy suddenly.

"Aye. If you keep me awake, I can keep him awake."

"Oh." She had almost hoped to hear something else. Seeing the gentle swell of his lips, she vividly recalled the feel of them on her mouth. Reminding herself to be wary was suddenly a challenge.

"Talk to me, Isobel," he said, leaning his head against the wall. "I am as sleepy as this hawk."

She began to tell him about her father's mews, and as he asked questions, his voice went hoarse with fatigue. When the hawk drooped his head, James wiggled his fist to stir him. Soon he asked about her childhood and her life at Aberlady Castle.

She spoke while he listened and held the bread on the bird's wing. He lifted a foot to the bench to rest his forearm, with the bird, on his knee.

"After your mother died, your father and the priest were the only ones to witness your prophecies?" he asked.

"And lately Sir Ralph. My father invited him to watch the sessions when 'twas agreed we would wed. He wanted Ralph to know what to do."

"What to do when the blindness comes?"

"What to do during the visions. My father and the priest talk to me and ask me questions. And Father Hugh writes down what I say. I do not recall it, usually."

He slid her a penetrating glance. "You truly recall naught?"

"Very little, as you have seen yourself."

His straight brows pulled together. "Who was with you when you prophesied about Wallace?"

"Those three men."

"The priest recorded everything that you said?"

"Aye. He presented some of it to his parish after that, and sent a copy to the Guardians of the Realm of Scotland. But he did not reveal all that I said about Wallace. He and my father felt it would cause distress, so they kept it to themselves. Then they let it out a week or so before it happened." She shook her head and sighed. "How were they to know it would happen so soon after that?"

"How, indeed." Hearing his cynical tone, she looked up. James slid a glance toward her. "Do you know what you said about Wallace? Do you know what you said about me, Lady Isobel?"

She looked away, feeling uncomfortable. "I know some of what I said. That bread must be cool by now," she said. "What else should we do for the hawk?"

She did not want to talk about the prophecies. She liked the peacefulness of the warm, dark cave, and she liked his soothing voice and gentle mood. To speak of the predictions only created tension between them. She felt that strain already.

He removed the compress and brushed the crumbs from the goshawk's feathers. "I thought you forgot what you see in a vision."

He was stubborn and intelligent, and would not be distracted. She rose to her feet and went to the brazier, holding her hands out to gather warmth.

"That time," she said, "I did my best to remember. I made Father Hugh read me every word of it, though he feels it is best if I do not know what I foretell. He and my father, Sir Ralph, too, were upset with me for asking about that vision."

"Why?" James spoke harshly, and the hawk ruffled his feathers in response. "Why do they want to keep you from knowing?"

She shrugged. "They say it is too stressful for me. And Father Hugh says the visions are too erudite for one of my small education and feeble female mind."

"What!" James huffed. "You have a distinctly female way of looking at the world, aye. But 'tis hardly a feeble mind. Just the opposite, I would say."

Flustered by his compliment, she looked into the bright heart of the brazier. "Father Hugh interprets the visions carefully to understand the symbolism. He says there is much deep meaning in them. He believes that the prophecies come from God, in the language of the patriarchs, and must be studied with care." She shrugged. "He is preparing a book of the prophecies, though I have asked him not to do that. But he says he will gain much respect through them."

"Let us hope he will share the honor with the prophetess," James muttered. "Tell me more."

"Since that day, I have tried to recall the visions myself, but only parts come to me. I begged my father to tell me what I had said. But I did not trust—" She stopped.

James sat forward. "Did not trust whom?"

She lowered her head. "I did not trust any of them to tell me the truth. And I wanted to know."

"Why would they lie to you?" His voice was gentle. She wanted to sink into its warmth.

"They have always protected me, so they kept secrets from me. When I was younger, my father felt he should guard me from the outside world. But as I grew older, he did not relax his protection."

"Have you always seen visions?"

"Since I was thirteen. I suffered a serious fever for several days, and nearly died. Afterward, I lost my sight for a month. During the worst of the fever, in a delirium, I described a battle between English and Scots that had not taken place. My parents and the priest were with me, for Father Hugh had come to give me the last rites."

James watched her steadily. "Dear God," he murmured. "Did the battle come about?"

"A few weeks later it happened just as I had said. Father Hugh told my parents that my prophesy was a gift from heaven, bestowed by the angels when I lay on the brink of death. He told my father such a gift must be used. He said the angels could speak through me to benefit all Scotland."

"And they realized that they had a way of predicting the war."

She shrugged. "I do not know what they thought. They told me little. I did as they asked."

"You were but a lass."

"My father and the priest, and my mother too, seemed to cherish me more once I became a prophetess. I was not just a tall, awkward, timid lass to be wed off to some knight. So I did what I could to please them. The visions came easily enough, but the blindness and the forgetfulness were horrible to endure." She looked away, bit her lip. "Father Hugh says 'tis the price I must pay for the gift."

James watched her. "Ah, lass," he said, sounding almost sad. "You are a rebel and a warrior, and do not even know it."

She tipped her head. "What do you mean?"

"You endure much, and you fight, too."

"How so?"

"In your blindness and forgetfulness, you protest being forced to prophesy. But you are the only one being hurt, I think."

Isobel felt a weight turn inside her gut as the truth of his words took on substance and force. She stared at him. "My God," she whispered, shocked. "Do you think so?"

James sighed. "Lady Isobel," he murmured. "Come here." He patted the bench. She did not move. "I would come to you, lass, but I am so tired I doubt my limbs will hold me upright."

Still she watched him, entranced by his gaze, stunned by the truth he had revealed to her about her visions and the aftermath.

"Come here," he whispered again, and held out a hand.

$$— \blacklozenge\!\cdots\!\bullet \quad \bullet\!\cdots\!\blacklozenge —$$

Chapter Fifteen

I SOBEL SAT BESIDE him, and James touched her hand. The quick, soft brush of his fingertips seemed to caress her entire being. She trembled as she looked up at him.

"Do you think the blindness and the forgetfulness could leave me, then?" she asked.

"They might, if you ever found peace with your gift," he said. "In the seminary, we studied the intricate symbolism that exists throughout life, the reflection of the heavenly and earthly realms in objects, in thoughts, in everything. Your blindness is a symbol of something. It may reflect your own struggle, within yourself."

"Father Hugh said it reflects my unworthiness to know the full truth of God."

He wrinkled his nose. "It could be that the blindness comes from your own fears. I have heard of cases of blindness that go away even when it seems hopeless. My uncle, who was blind in one eye, once had a bout of blindness in the other eye. A wise-woman brought him herbal medicines and told him his sight would improve only when he stopped being afraid of the blindness in the other eye. He thought about what she said. A week later, his sight was restored—quite miraculously."

She frowned. "I do not fear the visions."

"You may fear the way others insist that you keep doing it." He shrugged.

She rubbed her fingers over her eyes. "Dear God. You might

be right."

He leaned his head against the rock wall. "Sometimes another can show us truths about ourselves we do not—see," he murmured.

"There are other forms of blindness," she agreed.

"True. Now tell me—why did you try to recall your prediction about Wallace?"

She sighed. The hawk chittered and shifted on James's fist. "I do understand my visions," she began. "I see their meaning clearly when they come to me, but then I forget it. My father and the priest think the symbolic meanings are beyond my intelligence. But I know what I see. That day, I knew I had to remember what I saw."

"Why?" he asked softly.

"I wanted to warn Wallace. I never doubt the truth of my visions. That much I have learned. What is harder to know is the exact meaning of what I see."

He watched her. "Did you warn Wallace?"

"I wrote a note with my own hand, and begged my father to deliver it." She twisted her hands together. "He said he would. But the three of them—my father, the priest, and Sir Ralph— acted strangely about that vision. The images alarmed me. I knew Wallace would come to a dishonorable fate, a horrible end." She sighed. "But my note was sent in vain. He died, just as I foresaw." She felt the sting of tears.

"If he received your note, he would have been grateful. He respected prophecy—he had dreams of his own that foretold events. He mentioned your prophecies to me once or twice. But I doubt Will Wallace would have heeded anyone's warning. He was headstrong. Passionate. A driven man."

"But I could not bear to know such a thing about a man's fate and keep silent about it." She frowned at him through a glaze of tears. A drop spilled down.

James touched his thumb to her cheek, then cupped her shoulder. She was glad of the warmth and weight of his hand, for she felt forlorn and remorseful.

"We both tried to help him, I think."

"We did?" she whispered. She leaned her head against the rock as he did, his face just a hand span from hers.

"Regardless of what else I have done, I tried to help Wallace the night he was taken. My attempt came to naught but trouble."

"How so?"

"I hid among the trees and shot one arrow after another at those who beat him and took him. I killed several guards. I do not know how many. I thought to reduce their numbers so that I could get to him myself, or provide him a chance to get away. I was half-mad with rage and guilt, I think."

"Guilt?"

"What you did, what I did, both came to naught."

She touched his arm. "You did help him."

He slid her a glance. "Help? He is dead."

"Did he see you there, fighting for him?"

"I think so."

"Then he knew you tried to save him."

His eyelids lowered pensively. He nodded. "Aye, but—"

"You helped him, James," she said firmly. "He knew that he was not alone. It would have felt like a blessing to him in the moment."

"I had not thought of that." He watched her. She rested her head beside his and returned his gaze.

Then he moved, shifting toward her to touch his lips to hers.

Isobel tilted her head backward, drinking in the soft, warm kiss. The brush of his mouth on hers brought a delicious shock that burst in her center and blossomed outward. She drew in a breath, wanting more. But he moved back to gaze at her. The goshawk perched on his fist made tiny noises.

She stared at James. "What—was that for?"

He smiled. "A gesture of thanks. You took the blindness from me this time."

"Blindness?" she asked.

"The scales from my eyes." His mouth quirked in a fleeting smile. "Mayhap I did help Will in a small way. You cannot know what it means to me to think that."

Her heart thumped. "I owe you a—gesture of thanks as well, for showing me what my blindness might mean."

His eyes crinkled in a private smile. Leaning forward, drifting her eyes shut, she paused, hoping for the divine touch of his mouth to hers once again. He slid toward her, his breath soft on her cheek. She waited, eyes closed, heart pounding. Then his finger touched her lips and lifted away.

"Nay," he whispered. "Nay, lass. I cannot be trusted."

"I trust you," she whispered, her gaze full of him now, taking in his deep eyes in the warm, dim light, the golden sheen on his hair, the curve of his mouth.

"If I touch you again," he said, his voice like a caress, "I might be guilty of more than taking a woman hostage."

Her heartbeat went to thunder. She cupped her palm against his cheek, his bearded jaw warm and prickly. "And if I touch you?"

"Best not," he whispered.

But she could not stop herself. Earlier she had been drawn in by the rhythm of his moving hand as he entranced the hawk and the thrum of his voice. Now it was the steady thump of his heart in the pulse beating against her hand that pulled her toward him. She felt the strong shape of his jaw and its grainy texture and slid her fingers downward to feel the outline of his mouth, the warmth of his breath.

"Isobel," he whispered. His lips moved on her fingers. She sucked in a breath.

James gave a low groan. He dipped toward her and pressed his mouth to hers, hungry and hard, kissing her as he had under the cover of the ferns. Rich and full, the kiss delved deep inside of her, overturning her like a wave takes a boat. She was lost, drifting, anchored only by his mouth, by his breath, by the touch of his hand upon her cheek.

His fingers slipped inside the curtain of her hair. He tugged gently, angling her head, opening his mouth over hers, his lips moving in a delectable rhythm, rising and falling, opening and closing.

Isobel tipped back her head and gave in to the shivers that plunged and swirled within her. She followed the rhythm he set, her lips moving in harmony with his.

The hawk shifted and squawked. James pulled back, murmuring a low oath as he turned toward the hawk on his gloved fist, propped on his upraised knee. He ran his fingers through his hair in an exasperated gesture.

Isobel folded her arm around her waist, heart thumping, feeling heat seep into her cheeks, enduring an agony of shame at her boldness. "I was foolish," she whispered, head down.

"Not you. My foolishness, lass. None of this is what I planned. None of it—the besieged castle, the hawk, you—"

"Me?"

"Especially you. I thought the prophetess would be easy enough to manage. A woman who did not care for me, nor I for her. I would steal her away, hide her, send a message to Sir Ralph, and have Janet back again."

She ducked her head, hair sliding down. "That is all you want of me. A means to get her."

He laughed, bitter, humorless. "I want far more than that of you, God help me for it."

She raised her head. He had pulled her toward him with a powerful kiss and now rejected her. "If Sir Ralph came here to offer Janet in exchange for me, you would be glad of it."

"I might be tempted to keep you and let the lass fend for herself. She could do it well enough."

"Keep me!" She huffed. "Am I some prize hawk to be mewed?"

"That is not what I meant."

"That," she snapped, "is what I took as your meaning. And how can you be disloyal to your Janet now?" Her voice rose.

The goshawk roused his feathers and lifted his wings at her sharp tone. James rubbed his hand over his jaw, murmuring to the hawk.

Isobel scowled, a tumult of thoughts and emotions assaulting her. The initial flash of fury was followed by a confusion of resentment, embarrassment, and undeniable attraction.

"Ho, Gawain," James said softly. "Look at you, we forgot about your hood." He reached up and plucked the hood free from the hawk's head. Gawain blinked, his eyes reddish in the dim light.

"There, now he can see again," James commented. "And we did not even have to kiss him."

At his wry tone, despite her sour mood, she laughed reluctantly. James chuckled, leaning back.

"I owe you an apology," he said.

"Several."

"I do ask your pardon on one matter," he murmured. "I doubted your visions. I doubted the sincerity of your purpose. I was sure you were part of some Southron conspiracy. But I know now you had naught to do with Will's betrayal." He looked away. "And I know you did not set the blame on me and ruin my name with malicious intent."

She blinked at him. "You thought me so evil-minded?"

He shrugged. "I did not know you then."

"Just as I did not know you, when I thought you a traitor."

"Ah, but I am," he said tightly. "That I am."

Isobel touched his hand. "I do not believe that."

He gave a curt laugh. "You have been talking to Alice."

"Some. But 'tis my own feeling. Why do you call yourself a traitor?"

He shook his head. "I will not tell you, or anyone, that foul tale."

"Jamie, please," she whispered.

"I am tired and do not want to tell it." He said it bluntly.

"Then tell me what I predicted about you."

He frowned. "You know that."

She shook her head. "Father Hugh told me what I said about Wallace. But it was different than I recalled. Mayhap he wrote it down incorrectly. But he never told me what I said about you. I only heard later that I predicted the Hawk Laird would take down Wallace. What was the prophecy?"

"This." He closed his eyes. "'The hawk of the tower and the hawk of the forest fly together to take the eagle,'" he began in a low, quiet tone. His voice seemed to reverberate around the small cave. "'The hawk of the forest is laird of the wind. He will betray his brother the eagle in his nest at night. He will loose the white feather and flee through heather and greenwood. And the eagle will lose his heart.'"

Isobel lowered her eyelids, her hand at rest on his forearm. "I recall those words, or something like them," she said. "Wallace was the eagle."

"He was much like an eagle."

"And you are the hawk. But I do not think I ever said Lindsay or Hawk Laird."

"The English began calling me Hawk Laird a few years ago. I live in the forests. I ran with Wallace, at his side. I fletch my arrows with white feathers."

"And the hawk of the tower?"

"'Hawk of the tower' is a falconry phrase that describes the height a hawk reaches just before the dive for the quarry. So hawk of the tower could refer to me too, you see—if the eagle was the quarry."

She nodded. "And laird of the wind? What is that?"

"I do not know. But word went round that the Hawk Laird betrayed Wallace."

"Dear saints," she whispered, stunned by her part in this. "I never meant to place blame on you. I never knew your name until recently. I am sorry if the prophecy fit you." She bit at her lip in regret.

"But I had a hand in what happened to Will."

"How? You only tried to save him."

He shook his head and turned his hand over to fold his fingers over hers. "What is done is done," he murmured. "Do not fret over this. This is my matter. I do not hold a grudge against you or your prophecy. I regret the loss of a friend more than the loss of my name."

"Jamie—"

"Hush," he said, as the hawk squawked on his fist. "Soft, you bird." He glanced at her again. "Lady Isobel, I must ask that you help me keep awake. Just through the night and through the morrow. Then will have our hawk trained."

"Our hawk?" She glanced at him. His eyes were midnight blue in the low light, shadowed beneath. She felt the slow current of his fatigue as if it flowed between them. "Will you let me hold him so you can rest?"

"I suppose I could. Hawks are solitary creatures, but they often accept more than one falconer."

"So why not you and I, then? He does not seem to mind my voice or my presence. Well, Gawain?" She looked at the hawk. "What do you think?"

The bird tipped his head, bronze eyes glowing.

"We can find out," James said. "In that chest over there are gloves and suchlike. Go through it and find a glove to fit your left hand."

Isobel went to the little chest, sifting through its contents to find a worn, thick leather glove. She slipped it on, stretching her fingers inside its padding. The glove was large, nearly reaching her elbow, and heavy, made of stout leather with thick cloth padding inside. She returned to the bench.

"Sit here," James said, circling his right arm around her shoulders to bring her close, her left shoulder supported against his chest. With his direction, she raised her left arm to echo the line of his arm, her wrist cocked and offered as a perch.

"Sir Gawain, will you accept master and mistress both?" James asked. The low murmur of his voice nearly melted her bones.

The bird blinked at them. Isobel held her left arm up, held her breath. The hawk was still. Then he stretched his wings and went into a furious bate.

AT LAST THE hawk sat quietly on her fist. Isobel shifted softly so as not to wake James, who dozed beside her after a long while spent convincing the hawk to calm down and accept the woman's hand as another perch. Propping her left elbow on James's arm, she watched Gawain. His eyes shone in the light of the brazier. He dipped his head to tuck it sleepily.

"Ho, bird," she said into the quiet. Gawain lifted his head to look at her. "Ho, there. Jamie said to keep you awake. But then he fell asleep, which he needed to do," she murmured. "Those were mighty bates you threw for us, Sir Gawain. I am impressed. How is your shoulder?"

She reached out with a fingertip and tickled his breast feathers as she had seen James do. The white and speckled gray feathers were divinely soft and warm underneath. Gawain chirred, and she felt the rapid vibration of his heart in his chest.

Not long ago, she had been surprised when, after a sequence of bates and another treatment of warm bread on his wing joint, Gawain had finally stepped onto Isobel's offered fist. He behaved as if he had always done it, puffing his feathers and blinking at her calmly.

Recently, though, the bird had grown more restive, lifting his wings and flattening his feathers. The grip of his talons on her fist was stronger, and she sensed his increasing anxiety. Isobel plucked a bit of raw meat from the pouch James wore, laid it on her thumb, and watched the bird dip to eat it. All the while, she hoped he would not bate or try to foot her while she sat with him.

On impulse, she drew a breath and began to sing the *kyrie*. Although she lacked James's gift for true notes, the sound was soft and serene as it echoed around the cave.

The bird cocked his head curiously. His eyelids came together like lightning flashes. He stilled.

Isobel smiled and looked over at James, who only shifted and tipped his head toward hers in his sleep. She rested her brow against his head, his hair a thick cushion, his breath gentle on her cheek.

"Oh, Jamie," she whispered. "Look at our bonny gos. He has decided to trust both of us. And here you are asleep and did not even see it."

Gawain roused his feathers, turning himself into a calm puffball, as if he was content. Isobel held the hawk, letting James sleep while she waited for dawn. As light began to stream through the cave entrance, she realized that she was a few steps away from freedom.

Beside her, James slept soundly, breaths long and full, body relaxed. He would not know if she rose, set the bird on a perch, and slipped out. She could be away to Wildshaw and Sir Ralph before he woke.

The morning light glowed like a pearl. If she was going to escape, she would have to do it now.

She eased her arm away from James. Gawain blinked and sat calmly despite the movement. The simple reliance in the bird's gaze and posture stopped her.

She glanced at James, and recognized in his strong, beautiful face a vulnerability, a state of faith. He trusted her enough to sleep beside her. He trusted her with the care of his tempestuous, frustrating, fragile goshawk. And though he was a secretive man, he had begun to share his thoughts with her.

She remembered then what the lad Geordie had said—that James Lindsay needed someone to have faith in him again. She had begun to do that, and so had the goshawk. If she left now, it would be like a betrayal.

Dawn bloomed outside, and Isobel sat with the hawk and the man, and heeded her heart.

Chapter Sixteen

T HE EARLY MORNING breeze sifted through his hair as James stood by the cave opening. He murmured to the hawk perched on his fist, then glanced behind him where Isobel now slept on the bench, covered with her cloak. James had eased her there when she fell asleep, exhausted, after a meal of bread and ale. He turned back to gaze over the expanse of treetops under a pale cloudy sky.

In the forest below he saw a flash of movement. The hawk, seeing it too, fluttered his wings. "You'll soon be flying," James told him. "I promise."

"He longs to be free," Isobel said behind him. She walked toward him, rubbing her injured arm as if to soothe pain. The light gave her face a delicate clarity, and her hair flowed over her shoulders sheened like polished jet. He longed to touch that dark silkiness and wanted far more than that. But such impulses were dangerous. He must be cautious around Black Isobel. He had almost forgotten that. Last night he had succumbed, overwhelmed with the desire to touch her, and could have gone beyond simple kisses—but he was determined to avoid temptation again.

"Look there." He pointed toward the woodland. "Two runners, coming along the path."

"I do not see them," she said, squinting.

"Watch." His sharp vision often showed him details others

did not see as quickly. He waited as two figures ran through the trees, blond and dark heads bobbing as they went. They men cleared the forest and began to climb the slope.

"Quentin and Patrick?" she asked.

"Aye, back from Stobo. Alice must have told them we were up here."

"What will you do now?"

"Send a message to Wildshaw—offering to barter one woman for another." He could not look into her wide ice-blue eyes just then.

Isobel sighed. "Your Janet is a blessed lady, to be loved so well."

"My Janet?" he asked, dumbfounded.

"I would give all for such a blessing." She stepped forward. "Quentin! Patrick! Up here!"

Then he had no chance to ask what she meant or to explain about Janet. Quentin and Patrick came toward them and they entered the cave together, Isobel greeting them with a smile. Quentin winked at her, and Patrick went red in the cheeks.

And Gawain, on the fist, lifted his wings as if to bate. James scratched the yellow feet gently, and the bird calmed.

"What word of Geordie?" James asked. "Is he recovering?"

"He will be fine," Patrick said. Not as tall as the others, his barrel chest and muscled limbs made him seem large as he fisted hands on his hips. "We have some trouble....but first, what are you doing with a goshawk?"

"Found him. Training him. What trouble?"

"We came through the forest and were chased by a patrol of ten men," Quentin said. "Henry and Eustace were with us. Both were caught by arrows. We took them to Alice Crawford's house and she told us we would find you here."

"Are they badly hurt?"

"They will be fine. Alice sent you some food—Patrick has it in that sack. This sack," Quentin said, handing James a bulky cloth bundle, "is for the hawk. Alice said you might have a hungry hawk here. There's meat for him."

"My thanks." James turned to Isobel. "We must leave, my lady."

"Leave?" She looked surprised.

"Aye. You lads, go back to Alice's house and guard it well. If those men were sent by Sir Ralph Leslie, they will return. They are looking for the lady. And Alice will need protection."

He went to the back of the cave and returned with bow, quiver, and sword. Looping the quiver on his belt, he slung the bow over his shoulder and positioned the long broadsword in a sheath strapped on his back. Then he gathered the hawk's a hood, jesses, gloves, and shoved them into a leather pouch at his belt. Feeding Gawain a chunk of the fresh meat Alice had sent, he turned to help Isobel drape her cloak over her shoulders. "Ready?" he asked her.

"Do we go back to Alice's house?" she asked.

He shook his head, took her elbow, and turned. "Quentin, Patrick. See that Alice is safe. I will take Lady Isobel to Aird Craig."

She turned with a questioning look. He tightened his grip on her arm.

"Leslie's men will not find you there easily," Quentin said. "Do you mean to hide the lass there?"

"I do," James said.

"So," Quentin said. "You will trade her for Janet?"

"What?" Patrick asked. "Trade her? It is not honorable, holding women like this."

"Tell that to Leslie," James said. "But he may make a trade for his betrothed."

"Wait," Isobel said.

"He might," Quentin agreed. "A wonder he's had Janet this long. That lass can be a trial."

"Not easy to keep her against her will, true," Patrick said. "A clever lass with the strength of two men."

"She has what?" Isobel asked, looking from one to the other.

"You ought to know," Quentin drawled to Patrick. "She was after you often enough. And I saw you go off into the greenwood with Janet a time or two." He wiggled a brow.

Patrick blushed. "She were never after me. She were always after Jamie."

"She favors you both," James said.

"Me for my bonny face," Quentin said, "and Patrick for his, ah...."

"For me courtesy," Patrick supplied with a grin.

"But bold as she is, she needs our help," Quentin added.

"Meet me on the height this evening." James led Isobel to the cave opening as he spoke. "I will have a message for Ralph Leslie that you can deliver." He took the girl and the hawk outside.

"THERE," JAMES SAID later, pointing westward, "is the Craig."

He glanced at Isobel, standing beside him on a hilltop overlooking the forest. They had walked a good distance in relative silence. Now, standing together, the wind whipped at their cloaks and hair. He knew the climb lay ahead, and he must make sure the woman and the hawk both got up there with him. As two grouse flew overhead, the bird on his fist suddenly pitched off the glove in a wild bate.

James sighed and extended his arm to give him room for his fit. "We may have to begin again with this laddie," he muttered as the bird fussed.

"We will go up there?" Isobel asked, looking toward the enormous crag rising high above the western side of the nearby stretch of forest.

"Aird Craig—the high crag. Aye," he said. The rugged flat-topped crag jutted out of the side of a mountain, swathed in a thick cover of trees, as if a rumpled green tapestry had been tossed over it. One towering side of gray rock was split by a foaming white waterfall whose long white watery tail tumbled into a wide burn skimming past the base of the crag.

Isobel stared upward. "Do you live up there?"

"Aye, near the top." Seeing that Gawain had calmed, James lifted the bird back to the fist. "There are caves all through the interior like a honeycomb. At the summit there is an ancient ruin. A fine place to live apart from others," he added.

"So the Hawk Laird has an eyrie."

He shrugged. "So to speak. The Craig is a difficult climb. The most obvious access goes up the mountain behind it. Still steep and dangerous."

"Do we have to go that way?"

"There is an easier way, a secret way up. Once we found it, we used the crag as a refuge."

She frowned. "But we must climb up?"

"We lack wings to fly," he drawled. "I hope your foot is well enough for the walk. Come ahead." Taking her elbow, he urged her ahead to walk along the ridge of a hill. Passing behind a screen of birches and gorse, James could hear the faint, dull, familiar roar of the waterfall that spilled down the crag.

"We have been climbing and walking for days," Isobel grumbled. "Through forests, up hills, down cliffs. And now you want me to climb that monstrous crag."

"It is not so bad as it looks."

"I do not want to climb a mountain." She stopped. "I do not have to go up there with you."

He halted. "Nay?"

"Nay." She fisted her hand on her hip, her right arm tucked against her. "I can go back to Alice's house. I could walk to Wildshaw alone, if I want."

"Do you want to do that?" he murmured.

She tipped her head. "Would you stop me?"

He felt tension thrum between them. She had set a dare before him, and he did not know quite what she wanted with it. "Do you think I would force you to stay?"

"You might." She gazed out over the forest. The wind lifted the glorious dark length of her hair, released it. "But I do not care to be a hostage, James Lindsay. If I walked away, what would you do?"

Silence hung between them. His heart thumped. Without the lady as a hostage, he had no chance of regaining Janet, and less chance of exacting revenge on Leslie.

But if he kept Isobel captive, he would lose the trust she had begun to show him. He would lose what respect he had left for himself. And he would lose her entirely.

The thought struck him like a blow. He understood her desire for freedom. He had been a comrade of the greatest rebel leader in Scotland; he had spent time in a dungeon; he had lost his inheritance and legal freedom through unfair means. He understood better than most the desire for liberty.

Despite all, he had taken Isobel hostage in his passion to revenge the wrongs done to him and to his. Nor could he ignore the irony of the jessed hawk on his fist. He had forced a wild thing into captivity and denied Isobel her freedom too. Her resistance was hardly surprising.

The wind stirred his hair and his cloak, and ruffled the bird's feathers, strong enough to blow a little sense into his wounded, blinded heart.

"Aye," he agreed. "You deserve your freedom."

"You cannot keep me."

"I cannot," he said tautly.

"When I was blind," she said, "you promised me safekeeping. I am grateful for that. And you made another promise—to let me go after my sight returned."

"I did agree to that." Foolish, he told himself, to speak from his heart that day. If he refused now, he would lose honor in her regard. She would never trust him.

"Go, then," he said woodenly. Rain began to fall in tiny, misted drops. He waited. But Isobel did not walk away. "Are you leaving, then?"

"I might." The wind buffeted between them. "Is Wildshaw west or east from here?"

He nearly laughed. "West."

"I could ask Ralph to release Janet."

"He will not."

"Then I will release her myself." She lifted her chin.

"Ah," he said, flattening a smile. What was it about her, that she could so innocently charm a smile from him and hurt him all at once? "That I would like to see. But if 'twere easy, Janet would have walked out already, believe me."

"You think well of her."

"She's a good lass. I want her safe."

"You love her." Isobel's voice was soft.

"In a way." His heart quickened as he looked down at her. "Not as you love Ralph Leslie. You promised marriage with him."

The wind ruffled the sheened curtain of her dark hair. "My father wanted the match. I agreed. A betrothal is not always a promise of love."

"Yet you are eager to get to Wildshaw and eager to get away from me."

"My father may be there. And I do not like being held for ransom. But I am not eager to get away from you."

"Ah." He listened to the lift in the wind, the rush of the waterfall far ahead. "Janet," he said then, "is not my betrothed, if you think it."

"You are willing to risk much to get her back. Clearly you love her. It is—admirable."

"Janet Crawford loves me in her way, as I care for her in mine. But that lass would not wed me if I begged her on my knees. Which I would never do."

Her eyes went silvery blue, taking on the gray overcast sky. "I thought she was your lover."

"She is like my sister." He considered. "Like a brother, at times."

"Aye?" Her eyes gleamed. "I should like to meet her."

"You might." Gawain shifted on his fist, cheeping and squawking, threatening to bate again.

"What bothers him?" Isobel asked.

"He is a wild thing. With all this moving about, we may have lost whatever ground we gained toward manning him." He plucked the small hood from the pouch at his belt and dropped it deftly over the bird's head. "He could bate all the way up the crag and hurt himself, or make the ascent difficult for us," James told her. "This will quiet him. But we might have to start over with his training."

"We?"

"We worked together to man this hawk." An idea struck him. A risk. "Lass, a favor."

"What is it?" She sounded wary.

"You do not want to be the hostage of a forest outlaw. You want to find your father, and you think you will be safer at Wildshaw. Even if you do not love the man, you feel safer with him than with an outlaw."

"I might," she said hesitantly. "What favor?"

"I want Janet safe. We can help each other."

"How?"

"I promise you will have what you want. I just ask a little of your time."

"My time?"

"Give me a few days to send a message to Leslie and ask for Janet in trade for you. Let us see if he will accept."

"You want me to remain as your hostage?" She stared at him.

"My guest. My—friend. I ask for your help. That is all."

She said nothing. The wind rippled her hair, lifted his hair from his shoulders. James looked away, feeling suddenly, keenly vulnerable. She could refuse and walk away, and he would let her go and see his hopes shatter. Forcing her to be his hostage now would condemn him as the worst of rogues in her eyes. He did not want that.

Her silence lingered. He glanced at her. "My lady, I want to rescue Janet without risking more lives. But I will not keep you if you do not want to stay."

She let out a breath and glanced toward the great crag. "You want an accomplice."

"I suppose so." He smiled a little. "Leslie need never know. He will think you were kept in fear of your life at the hands of an outlaw."

"He would kill you for that."

"Lass, he means to kill me regardless. He needs no further reason."

She glanced at him, her hair whipping across her face. He reached out to draw the strands back.

"What do you say, Black Isobel?"

"Why would you let me go, if I want that?"

"It is unchivalrous to hold a woman for ransom," he said lightly. "Someone told me that recently."

"You once said I was your only hope of gaining what you wanted. Rescuing Janet, I think."

"My only hope, aye. But I cannot jess you as I can this bird. So I humbly beg a boon of you and wait upon your good will." He kept his tone light, though he felt tension within. He was gambling all just now, placing his wager on her trust.

She tipped her head. "What changed your mind?"

"You. I ask your help. But I will not keep you against your will." He paused. "Yet if you cannot trust me, I understand. Wildshaw is that way." He pointed.

"Very well." She turned. "Show me your wild craig. I will give you a few days. But you must treat me kindly," she added.

His heart gave a surge, but he nodded and turned to walk ahead. "I can do that. I have learned a few manners from hawks."

"I have noticed," she said, and followed.

Chapter Seventeen

"**T**AKE OFF YOUR shoes." James spoke loud enough that Isobel could hear him over the pounding din of the waterfall.

She blinked at him. "My shoes? Must we scale the cliff in bare feet?" She glanced up, dreading the climb that lay ahead on the towering crag that rose up from the far bank of a rushing stream. A short distance away, the high, narrow waterfall plunged down into the burn with considerable force, water churning and spilling over rocks as it sped past them. She scowled.

"Shoes and hose too." James set the hawk on a branch and sat to pull off his boots and hosen. Then he retrieved the hawk and stepped into the burn. The water rushed and swirled around his bare, muscular calves. He took up the hawk on his glove and held out his other hand to her. "Hurry, lass."

She sat to pull off her hose and her low boots, awkward with the wounded arm still stiff and sore, and crammed the things into her belt. Standing, she lifted the hem of her gown and tucked some of the fabric into the belt too. Then she stepped gingerly into the swirling stream, gasping at the cold. Moving ahead, she was soon knee-deep in the water.

James took her hand in a firm grip to guide her over the slippery stones littering the streambed. Reaching the opposite bank, she stepped out without needing his help. On the bank, he steadied the hooded goshawk.

Isobel looked up at the soaring cliffside. "Have you a rope? What about the hawk?"

"This way," he said, leading her toward the waterfall.

Puzzled, she followed, picking her way barefoot over mossy rocks and waving grasses. James led her so close to the waterfall that the spray dampened her gown and slicked her hair against her brow. She wiped her arm over her face and followed. Quickly he turned sideways and then slid behind the rushing foam of the waterfall. Then his arm thrust out and he grabbed her hand, pulling her through the beating rush of water to stand entirely behind the waterfall.

The sound was deafening, the light inside the crevice diminished. Seeing the outline of his head and shoulders, not sure where to go, she paused. He sluiced water from his brow. The hawk gave a long, nervous *keee-keee*. Then Jamie disappeared with Gawain, slipping into shadows with wildcat grace.

Isobel stepped hesitantly into the darkness, and again saw his beckoning hand. He went into a dark crevice. She followed into a black depth, the wet rock underfoot slick and cold.

She felt panic overtake her—the darkness was like blindness, the roar of the waterfall so loud she could barely think. Turning, she bumped against a rock wall. "Jamie!"

A dim golden light flared, lining a narrow passage. She went that way, finding a dry floor that sloped upward. She put out a hand for balance on rough rock and ducked her head to avoid hitting the low ceiling of an apparent tunnel.

"Jamie!" Her voice was a watery echo.

"Here," he said. The light bloomed brighter. She followed the twisting tunnel.

He waited along the passage, the bird in one hand. He held a flaring pine splint that he stuck into a crease in the rock. Sitting he pulled on his hose and boots, stood with head and shoulders hunched, and gestured for her to sit.

"We keep a flint and torches here," he explained. "Put your shoes on before we continue. 'Tis a bit of a walk, but better than climbing straight up the cliff side."

Isobel sat, yanked on her stockings and gartered them, not even caring if he watched, but he did not. She pulled on her boots and then followed James, who carried hawk and torch and loped up the incline. In the long, narrow crevice, the rock walls were pinkish sandstone and looked as if some stone-devouring dragon had carved a tunnel.

"A secret passage up to the crag?" she asked.

"I hope it is secret," he drawled. "We have used it for years. The tunnel is as ancient as the broch tower that sits high on the crag. Wallace and Patrick and I discovered this cave and tunnel a few years ago when we were being chased by a patrol. We leaped behind the waterfall to hide and found this. Only we few know about it. Quentin, Patrick, a few others." He walked on, then spoke again. "Pray God the English never discover it. Nearly a hundred men followed my lead at one time," he added. "But less than ten know about this route."

"Do the Southrons know you live up on the crag?"

"They know the Hawk Laird hides up there, but they do not know how we come and go. But now that you know—" He turned. The flare highlighted his face. He looked rugged, strong, unyielding. "Give me your solemn promise to never reveal this passageway."

"Upon my heart, I promise."

"Will you risk your heart? Then I will hold you to it." He moved ahead. The torchlight poured gold over his hair, his powerful back and shoulders, turning the hawk golden too.

For a moment Isobel felt an intense yearning bloom inside her, a feeling unlike any she had ever known. It was as if she had just made a deeper promise than he had asked—as if she had indeed pledged her heart, not for the man's secret here, but for the man himself.

The feeling was wrenching, so powerful she nearly faltered, placing her hand against raw rock. A sudden memory flooded her mind—a vision, the misty image of a church, a rain-soaked yard, a hawthorn tree. A man, cloaked and hooded like a pilgrim, a hawk on his gloved fist. He turned, and she saw his face. James. And she was there, too.

She had seen those images months ago, the day she had seen Wallace's death. She had not understood then, and still was not certain. Why had she seen James and herself together by that tree?

James looked back. "What is it? You are pale as the moon."

"Naught," she said, and came toward him. "I am fine. How much farther?"

He handed her the torch, one hand occupied with the hooded hawk, and took her elbow to lead her forward. "A long, steady climb that winds through the heart of the crag."

"Was this cut by hand? Who did this?" She looked around the narrow tunnel with its low ceiling, curved floor, rough walls, pinkish rock gleaming in the torchlight.

"Much of it was tunneled by ancient men, I think. There are deep, old chisel marks. But it was begun by the hand of God—there are numerous caves connected by crevices large enough to be tunnels. In places, it is as open as a dovecote, and there are small wells and even a spring, all inside the crag."

"How can that be, up this high?"

"The spring thaws funnel off the mountain. You will see for yourself as we go higher."

They resumed walking. The climb followed the narrow tunnel in a snaking path that turned, ascended, dipped and flattened and stretched upward again. As they went higher, Isobel saw small caves off the tunnel like honeycomb crevices. Farther on, she saw a larger cave.

"Do you live in these caves?"

"We use them as hideaways. But we live on the summit." The torch sputtered as they made a sharp turn and bent their heads to avoid the low ceiling in that section. Then the tunnel split into two arms, and Isobel heard the sound of trickling water, its echo magnified by stone.

"There is a spring over there," he said. "But we go this way." He turned left to follow the incline. Isobel went with him, her legs tiring. She yearned to rest. Then he rounded a corner, ducked beneath an overhang, and turned to beckon.

Stepping forward, she saw a flight of stone steps and the pale glow of daylight.

He took the steps two at a time. Isobel came more slowly, holding her skirts, wary of the uneven steps. Though she was long-legged, the stairs seemed cut for giants.

They emerged at last into the gray light, the wind fresh and full. Isobel set her foot on grass and looked around. James went ahead, disappearing beyond a stacked stone wall.

A huge, curving stone wall surrounded the grassy area. Blocks and slabs of the same rosy sandstone inside the crag were layered to rise to a remarkable height. She saw small tiny window openings and one rectangular door in the lower part of the high rounded wall.

She walked around the circular yard inside the walls. Sections had fallen, revealing the double wall construction of the circular tower. The space between the walls was divided into cells and floors.

James came toward her, holding the hawk but without the torch. "This is an ancient broch," he explained. "A fortress, abandoned ages ago, built by a people who they say have vanished from Scotland. The Romans called them Picts."

"They must have been a race of giants, judging by this huge place."

"No one knows much about them. And no one seemed to know about the passageway," he said.

"Their secret was lost," she said, feeling touched, saddened, somehow, and yet astonished. Overhead, the sky was like pewter and she felt raindrops on her cheeks.

James took her hand. "Come out of the rain," he said, taking her with him. He stepped over some collapsed stones to enter the hollow core of the double walls and drew her up a rough staircase inside the wall.

They stepped out onto a gallery with windows overlooking the courtyard. Between the double walls here, she saw a few small chambers, snug and swept clean of rubble. James entered one of the cells, ducking beneath the door lintel. Dim light filtered into the windowless room, which held a stone bench and three wooden perch stands. He set Gawain on one of the perches.

"This was a mews," he said.

"For Astolat?" Isobel asked, remembering the name of his other hawk.

"Aye. We will let Gawain rest, but not long. He could go feral again. Come with me."

She followed him out and then up a low flight of steps to a higher gallery and into another chamber. A square window shed light into the room, illuminating a stone bench, a table, and a bed that held a flat mattress and fur coverings. A small stone hearth in the corner, cold now, hinted at comfort.

"Is this your chamber?" she asked.

"Aye."

"Grand for a brigand." She wandered about. "I thought outlaws lived in caves or hollow trees."

"Some live in coziness and luxury inside ancient fortresses. But none have true homes. There is another chamber there," he said, pointing to a narrow door. "You may use that."

She peered through the doorway. The adjoining chamber had a view of the inner courtyard and held more crudely assembled stone furniture. The stone bed had a rudimentary mattress and no coverlet.

But the stark space had a peaceful simplicity. Isobel sat on the bench and looked out over the courtyard. Rain pattered over the stones and the grass below. She shivered.

"I will make a fire. And we have stores of goods and food, so you will be comfortable here."

She nodded. Fatigue and hunger, and the rigorous climb, had sapped her strength. He left the chamber and she leaned her head beside the window, watching the rain thicken to a downpour.

Enclosed in a stout tower on an inaccessible crag, she was firmly imprisoned.

Her best chance for freedom remained with the outlaw—and her only hope lay in trusting him.

"THE RAIN HAS stopped," Isobel said.

James nodded, silent as he focused on the hawk throwing yet another bate. He and Lady Isobel sat in the small stone chamber that sheltered them from the rain as they shared the bread and cheese Alice had provided, along with a small flask of red wine he had found in storage. A low fire crackled on the stone hearth, filling the room with warmth.

Sighing, he held out his arm, waiting for the blur of the hawk's wings to settle as Gawain worked off his displeasure over something. James shook his head, beginning to despair of training this hawk.

"He has been ruined, this gos," he murmured. "Whoever had him before spoiled him utterly."

"Then he is not from my father's mews. Papa raised hawks properly. As you do," she added.

The wing beats stopped, and he scooped the bird back to his fist. "I cannot right damage done by a poor falconer. There is not enough patience in the world for that."

"If anyone has the patience, it is you."

He huffed. "This bird may be hopeless."

"He is not—are you, Sir Gawain!" She looked at the bird. "Tell the man you can be reclaimed."

"I thought you wanted me to set him free."

"When the time comes, aye. But his wing must heal before we let him go."

We. He noticed that. "Every bate he makes delays his healing."

Isobel plucked up a deck feather lost by Gawain in his tantrum and handed it to James. He used it to stroke the bird's breast and legs. The hawk glared, bronze eyes resentful, and perched with wings hunched forward, talons flexing restively.

"He is hungry," James said. "See how his talons clench. Exhausted, too, yet he will not sit the fist quietly." He reached into the hawking pouch, found a scrap of raw meat in a cloth, and fed it to the bird. "Look at you," he told Gawain. "Just as bedraggled as when I first found you in the tree. And you have twisted your tail feathers with all these bates. They will have to be straightened, and that is not a merry process," he told Isobel sourly.

"Let it wait. You both are exhausted. You need rest, and can start afresh with the training."

He sighed. "I have to train him. It is harmful for him to behave wildly, and I cannot let him go with a weak wing. He must be able to hunt or he will die."

"You are an honorable man," she said quietly, "to rescue a hawk and train him for his own well-being, and at a cost to yourself."

Surprised and pleased by the compliment, he gave her a wry look all the same. "This from the lass who thinks me a wretched traitor?"

"I think you are like that goshawk." Her eyes were gray as the rain.

"Foul tempered and bedraggled?"

A smile played over her lips. "That too. As well as wild, strong, and stubborn."

Despite discouragement and fatigue, he felt his mood lighten at that hint of respect from her, as well as the easy humor she began to show toward him.

"Stubborn," she continued, "for neither of you will give in."

He huffed. "I seldom relent over any matter, but this goshawk may defeat me."

"I do not think anything could defeat you," she murmured.

He glanced at her, curious, touched, seeing a glint of admiration in her remarkable eyes. For a moment he remembered a sweet, lingering kiss shared among the ferns. Grateful for her trust, he felt discomfited too, sensing he did not deserve it.

"Oh, I have been defeated before," he drawled. "I just keep it to myself."

Isobel tilted her head, her gaze gentle, though it pierced through him. His blood surged with the need to touch her, sip some of the sweetness he saw on those lips, in those eyes.

Fatigue blurred his thoughts, blurred years of self-discipline. If he stayed with her longer, he might do something he would regret. Something kind and caring that he could not step back from easily.

"Come outside." He stood. "I will show you the Craig."

Chapter Eighteen

THE WIND ON top of the crag was fierce, beating her hair about her head, whipping her skirts against her legs. As her hair blew back, Isobel tried to capture it, wishing she had the use of two hands to braid it. She stood beside Jamie Lindsay on the summit of the crag, looking out over a glorious view, the sky bright after rain, dove-gray clouds rolling overhead. The forest stretched out below, its deep greens muted under veils of mist. Beyond its expanse lay lochs and streams like shining ribbons.

Isobel smiled at Jamie, who held the hawk on his gloved fist. "'Tis beautiful," she said in awe.

"This view extends for miles." He pointed with his free hand. "Over there are the Border hills, round and green and gold. There"—he indicated a meandering river—"is the Yarrow Water, which flows toward the Ettrick Water. Down there, beyond that rocky hill, is Alice's house. On sunny days, we can see the three peaks of the Eildon Hills from here."

"The Eildon Hills, where Thomas the Rhymer once lived?"

"Aye. His home, Learmont Tower, is near there. His family lives there now, after his passing."

"Into those hills, they say, he followed the Queen of Faery and stayed for seven years."

"And came out again, a prophet and a seer." He glanced at her.

She nodded. Thomas of Learmont's prophecies had earned

him renown—no one had tried to control him for their own purpose. She pointed west. "Can you see Wildshaw Castle from here?"

"The castle is beyond the forest, past that hill over there, see? It overlooks a river valley."

"It must be a very beautiful setting." She glanced up at him.

"Aye." A muscle beat in his cheek briefly. He stared out over the landscape.

"This wide view of the forest and land must be useful—for you," she ventured.

"From up here, we can see English patrols riding into the forest and over the hills, and we can see them heading to and from Wildshaw, and so on. It is useful to see our foes, true."

"Do they know you are up here, safely hidden where they cannot find you?"

"I suppose they do." He shrugged. "Watching from up here is like looking into the future, in a way. We can predict who we will meet down there. We can choose our skirmishes. But we cannot foresee the outcome."

"A more practical way to know the future than I can offer. This eyrie offers protection."

"It does. That has been fortunate. When I was captured months ago, it was elsewhere. They would not have found us had we been up here."

"Us?" Isobel studied at his strong, handsome profile. "Where were you taken?"

"West of here, traveling to meet others loyal to Wallace when we were ambushed by a Southron patrol." He drew a sharp breath. "A few of my men were killed, my cousin Tom Crawford—Alice's youngest—with them. One friend got away, Sir William Seton—he carried the word to others and help came, but too late. Janet was taken also."

"She was with you that day?"

"Aye, she was often with us. A strong and fearless lass, nor would I refuse a good bow arm just because it belonged to a woman. But that day was ill-fated. We were taken down to Carlisle, where I was held until July. Janet was put in Leslie's custody. He is sympathetic to the English," he added, with a glance at her.

She frowned. "Was that when you lost Wildshaw to the English?"

"Not then. The castle had been taken years earlier. My brother was baron and laird then, but he died at Falkirk, and Wildshaw became mine by right. But Edward of England dispossessed me along with other barons. I was declared an outlaw, if nothing else, for refusing to sign an oath of fealty."

"As if Edward Longshanks has the right to demand fealty or reassign Scottish lands."

He lifted a brow. "This, from a lass about to wed a Scots lord gone over to the English?"

"This from one who knows right from wrong. Marriage will not change that." She turned. "You cannot gain it back, as laird of Wildshaw?"

"I tried," he said. "It came to sorrow." He was silent for a moment. "King Edward's commanders installed a garrison at Wildshaw. They stock the castle with supplies and war machines to aid them in fighting in the Borderlands."

Isobel remembered, then, standing in the bleak, threatened garden at Aberlady, cradling a white rose while James told her that he, too, had lost a castle and loved ones to the English. And she recalled that Alice had hinted he carried a burden on his heart since Wildshaw.

"What happened, Jamie?"

He sighed, stroked Gawain's breast feathers. She marveled that such a wild bird would tolerate a man's touch. But the man was wild, too, in his way. They understood each other. She waited.

"I would bring Astolat and come up here to watch," he said. "I would watch for Southrons and she would watch for prey. If I released her to fly at quarry from this height, she would bring it back to me. If I did not set her to flight, she would perch calmly, even if a tempting bit of bird went by."

"Astolat was a remarkable hawk."

"She was." His eyes narrowed as he scanned the forest. The wind lifted his hair from his shoulders. "From up here, I could see who went through the forest to Wildshaw. I spent a good deal of time up here with Wallace and others while my brother held Wildshaw. But that day was shortly after Falkirk, where my brother and two cousins had been killed, Alice's older sons. I went to Wildshaw, then visited Alice, and came back to the Craig. And saw Southrons riding through, fitted for war. I went down with a patrol of a few men. We saw they were headed for Wildshaw. Astolat was with me."

The goshawk shifted on the fist, flapped his wings. James whispered to him, his patience preventing a new bate. He began to speak again.

"Astolat saw my attacker first. She raised her wings, seated on my fist, and took the arrow aimed at me." He paused. "Straight into her breast."

Isobel gasped. "Did she try to protect you?"

"I doubt it. Hawks are too wild for that. But she was always different, that gos. My men were convinced she sacrificed herself. Either way, a hard loss to bear."

"You loved her."

"As much as one can love a hawk, for they do not love us back. But she was as strong-willed and loyal as any I have done. But for one man, and one lass, long ago."

She knew he spoke of William Wallace, yet wondered about the girl. An empty ache bloomed inside her and she realized that she felt jealous—toward the hawk and the girl he had loved.

"Loyalty means much to you," she murmured.

"It is essential to me," he said bluntly.

"Did you love the lass too?"

"In my way. We were young and did not know much of love, but I was fond of her. She had a kind nature and a fine laugh." He smiled, rueful and fleeting. "We had been betrothed for years on our parents' wishes, when I gave up on the notion of the seminary. But the wars and my commitment to Wallace delayed the marriage."

Silence spun out. The goshawk chittered. "Elizabeth died unfairly, after Astolat was killed." His voice had a new edge. The air felt weighted with regret or sorrow, and Isobel saw the glimmer of hurt in his eyes. "She was at Wildshaw then. Sometimes she acted as chatelaine, since my parents were gone, and my brother and I were often absent."

"She was there when Wildshaw was taken?" Isobel whispered.

"Aye." His face was set hard. "An English arrow took Astolat in the morning. By afternoon, Elizabeth was gone too, in a fire set by flaming arrows. The English marched through the burning gates of Wildshaw and killed any they did not take prisoner. One man escaped and found us, told us."

"Dear saints." What he had endured that day went through her like a punch to the gut.

"But we did not sit idly by after that news. We took as many English lives as we could. But we had just suffered a great loss at Falkirk. We lacked the spirit, and the men, to win much."

"Do you know who was behind the attack on Wildshaw?"

"Some. I know Sir Ralph Leslie was with the English commander. And he was with the party that captured us months ago. I recognized that he had been at Wildshaw. Some of those faces are seared into memory," he added.

"So you have a bitter quarrel with the English. And Sir Ralph."

"I do." He closed his eyes. "At Wildshaw, we tried to get through the gate. I would have walked through fire for Elizabeth, and for any of them caught in the fire. But I was wounded, and dragged back by my men, or I would have thrown myself in, I think."

Isobel gasped. "Sir Ralph told Alice he did that for me at Aberlady! He must have seen you at Wildshaw, and then gave himself credit for such—nobility."

"Did he?" he muttered. "Brave lad, your intended."

"He lied, but you were the one had the courage." She saw a muscle twitch in his jaw, saw a flush spread in his cheek. Sympathy washed through her. She set her hand on his hard-muscled arm.

"What happened at Wildshaw could not be prevented. You would have died there too. I am so sorry that it happened. But I—I am glad you survived."

"I avenged her death," he said fiercely. "Without mercy. For weeks afterward. For months." He drew a breath. "I may still be avenging it even now. But bloody deeds cannot appease that sort of anger, or change the hollowness inside. Prayer and time—may mend it. Or perhaps I will never find peace."

"Jamie." She moved her hand, her fingers touched his, and he grabbed her fingers swiftly.

"But I grew stronger. Cold inside. Fierce. English vowed to capture me, but could not for years."

"So they want you still."

"They had me once." His voice was near a growl. "And nearly took my soul."

"What do you mean?" she whispered.

He let go of her hand and looked at the goshawk. "I swore I would never keep another hawk. I thought a hawk would only remind me of what I had lost."

"But now you have a silly wee hawk that needs you."

He huffed at that. "I suppose I do."

Isobel watched him, wary and sympathetic and glad that he had opened up his past a little to her. But doors were still closed between them, a darker part of his life. And she knew he would not answer questions related to what had caused him to be called a traitor. But the more she learned about him, the more she knew he was a good, caring man. She would never believe, now, that he was truly a traitor.

"After Wildshaw was taken, you stayed here at the Craig, and also ran with Wallace?"

He nodded. "More men joined me in the forest—Wildshaw's tenants and others made homeless by English attacks. We followed Wallace, and also acted on our own. Liam Seton and others would meet with me, and we would do what we could. A simple band, with naught but the clothes on our backs and the weapons in our hands. We lacked might, but we were clever. Yet there were always more soldiers to replace the ones we eliminated."

Isobel looked out over the vista of forest and hills, and saw a hawk circling above. It rose higher, riding the wind with easy grace, then swooped and disappeared into the forest.

"One day you will gain back your property and all that belongs to you," she murmured.

"I hope that is not a prophecy. Because if I regain Wildshaw, I will have to destroy it."

She stared at him. "Are you that bitter?"

"Practical," he said. "Scotland lacks the soldiers and supplies needed to keep castles garrisoned against English attack. We defend only the most important strongholds—those we call the strengths of Scotland. It is what Wallace wanted. What Bruce and others want, now. So we render the rest useless to the enemy by destroying structures. Aberlady is not a major castle. Neither is Wildshaw."

"But both were homes once and could be that again. You could be laird of Wildshaw again."

"Laird of what?" He made a sweep with his hand to indicate forest, hills, sky. "Of a castle I have not set foot inside for years? Of a forest filled with Scottish deer that an English king claims for his own? Of tenants who have no homes now?" He barked a laugh. "I am laird of naught, lass. I am a brigand, an outlaw. A broken fellow."

"You are far more. You have a name here. You are a legend in the Ettrick Forest."

"But I have lost all claim to that. Laird of naught that can be kept, measured, or protected. Like the wind." He waved his hand impatiently. "Impossible to hold."

She looked at him, startled. "Laird of the wind." She gestured too, echoing his sweep. "You have dominion over this high, windy place. You command your freedom. The Southrons cannot reach you here, cannot force you to surrender or to say a false oath. They cannot climb up here, weighted down by armor and weapons. Weighted by greed and the anger of their king. You fight for liberty, and you are helping to make that possible for others."

He gazed down at her. "Laird of the wind. Hawk of the forest. Your prophecy."

"And I just realized what it means. Hawk of the forest, laird of the wind—they describe a free man, one who does not bow down, one who rises above the rest. Like that hawk you hold, or that hawk out there, flying above the forest."

His eyes crinkled, cheek pulsed. "So it is me in your prophecy after all."

"But I was wrong if I named you a traitor. You are only a man of honor."

He regarded her steadily. "Nay, lass. Just to you. Then I am a hero, a champion of maidens, one who rescues Scotland and— can kiss the blindness from your eyes."

"Any who call you a traitor do not know you. You have a noble heart where honor dwells."

He frowned. "You called me a wretched traitor. I took you from your castle, made you a hostage, and now I ask you to deceive your betrothed in a ransom scheme."

You are the man who took my heart. "Aye. And you are honorable."

"Are you so sure, Black Isobel?" His quiet voice, low and soft, was powerful.

"I am. And I am here with you because I have faith in you."

His eyes turned a dark, penetrating blue. "Faith in me," he

repeated. The wind whipped at him. The hawk chirred at him. But he did not take his gaze from hers.

"I do. So does Alice, and your men." She leaned toward him. "Are you so blind you do not see that? None of us believes you a traitor, though you think we should."

He looked down at her. "None of you know the truth."

"Then tell me."

He looked away, his hair blowing softly in the breeze. Then he shook his head.

"You trusted me with some of what haunts you. Trust me for the rest."

He smiled and lifted a hand to trace the curve of her jaw. She closed her eyes at his touch, and he leaned closer, hand warm on her cheek in the cool wind, his fingers then cupping the side of her head. The wind fluttered her hair like a black banner around them.

"I trust you, lass, and I do not do that easily. But if I told you all the truth, your faith would vanish. And I need it from you." His mouth was close to hers then, and she tilted back her head, welcoming. "God, I need it," he whispered.

His lips covered hers in a kiss that was stirring, hungry. He pulled her to him with one arm, the other balancing the bird. His fingers delved into the windblown mass of her hair as Isobel leaned into his embrace, tipping her head for the deepening kiss. The wind rocked her, and he held her steady while his lips caressed hers, softening, tensing, coaxing. She felt as if the world tilted and the wind lifted her.

Then Gawain leaped off James's outstretched hand like a frog off a sunny rock. But the jesses caught him, as always, and he battered wildly, his wingtips brushing against her arm. Isobel broke away from James to leap back.

With a deft flick of his gloved wrist, James gave the tiercel room to fuss. The bird then clambered back to the fist, squawking. James shook his head in disgust, then spoke gently to the bird, and sang a few notes of the *kyrie* until Gawain settled, blinking, feet planted on the glove.

James gave Isobel a wry smile. "This dim-witted hawk has more sense than I do. Let me ask your pardon once again. I should not have—"

"Do not beg pardon of me." Still reeling from the shimmering strength of the kiss, she shook her head. "I was part of that, too."

"You have placed yourself in my care and are on your way to meet your betrothed. So that lacked grace on my part. I will not give Leslie any more reason to seek my head. Nor will I give you reason to regret—time with me."

"See, you are a man of honor."

He took her hand, and turned to look out over forest and sky. "Do you see the hawk there?"

"Is that a hawk off to the west?"

"Aye. A red-tailed hawk. A large one, so likely a female. But it is not wild. There must be a hunting party down there."

"She is beautiful!" She watched the hawk soar over the trees, circle, bank, sink among the trees. "Soon your Sir Gawain will fly like that."

"This sorry gos?" James tilted a doubtful brow at the bird on his fist. "He may never fly for me or any owner. I may have to give in and let him go to the wild when his injury heals."

"James—are those riders beneath the tree cover? I see red and white moving there." She shaded her eyes.

"Soldiers, coming along the path from Wildshaw." James tugged on her hand. "Come on. If we can see them, they might see us. And there is something I want to show you."

She followed, her hand captured in his, her heart beating like a wild thing, and knew as they walked away that she never wanted to leave the crag, or let go of the outlaw who lived there.

And she knew for sure that she did not want to be sent to her betrothed.

$$\longrightarrow \blacklozenge\cdot\cdot\bullet \quad \bullet\cdot\cdot\blacklozenge \longleftarrow$$

Chapter Nineteen

I SOBEL FOLLOWED JAMES along the promontory toward the mountain that rose solid and dark on the eastern side. He led her with swift steps to ease behind an outcropping formed by a rockslide that must have spilled off the mountain long ago.

"This way," he said. "Careful, now."

He preceded her down a narrow sloped path edged with scrub and gorse. A plateau jutted out below the high crag, just where the crag split from the mountainside. Runnels of water creased the slope, narrow streams trickling along to disappear behind a cluster of yellow-flowered gorse.

"Look here," he said, dropping to his haunches beside the gorse hedge. Isobel leaned forward.

A jumble of rocks, broken by some long-ago avalanche, blocked the way but for a gap that opened into the body of the crag. Rills of water poured thinly over the break in the rocks.

Isobel heard the echo of water on stone, and peered into the opening. "What's there?"

"A cave and a spring. Can you climb down that ladder with one hand?" He pointed toward a wooden ladder, a curious sight that leaned against the rock to sit inside the gap.

She nodded. James maneuvered to catch the side of the ladder and descend carefully, still gripping the hawk's jesses in one hand. Gawain flapped his wings and squawked, but James was able to climb the short distance to the cave floor. He looked at Isobel and beckoned.

She sat on the rock, set her feet on the wooden rungs and came down, also using one arm, balancing herself lightly with her injured arm as she went down. James caught her round the waist and set her on the rock floor.

"Careful, 'tis wet." His voice had a muted echo. Isobel turned, and caught her breath in wonder.

Soft daylight, damp air, and the rush of water filled her senses. A sparkling fall of water poured over the rim to collect in puddles on the uneven floor and spill into a small pool. Water seemed to cascade from the rock itself, issuing in clear trickles from crevices to splash into the pool. Another wall had a crudely cut entrance.

"Beautiful," she murmured in astonishment.

"The shallow end of the pool," he said, "goes warm as a bath when the sunlight shines here. The other side of the pool is deeper, and in shadow, and is quite cool."

"This place is miraculous," she breathed. "I did not know such things existed."

"Aye, though they are rare. 'Tis said that springs and pools like this can have healing powers. There are some legends about the Craig, but only my men and I know this place is here."

She nodded, looking at the falling water. "Does the water run down with the rains?"

"The rain increases the flow, but there is always a small stream coming down from the mountain. In summer especially, and on warm days, it is a bit of paradise here."

"Oh, aye," Isobel agreed. She lifted her skirts to walk around the pool's rim, which looked like a large, luxurious tub for a giant, scooped out of living sandstone.

James knelt beside one of the puddles, and extended his arm to allow Gawain to come close to the water.

"Will he drink?" Isobel asked.

"Nay. They do not drink much unless they are ill. But they like a good bath. Aye, laddie, try it," he urged. The hawk pecked suspiciously at the water, then dipped a talon into the wetness, and soon stepped off the fist to plop into the water. He stretched his wings and spread his tail feathers.

Isobel laughed. "He likes it."

"He might be a useless hawk, but at least he will be clean." Isobel laughed again as Gawain splashed, and James laughed with her. She glanced up at the man and felt her heart open like a rose in the sun. She was glad that he did not look at her just then, for she felt the glow of her feelings, and could not hide it.

He watched the hawk splash in the puddle. "You can bathe here, too," he said then.

"In the puddle, with the hawk?" She blinked at him.

"In the pool. If there are healing properties here, it would help your arm."

No one had ever showed such concern for her welfare, even during her bouts of blindness. "Is it warm enough?"

"Might be. How does your arm feel, lass?"

She flexed her arm and winced at the ache. "Better unless I move it too much. Alice suggested hot poultices to draw the stiffness out. Hot bread, I suppose," she said, and he laughed.

"We can tend to that later tonight, if you want."

She stared at him, realizing she would be alone with him that night, sleeping in a room next to his. The thought of him touching her to help her with her wounded arm—indeed, touching her, peeling away her clothing to help her—made her suck in a breath.

She nodded slowly, surprised that he seemed to care about her. The man who had taken her hostage was at heart compassionate. The day was filled with revelations, with proof that she had been wrong about him. So wrong.

"Let me see," he said. While the hawk dabbled in the puddle, James drew off the falconer's glove. Then he took Isobel's arm and gently lifted away the sling. Her breath quickened.

"Push against my hand," he instructed. "Now pull up." He put a little pressure on her arm, but she winced. "Well, the muscles still have strength. The broadhead did not cause permanent damage, I think. Use it more and it will get stronger. But rest it for now." He replaced the cloth sling.

As he withdrew his hand, he tugged on her fingers to pull her forward. He brushed away a drift of her dark hair where it shifted to drape over her shoulder.

"Is that why they call you Black Isobel? Your hair?"

"Did you think it was for my bad temper?" She smiled as he did. "I usually keep my hair braided back and under a veil," she went on. "But I cannot do it myself with one arm." She shook the mass of her hair over her shoulders. "The wind has made a tangle of it."

"I can braid it, if you do not mind a clumsy hand. Turn." He urged her around. His fingers soothed through her hair, lifting, tugging, grazing against her neck and shoulders as he made a thick plait. Shivers traced through her from head to foot, pooling and swirling in her breasts and abdomen.

The heat of his body was close and welcome in the intimate, damp cave. Her heart thundered. She kept still, loving the delicate web of feelings running through her at his touch.

He patted her shoulder them. "A sorry sort of braid, but 'twill do."

She half turned her head. "You have a gentle hand."

"I have learned well from hawks." He smoothed a tendril of hair over her ear, his thumb caressing down her neck, sending tremors through her. She wanted to turn in his arms, her body pounding with an urgent, startling need. But she stayed still, trembling, waiting.

"Ah," he said, lifting his hands away. "I will regret sending you to your betrothed, I think."

"Will you?" she breathed.

"But you must go back—for your father, and for Janet." He paused. "And for Leslie."

She bowed her head, feeling a sad weight upon her shoulders. "Not for Sir Ralph." She heard his indrawn breath. "He only means to use me—for the prophecies."

"The others used you too. They kept you away from the world, caring more about the prophecies than the prophetess."

"I know that now." She glanced at him. "Thank you for—showing me kindness and patience."

He sighed. "Lass, I mean to use you as well, to barter for Janet. I am not a champion or a saint. I am a rogue and will not change."

"But you never forced me to your will, as a true rogue would have done. And when I insisted on freedom, you were willing to give it to me, even if it deprived you of what you wanted. And you—"

"What?" His voice was soft. She wanted to melt into its warmth. And though she bowed her head protectively, she spilled her thoughts like the water pouring over the rim of the cave.

"You asked me to help you. I valued that. So much, you cannot know. I have—few friends."

"And so you want to stay with me, as a friend?"

Only in part, but she did not say. She waited, heart pounding. What she wanted, what she needed, crystallized then—as if she had been blind for a long time, and now saw a ray of light.

But she did not have the courage to say that she wanted to stay. And she hesitated to name the reason for the urge. She did not want to seem foolish or needy.

He touched her hair. "Isobel," he said. "I have been a fool."

Now she looked at him. "A fool?"

He nodded, tilting his head. "I should have kept you a hostage."

Disappointment plunged through her. "Oh."

With a finger, he lifted her chin. "I should never have let you become a friend. Become close. Now I cannot so give you up."

"You do not have to give me up."

His thumb traced her jaw. "I must."

She drew a breath, leaned toward him. "Jamie, you—"

"Och!" A voice called from above. "Look at that! Janet will

not like that!"

Isobel jumped as if stung. James turned and they both looked up to see Quentin and Patrick peering down at them with delighted grins.

"Aye," Quentin told Patrick. "She will not like it at all."

"Then we will not tell her," Patrick said. "Can we come down, or do you want to be alone?"

Isobel felt a hot flush spread into her face. Quentin winked at her and Patrick grinned.

James scowled. "We will come up. Did you ruffians bring supper?"

Patrick held up a brace of rabbits. "Two to share, and one for that surly gos."

"It is more than foolish to walk up to the yett of Wildshaw Castle and offer a message from the Hawk Laird," Patrick grumbled, his mouth full of roasted meat. He wiped his chin on his sleeve as he sat cross-legged on the floor James's snug bedchamber inside the broch wall. "We would be grabbed for hostages or slain on the spot."

"We can conduct the whole of this business from Stobo." James sat on the floor opposite the others, leaning back against the bed.

"Ah, the priest?" Quentin asked. "Father Hugh knows Sir Ralph Leslie and Black Isobel both."

"Exactly. So I want you two to ask him to convey the glad news to Sir Ralph Leslie that Lady Isobel is alive. He believes she died at Aberlady. And ask Father Hugh to deliver our demands."

"Just what are your demands?" Isobel asked.

James glanced at her. She sat alone on the stone bench by the crude-cut window, where moonlight cascaded along her face, and the glow of the fire highlighted her skirts, her graceful form.

"We will ask Leslie to meet us at the village church in Stobo. Sunday next is the feast day of Saint Ursula," James answered.

"How fitting," she murmured. "Saint Ursula, patron of virgins, ran away from a marriage she protested. She took her female companions with her. Eleven thousand of them."

"Och," Patrick grunted. "At least we only have to look after Lady Isobel and Janet."

"Tell Father Hugh," James said, "we will meet Leslie after Mass, in the presence of others, since the villagers will be gathered outside the church. Isobel will wait for him inside the church. He is to bring only two men, and Janet. He is to send Janet into the church alone. Lady Isobel can go out to him when Janet is safely inside."

"You will claim sanctuary, then," Isobel said. "The safety and protection of holy ground."

"Aye. We cannot trust Leslie. He could escort Janet to Stobo with a hundred men."

"If he would take part in betraying Wallace, he will not let a church door stop him from getting to Lady Isobel, or you, Jamie," Quentin said. "He will want the Hawk Laird's head."

"But he wants Isobel, so he must agree to a peaceful exchange." He sat scowling at the others.

Isobel was silent, looking out at the moon. James felt a deep tug in his heart to see her. He sighed, reluctant and torn. He tried to tell himself that she was wrong to think him her champion. The best course was to send her away quickly and for good.

But he did not want to do that. What he felt for her burned within him now, stifled and discouraged, though he felt the flare of passion whenever he was near her. And that was often now.

He could not bear to send her back to Leslie, but his plans had been formed before he knew her. She had altered the scheme, unwitting and wholly charming. But he had to stoke his determination and sheer will to see this through. This was the best way to rescue Janet. But exchanging Janet for Isobel felt like an unholy, heart-rending choice.

But, he reminded himself sourly, Isobel had been promised in marriage. She deserved a home, and a man who could safeguard her—even an English sympathizer whom James loathed. She did not need a forest brigand.

"You will be safe at Wildshaw, Lady Isobel," he said, trying to convince himself as much as her.

She shrugged a shoulder and did not look his way.

"You will be reunited with your father," he went on, "if Sir Ralph keeps his word."

"Aye," she said, staring at the moonlit sky.

"The lass is tired," Quentin murmured. "Lady Isobel, I set blankets on your bed and hung a curtain. And Alice sent along the satchel of your things."

"And I brought some French wine out of storage," Patrick said, "if you would care for some."

She rose from her seat. "Thank you. I will not have wine, but I do need some rest. Good night."

She drifted through the shadowed room like a wraith, pushed aside the cloak that served as a curtain, and disappeared into the darkness beyond the narrow threshold of the adjoining room.

James watched her go, feeling his heart sink a little with each step she took. Now that bartering with Leslie had begun, he felt even more dishonorable and traitorous. She had given him her trust and he was sending her back to the lions to be devoured.

Patrick poured wine from a jug into clay cups and handed one to James, another to Quentin, then noisily swallowed the contents of a third cup himself. James downed the wine quickly and leaned over to refill his cup. "Get to Stobo by mid-morn."

"Aye," Quentin eyed him. "And what will you do? Take the lass to Alice?"

James shook his head. "I will not risk Alice in this. I can keep Isobel here."

"Ah," Quentin said. The sage note in his voice made James frown at him. "Then while you have the chance, you can solve whatever stands between you and that lass."

"There is naught between us," James growled, and set down the cup.

"We are not fools," Quentin said. "I wonder if you can give

her up to Leslie."

"I can," he snapped.

"But will she go?" Patrick asked.

"Aye." He stood. "I must see to the hawk."

"The hawk is asleep on a perch in the mews with his head tucked to his wing," Patrick said. "I looked in on him when I came up with the wine."

"Leave him be," Quentin said. "He is jessed and tired. He will sleep."

James nodded and rubbed a hand over his jaw, shoved fingers through his hair, feeling unsettled, as if he must do something and could not think what it was. "I need to work with him more. His wing will not heal unless he stops bating and fussing. He has to learn to stay quiet."

"He will, but he is spoiled," Quentin said. "I have never seen any man with as much patience for a hawk as you have. But you look as ragged as that hawk, as if you have not slept for a week."

"I have not. Well. You know the message to deliver to Father Hugh."

"We know," Quentin said. "It will be done. Jamie, this is a dangerous scheme. Father Hugh knows Leslie well. We can only trust him with caution."

"I know. We will let him deliver the message, but we cannot tell him our business. And I want you to get Geordie out of his hands before this exchange takes place. Father Hugh will not let harm come to Isobel, but we must not trust Geordie to a friend of Leslie's for long."

"The lad will be able to travel by the time we go back to Stobo," Patrick said.

"Good. I need one more favor," James said. "I want you to travel to Dunfermline Abbey to see Brother John Blair. Find out what more he knows about Wallace's betrayers, and any other news he might have. If Geordie needs further rest, leave him with John Blair. I will not endanger that lad by bringing him here until he is strong enough to wield a bow and a sword again."

Quentin nodded. "Do you have a message for Blair?"

"Tell him I have the prophetess. Tell him she will serve as payment for my cousin."

"I think," Quentin said, "you will pay more dearly in that exchange than you expect."

"So you make predictions now?"

"Anyone could see that one," Quentin murmured, and took a swallow of wine.

$$— \blacklozenge\cdots\bullet \quad \bullet\cdots\blacklozenge —$$

Chapter Twenty

J AMES SAT ON the edge of the broch wall, watching as Isobel stood facing the wind on the crag. Her gown blew against her slim form and her braid loosened in dark tendrils as she lifted her head proudly. She had an elfin, beautiful appearance. He tipped his head, considering her. Scarcely a word had passed between them since they had shared a simple breakfast of porridge.

Sensing her silent, cautious mood, he did not know quite what to say, and kept his thoughts to himself. Perhaps she was preparing herself to return to Leslie while James bartered her for Janet. Just as well that she distanced herself from him now, he thought—and he should do the same. Being with her was changing him, altering his view of what he wanted, who he was. What he needed.

She would leave soon, and so there was not much wisdom in strengthening what had begun to forge between them. Isobel had retreated within. He should do the same. It would better serve them both. And as much as she dreaded the exchange about to take place, he did as well.

When this had started, he had only wanted Janet back safely. Now he wanted Isobel safe as well, and that was the crux of a problem he could not easily solve.

The tiercel chirred on his gloved fist, eyes sharp, movements calm. The bird's temper was improving, for he had bated only once that day. A night's rest had helped the bird, who perhaps was beginning to accept his new master's fist. Whatever the reason, James felt more confident that the tiercel could be manned.

A flock of larks flew past, and Gawain scarcely moved. That was a sign of progress. The time was near when he could begin to train the goshawk to jump to the fist from a leash, then fly on a creance line long enough to allow the bird to fly away from the fist and back again.

But the injured wing needed more time and treatment, and the bent tail feathers must be straightening if the goshawk was to fly. James would need Isobel's help for that.

He stood, about to call out to ask Isobel for her assistance, but he paused. The urge to be near her was suddenly strong. Too strong. His blood filled with fire. Watching her lonely, wind-blown figure, he held back.

He realized that he had begun to treasure her; God help him, he might even have begun to love her. The feelings that rocked inside him now were too difficult to define. This turn in his attitude toward the prophetess of Aberlady was wholly unexpected.

But one certain fact remained. No matter his feelings, soon he would need to let her go.

FEELING THE PUSH of the wind and the warmth of the sun, she stretched out her arms, despite the ache of her wounded arm. The sun's heat felt good on the stiff muscles. Standing so high, above the veils of mist floating over the trees, she felt free and unfettered for perhaps the first time in her life.

Only recently had she realized how closely her father had protected her at Aberlady, keeping her inside its walls. She had never questioned being confined and supervised, seeing few people, having few true friends. At Aberlady, she had read poets and patriarchs, embroidered fine work, practiced the skills of running a castle household—and prophesying whenever her father had deemed she should.

But the siege had brought a new education for her, one that James Lindsay continued. She was discovering untapped strengths and a craving for freedom, understanding that urge more sharply because of a sheltered life and then captivity.

Now James Linsday would send her back to a protected life with a husband for a guardian, a man she did not want. A life she no longer wanted. No longer did she want to be obedient or allow her abilities to be use by men who saw her as a weak female to be directed—and as a political advantage.

Her visions were precious to her, and she endured bouts of blindness for the privilege. But increasingly she wanted her gift to flow from within, from the will of God and not the will of another.

Without the siege, without James Lindsay's action in taking her away, she might never have realized independence. She would still be a pawn of Father Hugh and Ralph Leslie in her father's stead.

She sighed at the thought of her father. A vision had shown her that he sat in a dungeon, and though she did not know if it was true in the moment, or true in the past, or simply symbolic, she had to find out.

And that meant returning to Sir Ralph. She hugged herself, looked down at the landscape spreading for miles in the sunlight. For a moment she felt as if she saw it from a hawk's vantage point, stunning and vast. She did not want to leave this place.

Nor did she want to leave the man who had brought her here. But that was inevitable now.

She glanced over her shoulder to see him standing near the wall, the goshawk on his gloved fist. An outlaw, a solitary figure, sun glinting gold on his head. A legend come to life, all wild untamed power and beauty. Yet inside, she sensed he was manacled to the past—as she was, in her way.

And in her way, she adored him now—for his kindness, the respect he had shown her. He had even erased the blindness from her. The wonder of that, and his kisses, his presence, filled her.

She could love him—if he would let her. If life itself would allow that for them.

He stood, lifted a hand. Her heart leaped, and she walked toward him. With him, she could find safekeeping, perhaps even happiness one day—but the forest outlaw did not intend to include the prophetess in his life. Yet before he sent her off to accept confinement again, she meant to cherish the bit of freedom that remained to her.

"Hold the jesses securely," James told Isobel. "Wrap them around your fingers, just so."

She twined the leather jesses around two fingers in a thick glove that swathed her hand. Gawain settled his feet squarely on her fist and blinked his bronze eyes, taking in man and woman both. Isobel shifted her hand a bit and the tiercel lifted his pale wings and squawked, fluttering in a partial bate.

Isobel ducked away, startled by the power of it. A wingtip batted her cheek and James reached out to assist. "I have him," Isobel assured him, straightening her spine, tightening her arm.

"Very well. I will warm some bread so we can treat the wing." He turned to rummage in the sack of food that Alice had sent with Quentin and Patrick, who had left it in the broch for them.

The bird's squawks echoed in the small cell. Broken stones were open to the sky, forming a wide window. Stacked stones served as a hearth and a kitchen area, James had explained earlier. The chamber was cozy with heat from the fire James had stoked that morning. He went there now to set an iron kettle on a hook, and placed Alice's bread loaf inside for warming. Then he took it out, tore it in half, and handed it to Isobel.

"Hold it on his wing, if you can. I need to fetch water to help in straightening his tail feathers."

"And fill another kettle, if you will," she said. "I will make us some food—I think we have oats and onions, perhaps some of the cooked chicken Alice sent along."

He nodded and left the chamber, while Isobel sat on a stone slab, glancing through the rubble that provided a window across the broch's grassy courtyard. She carefully applied the warmed bread over the joint of the bird's wing and shoulder, and Gawain tolerated it, perhaps welcomed its comfort. He sat quietly, but after a while grew restive, jerking about.

Drawing a breath, she began to sing the *kyrie eleison* that James used so often with the bird. She kept her voice low, soft, repetitive and calming. Gawain responded, recognizing the sounds. He grew motionless, watching her, piercing and keen. Remembering that hawks hated to be stared at, she glanced away, still singing.

Then she noticed James in the doorway, leaning a shoulder against the frame as he listened. She stopped singing, blushing, and he entered the chamber, setting two kettles by the hearth.

"Lovely," he said. "Do not stop. It calms the bird."

Still feeling heat in her cheeks, she resumed the song as James set a kettle of water over the fire and turned to pull on his falconer's glove.

"Let me take him," he said. "You could make us some supper if you like." He smiled.

Her heart gave a curious lurch as he came toward her, lifted the bread away, and motioned for her to transfer the hawk. Gawain, startled somehow, shrieked and clenched his talons tightly on her finger. Isobel gasped, at the fierce grip and the pain. Panicking, she reached toward her gloved hand.

"Stop!" James hit her bare hand away. "Open your fingers and cast him off!" He slid the jesses off her fingers, and she opened her fingers, giving a tossing motion to release the bird.

The goshawk spread his wings and fluttered upward, kakking, only to be brought up short when James pulled on the jesses. Gawain flapped down to his fist and fixed him with a glare, turning the same cocked-brow look on Isobel.

"Naughty lad," James told the bird. "Isobel, let me see your hand."

She sat beside him, drew off the glove, and held out her finger, which was bruised and beginning to swell. He took her hand gently. "Can you move your finger?" When she wiggled it, he nodded. "Good. A hawk can break a bone like kindling even through a glove. The only way to break a talon's hold is to cast them off and let them think they are free. You were lucky, lass."

"Why did he do it?" she asked. "I thought he was growing more tame."

"He will never be tame." He held her fingers in his, warm and soothing. "He is wild, and manning a bird will never change that. So we handled them gently with patience, respect, and caution. I know you did that," he added. "But goshawks are hot-tempered creatures. And there is always some danger in keeping a short-winged hawk."

She nodded. "Naughty lad," she repeated to the bird. James chuckled, still cradling her fingers.

"He will always be a rogue, this gos." He let her go and stood, going to hearth to fetch a bowl and ladle, then scooped water from one of the kettles, bringing it to her. "Soak your hand. The water is still cold from the well."

With a sigh of relief, she dipped her fingers into the cool water while James moved around the makeshift kitchen, the hawk on his fist as he went through Alice's sack of food, and began to dump handfuls of oats, an onion, and the cooked chicken. He tore off a bit of chicken and fed it to Gawain.

"I can cook the meal," Isobel offered.

"I have cooked for myself and the lads for years. With a hawk on my fist, I think I did well." He took a stick from a stone shelf to stir the pot, then went toward a pile of stones stacked in a corner of the room. He carried several, back and forth, to the hearth.

"What are you doing?" she asked, soaking her fingers as she watched him.

"When the stones are hot, I will take them to the spring so you can have a warm bath."

The feeling that flowed through her at his care and thoughtfulness had naught to do with hearth fires. "Thank you," she murmured.

He peered into the kettle hanging on a hook over the fire. "Can you help me with this?"

"What do you want me to do?" She stood.

"Cook a naughty gos," he said, laughing when her jaw dropped. "Of course not. We need to straighten his crooked tail feathers."

He ladled boiling water into another wooden bowl and carried it to set it on the stone slab. She sat again as he did. Then he shifted the recalcitrant hawk closer to him, smoothing his free hand over Gawain's back plumage gently as he murmured softly to the hawk.

"Look at his tail," he told Isobel. "The deck feathers in the middle are twisted. A quick dip in boiling water will straighten them out."

"That sounds risky!"

"We can manage together. When I move him toward the bowl, grasp his tail and dip it quickly."

Isobel grimaced, then nodded, holding out a hand, ready to help despite her aching arm and now the bruised finger. But she would do whatever the man asked, and whatever his bird needed.

He lowered the hawk, murmuring and soothing and distracting him until the goshawk spread his tail in a wide fan. "Six bars out," he said then. "See the gray bars across his tail feathers? That tells his age. He will have seven bars when he's full grown. Aye, you gos, you're a young lad still. A bratling."

"He does act like a bairn who does not get his way," Isobel said.

James huffed agreement and lowered the bird's tail toward the water. She took hold of the tail feathers carefully and dipped.

Shrieks, footing, a wildly flapping wing, and the ordeal was over. James pulled the bird up on his fist, reached into the pouch at his waist, and fed him a bit of raw meat quickly—Isobel recognized a segment of the rabbit that Patrick and Quentin had provided for the hawk.

"What a fine tail you have now," James said. "Soon you will soar out there where you belong. Soon, lad. *Ky-ri-e e-lei-son. . .*" He sang the melodic phrase while the bird devoured the food clenched in his talons.

Isobel leaned against the stone wall and listened to his mellow, serene, rich voice, the sound soothing through her and the bird as well. Its peace eased her fears, her sadness. She never wanted to leave this place, this man, this outlaw and his naughty gos. Never.

Drawing drew a breath, she sang with him, her voice blending with his, filling the air with sweet power. His voice vibrated through her in a glorious thrum.

Then he stopped. "Isobel. My porridge is burning."

❖┄• •┄❖

Chapter Twenty-One

THE WATER IN the shallow end of the underground pool was indeed warm, Isobel found when she tested it with a bare foot. After their meal of porridge with chicken, overcooked but hearty, James had carried the hot stones to the pool and stacked them in the water. Now she stripped out of her gown and shift and set them beside her boots. The afternoon sun cast amber beams into the cave space, creating a warm rainbow sparkle in the water. She eased herself into the pool, sighing.

Above, on the crag's summit, she heard James whistle to the hawk as he worked with the tiercel. She sank deeper into the pool and leaned back against the rim of the wide, natural stone bowl that had been rubbed smooth in places by flowing water. Stretching out, she dipped down, finding a comfortable niche. Water lapped in a soft cadence against the stone and trickled along furrows in the rock wall. She relaxed, tension flowing out of her, aches easing. A current of cool water, carried from elsewhere, swirled among the pocket of warmth created by the hot stones. She leaned back to wet her hair and closed her eyes. Somewhere overhead, James sang plainsong to the hawk.

Splashing gently over herself, Isobel smiled, knowing she could easily spend her life in this solitary, beautiful place. The warmth, the rippling water, the trickling harmonies eased her further. The edge of her awareness dissolved.

Within moments, she could not dispel the shimmering images that began.

A MAN SAT in a dark corner of a dank chamber, leaned against the wall, ankles manacled. His large frame was too thin and his long gray hair was grimy. His striking blue eyes, so like her own, were hollow. Then shadows closed around her father's image and Isobel saw horsemen riding along a forest track.

Ralph Leslie was in the lead, bull-like, his back straight as he rode a dappled horse. He turned to the woman riding beside him, her black hair braided beneath a gauzy veil, her gown blue silk.

"Wife," he said.

Gasping, Isobel gripped the edge of the pool. The woman was herself. Opening her eyes, she only saw a field of darkness. The blindness was back.

Next she saw the pilgrim, cloaked and hooded, walking toward a church in the rain. He pushed back his hood as he neared a hawthorn tree. He knelt by a green mound under the tree and clasped his hands in prayer. A goshawk fluttered past him to perch in the tree.

Isobel saw a woman approach him. Herself. Her gown whispered over damp grass. He looked up, but when she reached out to him, he vanished into the mist and the rain.

Now she saw a flurry of battle scenes, men struggling on a field, wielding weapons, swords and maces and lances, blows hard and heavy, armor bloodied and shimmering in a misty dawn—then in a shaded wood—then beside a wide stream. The sight and sound of the battles faded, and she saw a lion, curiously calm, standing on a hill overlooking a Scottish loch.

She drew a sharp breath, held the edge of the pool, and vividly saw a skirmish in the forest. Men on horses, men on foot. James was there, sweeping his sword around as riders closed in on him. He fell.

"JAMES!" ISOBEL SCREAMED. *"Jamie!"* She lunged out of the pool, splashing and puddling water on stone. Darkness enveloped her, and she trembled, less alarmed by blindness than by a deep fear for James, wounded and defeated in her vision. Falling to her hands and knees, she prayed she had not witnessed his death.

Groping for her clothing, she found her things and struggled into them, damp and shaking. The murmur of the water seemed louder because she was sightless. She stood, spinning, trying to find the direction of the ladder that led out of the cave.

"James!" she called. "Jamie!" The echo of her voice seemed lost amid the rush of the water. She took halting steps forward, her foot slipping in a puddle. Making her way forward, she met the wall and fumbled her hands over its slick, knobby surface, following it. The sound of the water confused her. Another step, another—and then she stepped into nothingness.

The shock of cold water brought her upright, gasping and choking, flailing. She had learned to swim as a child, and it came back to her now as she pushed forward through chilly water, seeking the edge of the pool.

JAMES TORE OFF his boots and tunic as he saw Isobel go under again. He plunged feet first into the pool and sliced through the water toward her with long, swift strokes as she thrashed, sputtering. Reaching out, he grabbed her around the chest, pulling her against him, then pumping arms and legs as he made his way to the rim of the pool.

He lifted her over the ledge and heaved out of the water, then pulled her out completely. She curled over and moaned, her breathing ragged. The wild, frightened look in her eyes alarmed him to the depth of his soul.

"Isobel," he rasped. He swept back the sopping fall of her hair. "I am here. Isobel!"

"Oh Jamie!" She reached out, fumbling. She was clothed only in the wet, diaphanous silk of a shift that clung to her bare form. Desire cut through him, but it did not matter. Seeing her glass-blue stare, he knew.

"Oh, God, Isobel," he whispered. With a sob, she fell into his arms, and he gathered her close, both of them wet, the girl shivering in his arms. "Soft, you," he said. He grabbed his cloak and wrapped it around her. "Be calm, lass."

"I had a vision—in—in the water," she stammered. Afternoon light poured into the cave, but the space was dank and chill now. He rubbed her arms, her back.

"Tell me later. We need to get you warm and dry." He stood, brought her to her feet, then snugged his cloak around her. Gathering his boots and her things, he led her out of the cave, up the steps, and along the stacked steps that would take them back to the broch.

ONCE INSIDE HIS bedchamber tucked between the broch walls, he wrapped Isobel in a blanket of plaid wool both thick and warm. Cloaked under it, she removed her wet chemise while he turned away to add wood to the fire. Then he stripped out of his wet tunic and took up his pilgrim's cloak against the distinct chill.

"Come sit by the fire," he said, guiding her there, where she sat with knees drawn up beneath the blanket. James heard her teeth chattering as he sat beside her. He pulled her into the circle of his arm.

"Wh-where is the hawk?" she asked, shivering.

"In the mews across the yard. He worked hard for the day and is resting."

"D-did he come to your fist on the leash?"

"Aye. You are cold." He rubbed her back. "He came like a dream, Isobel. He flew the length of the leash, a few feet, though it took many attempts before he did," he admitted. "So I fed him and put him on a perch for the night."

"Will you stay awake with him?"

"Not tonight. I will let him sleep, and carry him all day tomorrow if he needs it. Then I will try him on a longer line, the length of the field, if he is ready. His wing is stronger."

"And he is finally taming."

"As much as he can. Tell me what happened, lass. Are you warmer?"

"S-some," she said, teeth chattering. "The visions came in the pool, though the water was lovely, and I was relaxing, and heard you singing. And then they came. And the blindness came too. I got out of the pool, and panicked."

"All is well now. What did you see? Do you remember?"

She hesitated. "I—saw my father, and you. You were in grave danger, Jamie. I know that." She ducked her head to her knees, huddling there. "My father was in a dungeon. I must find him."

"Ralph Leslie can likely help you. He may know."

"Aye," she whispered. "I saw you. It seemed like an ambush. I know there was danger. And there were other images—battles, men fighting. And you and I in a garden. By a hawthorn." She shrugged.

He frowned at that, but said nothing of what came to him. "Isobel," he murmured. "Your father and the priest would ask questions of you, so that you could describe what you saw."

"During a vision. Not after it."

"Bring it back," he said quietly. "Tell me what you see. I will help you remember."

She nodded. Then she lifted her head and closed her sightless eyes, breathing deeply. For several breaths, he listened to the crackle of the fire.

"A pilgrim on the steps of a church in the rain," she said. "He walks toward a hawthorn tree. He is a laird . . . and the tree guards a secret."

James felt struck to his soul. He had heard something of the prediction that had circulated throughout the Borderlands—but now, hearing it from the seeress stunned him.

Her description of the church matched Dunfermline Abbey, even to the hawthorn tree that grew close to it, yet she had never been there. He had walked past that very tree not long ago, cloaked as a pilgrim. The tree had a secret—for it sheltered beneath its branches the hidden grave of his friend's beloved mother, protected from any who might disturb her rest.

"A battlefield beside a wide stream...." Isobel continued, detailing what more she saw.

"A lion protects the hills of Scotland?" he repeated. "Who is the lion?"

She turned her head back and forth. "He is . . . Robert Bruce, earl of Carrick. He will take the crown for himself, but years will pass before his leadership triumphs. But Scottish independence will be broken again, hundreds of years from now. Centuries will pass before Scotland and England live in peace. Roads will cover the land and wagons made of steel will speed past without horses."

He stared at her, dumbstruck. She was quiet for a bit.

"The laird of the wind will be taken," she said then. "The hawk of the tower cannot be trusted."

"When will the laird be taken?"

"Soon." She stilled as if something new came to her. "A folded parchment drops from the hand that holds it. The laird protects the lion's secret with his life. Another parchment"—here she frowned—"but the ink on the page disappears."

A chill went through him. No one knew about the creased and folded parchment that Wallace had dropped the night he was taken. James had found it later.

Isobel drew a long breath and opened her eyes, tilting her head as if listening for him. "James?"

"I am here." He took her hand. "Dear God, you are a true visionary with a rare gift. No wonder your father protected you, and the priest wrote down every word. Do you recall what you said now?"

She shrugged. "Something about you. And battles, and Scotland." She drew the blanket higher.

He gathered her close to warm her and murmured what she had said, speaking calmly to hide his astonishment and his own puzzlement.

"You are in danger if you go through with the exchange," she said. "The laird of the wind will be taken—"

"Danger always exists," he said. "We who fight as rebels accept that. Nor did your vision reveal when this could happen. I could be in a skirmish days—or years from now." He tucked her closer. "And it might be symbolic. There are other ways a man can be taken down."

She frowned. "How so?"

"He might never meet danger, yet lose his heart."

"It was no symbol," she whispered. "The danger is real."

"Mayhap," he said. "Isobel—that parchment you mentioned. I have it."

Her eyes widened. "What do you mean?"

"The night Wallace was taken, he dropped something hidden in his hand, though his hands were bound together. Later I went back to find it. A folded parchment, just as you described. But you could not have known that. No one knows that."

She sat up, interest caught. "You still have it?"

"Aye. It is a letter from Bishop Lamberton of Saint Andrews to William Wallace that mentions a pact between the bishop and Robert Bruce, a promise of support against the English. The bishop invited Wallace, with Bruce's sanction, to join in a secret bond. The Scottish Church declared their stance against the English, but the letter reveals that Bruce of Carrick, who gave his oath of service to King Edward more than once, is a key part of the rebellion as well, and supported Wallace."

Isobel looked stunned. "And if the English had evidence of Bruce's loyalty and intentions, it would be the end of him. And the future of Scotland might be lost."

He nodded. "I kept the letter, fearing that if I sent it to Bruce or to Lamberton, it might be intercepted. Perhaps I was the one guarding the lion's secret, as you hinted—Bruce, if all goes well."

A crease formed between her brows. "I think you keep many secrets."

"I trust few people. And few would trust a traitor."

"And you do not trust me, when I have faith in you."

"I do trust you," he whispered, and felt awe, gratefulness—and love—pour through him, and with it a current of regret. Soon he must give her up and ruin what faith she had in him.

She laid her hand upon his bare chest. He wondered if she could feel the wild beat of his heart beneath her fingers. "Why call yourself a traitor? All I see in you is honor."

He sighed. For a long time, he had kept those dark memories private, but the urge was strong suddenly to tell her—only her. No one knew the full tale, and it would take more than trust for him to reveal it. He drew a breath.

"The English took me prisoner last spring. I was held in Carlisle," he began.

"And released in the summer." She nodded.

"I was with other Scots nobles, and when they took some of us north, I escaped from the escort. Janet did not get away with me. That was when Ralph Leslie took her to Wildshaw."

"And so you must get her back. I understand. None of this makes you a traitor."

"While I was in Carlisle, King Edward sent orders that some of us must sign a statement. We would be executed unless we obeyed. A few of us signed it, never meaning to keep it. Those who signed were released shortly afterward. I was given into Leslie's custody. He was ordered to let me go on the promise that I would fulfill what was asked. But he decided to keep me a bit longer. But I did not agree with that." He shrugged. "So I left his patrol once we were in the forest."

"What was the parchment you signed?" she asked quietly.

"An agreement to—hunt down Wallace and deliver him to the English."

She caught her breath. "I do not believe you would ever make that promise."

"Believe it. We signed the pledge, but none of us intended to keep it." He watched the fire. "But I kept it. I led them to Will."

"That cannot be all the truth. Not you, Jamie."

He lifted a shoulder. "I escaped and heard that Wallace was

north of here, so I set out to find him, disguised as a pilgrim. But I was followed. Leslie sent a man after me. Had I known," he muttered, "I would have taken a different route or changed my guise. But all unawares, I led them to Will."

"You could not have known what would happen."

"This from a prophetess." He gave a bitter laugh. "Soldiers followed me to a house where I had heard Wallace could be found. I tried to lead them away when I discovered—but I was too late."

She touched his face, and he realized her vision was not yet restored. "You did not betray him."

"I did." He closed his eyes, feeling the anguish, feeling her butterfly-soft touch assuage it some. "I led the bastards to him. If I had not gone there, he might be alive today."

"And might not. Listen to me—we both tried to warn him. You did not betray him on purpose."

He sat silent, lips pressed together. He had believed for so long that he had betrayed his friend, through folly or carelessness. He did not want that burden, but he could not cast it away.

"You said that my prophecy mentioned a parchment with ink that had vanished. I wonder if that was the page you signed."

"Symbolically, perhaps."

"If the pledge you took was not real and intended, then the guilt need not exist. You had no role in the betrayal. They would have taken him sooner or later. That was his fate. I know it, I do."

As he listened, he felt the hard casing around his heart crack a bit. His throat was tight when he spoke again. "One thing more. No one knows this. When they rode away with Wallace," he said, "I used the last arrow I had—and tried to take his life then and there. But I missed."

She gasped a little. "You tried to save him from what would be a cruel death." Her hand found his. "That was an act of love, Jamie," she whispered. "Nothing less."

He had not felt the sting of tears since he was a child. He blinked them away.

"It is not in you to betray a friend. Those who love you know that. We have faith in you."

He sucked in a breath. *Those who love you.* He dipped his head, touching his cheek to her hair. She tucked close under his arm. "And you saw this before it happened. If I had only known you then, perhaps we could have changed the outcome."

"Nothing changes what God decides. But if we had met back then, I would have tried to help you, I think. And now I know I would do anything for you."

His heart bounded. He drew her close, savoring the warmth and the truth of her there in his arms. "A prophetess would not want the trouble of an outlaw."

She laughed softly. "She would. But an outlaw might not trouble with a prophetess."

"If he troubles himself with a silly wee hawk, a wee prophetess is easy." Sliding his fingers through the silken mass of her hair, he tilted her head back and took her lips with his, gentle and then with swift craving, as if he could take some of her sweetness into his soul.

— ◆··• •··◆ —

Chapter Twenty-Two

HER HEART THUNDERED and she sighed beneath the pliant caress of his lips, surrendering gladly to that strength. As he leaned, she tilted back, the flow between them a silent play of taking, giving. For an instant, tiny lights spun in the darkness inside her eyes. Then the light grew until it filled her sight. She opened her eyes. Firelight, at last.

Gazing over his shoulder at golden flames, she gasped and pulled back to look up at him, blinking. She touched his bristled cheek and looked deep into his dark-lashed indigo eyes. He tipped a brow in question.

"Aye," she said with a soft laugh. "It is back again. I can see you now. Whatever magic you possess, 'tis wondrous."

"The magic is not mine." He dipped to kiss her and she shaped her mouth to his.

"Nor is it mine," she whispered then.

"Ah well," he murmured. "Perhaps we create it between us."

"Perhaps we do," she breathed, as he took her down to the floor in a nest of fallen blankets and cloaks. He stretched out beside her, and she shifted toward him, the hearth fire feeling warm on her bare feet and shoulders. As James gathered her closer, leaning to kiss her softly, he then drew back.

"All is well?" he asked.

"It is. And I am thinking—only you could kiss the blindness from me."

212

"I am thinking I would take to task any man who tried." His voice was fierce.

"Only you. Another man could never kiss me as you do. I swear. Only you have that magic." She looked at him intently.

"Isobel," he said on a breath, taking her lips again. She sighed as he delved, his tongue moist and gentle, and she felt her body whirl and spin. The fervent truth of what she said—only this man could bring her back from the physical darkness the prophecies stirred in her. He alone had done that, and that felt profound, like a promise and a bond between them. She wanted to give herself to him utterly, heart and body, now—and she fiercely wanted to stay with him always, though it might prove impossible.

She did not want to close her eyes to darkness again, and pulled back to look at him, taking in the beauty of him, the waves of his hair reflecting golden firelight, his broad, muscled shoulders, the strength in his neck, where a pulse thumped. But sight could not satisfy what she wanted of him. Blindness had taught her that touch could bring more, so she traced her fingertips over his face, the corner of his jaw, the firm curve at the chin, his beard textured like sand; his nose, straight and long, his lips full, firm, breath escaping in warm caresses.

He took her exploring fingertip between his lips and she caught her breath. Then she slid her palm along his neck to his hard-sculpted chest and rested her fingers over his heart. He pulled her even closer, his hands cupping her waist. Even with blanket and cloak bunched between them, she could feel the heated hardness of his body, and felt her body answer, a startling and exciting quiver deep within.

His hands were warm pools of touch, his voice low. "Do you want this, now, between us?"

"Aye," she whispered fervently. Though she had never done this before, she felt no fear or conflict, only a growing desire and a sense that it was right, this. Oh aye.

But when he pulled her snug to him, pushing the blanket aside, she hid her face against his shoulder. The danger she had foreseen for him, the marriage to Leslie that she dreaded, loomed for a moment. Yet all she wanted was the comfort of his arms, of him. It might be all she could have.

Skimming her hands over his shoulders, pressing her body to his, she opened her lips beneath his as he sought deeper kisses. Thought and logic began to fade as she immersed herself in feeling, the warmth of his hands, his tender lips, the pulsing that stirred in her body. As his fingers glided lower, her heart pounded, a begging drum as his hand cupping her breasts teased shivers all through her, and she arched into him, breath quickening. He wound the mass of her hair in his hand, tugging her head back, his lips tracing along her throat, finding her breast, so that she pearled there and gasped, wanting more, seeking him in turn with her hands and lips, curious and thrilled, delighted and allowing.

When he pulled away his trews and drew her even closer, his body heated and solid along the length of hers, his hands warm and soothing along her back, her hips, his breath hot against her throat and breast—she moaned, his fingers enticing, sliding, teasing downward until his hand delved into the hidden recess of her body, his touch easing into her, over her, in exquisite caresses. She lifted toward him as liquid fire poured through her in a shimmering cascade. She yearned, ached, hovered on the verge, fervent, seeking more of what her body promised and her heart now craved. As new as this was, every touch a discovery, she felt as if this was perfect, what she had needed from him all along, now coming into focus.

Slipping her hand over his abdomen, following the warm path of his musculature, easing down as he pressed close, she found the hot, rigid length of him, and he groaned low. Shifting, he lay back and pulled her over him until her legs hugged his hips and his body fit intimately to hers.

"Are you—" he whispered hoarsely.

"I am sure," she whispered, her breath over his lips in a lingering kiss, her heart pounding. The quickening cadence of his breath matched hers as his hands settled on her hips, guiding her over him with gentle, fervent fingers. With a deep exhale, she felt her body slip over him like glove to hand, and with push, she gasped, her little cry smothered against the column of his throat. She arched her back, his hands on her hips, her back, easing her into his rhythm, his touch warm and tender and shepherding her along with him in a sweet, hot merging of body and soul, a pledge of trust and giving. An irresistible force flowed through her, a craving that was compelling—a hunt after satiety, but more, a craving for love, for him, for the sanctuary of the heart that existed wherever he was.

Leaning forward, she sighed and laid against him. He wrapped her in his arms, breathing in tandem with her, while her hair fanned out to cover them like dark, outspread wings. She could not leave him—she knew it with certainty now. The thought echoed, spun within her as she closed her eyes and savored the feel of his arms around her, his lips, his soft whispers.

COLD AIR AND dawn light sliced through the window gap in the stone wall, stirring him awake. Shivering, James drew the blankets closer, keeping Isobel in the circle of his arm, her body warm and soft against his. Her gentle snores made him smile, and he tilted her head to quiet her breathing.

They lay together in a nest of blankets and cloaks; he wished he had thickened the straw mattress and constructed a curtain to keep out the draft. Though he was used to a hard bed, grabbing sleep when he could, here or in the forest, she was not accustomed to such.

He took in a quick breath, remembering the joyful, sensuous loving this stark bed and stone chamber had supported. As the embers had faded in the hearth and the cool breezes increased, they had sought the shelter of the bed, dozing a little and then waking to readily explore and share, deeply and completely. His body surged at the memory, and he pressed his lips to her hair as she slept.

This day or the next, his friends would return, and too soon, Isobel of Aberlady would step into the church in Stobo and disappear from his life.

He had endured the sacrifices that came from his choices in life—but this one would be the hardest.

"THE CREANCE IS such a long line," Isobel said, standing beside James as he wound the length of twine over his arm. "He has only hopped to your fist from a little distance. This line is a hundred feet long, you said."

"Nearly. But that is not the problem," he answered, walking with her across a grassy stretch of the crag's summit. Gawain sat on his fist and chirred. "The problem is getting the bird to come back to the fist. Once he does, he will do it from a foot away, a hundred feet, or as far as he can see the falconer without a line between them. The distance is naught to the hawks. Trust is all."

She nodded, and stood where he indicated, waiting while he checked the knots that attached the creance to the jesses. He tied the other end of the line to a wooden peg and shoved it into the grass. Then he walked the length of the field, letting the creance unfurl as he went, and set the bird on a rocky ledge. Returning to stand with Isobel, he called to the bird, whistled, and sang the notes of the *kyrie*.

Gawain was busy preening his feathers, but at the sound of the melody, he fluttered up, then down to perch on the ground. James sighed and walked over to pick the bird up, carrying him back, looping the creance again. Then he thrust out his arm to cast the bird off his fist swiftly.

This time, Gawain took to the air with a broad sweep of his wings, flying out and upward, the creance spooling out behind him. His wings rowed, glided, rowed the air as he crossed the field.

Isobel gasped with delight. The sun glinted silver on his back as he sped along. The hawk was beauty and grace, yet possessed a keen, dreadful power too, a master of the air, an archangel in his realm. He gained height. The creance waved and soared with him, then tightened. The goshawk glided over to perch on a high rocky outcrop on the crag's summit.

"Now we will see if he comes back," James said, and raised his head to sing again. Isobel caught her breath and waited.

Gawain cocked his head and turned. James sang again, arm extended. Then, as if he had considered and decided, the bird sailed back toward them, wings spread wide as he floated on a current.

Seeing his fast approach, Isobel stepped back. James stood rock still and waited, arm out. Moments later, the hawk tipped and slowed and settled to the glove with a nonchalant flutter.

James offered him a bit of meat. Then he grinned at Isobel. "Now that," he said, "is a goshawk."

She smiled. "That was beautiful! Sir Gawain, what a bonny lad you are!"

"Bonny indeed. Now we shall see if he will do it repeatedly. This may prove a long day, lass."

"Ah well. What else do we have to do up here?"

"I could think of something." He gave her a twinkling look, and she suppressed a smile, heat searing her cheeks, a small rush of pure joy streaming through her as she imagined being in his arms.

The afternoon spun out, delights and disappointments as the hawk flew or did not, bated or perched, ate or declined, according to his whim. Isobel watched as James soothed and cajoled and so very patiently tried again and again. As the shadows on the crag grew longer, the bird complied more and misbehaved less, always responding in some way to the serene notes of the song.

At sundown, with pink-edged clouds spreading overhead, Isobel gazed out over the forest, struck by the blend safety and power she felt high up in their eyrie. James tucked the looped creance in his belt and came toward her, Gawain calm on his fist.

"I love it here," she said as he joined her. "Far above the world. No one can threaten us here. No one can find us unless they know the secret way in."

"It is an excellent sanctuary.".

"I spent years inside a castle, seeing little of the world outside. I thought I was protected, but it was false. A prison. Here I feel safe. Free." She glanced at him. "I want to stay here with you."

He was quiet, then sighed. "You have a gift, Isobel. Your words should be heard by many, though some might use you for that gift. So your father did what he could to keep you safe. The marriage he arranged with Leslie is intended to continue that protection. Consider that."

"What are you saying?"

He stared outward and did not meet her gaze. "I cannot give you what you need. Safekeeping, and a true home. You deserve a walled castle, a rose garden. A place to raise children in peace and plenty, a place where you can use your ability to benefit others. That is important for you."

"Love is important to me. Freedom is important to me. *You* are important to me."

"Your gift is rare. It is significant. If you shut yourself away with a man who hides from the world, your visions will not be known." He shook his head. "A homeless outlaw cannot guard such a treasure. A lord who commands a stout castle and has the might of England on his side—he can."

"I thought you regretted sending me to Sir Ralph." She could not keep the tremor from her voice.

"I do regret it. But I want you to go."

She scowled. "You want Janet."

"Och, now," he murmured. "You know the truth of that." He glanced at her, then away. "My lass, if you stayed here, we would always be hunted. You might never have peace, plenty, or a home."

"This is a home. Here," she insisted. "I—I could not bear to be Sir Ralph's wife. Not now." She reached out, took his hand, felt his grip hard over hers. "And he would make sure that I make prophecies for King Edward. For the English."

"Then say them well. You will have all you ever need or want."

"All I want!" Fear and anger flared. She released his hand. "All I want is you!"

"And all I want," he said sternly, "is your safety. I have thought long about this. It is the only way to save you, and your gift."

"And Janet."

He was silent. The hawk kakked, shifted, stirred his wings.

Her heart slammed. "There is one problem in your scheme to barter for Janet."

"What is that?"

"I will not go."

He cocked a brow and glanced down at her. "But you will."

She scowled. "When we go to Stobo, you keep Janet in the church after Sir Ralph sends her in. Then I will go out and tell him I will not go with him."

"That would start a bloodbath."

"Do not make me go. Please," she added.

He blew out a breath, an anguished sound, and reached out to pull her close with one arm. She wrapped both arms around his waist—she had taken off the sling at last—and held him. "Listen to me. I have to let you go. The prophetess of Aberlady has too much worth for an outlaw to keep to himself. And what about your father?"

"Leslie will want to control my visions like sacks of wool for the market. There must be another way to help my father. Father Hugh can help us, or some other friend. We can get him back. I know it."

"Perhaps not," he murmured. "He is at Wildshaw."

"But—" She straightened as a thought occurred. "What if I go with Sir Ralph to Wildshaw, as he expects, so you can rescue Janet? And then, if my father is there, I will find a way to leave Wildshaw with him, and come back here to you."

"Nay," he growled. The wind ruffled his hair, and his eyes

were deep blue in the sunset light. "Remember our bargain. You made me promise to let you go. I will keep my part of it."

"Then I will come straight back here to you."

"You must not."

"I will," she insisted. Then she suddenly understood. "Your freedom," she whispered. "You have freedom here, and think you will not have it if I am here."

"Not true. I want you. But I cannot keep you. You will forget me in time. We have different paths, you and I."

An ache began in the center of her body, her being. "We have the same path. The same needs. Sanctuary. Love," she whispered.

"If I had stayed simply the laird of Wildshaw, and you had been simply the Maiden of Aberlady—aye. But that is not what we are."

"Jamie," she said, taking his arm. "Do not do this." She blinked away tears.

"Soft, you," he murmured. "Hey, my lass. Look down there."

She searched the forest, narrowed her eyes. "I see only trees. Your eyes are sharp as that hawk's."

"Quentin and Patrick are coming toward the crag. They are back quicker than I thought."

After a moment she saw the distant figures running toward the crag. "I am afraid what tomorrow will bring," she said.

He kissed her head. Then he turned and walked away to meet his friends, the hawk on his fist.

◆┄• •┄◆

Chapter Twenty-Three

"FATHER HUGH WANTS to see Isobel in return for taking our message to Leslie," Quentin said. "He is not assured of her safety from just our word."

"We do need his help." James looked at Isobel, who sat with them in the simple kitchen area of the broch, sharing a meal of barley and onion porridge.

"Father Hugh has always been careful on my behalf." Isobel poured wine into cups for each. "Where is he now?"

"He rode to Wildshaw with our message," Quentin answered. "We came back from Stobo with the priest and Geordie. Father Hugh says he will meet us in the morning to see Isobel. He will stop by the huge old oak along the road, the one near Alice's house."

"Good," James said. "We can defend her there if he brings soldiers."

"He swore to come alone," Patrick said.

"Still, I do not like it," James said.

"I must go if we are to free Janet," Isobel said. She wiped crumbs off the stone table with her hand as she spoke, keeping busy. James was glad that she seemed to be more accepting of the plan to help Janet and her role in it. "I can go alone. I trust him."

He wanted to reach out, keep her here as she asked, but he would not show it. He had held back his feelings from the start and would not upset the cart now. "I fear a trap. We will escort

221

you."

She shook her head. "You must stay away."

"You will not go alone," he said firmly, but knew she was bothered by the possibility of danger to him, as in her prophecy. He did not care about that.

"But I will not go with you, James Lindsay," she said, and then rushed out of the room.

"What was that?" Quentin Fraser asked. "The lass is upset with you."

James rubbed a hand over his eyes. "She is concerned—that they will try to take me."

"She has a point. We will go with her, do not worry," Patrick replied.

"Aye then. You two returned more quickly than I expected," James said.

"We did what was needed and came back fast as we could. Jamie, in Stobo, two monks came from the abbey with a letter for Father Hugh," Quentin went on. "One said Brother John Blair is making progress on his chronicle of Wallace's life. They had news of some who might have betrayed Wallace."

James looked up with keen interest. "Sir John Menteith is the name I have heard."

"They mentioned that, but said it is likely he sent servants to do the task for him, to keep him clean. There seems little clue about other names."

"But for mine," James said darkly.

"We also heard the possibility that Leslie was involved."

"That would not surprise me." He suspected that Leslie knew about the pledge James and other captive Scottish lords had signed. And he was sure Leslie had sent men after him when he escaped Leslie's patrol and sought out Wallace.

"Now that Robert Bruce has been named one of the Guardians of the Realm of Scotland, they say he is determined to convince King Edward to appoint a Scottish bishop to work with him."

"There is more news of the Earl of Carrick?" James remembered Isobel's prediction about the lion of Scotland, and that Bruce could gain the throne soon.

"Aye. He renewed his pledge to King Edward, but rumors grow that he secretly aids the rebels. They are never caught if Bruce rides out to find them. Edward does not trust Bruce any longer."

"Then the cause of Scotland has a strong ally in Robert of Carrick," James said.

Quentin frowned. "Something else we heard—the English put Wallace's remains on display."

"Did they," James said flatly. "Where?"

"Piked his head above London Bridge, crowned with flowers. Sent his limbs north to four locations. In final insult, they set his right arm above the sewers in Newcastle. But they say that his finger rose to point toward Scotland, and there it stays. Better we tell you than others."

"Jesu," James said, fighting a rise of grief and anger. "He deserves peace and honor."

"King Edward should be damned for this act," Patrick said.

"Among his other deeds." James huffed bitterly.

"Will Wallace deserves a proper burial," Quentin said.

"Someone should see to it," James snapped. Hurt and rage surged raw within as he turned and strode out of the kitchen.

Long after dark, he sat in the mews with Gawain on his glove after walking endlessly around the summit of the crag. The torment had calmed; now he felt grim and solitary.

He heard Quentin and Patrick walking past, talking low, likely gone to seek their pallets elsewhere in the broch ruins. No sound came from Isobel's small cell nearby. When she did not return to the kitchen, James thought she had decided to keep to her chamber.

Gawain sat staring at James with bronze-tinted eyes. He puffed his feathers and balanced on one leg, looking silly but content. Far from content, James blew out a breath, startling the tiercel.

The news of Wallace's further humiliation rocked his feelings from remorse to anger and back again—anger at the English for brutality and callous lack of respect; at Will Wallace for his stubbornness; and anger with himself for having had any part in the tragedy. He could never repay the debt he owed Wallace. And now he had delivered a blow to Isobel, too, rejecting her when he only wanted to keep her safe and give her a chance at a peaceful life. He despised Leslie, but the man could provide for Isobel what James could not.

He would never forget her, and he had to face that truth too; he wanted her, needed her rather desperately in certain moments. His original plan called for abducting the prophetess, trading her to Leslie for Janet, and going on his way. But the plan went awry, and now he had lost his heart to her.

Setting the bird on a perch, he left the mews and headed for his own chamber. But he stopped by the opening to Isobel's adjoining nook. He could hear soft snores. So her head was tilted poorly again, and she would not sleep well. Nor would he, with her so close, and him aching with regret.

The curtain that separated their rooms was but a cloak. He shoved through it and went to her bed, kneeling there to cup her face gently and shift her head to ease her snores. Her cheek was warm and her face was beautiful enough to break his sorry heart. He was not accustomed to needing anyone.

She had foretold that the laird of hawks would be taken. He should not forget that.

He kissed her lips. Then he stepped back and shouldered the curtain aside.

DAWN LIGHT STREAMED through the cold as Isobel walked with the others along an earthen path that led through the trees. None of them spoke much as they left the crag and moved through the forest. The goshawk rode on her glove.

Earlier, James had said that Gawain might slip back to half-wild if left too long in the mews, so the bird must come along. He let her carry the tiercel after he fed the bird to ensure his crop was full and his behavior more complacent. But Gawain's piercing eyes seemed to see all as they went.

She and the others followed James's long stride. The hilt of his broadsword glimmered, strapped to his back, and he carried his bow. His head was draped in a chain mail hood, his body covered in heavy leather hauberk and a long tunic and cloak. He was prepared for battle. So were Quentin and Patrick, walking beside him. Their preparedness both assured her and frightened her, for she could not tell what the future would bring to them that day.

After a while, James paused. "They are waiting for us."

Looking past him, Isobel saw a few people standing like shadows outside Alice's house. She walked forward with the men, and saw Alice in the yard, along with Eustace, Henry Rose, and Geordie Shaw, whom she had not seen since the day of the skirmish in the forest, when her horse had run away with her.

Alice came forward to envelop her in a warm hug that brought unexpected tears to her eyes. She hugged James too, and then Gawain, on Isobel's fist, began to bate. James turned to take the bird.

Seeing Eustace, Isobel grasped his hands, smiling. "You look well," she said, smiling.

"My lady," he said, smiling. "The life of a forest brigand has been good for you, I think. I have not seen such roses in your cheeks or such a sparkle in your eye since you were a wee girl."

She felt a blush rise. "I am rested and healed. I am stronger." She meant it more than Eustace could know. Then she listened as he told her of his time at Stobo and then at Alice's house recently, and turned to greet Henry and Geordie, glad to see the lad recovered too.

"Lad, I want you to stay here for Alice," James said. He looked at the others. "We should go. The sun is nearly up and we are to meet Hugh in the morning."

"I will go alone," Isobel said. "I have known this priest all my life."

His eyes were dark in the half light, his face lean in the steel mesh frame. "But you do not know where the old oak is, do you."

"Jamie, let me keep that hawk while you both go," Alice said.

"Let Isobel keep the hawk with her," he said. "If there is trouble, he will bate, and then no one would come near her while he frets. She could get some distance. And we will be close by."

"I will be fine," Isobel insisted. "Keep your distance. Keep safe. I do not have a good feeling."

He leaned down. "You can be thick as a stone."

"You are the thickheaded one, you great brigand," she whispered. Amusement flickered in his eyes, but he shook his head and handed the hawk to her.

"Here is your guardian, my lady." Turning, he beckoned the others. "Come ahead."

Chapter Twenty-Four

THE ANCIENT, MASSIVE oak dominated the center of a grove, its wide, leafy canopy casting shade around younger trees that formed a circle around it. Beyond lay forestland, and in another direction, open moorland. James headed toward the oak and the others followed.

He waded through tall green ferns and ducked his head beneath low-hanging branches. Partly hidden by leafy boughs, a large knotty crevice in the great trunk of the tree formed a long, hollow niche where he and his men had hidden at times.

Taking Isobel's hand, he pulled her inside the narrow cavity, pressing close in the confined space. Quentin and Patrick swung up into the boughs to find perches along the wide, thick branches. Eustace and Henry went into other trees.

As Isobel looked up and around, James rested a hand on her shoulder and watched the grove. On Isobel's glove, Gawain stirred. She shushed the bird—she had a way with him now, James noted. Her body was warm against his in the tight space. Time seemed to suspend, his awareness of his need for all to be well in her world grew. He felt that responsibility on his shoulders. He wanted it there.

"Father Hugh should be here soon," she whispered.

"I will go with you," he said, but she shook her head. "Then know we are here. Should the priest bring someone else—"

"He would not do that. I do not want you to be seen. Stay

away."

He gazed at her, touched her cheek, and felt a wave of love, purely that, pour through him. It stunned him in its power. He leaned to kiss her, regardless of the fellows above who might see. He did not care. She seemed to share the notion, kissing him with such fervor that his heart pounded.

He was a fool to let her go with anyone, anywhere. He would survive without her in his life, he was sure of that. But he would not flourish.

Years ago, he had not protected Elizabeth as he should have. That would always haunt him. For Isobel to be safe, she would have to leave him. But for now, he held her.

"Jamie," she whispered. "I do love you."

Her words sank through him, warm and welcome. He loved her, he knew that now. But if he declared it, had that distraction, he would find it harder to do what he must. He only kissed her hair.

"The priest is in the meadow," Quentin murmured, above them. "He is alone."

Isobel pulled away, the bird quiet on her glove, and edged away from the niche in the tree. James watched her go. Beyond the trees, the sun brightened over the moor. Isobel moved into the sunlit grove, her grip on the hawk's jesses as secure as her hold on James's heartstrings. He felt the tug of it.

A man rode to the middle of the moor and dismounted to walk toward the grove, dark-robed and short, his wide face pale beneath the shelter of his hood. Isobel greeted him and they stood talking. The priest took her arm, urging her to walk with him. She hesitated, but then went with him.

James grabbed his bow. A shiver went through the small hairs along his arms and neck. Isobel might trust this man, but he did not. Hefting the bow, he edged out of the hollow in the tree.

Out on the moor, Gawain bated off the glove, lifting his wings and squawking. Isobel stopped to calm him, and the priest stepped back. But he reached for her arm and tried to urge her along. The bird continued its fit.

James ducked under a low oak bough and whistled softly. One by one, he heard them thump to the ground one by one behind him—Quentin, Patrick, the others. And before he could call out a warning, men on horseback pounded out of the forest and crossed the moor at a thundering pace. James snatched an arrow and nocked it in the bow even as he began to run.

Three men rode toward Isobel. The rest cut across the grove. The priest stepped back as they came near, as if he expected them. One rider leaned down to grab at Isobel, hauling her onto his saddle as he rode past, his horse's hoofbeats digging up heathery clods.

The hawk fluttered his wings wildly, and as Isobel was yanked roughly upward, she lost her grasp. The tiercel separated from the glove, soaring above the moor, slanting high, and vanishing.

Isobel and the goshawk, both swept away in one swift and awful moment.

James roared out and ran forward. He only let himself think about how many arrows, how long the bowshot, how many men. The white horse carrying Isobel disappeared into the forest, and the other riders neared the grove.

Behind James, his friends arranged themselves, bows and weapons drawn. Henry Rose lifted his longbow and released a shaft that sailed between the trees and struck one of the soldiers in the armpit, where the mail was vulnerable.

James shot too, nocked, pulled again. The horses came at him so fast that arrows were soon of little use. He drew his sword from the scabbard at his back and swung it brutally, his teeth bared, legs planted apart as the first rider came toward him.

Horses circled him, and he fought ferociously, strength stoked by rage. Isobel had trusted the priest and had been betrayed. She was gone. The hawk was gone too. James had no time to think past a gut-deep need to get past the men who confronted him, who prevented him from going after what had been torn from him. Fury burned like a yellow-red glaze and his vision took on a slow and terrible grace, as if he looked through the golden irises of a hawk.

Horses and soldiers surrounded him. He swung the two-handed sword savagely, driving the horses back, slicing at the thighs of riders, his blade striking steel, arcing back and down again. His sight filled with heaving flanks and faceless men, glinting steel and blood-red English surcoats. He ducked and swung and turned, cut the blade upward, turned again. He knew his men were there somewhere, fighting with him.

Then the spiked steel ball of a mace came down from nowhere in a terrible arc. He felt the shock of the blow to the side of his head. As he slammed to hard earth, he heard the cry of a hawk.

ISOBEL LOOKED FRANTICALLY over her shoulder again and again, past the shoulder of the knight who carried her across the front of his saddle. They rode fast and steady through the forest, while she sat trapped in his beefy, steel-covered arm. She had never seen him before; his face was bearded and his dark eyes somber, and he seemed young. He scarcely spoke.

Far behind them, she saw Father Hugh riding with other guards along the forest path. She looked away, ill with anger to realize that the priest had broken her trust. He had known that Leslie's patrol waited in the forest ready to steal her away and attack the outlaws who might come with her.

She had caught sight of James just once, when she looked back wildly to see him running through the trees, bow drawn, face fierce. Then a phalanx of horses had surrounded him and the trees had obscured her view.

She knew James had gone down, fallen in a circle of horsemen. She had seen something similar days ago. She gasped, feeling as if her breath might stop. Yet she had to think, had to find a way out of this. She still wore the hawking glove, and the awful realization that the hawk had escaped hit her with awful force. Squeezing her eyes shut, she fought tears as her captor rode on.

Kee-kee-kee-kee-eerr.

Hearing that, she looked up at the vast, swaying canopy of leaves overhead. A hawk swooped there, slanting his wings as he cut through the treetops. He glided like a sylph, the sun touching the fingers of his wingtips. His jesses trailed behind him like ribbons.

Excitement and hope stirred in her, and she held up her gloved hand. "Gawain!" she called. "Sir Gawain, to me!" She began to sing the kyrie.

The guard, cantering along, looked at her as if she had gone mad. "Gawain?"

"My hawk. Up there."

He looked around. "The goshawk?"

"My bird. I must have him back."

"Gosses are trouble to train, but they are worth much." He shook his head. "He will not come back now he's free. Soon he will be as wild as the day he was born."

"He will come back! He will. Stop. Let me call to him. Please, I beg you!"

The guard glanced over his shoulder at the others riding a fair distance behind them. "A hawk named Gawain ought to be saved," he muttered. He drew rein and paused the horse. "But you must stay with me. Sir Ralph charged me with your safe arrival."

"What of the outlaws?"

"We understood they held you hostage, my lady. Our orders were to rescue you and deal with the brigands."

"I was not a hostage. What happened to the men back there?"

"I did not see. But Sir Ralph demanded the leader be brought to him. Lady, look there. Your hawk is up in that tree, I think."

She felt a surge of relief, thinking James might yet be alive, and then seeing the goshawk. He was perched on a high, dead branch, looking like silver in the morning light. She lifted her gloved fist and sang out again. The tiercel did not move.

"Gawain," she called. "Here to me!"

The guard looked up. "Gosses are stubborn birds, always wild. But you must have your bird. And Leslie would not want a good hawk lost, if it can be useful for hunting."

Isobel coaxed the bird, then reached into the pouch at her waist, remembering that James had given her some food for the goshawk. Taking a slimy piece, she waved it about.

"Not like that," the guard said. "Use it as a lure. Have you got a creance in the pouch?" She nodded, glad of his unexpected help, and withdrew a twine leash. The knight took it and tied the meat to it. "We need feathers to disguise it."

She dipped into the pouch again and found small feathers that James kept in the pouch. The guard thrust them into the meat like wings as a false bit of prey. Then the man tossed the line out and began to spin it overhead. "Call your bird, lady."

She did, singing, whistling.

Then Gawain lifted his wings and soared away, banking out of sight. Isobel sighed, devastated. The guard gathered the reins and rode on. A while later, he stopped again.

"There," he said. "See him in that tall elm? He almost seems to be following you. Call out." He lifted the lure and spun it again as Isobel sang and called, holding her gloved hand high. Then she saw the goshawk cutting through the trees, streaming toward her. She held the glove high and waited, heart racing. The guard spun the lure.

Gawain plucked the meat out of mid-air with his talons, and dragged it with him to alight on her glove, as if he had done it a thousand times. Slanting her a bronze glare, he dipped his head and began to tear at the meat. She grabbed his jesses in a trembling hand and wrapped the leather around her fingers.

"Look at that, he came right to you," the guard said. "A good hawk indeed. Come, Lady Isobel. Your betrothed wants you safe in his castle." He urged the horse onward.

"Oh, you bonny gos," Isobel said, her voice thick with tears. "Thank you."

Chapter Twenty-Five

Through the morning mist, Isobel saw a tower of gray stone encircled by high stone walls set on the green crest of a hill. As she and the guard rode closer, she glanced back to see Father Hugh and a few soldiers following. Then the guard's horse pounded over the wooden drawbridge spanning a rushing stream and passed under the iron teeth of the portcullis.

Wildshaw. She could only think of it as James Lindsay's castle, though Sir Ralph held it.

In the bailey yard, she saw the early morning bustle of soldiers and servants hurrying about on various errands. Dozens of English soldiers in chain mail and surcoats stood about or walked past, while lanky boys and dogs ran with them, and a servant guided a cart drawn by an ox across the yard. Smoke twined upward from a slate-roofed open smithy, and the tempting fragrance of baking bread wafted from a smaller building nearby.

Above the busy yard loomed the massive tower keep, where wooden steps led up to a wide arched entrance. A man hurried down the steps, chain mail glinting, his wine-red surcoat a rich burst of color in the morning mist.

Sir Ralph Leslie lifted a hand in greeting as he came near, pausing to fist his hands on his hips with a stormy expression. He had always reminded her, in build and temperament too, of a dark bull, and that was true now.

"Lady Isobel, thank heaven you are safe," he said. "You

brought a hawk!"

She gave him a grim look in silence. The guard who rode with her swung down and reached up to help her dismount, taking extra care as she held the hawk. A boy ran forward to lead the horse away.

"I appreciate this, Sir Gawain," Sir Ralph said brusquely.

Isobel turned, surprised. "Gawain?"

The young knight gave her a quick, warm smile, and she noticed for the first time that he was a handsome fellow. "I share a fine name with your hawk, my lady." His dark eyes twinkled. "So I was pleased to help you. Good day, Lady Isobel. May you be content at Wildshaw." He tipped his head and turned away. Isobel smiled slightly, grateful for one friend in this place.

Ralph Leslie looked up at her, for Isobel stood a handspan taller than he did. But in contrast to her slender build, he was broad as an oak, with a round face and a wide torso, his fisted hands tough and sure, his brown eyes smoldering beneath a thatch of iron-gray hair.

"Are you harmed?" His tone held a flat irritation.

"I am fine. Does it matter?"

"Of course it does." He looked at the goshawk on her fist. "I see you brought my goshawk all the way from Aberlady. A gesture of good will, I see."

Her mouth dropped open. "Your hawk?"

He nodded. "Aye. I left him with your father's falconer. He is a stubborn and hot-tempered bird. I had no success training him, though by nature I am a most patient man," he added. "How is it he sits the glove for you? I did not know you cared for hawks."

She blinked at him, still astonished. "I—we—Sir Eustace set the hawks and falcons free from Aberlady's mews. We had no choice during the siege, but for the few we ate. We...found this one in the forest later. I did not realize he was yours."

"What! You *ate* trained birds?" He glared at her.

"We were starving, under siege by Clifford's men!" she retorted. "No one came to our aid." She narrowed her eyes at him.

"You mean me? I did not hear of the siege until later. I went there, but found it burned. I would have come to you sooner had I known." He took her free hand in his. "You know I care for you."

"Do you? Where is my father?" She pulled her hand away.

"He is here."

"Thank God! I must see him. Where is he?" She looked around as if he would appear.

"He is unwell and not ready for visitors. You will see him later. First we must talk."

"He will want to see me no matter what."

"Not yet," he replied.

She frowned, puzzled. "Soon, then. I trust you have a chamber prepared for me, since you took the trouble to have me escorted here."

He turned to walk with her. "Someone will take you there. Janet! Come here, girl!"

Isobel looked up in surprise to see a tall young woman coming toward them with a bold, quick stride. Her russet gown molded to her lush, large-boned figure and matched a thick mass of red hair barely tamed by two plaits pulling it back above her ears. As she came near, she smiled, her golden brown eyes warm and intelligent.

"This is Lady Isobel Seton," Leslie said. "Take her to the chamber made ready for her."

"Lady Isobel, welcome to Wildshaw. I am Janet Crawford."

"Janet!" Isobel extended her hand. "I am so glad to see you!"

The girl looked confused; so did Ralph Leslie. "Come with me, my lady. You must be tired after your journey."

"Journey?" Isobel looked at Leslie. She would not be part of any mummer's play he designed. "No journey. I was taken by force from my friends. I had faith in Father Hugh, and in Sir Ralph, but no longer." Beside her, Janet gasped.

Leslie only scowled. "You needed a rescue and I provided it. Go inside. You are distressed after your ordeal—taken by outlaws and held these weeks. Someone will pay for that. Ah, here he is, delivered just in time."

Isobel turned, hearing a commotion at the gates. The rest of the patrol, including Father Hugh, rode beneath the portcullis into the yard. A man walked between two horses, tied there, his arms stretched, long legs dragging in the dirt. A tangle of brown-gilt hair obscured his face and bowed head.

Her heart lurched. "Jamie!" She started forward but Leslie grabbed her arm, yanking her back, sending a shaft of pain through her arm. "Let him go!" she cried. "What will you do with him?"

"Do you care what happens to the brigand that took you?"

"He never harmed me!"

He ignored that. "Janet, escort her to her chamber. Janet!"

The girl sprinted across the yard and clasped her arms firmly around James to help support his sagging weight. His head lolled, and Isobel saw that his face was half covered in darkened blood. Though she pulled against Leslie's grip, he would not release her.

But on her fist, Gawain launched backward in a furious bate, beating his wings and squawking. She extended her arm to give him necessary space.

"By hell, that is indeed my own damned hawk!" Leslie muttered. "Guards! Get that girl away from the prisoner. Take him to the dungeon, if he yet lives."

"He lives," a soldier answered. "Might survive."

"We shall see about that," Leslie growled.

Isobel swallowed back a sob, but she could not reveal any feeling for the outlaw. Stifling her urge to react, she focused on the hawk, who tired of his fit and let her lift him back to the glove. Quickly she took his little hood from the pouch at her belt and pushed it over his head, shutting out the world.

Janet, pulled by a guard, snarled in a way that caused the man to step back. Then she whirled and stomped toward Leslie with a thunderous scowl. Standing taller than him, she pointed at him, then at James Lindsay. "You know that is my cousin! Let him go,

Sir Ralph!"

"I cannot do that," he murmured. "And this is none of your concern," he snapped. "Lindsay has committed crimes and offenses against the Crown, and against me." He turned, yanking Isobel with him. The goshawk shrieked but held his position, the hood enough security to keep him from bating.

"If you put him in your dungeon," Janet said, striding after with them, "I will never go to your bed again."

Isobel gaped at Janet, stunned.

"Hush!" Leslie stopped and patted Janet's shoulder, keeping hold of Isobel. "Easy, lass." His voice, Isobel noticed, gentled. "Lady Isobel is my betrothed. I will explain it all tonight."

"Betrothed? You never said—you will not see me in your chamber tonight or ever, sir!"

He leaned toward her. "Will I not?" he snarled. Janet lowered her eyes and looked away, surprising Isobel further. What power did he have over that bold girl? "Now take the lady to the tower chamber. Your eyes go the color of honey when you are angry. I like that. Go on, and come to me later."

Still holding Janet's arm and Isobel's too, he turned. "Lady Isobel, you and I will talk as well. Go on. My falconer will take the goshawk to the mews."

"The gos stays with me," Isobel said. "Have a perch and fresh food brought up to the room."

He tipped his head. "Very well. Janet, you know where to take her. And do not go to the dungeon." He let go of both girls, spun on his heel, and stalked away.

Isobel looked at the tall girl beside her. "Janet, I will not wed him, no matter what he says."

Janet's eyes brimmed with tears. "Come with me," she said stiffly, and went toward the keep.

For a moment, Isobel glanced back to see two guards half-carrying James slung between them. They disappeared into a doorway in the base of a corner tower in the curtain wall; likely steps inside there would lead down to a dungeon area below ground.

Fighting her own tears, she followed Janet up the steps to the door of the keep.

JANET STOOD BY the door of the small chamber, arms crossed like a determined guard, as Isobel crossed the creaking floor planks to peer out the single narrow window in the stone wall. The room held only a bed, draped in dusty red cloth, a leather stool, a brazier, a small cupboard, and a tall wooden perch in a corner. She set the hooded goshawk there, drew off the falconer's glove, and turned. "I will go, then," Janet murmured and set her hand on the door latch.

"Wait, please!" Isobel said. "I know you are unhappy with me. You did not know about me. But I have heard much about you."

"What do you know of me?" Janet scowled. "I have heard of the prophetess of Aberlady. Many know that name. Sir Ralph said that he knows you, that you prophesy for him. But he never said he had promised to marry you."

"My father arranged it, but I never wanted it. I love another," she replied soflty.

Janet shut the door and moved toward her. "Does Sir Ralph know that?"

"Not yet. But you know the man I care for. James Lindsay— of Wildshaw."

Janet set a hand to her chest. "Jamie! But how—when? My cousin only mentioned your predications. He was not happy about them," she added.

"I know that now. I met him—recently. Janet, do you know why I am here today?"

"Sir Ralph said he rescued you."

"Hardly. He ordered his men to abduct me from a meeting with a priest." Though Janet looked confused, Isobel rushed on. "James Lindsay has been desperate to get you back. He—took me away from danger and Aberlady, and planned to barter me for you. But Sir Ralph deceived him, and all of us."

"What do you mean?"

"Sit down," Isobel said firmly. She sat on the edge of the bed, while Janet took the stool. Quickly and simply, she explained to the girl how she met Lindsay in the besieged castle, and went with him into the forest. She told her about the hawk, and mentioned Alice and Quentin and the others.

"He took you to the crag? He would not take just anyone there. He is very protective of that hideaway." Janet shook her head. "I am bewildered. Why would he barter you for me?"

"Your safety was all to him. He did not have enough men to bring force against this castle, so he meant to use me as a ransom payment. But—we spent time together and we—we came to care for each other. I wonder, now," she went on, "if James thought you were in danger when you were here by some sort of agreement with Sir Ralph," she said tactfully.

A pink blush filled Janet's freckled face. "I am a prisoner here," she confirmed. "But I bought myself some privilege at the price Sir Ralph—suggested."

"Oh, Janet," she murmured softly.

The girl shrugged. "When he first brought me here, I was angry and frightened. Jamie had escaped—he tried to take me with him, but the guards had me, and I screamed for him to flee. I knew he would come back for me. I knew I need only wait. But—" She sighed. "Leslie gave me a choice between a horrid wee dungeon cell or the room beside his bedchamber. I spat in his face and took the dungeon."

Isobel nodded, waiting.

"He never forced me, you see," Janet explained. "He had me brought up to him each evening and let me sit by the hearth in his chamber. We spoke about many things." She paused, shrugged. "He was—kind, in a way. After a time, I let him—it was not force. Nor my first time, if I am truthful. But I am a plain lass, and men do not find favor with me as they would gazing at you, my lady. I—was grateful."

"Plain? You? You are a strong and beautiful girl, one to admire. And Patrick Boyd seems smitten with you," she added.

Janet blushed again. "Patrick is a rough lad, but tender in his heart. But he thinks of me as a comrade. Like a sister to him. They all do, for I followed them everywhere when we were young, and my own brothers were with them. I love them all, but—none love me. Not in that way."

"I think you are wrong. Jamie and the others care so much for you that they would risk their lives to rescue you. They would even risk my life to get you free. At least they thought about it," she added.

Janet smiled a little. "I am their compatriot. I have always liked the ways of men, their freedom, their strength. I like shooting a bow and running free, even wearing breeches when I was with them in the forest." She fiddled with the fine wool of her gown. "But I am a woman, and Sir Ralph has been good enough to me. I might have been unwise to succumb to him, but it has been nice to be treated well and kept close."

"You did what you had to do to protect your life."

She made a face. "I suppose. And I do want to be let loose from here."

"I was confined, in a way, at Aberlady by my father and the priest. And Sir Ralph as well. But I never felt—free until James Lindsay came for me. I did not have a life beyond the castle. And I—well, I have grown to love the life he leads. I would live like that with him. But he will not hear of it."

"Ah, Jamie would always let a woman make her own choices—he was practically raised by Aunt Alice, who is as independent a soul as a woman could be." Janet chuckled. "But if Jamie wants to keep you away from the life of a forest rebel, he has good reason."

"The prophecies," Isobel explained. "And because he thinks I prefer to be the lady of a castle."

"Do you?"

Isobel began to speak, but tears constricted her throat. "I just want to be with him," she blurted.

"Oh, Isobel," Janet murmured. "I think Jamie must love you as much as you love him."

Isobel smiled wanly. "I am not certain of that. There is—Sir Ralph, after all. But I will tell Ralph Leslie that I will never marry him." She paused. "But do you—love him? Would you choose to stay?"

Janet shook her head. "He treats me well enough, but I am here against my will. He binds my ankle to his bed at night, and sometimes during the day."

Isobel gasped. "As if you were a beast?"

"A prisoner. After all, I was captured by English when I was with a band of Scottish rogues. But if you had seen that dungeon cell, Lady Isobel—you might have considered the same choice I made."

"Janet, we must get down to the dungeon. Can you help?"

"I will tell Sir Ralph I want to see my cousin, and then convince the guards to let both of us in."

Isobel nodded. "Good. Janet—is my father here? I have heard so. Sir John Seton? He was a guest of Sir Ralph, but I do not know if he is still here."

Janet drew her brows together over her tawny eyes. "He is your father? I should have realized from the name." She heaved a sigh. "Your father was a prisoner at Carlisle Castle when Jamie and I and the rest were taken there. He is not a guest at Wildshaw. He is down in the dungeon."

Chapter Twenty-Six

A GRAY HAZE intruded into a dream of floating on a dark river scattered with flower petals. James opened an eye and blinked, seeing dim surroundings. The dark peace of the dream was replaced by shadows, cold dampness, and pain.

He reclined against a cold stone wall, and now felt the weight of the iron cuffs on his wrists, attached to a heavy chain. Over his boots, iron cuffs circled his ankles. The straw beneath him had a musty, unpleasant odor. His head ached and he could scarcely see out of one eye. His jaw felt bruised, and his right side felt as if a rib might be cracked. Every muscle in his body seemed to ache.

Vaguely he recalled the spiked ball of a mace coming toward him, and the awful sound when it struck the side of his head through his chain mail hood. Blackness had followed.

With effort, he sat straighter, looking around at dark, slimed stone walls and a narrow door of latticed wood and iron. Through the gaps he saw torchlight and rough stone walls. He shifted, the pull of the chain limiting his movement. Licking his dry lips, he searched the shadows of the cell.

A man lay in the corner, chained as he was, wearing a torn tunic and what had once been a fine surcoat. He looked thin and hollow, with a wild tangle of gray hair, but his eyes burned blue with sharp awareness.

"Name?" the man rasped out.

James blinked at him. Name? He thought about it. Ah. "Lindsay." That was it. "James Lindsay."

"The forest outlaw?"

Was he? "Aye," he said slowly, as certainty dawned.

"Jesu," the man muttered.

"Good to meet you, Jesu." James felt almost drunk with wooziness and pain.

"Nah," the man barked. "John Seton."

"Seton?" James sought the mental niche where the name belonged. "I know a William Seton of Dal—Dalrinnie. And a Seton—a lass—of Aberlady."

"I am Aberlady," the man rasped. "Sir William is a cousin. The lass—is my daughter."

James stared at him. "The—prophetess. The—" What was she? Oh God. His own heart, she was.

"We were at Carlisle together, remember?" John Seton went on. "I saw you there. You and the lass Janet and others. We were taken north by Leslie's patrol. You escaped. I know who you are."

James scowled as he pieced it together, his head and eye throbbing. *Isobel.*

He narrowed his eyes to focus on the man. Those startling blue eyes, nearly luminous—just like the lass. "Jesu," he breathed.

"Nah, John, I told you."

"Ish—Ishbel," James murmured, his swollen lip clumsy. "I know her."

"What do you hear of Isobel? Do you have news?"

He nodded. "I remember now. Aberlady was besieged. Burned. I am sorry, sir. I was there."

"So it is true. The guards told me."

"We had to torch it to keep the English out."

Seton drew a sharp breath. "What of Isobel?"

"I took her away safely. She is here—at Wildshaw." He looked around again. Wildshaw was his home. He knew where he was now—in the base of the northwest tower, where two dungeon cells were located.

"Here? How do you know?"

"Leslie has her." James leaned his head against the wall. "I tried to reach her. But they took her faster than—"

"What do you mean?" John Seton growled. "Lad! Wake up!"

The ache in his head swamped his reason, and darkness returned.

COOL, GENTLE HANDS stroked his face. Then a damp cloth sponged his brow, slicked over his eyelids and temple, stinging and cleansing. He winced, opened his eyes.

"Jamie." He loved the sound of her voice. "I am here," she whispered. "Papa is here too. Dear saints, at least you are both together. But—"

"Ishbel," he muttered. His lip felt like a sausage.

"Aye, Ishbel," she laughed softly, and caught back a sob. She kissed his brow, and he realized she was kneeling on the awful straw beside him. "Are you hurt badly?"

"I am fine," he lied, sitting up, stiff and awkward, and accepted the cup of water she tipped to his lips, though it dribbled as he swallowed. He looked at her. God, she was beautiful. An angel. His angel. "Love you, Ishbel. I do."

She gave him an exquisite, watery smile, tears in her eyes, and touched his cheek. She smelled like flowers and sunshine, a font of blessings. He raised a hand to touch her arm.

"The goshawk—" he began.

"Isobel, we must hurry," a woman said.

"Listen to the lass," a man said. "Do not stay here."

Isobel nodded, then touched his face, a healing butterfly skimming that somehow took pain away just because she was there. "The goshawk—he is free." He remembered it now. "Do not fret. He will be happy in the woodland—"

"I have him. He came back. He is here."

Relief surged through him. "Ah. Keep him safe, then." He reached up to touch her cheek, the chain jangling. Her skin was damp with tears. "Keep yourself safe too," he whispered.

"Isobel," John Seton said from across the cell.

"I must speak with Papa again," she said. "He is here with you. Did you know?"

He frowned, nodded, stirred to sit up straighter. "Aye." Awareness was sharpening now.

She smiled, wan and loving, and got to her feet. Her skirt brushed his legs as she turned. He caught at the hem in his fingers, reluctantly let go.

Another skirt came into sight. The woman knelt beside him. "Jamie!"

"Janet! Dear God, lass—you are well?"

"Well enough." His cousin and leaned forward to kiss his brow. "I am so glad you are awake. When they brought you here, I feared the worst. But I was able to bring Lady Isobel here to see you and her father. We cannot stay long. We brought food." She indicated a sack nearby.

"You brought Isobel and yourself. It is more than enough."

"I heard about your plan to ransom me with Isobel. And she told me about you—and her." She glanced at Isobel, who was talking with her father. "I like her. If you would not have me, that is." Her eyes twinkled, but he saw sadness there, too.

He tried to smile. "Oh, you would not have me, lass," he drawled.

"You, a brigand? Surely I would not. But that lass. She has a good and gentle spirit. You need her far more than you ever needed me."

"You have fire," he said. "We all need that from brave Janet."

She squeezed his hand. "I am so sorry. You are hurt because of me."

"I should have attacked these gates weeks ago. Should have demanded your release. But I thought he might release you in exchange for—his betrothed."

"The garrison is large here. Your plan was better, and would have worked, if Sir Ralph had any honor. Isobel—wants to be with you, you know."

He closed his eyes. "That lass—can do better. I just want you both to be safe. She should be with someone who can protect her and her gift."

"She should be with you, you dimwit," Janet said crisply.

"She is a true visionary. I thought Leslie would provide for her and keep her well. But—"

"But you were wrong. He only cares about keeping himself well." She wiped the damp cloth over his face as she spoke. "When will you listen to your heart, you great loon? Who best to keep that lass and her gift secure—but the man who loves her, the man she loves?"

"She wants a peaceful life, a home, a refuge. I cannot ensure that."

"She wants and needs you more. Do you not see it?"

"I am an outlaw," he said hoarsely.

"And a great bonny fool." Janet scrubbed at his temple. He winced and caught her hand.

"Ow! And how am I a fool, when I want what is best for her?"

"What gives you the right to choose what is best for her? Let her decide that. And you," she went on, "there is tragedy in the past, and not to be belittled, I know. But if you can drop that burden from your mind and your heart, you could have some happiness at last. Do you realize yon lass would risk all to be with you? And you would send her away, thinking it is right? So you are a fool, sir."

James made a wry face, wincing again, and glanced toward Isobel. She was watching them now, eyes wide, cheeks pink, a deep stillness around her. "There is still the matter of you and Sir John, trapped here," he said.

"Och, I am working on that." Janet waved a hand in dismissal.

"Isobel, what is this?" John Seton asked. "I can see you are fond of the outlaw, but—"

"I am very fond of the outlaw," she said, her gaze on James.

"Even if he is a fool?" James murmured, watching her steadily.

"Aye," she said.

"You, Lindsay! If you care about my daughter, would you have her live an outlaw's life? She has a precious gift. She deserves a fine life. I did my best to see to it."

"I do love her," James said. "And she does deserve a good life."

Isobel stood, silent, looking from one to the other. Janet sat equally silent beside James now.

"Isobel, I was wrong to expect you to marry Sir Ralph," John Seton said. "He has shown himself to be treacherous. We can dissolve that agreement. But I do not want you to yoke yourself to an outlaw."

James frowned, only watching Isobel. She looked from one man to the other, twisting her fingers together. She said nothing.

"Her gift is hers to use as she wishes," James said. "Not as others deem proper."

John Seton sent him a glare, then looked at his daughter. "You need a proper husband. Rumor says this one betrayed William Wallace. I had great respect for Wallace and all he did."

"James Lindsay did not betray him, Papa. He is an honorable man."

"But not a husband for the prophetess of Aberlady," Seton said.

"Have you forgotten?" Janet asked. "Jamie is not just an outlaw. He is the rightful lord of Wildshaw, and by rights it should come back to him."

"Interesting," Seton said.

"What do you want, Isobel?" James wondered what thoughts tumbled through her troubled eyes. That was all that mattered to him just then.

"Aye, tell us what you want," her father barked.

She fisted her hands at her sides. "I want both of you to be free," she said fiercely. "I would give anything to see that. I would give my own life to see that." Her chest heaved, her eyes burned blue. "I thought I needed a sanctuary for my visions to come to me. But now I know they will come no matter where I am. And I know I am safe—and happy—with this man. I have learned that I need freedom even more than a safe place." She flattened her hand on her upper chest. "I want to decide for myself what is best for me—and my gift."

"What a bonny speech, my dear," a man said. "I think we can find a solution to suit you."

AN ICY CHILL plunged through Isobel as she whirled to see Ralph Leslie on the other side of the latticed door. He inserted a hefty iron key in the lock and swung the door open. Two guards stood behind him.

"In fact," he said, stepping inside, "your conversation was very enlightening." He reached for Isobel and took her arm. "But it is not too late for you, my dear."

"Get your hands off me," she said through her teeth. She heard the chink of chains as James shifted, helpless to rise to her aid.

Leslie inclined his head. "I would never mistreat the prophetess. Now, bid your father farewell. Your lover too," he added in a growl. He looked at James. "Did you touch her, when she was in your keeping?"

James gave him a flat and silent stare.

"Lady Isobel, return to your tower chamber. Janet, take her there," he barked. The girl stood beside Jamie and made no move to leave.

Snatching her arm out of his grip, Isobel backed away. Beside her, James rose slowly to his feet, sliding his back against the wall. His gaze was stony, made more fearsome by the bruises. He clenched his fists beneath the iron bands. Even weakened, he radiated anger and stubbornness. She took a step closer to him.

"Isobel," Leslie said. "Get away from him. Go you to your chamber."

Anger surged through her and she fisted her trembling hands. "You played us false," she said. "You kept Janet dishonorably. You and Father Hugh betrayed me. And you were holding my father all this time. I trusted you. My father trusted you!"

He shrugged. "I accepted the command of this castle from King Edward in return for my fealty. If I am ordered to imprison rebels, that is what I must do. You, Lindsay—" He turned toward James. "You escaped before, but you will not do so this time."

"Do not be so certain," James replied.

Isobel stepped in front of him, facing Leslie. "You could have treated my father with courtesy. He was always a friend to you. You have no loyalty!"

"I place my loyalty where it does the most good—with King Edward in the king's peace. Seton has been involved in rebellious activity. Once I had the betrothal promise, there was no reason to court his favor any longer."

"None of you knew of my secret politics," John Seton said. "My loyalty to Scotland will never waver. But you, Leslie, led me to believe even if you declared for Edward, you chose Scotland in your heart—your own land and people."

"Papa, why would you trust him?" Isobel asked.

"For you, lass," he said quietly. "I thought you would be safer with a Scottish knight with an English alliance. I thought that would protect your gift better than I could. I thought him a practical man. Father Hugh praised him."

"We were all deceived," Isobel said. "Father Hugh betrayed us too."

"You never liked either of them, it is true. That perhaps was your gift, and I did not listen. I trusted them because they seemed to have your welfare in mind. Sir Ralph said he could love you," he added low, "and that he would never let harm come to you. So I gave him your hand."

"I only said what you wanted to hear," Leslie interrupted. "But I do care for Lady Isobel. That is why I accepted the command of Wildshaw. You wanted to wed her to a man of power. I have that now."

"Wildshaw belongs to my cousin," Janet said.

"Not anymore," Leslie said.

"I wanted my daughter to wed a man of honor," Seton growled, getting to his feet. Janet, nearly as tall as Seton, stepped forward to put her arm around his waist, seeing him slip against the wall.

"Honor is not practical. Is it, Lindsay?" Leslie drawled. He took a step toward James.

"You do not understand honor. He does," Isobel said.

"Truly?" He narrowed his eyes in a hateful glance that made Isobel lean away. "I have seen a letter with Lindsay's signature—on a pledge to give Wallace to the English. And he led us there nicely." He glared at James. "I allowed you to escape that day, Hawk Laird, or so they call you. I trapped you into taking us there. We followed you. And I caught one of your own arrows myself." He clapped a hand on his shoulder.

"Good to know it," James snarled.

"'Twas simple enough to start the rumor." He jabbed a finger toward Isobel. "Her prophecy had already suggested it, and I saw the need to get rid of you. So I attached your name to Isobel's prediction of Wallace's fall. You two," he said with an ugly laugh, "have been tied together since then."

Nostrils flared, eyes like steel shards, James pressed his back to the wall, sank his weight, then lifted his booted, manacled feet and slammed them into Leslie's gut.

Flung backward by the force of it, the man lay gasping on the straw-covered floor. Then he rolled to his side, groaning, as two guards rushed into the cell. One helped Leslie to his feet. The other stepped toward James with a hand on his sword hilt.

Isobel cried out and threw herself between them, pushing back against James, who leaned against the wall. The guard halted, then looked at her.

"Sir Gawain," she breathed.

The knight stepped back, taking his hand from his sword.

"Gawain?" James murmured.

"What stops you, man!" Leslie gasped out. "Toss the woman aside and take him down!"

"I will not harm a woman," the knight said, "nor punish a man for doing what I would like to do myself." He spun on his heel and walked out of the cell.

"Damned chivalrous bastard, always been like that," Leslie muttered. "Isobel! Get back! I will take him down myself—" he said as he stumbled forward, drawing a dagger from a sheath at his belt.

"Move," James murmured, pushing her aside, though she turned to embrace him, then faced Leslie, forced to stop his advance.

"If you harm him or my father," she said low, "I swear I will never utter a prophecy again."

His glare was cold and hard. "We shall see," he growled as he grabbed her wrist and wrenched her away. Pain seared through her weakened arm and she cried out.

"Bring the other woman too!" he yelled to the remaining guard as he dragged Isobel out of the dungeon.

Chapter Twenty-Seven

Pushed inside the tower bedchamber, Isobel stumbled and scrambled away from Leslie, hurrying to stand beside the goshawk's perch. Gawain kakked loudly and clenched his talons. Isobel picked up the thick glove that she had left with the falconer's pouch on the wooden chest. She turned.

"He is hungry," she said, "and he has been here too long. He reverts to wildness quickly." Remembering that James had said the goshawk might act as protection, she shoved her hand into the glove and nudged her fist toward Gawain. The tiercel stepped to the glove, his bronze eyes glinting as he focused on Leslie.

Keeping a wary eye on Leslie herself, Isobel removed the last strip of raw meat wrapped in the pouch hours before, when she had stood with James on the crag. The hawk clutched it quickly and tore at it with his beak.

"You have become a falconer since I last saw you," Leslie said. "But I know this bird. He is spoiled and truculent, and too wild to train. He'll never learn to hunt for a master. His temper is too hot. I would have released him, but John Seton said he would train the bird."

"James Lindsay found the bird wild in the woods after Aberlady was taken. He determined that the original owner ruined him. That would be you," she said. "He comes to Jamie easily."

"Jamie, is it? And you? Do you obey his every command too?" He advanced toward her.

"Do not stare so. The bird does not like it. See how he glares at you. He does not like you. Mayhap he remembers you." Gawain finished the food and gave a raw squawk.

Leslie folded his arms and did not come closer, Isobel saw with relief, but the tension in the air was palpable. The tiercel sensed it too, for he drew in his feathers and swiveled his head, eyes gleaming beneath slanted brows. She murmured softly, aware he might be about to bate.

"Lindsay showed you how to handle the bird? What else did he teach you?"

Isobel cooed softly to the bird. "He taught me to relish freedom," she said carefully.

"Freedom! You learned that while hiding with an outlaw? He held you hostage and called it noble, and you believed it." He shook his head. "You are a poor judge of men, Isobel. Too innocent."

"Freedom," she said, "was what you, and Papa, and Father Hugh took away from me."

"We took naught. We guided you and gave you sanctuary."

"I see it differently now."

"What else did you learn from this brigand? I suppose, being naïve, you were a keen pupil." He came closer, threat rolling off him like heat from a fire. He reached out and touched her arm. She flinched back. Gawain rustled his feathers.

"You had best leave," she said firmly.

His hand fell hot and heavy on her shoulder. "Did he touch you?" His fingers flexed like talons. She suppressed a wince, returning a stony gaze. His fingers traced down her arm to her waist. "Did he touch you like this? Or this?" His hand slid up, his thick thumb grazing over the side of her breast.

She gasped and stepped back. The bird kakked. "Get you gone, Ralph Leslie," she said.

"You have a wild spirit. I saw a touch of that at Aberlady," he murmured. "But you were more biddable. Now something has changed. You tasted freedom—and perhaps a man's touch?" He smoothed his hand over her hair, then grabbed a fistful, yanking painfully, pulling her head back. "If that rogue has cuckolded me," he growled, "I will make him scream for mercy before I kill him."

Gawain shrieked then, launching off the fist in a fury of flapping wings, caught by the jesses. Isobel raised her arm and locked her muscles, letting the bird's frantically flapping wings brush toward Ralph Leslie, who stepped back.

"That is a damned troublesome hawk!"

"He would be fine if you were gone," she said. "As for betrayal, you should beg forgiveness of James Lindsay for what you did against him—and against Scotland too." She had to remain calm because of the bating hawk, no matter what she said, or wanted to say.

"Wallace was a firebrand. Many wanted him stopped. Lord Menteith and others—were in agreement. There were several who conspired toward his fate. And I will continue to see that his compatriots are brought to justice. King's peace must come to Scotland."

"Peace will come to Scotland with an English king," she said. "King Edward will never rule Scotland. Never. I know this."

He looked as if he had been struck. "When did you see this?"

Isobel walked away, legs trembling, carrying the hawk, who slowed and calmed, hanging upside down. She righted him and sat on the wooden chest by the window.

"By God, did you prophesy for him?" Leslie crossed toward her. "What does he know?"

"Does he know secrets that you do not? I am not sure. I have forgotten what I saw."

He grabbed her arm, fingers pressing deep. "Tell me. I must know what you predicted."

"Why should it matter to you? You do not own me or my gift. I will do with it what I please."

"That will be mine more than yours once you are my wife. I promised your services to King Edward." He frowned to himself, nodded. "I will send for the priest. He will sit with you, and you will say again what you told Lindsay."

She stared at him, horrified. "What did you promise the king?"

"That what you say belongs to him. He is keen for prophecy—hungry for any news and reassurance that Scotland will be his. He has promised to reward me. As my wife, you will benefit."

A chill went down her spine. "You would turn me over to him as if I were a bag of gold or a bit of property?" Her voice rose indignantly. The hawk, exhausted from his recent fit, stirred restlessly.

"I will take you to King Edward when we are wed and introduce you. When you prophesy for him, he will be generous. You are to predict a golden future."

"You are mad. I will not do that."

"He has already summoned me. We must go soon. I have been desperate to get you back." His fingers felt like claws on her arm, hot and sharp. Once again, she could not free herself, though she could feel the bruises rising.

"Edward sent his lieutenants to besiege Aberlady to get to me," she said. "Did you advise him to do that?"

"I sent word to the king that I had access to you—that you were my wife. A betrothal is as good as a marriage."

"Presumptuous."

He waved his hand in dismissal. "Father Hugh will wed us soon, and I will take you to Carlisle where the king is currently planning another push in his Scottish campaign. He expects to see you. You should be honored."

"I will not prophesy for him."

"I have no choice, therefore you have no choice."

She stood, yanking on her arm. His grip set her teeth on edge. "I refuse," she said. Even standing taller than he did, she felt little confidence over him, though she lifted her chin to pretend it.

"You will see the future for Edward of England."

"If I told him what I know, you would not like your reward."

"Then I will report to him what you see. You can do that today." He let go of her arm. Physical relief flooded through her. Then he pushed her toward the perch. "Put the hawk away and we will begin."

"Nay!" She stood her ground, though her limbs trembled in sudden fear.

"You always did what was asked of you. I expect the same. Your little taste of liberty will not help with me." He set a hand on his dagger. "If you treasure freedom so much, then I will cut those jesses and let that cursed bird go free. If you do not want that, then put the bird away and do what you are told."

She had no choice. Turning, she set the bird on the perch, but kept her glove. Leslie grabbed her upper arm this time. She knew the bruising would be fierce. Tears of rage and frustration stung her eyes.

He pulled her toward him with inexorable strength, then slid his hand to her lower back to press her against him, her breasts flattened against his broad chest, thick wool and chain mail the only barrier. His dark eyes went darker, became frightening pools.

"The priest warned me that taking my pleasure of you could affect your gift." His breath blew hot and sour in her face. "But if you gave yourself to the outlaw and still foretold for him, then your gift is safe. For that, I suppose I am grateful," he murmured, nuzzling his lips along her cheek now. "But I still mean to kill him."

She leaned her head away and pushed against him. "Stop! I never said I gave myself to him."

"Did you not? I saw when you looked at each other down in the dungeon. I might forgive you someday, but first I want guardianship over you and your power as your husband." He gave a taut smile.

"You will have naught of me," she gasped, as he dragged his lips hot and slow along her cheek, her neck. She shivered and pushed against his strength. On the perch behind her, Gawain kakked.

Ralph Leslie snugged her hips hard against him, his grasp iron-hard. "Tell me what you told him." She did not answer, struggling against him. He raised one hand as if to strike her.

His hand was too high—for the tiercel spread his wings and leaped off the perch, jesses pulling, to land on Leslie's hand, inches from the perch. The bird beat his wings furiously and shrieked, his muscular yellow feet clenched convulsively, talons digging deep.

Ralph roared and let Isobel go, stumbling back, batting wildly at the bird, the perch knocking over, the knots in the jesses loosening. Isobel watched in horror.

"Cast him off!" she called. "He will let go if you cast him off!"

Ralph flung his arm outward in a frenzied castoff. The goshawk released him and rose toward the ceiling, then flew about the room while Leslie fell to his knees, howling in pain.

Still wearing the glove, Isobel leaped up to the wooden chest to stand as tall as she could, waving her arm until the bird decided to obey. He settled to her fist with a quiet flutter and blinked a bright eye at her, then began to preen his feathers.

Ralph Leslie sucked in air, examining his bloodied hand and spewing vicious oaths. "He broke my finger! Curse that bird!"

"You should be more wary around a goshawk. He did not like you so close to him." She was not certain why the bird had leaped to the man's bare hand, but she was grateful for the intervention.

"What is the trouble here?" a man's voice asked from the door. "I heard the screams from the down the stairs." Isobel whirled to see Father Hugh entering the room.

"That pestilential bird broke my finger," Ralph muttered, holding his wound up for display.

Father Hugh winced as he saw it, and head, gray hair partly shaved. "Hawks never favored you, Ralph," he said. He glanced at the tiercel on Isobel's fist. "Is that the gos that you left at Aberlady?"

"Aye, and he is not long for this world. You should have eaten him when you had the chance, Isobel," he growled, and stepped forward. She gave a little shriek and retreated.

"Enough! It is just a bird. Have some sense," Father Hugh snapped. "Wrap the finger and stop complaining. I came to tell you that Janet is waiting for you in your chamber. She's complacent. Ready to beg your pardon and tell you what she knows."

"What? Janet is incapable of complacency. It would be lies." Leslie shot him a dark look. "I want a proper wife—this one. You will marry us."

"Be patient." Father Hugh turned to look at Isobel. He was her height, built slight, his jowled face pleasant enough—but now she knew he was deceptive. "Sit down, lass. We must talk. Set the bird away." He helped her right the perch and waited as she set the calmed bird there. Then he took her arm gently to lead her to the bed, seating her on its edge, standing in front of her. He folded his hands inside his tunic sleeves.

"You betrayed my trust," she said.

"Isobel, I only agreed to bring a patrol with me because I was concerned for your welfare. We had to rescue you from the outlaws."

"What about Janet Crawford?" She glanced at Ralph Leslie, who sat on the leather stool nursing his wound, which he had wrapped in a cloth he found in the wooden chest.

"She is content here, though Lindsay wrongly believed she was held here against her will. She has been. . .a willing companion for Sir Ralph these weeks."

"You know better than that," she retorted. "You condoned it, even as a priest."

"I am more concerned with your well-being than hers. Your honor was threatened. You should be grateful we took you away. Sir Ralph wants you for his wife, and wants you to be a king's prophetess. It is a great honor." He reached for her hand, but she snatched it away. Her muscles ached from Ralph's rough handling.

"He told me. I refused."

She saw the priest exchange a quick look with Sir Ralph, their determination clear. But she could let them control her again. Those days were over.

"Isobel, listen to me," Father Hugh said. "For years I carefully wrote out your visions, and I knew they were too significant to keep to ourselves. I began announcing them from the pulpit—this you knew." She nodded. "And I sent copies to the Guardians of the Realm of Scotland and to other Scottish nobles."

"Why?"

"Because I believe they are extraordinary and the work of God. You could speak for kings, and now you will. I have been preparing a volume of what I have recorded and notated so far. I mean to send it to the Pope. I already sent a collection of your words, bound in leather, to King Edward."

"When you die, you could be a saint," Leslie snarled.

She stared from one to the other, incredulous. "Without my knowing? Those words belong to me, Father. I endured blindness and—and restriction to speak them."

"We did not consult you, knowing you would refuse in appropriate humility."

"Then you are also to blame for Aberlady being besieged," she said.

"We could not know the king would respond in that way. Your father only wanted your words shared with a select few. Robert Bruce. Wallace," the priest said sourly. "Sir Ralph and I decided they should go to King Edward." He had the audacity to beam at her, though she felt shocked. "We are fortunate in this patron."

"Patron!" She stood. "You want to gain status and goods in return!"

Ralph came forward to stand with Hugh. "I would be honored to see my wife so favored."

"To see yourself favored," she nearly spat out.

"The prophecies are most important here," Father Hugh said.

"I will never be part of your plan."

"You need us," Father Hugh said. "You understand little of your power. You are like ink for a pen, clay for a hand. Someone must take over from there."

"Father Hugh—the lass prophesied for the outlaw, but refuses to say what it was. We must find out what she said. She must tell us all she knows. I can convince her, I think."

"Aye, then," Father Hugh said.

Isobel stood, edging toward the door.

"I will get the damned hawk," Sir Ralph said, striding toward the perch, then rummaging through the falconer's pouch to pull out a small leather hood.

"He will foot you," she warned.

"Let him try," he said, managing to hood the hawk in one swift, forceful movement. The bird squawked but stilled on the perch. "Father!" he called.

Father Hugh nodded and pulled out a piece of dark cloth that was tucked in his belt that she had not noticed. He whipped it over her head and tied it firmly behind her head.

Darkness descended suddenly, and though she pulled at the blindfold, the priest took her hands and held them.

"If the blindness is forced upon you first, you might prophesy more readily," Father Hugh said. "Sir Ralph—do not hurt the lass. Stay back. Here, Isobel, sit."

Someone guided her back to the bed and pushed her to sit. She knew Leslie's rough, strong hands and the grip of a man who worked with weapons and gear and horses. Then he tied her hands behind her.

"Why do you do this? Father Hugh, I thought you a worthy priest! Why join in this treachery?"

"John Seton looked after the welfare of his only child," he replied. "Just as I cared for mine."

"Your—child?" She tilted her head, frowning. "Sir Ralph is your—son?"

"Aye. I watched him struggle in his youth, the bastard of a

priest. So I found a noble household to foster him, and made sure he was instilled pride and ambition in this temporal world. Now, Lady Isobel," he murmured, "with the darkness upon you, you can summon the visions."

She turned her head to shake off the blindfold, shake off the fear. "I will not."

Sir Ralph's hand clapped heavy on her shoulder. "All this talk of freedom and wildness and that devil of a gos over there has shown me the way to tame you."

"Tame me?" Her heart pounded. Now that she knew their relationship, she could not trust them to be anything but cruel, grasping, and in agreement.

He bent close. She could smell his breath. "I will keep you awake for days and nights, without food, without sleep, listening only to me." He caressed her shoulder as if it was a bird's wing. His whisper was cold as ice entering her veins. "When you are ready to obey me as your master and your husband, we will have prophecies great enough to please a very demanding king."

"Nay," she whispered, bowing her head. He laughed.

Chapter Twenty-Eight

J AMES GRIPPED THE chains, and with the strength in his arms and shoulders, raised his body weight so that his feet cleared the floor. He lowered himself, pulled up again, repeating it until his muscles ached for release.

"You will exhaust yourself," John Seton observed.

"What else is there to do?" he muttered. Wrapping his hands around the chains, he set his bootsoles against the wall and stretched his legs. "I have grown weak in here on a thin porridge and sour watered ale. I need my strength to get us out of here, and get Isobel and Janet free too."

John Seton grunted. "True, we have lost brawn and will in here."

"Not will. And I am gaining back the brawn. Especially when crumbs fall down in here from above." He extended his legs against the wall again, glancing up at the wooden planks that formed the ceiling—those same boards were part of the floor in a chamber overhead that was used by garrison soldiers as a dining hall. Sometimes when the men gathered for supper, small scraps of food would trickle down between the planks and fall to the dungeon floor. John and James would harvest the bits before mice could scurry in to grab the feast.

John looked up. "I hope they drop some chicken bones with a little flesh on them tonight. Your eye looks better and the bruises are fading."

James sat and squinted. "It is improving. I no longer see an old fool, but a friend."

Seton huffed. "And I see no outlaw, but the man my daughter loves. And I am thinking she is right to do so. I was wrong about you, lad. I treated her unfairly and she has rebelled. She was a bold child but became a timid woman. But she has changed recently. Bolder again."

"She has a strong will." James pinched back a smile. "And I intend to get out of here to help her and all of us."

"What is the plan?"

"I am thinking that if Janet comes back, she might be able to get a key. If not, when Leslie returns, and I trust he will, I will be ready for him. Let him try to come at me again," he said, drawing out the chain between his hands in a slither of steel. "If threatened, he may collapse and order us freed. That would give us a chance."

"But there are a hundred soldiers in this place."

"And one guard who showed us some favor. That may be enough. With even a few on our side, we can get free." Seeing Seton's doubtful expression, he sighed. "What other hope do we have?"

Once again he placed his feet to the wall and sat up, leaned back, curled forward, feeling his abdomen tighten, his legs work, feeling power and resolve surge through him.

He would be ready.

SHE WANTED A bath desperately. Isobel turned again to walk the length of the room, counting the steps, reaching the bed on the eleventh step, turning walking back to the bird's perch. With her hands tied behind her back, she twitched her messy, loosened hair over her shoulder and turned again.

She wanted a bath, a fresh gown, a meal in her belly. Most of all, she wanted to see James Lindsay again, wanted to know he was well, wanted to feel his arms and his love wrap around her like a cloak—and she deeply wanted to do the same for him.

Tears pricked her eyes behind the blindfold. She sucked in a breath. Ten steps, eleven.

Her toe caught the base of the perch. Gawain chirred, and she stood there, singing the *kyrie* softly, its haunting strain calming her as well as the bird. Turning, she walked again in darkness. The sound of larks and the newborn coolness of the morning wafted in through the window. Soon Ralph Leslie would return.

Her knees were wobbly with exhaustion, but she stayed on her feet. If he came in without warning again and found asleep, he would pull her to her feet, continuing his quest to treat her like a wild hawk to be broken.

For days, she had slept little, had scarcely eaten, had remained blindfolded and constrained. When Leslie was there, his voice was soft, cajoling, nauseating to her as he tried to convince her to rely on him, trust him, give in to him. His hands soothed over her and his voice murmured at her ear in a travesty of James's patience and kindness with the hawk—and with her.

Heeding his father's advice, Sir Ralph had allowed Janet to come to her briefly a few times a day, to assist her in whatever she needed, but Janet was forbidden to speak. Either the priest or his son, perhaps both, stood outside the door, listening. Isobel could almost feel the malevolence and control seeping through the oaken door. But Janet's whispers and bracing hugs brought solace and a little joy.

This morning, a couple of hours of sleep had managed to clear her head as she paced through the darkness of the blindfold, ignoring the sharp hunger in her belly and the equally keen fear in her heart.

If she prophesied for him, she could have anything, she knew that. He had repeated that he would allow her almost any request, even as his hands traveled the contours of her body. He had made only sweeping caresses, promising more when she became his wife. She could not bear to think about it.

The door latch rattled and she heard the creak of hinges. She whirled around.

"Isobel." Dear God, how she hated that voice now. "Come eat. You must be hungry."

She shook her head and backed away, counting steps until she reached the bird's perch. Ralph crossed the room.

"You are more stubborn than I thought." His hand touched her head. She leaned away. "But I have no time to wait upon your whim. You must give up. Tomorrow we journey to see the king."

She said nothing, her head lowered. She heard the goshawk stir nervously on the perch.

"Today," he said, "we will let that hawk go."

Isobel swallowed heavily. She sensed Ralph reach out to the bird—the sound of leather, the chirr of the hooded bird, blinded as she was. Other sounds told her that Gawain tore at some meat as Sir Ralph fed him.

"I will let the hawk go, and go to the dungeon to set your lover free—so he can go to God. If God will take him."

She licked her dry lips. "You—you will kill him?"

"I told you I would unless you do what I ask. My patience has gone. The king awaits, and there is no bargaining there. He will not show you any tolerance."

She brushed past him quickly, crossing to the bed, taking the moments to think. She did not doubt he try to would kill James, and her father, too, for the man had loyalty only to himself. Even Janet might fall victim to her lover's evil nature. As a last blow, the hawk would fly free.

She would lose everyone she loved if she clung to stubbornness now. But if she acted, she might be able to save them. Her own fate hardly mattered, suddenly, compared to the immeasurable value of those lives. Sir Ralph would be generous with her—she would not be harmed. She would only lose freedom. And love.

But if Jamie died, she would surely wither inside. At least she would know he was alive. She would exchange her chance at joy and peace for the good of those she loved. But she must speak now or lose the courage of the moment, for an empty feeling crept through her, sucking up hope and the future.

"What do you want?" she asked in a hollow tone. She knew well what it was. The question was her indication of surrender. She felt detached. Numb.

"Prophecies. And marriage, this very day."

She lifted her blindfolded head. "Then I ask a marriage boon." He waited. "I want them released. My father, James Lindsay, and Janet Crawford. If you let them walk away unharmed, I will agree to what you want."

She heard him approach, and she turned to walk to the window, feeling its soft, cool, early air on her face.

"Reasonable enough," he said, surprising her. "After we wed, I will release them."

"And leave the goshawk with me. He is mine now."

"Very well. If you promise all that I want, that is your marriage boon. I will tell Father Hugh to prepared for our wedding. Isobel—" He paused. "I hope to make you proud. You will be admired in the years to come."

She kept her back to him. "I do not care. I love another, and I want you to know I will only marry you in barter for his life, and the lives of Papa and Janet. I must have your solemn oath of honor."

He was silent.

"Swear it to me."

"I swear they will go free," he said. "On pain of my love for you." He opened the door and left.

ISOBEL'S HAIR GLEAMED like a skein spun from midnight as Janet combed it out before the brazier's glow. The girl had assisted Isobel through a bath, weeping freely, while Isobel sat nearly silent. Now she watched the goshawk on his perch, feeling as trapped as the bird.

Freed of her blindfold and wrist bonds, she took no satisfaction in any of it. Sir Ralph had provided a clean gown and a surcoat of deep blue samite, trimmed in embroidery and glass beads. The pretty things, along with a silk shift and a gauzy veil, were exquisite. He had said they were purchased and made in Edinburgh months ago in anticipation of their wedding.

She would not have cared if they had been rags. She stood passively while Janet dressed her. Through her own pain and disappointment, she sensed Janet's misery too.

"I am sorry," Isobel whispered. "I know you care for the man more than I ever could."

"I have no more affection for that priest's bastard," the girl hissed. "I weep for you, Isobel. And I do not know what to tell Jamie if Ralph truly lets us go."

"Tell him—that I wish him peace in his life. And freedom." She looked away.

Janet nodded and finished combing Isobel's hair, then arranged the veil over it, draping it under her chin and bringing it up, fastening it with a circlet of rolled white silk.

A knock on the door preceded Sir Ralph and the priest. Leslie, who carried something covered in a plain cloth, wore a surcoat of black wool trimmed in fur in honor of his wedding. Seeing Isobel, he widened his eyes. "You are—a beauty."

"Is it time for the ceremony already?" she asked.

"Soon. Janet, tell the guards to fetch our guests out of the dungeon and to the chapel."

"Guests!" Isobel burst out.

"Surely you want witnesses for your wedding," Leslie said.

Isobel stared flatly at him. "I do not."

"Nonetheless. Janet! Go now," he barked. With an uncertain look for Isobel, Janet left the room.

Father Hugh turned. "Lady Isobel, we must know what you told the outlaw. You will need to summon a vision for us before we go to the chapel."

"I cannot—"

"As a token of the promise you gave me," Leslie said, "you will do this now." What he carried was a bowl; he whipped the cloth away to reveal a gleam of water. "Sit there, and gaze into this."

Isobel sat in the leather-seated chair, but did not look at the water. Instead, she closed her eyes and saw, in her mind's eye, a pool deep inside a cave; and she heard the sound of water trickling down a rough stone wall. She might never enter that paradise again, yet its peace streamed through her. In memories, at least, she could still feel the refuge of love surround her.

Tilting her head, she watched new images form in her mind. Men in bloodied armor, wielding broadswords and axes; a tall, white-haired, old man on his deathbed; a nobleman in plaid and rags running through heather and bog; and the banner of Scotland whipping over a field beside a wide burn. Kings, rebellion, murder, battle—freedom.

She began to speak, and the darkness fell over her eyes.

Chapter Twenty-Nine

JAMES REACHED OUT, chains jangling, to assist John Seton in climbing the steep stairs, both of them wearing ankle and wrist cuffs and chains. At the top, they stepped into a yard. The dusty expanse was filled with sunset light. Several guards stood nearby.

He looked around warily. One of the soldiers who had brought them out of their cell had muttered that they were to be taken to the yard, but had said no more. Soldiers gathered to one side of the tower keep, where a small stone chapel jutted into the bailey. His parents had been married in that small church; he and his brother had been baptized there. He had knelt in prayer there countless times.

Now guards escorted James and John toward a small crowd that gathered along the steps of the chapel. On the steps in front of the arched entrance, he saw Isobel, Sir Ralph, and the priest he recognized from that ill-fated meeting in the forest. As he walked closer, he realized why they had been brought up here.

"Dear God, she is being married, here and now, on the steps of the church," her father said.

In silence, James moved ahead slowly. The profound weight of his sinking heart was a thousandfold heavier than the chains he wore.

The ceremony had already begun. He could hear the priest speaking the Latin of the ritual. He heard Sir Ralph's reply. After a moment he heard Isobel's uncertain answer.

She looked like a queen or a saint, framed within the curve of the arch. Gowned in sumptuous blue, with glints striking off sleeves and hem, she was willowy and elegant beside Sir Ralph's husky, vigorous form. The shimmering folds of the gauzy veil lent her face a fragile, ethereal beauty.

He stared, stunned and enthralled, struck deep to his soul.

Sir Ralph took her hand and slipped a ring on her finger. When he bent to kiss her, she leaned away, turning it awkward. Her groom turned to look out over the soldiers gathered there, saw James, and smiled, bitter and triumphant.

Isobel looked at no one. Leslie took her arm and spoke to her. She ignored him.

"Bastard," John growled. "He delayed bringing us here. I am her father, and he knew I would raise an objection. So would you."

James spun away in silence, feeling a tide of rage and anguish plunge through him like a killing blow, as when innocent Elizabeth had been killed; as when Wallace had been taken. He had survived those moments. He would survive this too, somehow. But he stood like a stone with his back to the church and the scene there.

"Jamie," Seton murmured. "Look at her. Look, sir. What do you see?"

James reluctantly glanced at her, so beautiful, so heartbreaking. Then he noticed the curious tilt of her head, the icy glaze in her eyes.

"Jesu," he breathed. "She is blind."

"Aye," John growled. "She must have prophesied for those bastards recently, and when she was defenseless, they led her into this marriage ceremony."

Rage rose within him, hot and nearly uncontrollable. He fisted his hands, felt his belly tighten. He looked about instinctively for a weapon, found none but the chains on his hands, which he would have wrapped around Leslie's throat if he could. Helpless and furious, he watched, unable to stop it.

"It is done," John Seton said. "They are bringing her into the church—the priest will bless and solemnize the occasion."

"There is no blessing in this," James growled. Hearing his name called, he turned.

Janet ran toward them, skirts flying, to grab Jamie's arm. "We will be released! They will escort us out of here now," she said breathlessly.

"What do you mean? Why?" As he spoke, four guards urged the three through the yard to the vaulted foregate tunnel, where the portcullis gate was being raised, pulleys squealing, to reveal the lowered drawbridge. The guards led them tromping across the wooden bridge to the grassy verge that stretched toward the woodland. James took in fresh, keen air, but the shock of the marriage ceremony had drained him and the iron cuffs weighed him down further. He merely stood, looking about.

One guard came forward with a large iron key and began to unlock John Seton's manacles, lifting the chains to hand to another guard. He did the same for James, who held out his arms in silence. The other sentries rested their gauntleted hands on daggers and swords in warning.

When cuffs and chains were removed, three guards walked back over the drawbridge, while the one holding the key stepped back, yet stayed. James recognized the same man who, days earlier, had refused to harm Isobel in the dungeon. He handed James a folded, sealed parchment.

"Safe passage from the commander of Wildshaw, allowing you to travel freely on his lands."

That bit deep—Leslie's lands! "Why are we being released?"

"I understand it was the bride's wedding boon. She required it as a condition of marriage."

Yet another blow, poignant and hard. "I see. Thank you for your help. Farewell—"

"Wait. Beware, Lindsay," the knight murmured. "Soldiers are hiding in the woods, ready to ambush the three of you. That, I believe, is a wedding gift from the groom."

James inclined his head. "Why do you warn us?"

"Your lady is much put upon of late. She would be further distressed by news of your death."

"She is not my lady," James said harshly.

"Is she not? She gave me that impression. And I am sorry you had to see her wed another."

James gave him a wary look. "Why take a risk in talking to me, sir? Though you have the chary look of a fine knight, not one to follow a man like Leslie."

"I am assigned and will fulfill my obligation. But I know Leslie, and do not trust him. I also admire what I know about the Scots. And I have heard of the bravery and cunning of the Hawk Laird."

"Good to hear, sir. But those are old triumphs. Few trust me now."

"Many still do. I was part of the guard the night Wallace was taken—and I saw what Leslie and the others, Menteith and such, did. I saw what you did too. That arrowshot was uncommon bravery."

"To no avail."

"Aye. I confess I felt fouled to be in their company that night. I have heard since how men trust and respect you. Inside Wildshaw there are Scottish soldiers who have given their pledges to Edward. But they know where their loyalty belongs." His eyes were a rich, sincere brown. "Many regret what happened to Wallace—and to you. Not all of us condone betrayal and injustice."

James stared in astonishment, then nodded to himself, deciding to take a chance. "Would those men—would you—step forward for the rightful laird of Wildshaw if he wished to reclaim his castle?"

The knight narrowed his eyes. "Possibly."

"Your name, sir?"

"Gawain of Avenel in Northumberland."

James huffed, amused. So this was the fellow. And weeks ago,

Isobel knew somehow that the name was significant when she gave it to the hawk. A sign to trust the knight, then. "I am pleased to know you, Sir Gawain. Should you ever be dissatisfied with your king and his deeds in Scotland, you are welcome to find me in the Ettrick Forest."

"I will consider it. One last thing. On the morrow, Sir Ralph will escort his bride south to Carlisle to see King Edward. They will pass through forestland—should you want to bid your lady adieu."

"I might."

Gawain pulled a dagger from his belt and tossed it away to land in the grass. "I dropped that. You might find it when I leave."

"We are sincerely in your debt, sir," James said, glancing at the two who had stood by and now nodded agreement. As Sir Gawain strode across the drawbridge, James turned to go with them.

His step had lightened with the chains removed. But as he shoved the dagger into his belt, he carried a leaden weight in the region of his heart.

"THAT HAWK IS getting fat," James said. He stretched out on the floor beside Alice's blazing hearth, leaned his head on his elbow, and looked up at Ragnell. The hawk perched on Alice's chair, her false silver foot shining in the firelight. She glared at him with a royal, reddish eye.

"She is fat because I overfeed her," Alice said. "I do not want her to fly away. And you, my lad, are drunk."

"Not yet," James said, as he took another sip of dark Rhenish wine from a leather flask.

Alice sighed and frowned at him. James cocked an eyebrow in response and took yet another swallow. His aunt turned her frown on all of them, one by one: his men, now including Sir Eustace, Sir John Seton, and Janet Crawford, who curled beside Alice's chair. The small room was crowded, dim, warm, a familiar and comfortable place that was yet tense and silent.

"What is to be done with him?" Alice asked the others.

"Leave him be," Patrick said. "He is heartbroke."

"If he wants to dive into his cups, let him," Henry Rose said.

"This is not like him," she told them.

"After what he went through this day," John Seton said, "who can blame him. We could all be dead inside Wildshaw even now. Leave him be. We witnessed an accursed marriage today. Pass that wine, lad, before you take it all down. I need some too."

James ignored them and sipped from the leather flask again. He disliked the stuff and had not intended to get drunk. But the more they discussed him and his state, the better the idea seemed.

"Heartbroken he may be," Janet said. "But he can do something about it."

"I have not decided what I will do about it," James drawled. A painful blend of anger, confusion, and hurt had roiled in him all day, barely faded by wine. He wanted to believe Isobel loved him. But he yet wondered about the choice she had made. "Lady Isobel does not want a forest outlaw, it seems. Naught makes that so clear as a wedding."

"Do not be a sodding fool," Janet said. "Go get her."

"I do not the sharp side of your tongue, my darling."

"Gawain of Avenel told you about Sir Ralph's route through the forest for a reason," Janet said. "He gave us the chance to win her back. We cannot ignore that."

"She chose luxury and protection—in my own castle—over life with an outlaw. Who could blame her?"

"Against her will," Janet said. "I told you that. Sir Ralph forced her into this by threatening all our lives."

"You said she wished me peace in my life, and went about donning wedding finery that I could never have afforded for her. She made a practical choice."

"She hates and fears him. He will use her for gain. Steal her back, you fool!"

"The English king will favor her. She will be honored. She will not be well kept."

"She will not be *happy*," Janet snapped. "Do you love her or not?"

"I will not take another man's wife. Even a drunken rogue has morals."

"Make her a widow," Quentin said quietly.

James slid his friend a long look. Quentin folded his arms, stretched out his long bare legs from under the wrapped plaid, and regarded him calmly.

"Make her a widow," Quentin repeated. "I will help you."

"And I," Henry Rose said. Patrick echoed agreement.

Eustace leaned forward. "I know Leslie well, and my loyalty has ever been to John Seton of Aberlady and his daughter. And James Lindsay, you have my respect." He gazed steadily at James. "I will help you as well."

"We are always at your back," Patrick said. "You know that."

"I am with you too." Geordie sat up where he lounged on Alice's bed. "I have a good hand with a sword and I am recovering."

"Now that I have a good meal in my belly," John Seton said, "I believe I could run with you lads myself."

James looked at each one, frowning deeply.

"And my hand is steady with a bow," Janet said. "Besides, I have my own grudge against Sir Ralph Leslie."

"As do we all, on your behalf," Patrick growled, looking at her.

"So, James Lindsay. If you want to know why your lady married that fellow," Alice said, "stop her escort and ask her yourself."

James felt his throat tighten. Their loyalty stirred him to the roots of his soul. The trust and support of these few willing, loving friends were riches enough for a lifetime.

But there was one whose shining, gentle faith in him was as elemental to his soul as water to his body. As long as she was missing from his life, as long as she was threatened or unhappy, he would feel it. And he would never find the peace that he craved without her.

"Aye, then. How shall we go about it?"

"My strong advice to you, my son," Father Hugh said, "is to wait."

"Wait!" Sir Ralph protested.

Seated in blindness on the edge of the bed in the tower chamber, Isobel listened to their conversation. Silent, she folded her hands in her lap and felt grateful toward the priest for that, at least.

"Wait," Father Hugh said. "The blindness does not last long. Soon she will be sighted again, and willing."

Never that, Isobel thought to herself.

"She is not a virgin, I vow, so what does it matter," Sir Ralph whined. Isobel suspected he was quite drunk, judging by the amount of wine and ale he had consumed at supper. She had heard a good deal of slurping and pouring beside her, while she had eaten and sipped very little.

"We cannot change her sorry state," Father Hugh said. "Although you could have avenged yourself rather than release the knave who did that. But remember, Ralph. Her gift is fragile. As long as she is blind, she is in a state of grace brought on by the holy word of God that comes through her."

"So I cannot touch her. Damn it," Leslie muttered.

Isobel sat straight and demure, and tried then to look innocent and saturated in grace. If she remained blind—or claimed she was—she would keep her groom away from her longer.

But both men knew the blindness would go away in a day or less. Her reprieve would end.

She heard Ralph's heavy step as he crossed the room, and she sensed him standing in front of her. "One kiss. She is my bride."

"One chaste kiss to mark the marriage," Father Hugh agreed. "But do not offend the integrity of her prophetic gift. You will not touch her until the blindness passes."

"By then we will be in Carlisle, visiting the king. A fine place for a nuptial celebration."

Isobel felt his fingers slide along her chin, felt him tip her head up as he bent forward. His lips touched hers, pressed, opened slightly. She closed her eyes, keeping her lips together beneath his. But he slanted his mouth over hers and she felt the repulsive flicker of his tongue as his hand slid over her shoulder. The kiss was wine-flavored and somehow desperate. She flinched away.

He lifted away and stood back. "Good night, wife." She heard both men leave the room.

Her eyes flew open. For once, she was very glad the blindness lingered.

—— ◆··• •··◆ ——

Chapter Thirty

MIST DRAPED BETWEEN the trees as the group made their way along the forest path. Leather trappings, chain mail, and the stomp and snort of the horses created layers of sound as the travelers moved through the cool, silent morning. Isobel rode at the center of a group of a dozen men flanked by Sir Ralph and Sir Gawain. Father Hugh rode in front with several soldiers; several more rode armed and mounted behind Isobel at the center.

She carried the hawk on her gloved fist as they rode through the fog-shrouded forest. With the blindness cleared, she savored the simple beauty of the morning. One night's sleep had restored her vision, and unfortunately, she had not been able to hide that from Leslie and his father. She tried to ignore Sir Ralph's eagerness and the spin of dread in her gut as they moved toward Carlisle.

Her groom seemed anxious, looking around, hand on the hilt of his sword. "The guards who went out yesterday have not returned. Do we know if they did what they were told?" he asked Sir Gawain.

"I do not know, sir," the knight replied.

Isobel gasped as a terrible feeling cut through her. "Did you send an ambush after my father and Lindsay? And Janet?" she demanded, horrified.

Ralph slid her a glance. "No need to concern yourself."

"We may need to worry more about the guards than the outlaws," Sir Gawain murmured. He cast her a glance that somehow made her feel reassured.

After a while, hoofbeats quiet and steady on the forest floor, a cloaked figure stepped through the mist to stand on the path ahead of them. Holding a large hawk on a gloved hand, the figure was tall and statuesque—and the hawk had a silver foot. Isobel gasped.

"Alice," she mouthed to herself, as the escort drew to a halt. The woman dropped her hood and stepped forward.

"Sir Ralph Leslie," Alice called. "I beg a word, please."

"Do not stop," Sir Ralph said. "We have naught to say to you, and we are in hurry. Stand aside, woman!"

As he spoke, Alice raised her arm and cast off the bird, who flew toward the escort. Leslie shrieked and ducked and the men leaned away in alarm as the huge red tail hawk swooped past. Then Ragnell slanted sideways to disappear between the trees, and Alice slipped away, too.

On Isobel's glove, Gawain, frightened out of his wits by the bird, fell into a ferocious bate. She extended her arm to accommodate him while Leslie snarled and looked around, his hand at his sword.

Next, a slight rumble of sound was the only warning as suddenly an enormous log burst out of the treetops, suspended sideways on long ropes, and swung down toward the front group of guards and the priest. The men guided their horses away, but the log crashed into them to sweep them off their horses like chessmen off a board. Among the mist-veiled trees, men on foot scattered like deer.

"After them!" Sir Ralph screamed, vying to control his startled horse amid chaos. Isobel struggled to hold both her horse and the frantic hawk, still hanging from her glove in a fit.

The soldiers to the rear could hardly control their frantic horses, some of them falling, others carried off into the woodland. Leslie, Sir Gawain, one guard, and Isobel, having been at the center of the group, remained mounted. Father Hugh and several guards lay moaning on the ground while their horses stomped and circled or ran frightened into the forest.

Then Isobel saw three men and a woman emerge through the trees to walk toward them on the path. They carried bows, stretched and arrowed and ready, as they advanced. James—with Quentin, Patrick, and Janet.

Isobel gasped to see them, while Sir Ralph swore hoarsely and grabbed the hilt of his sword. Trembling, Isobel shifted the exhausted goshawk to her fist and watched the others, her heart pounding in anticipation.

Quentin, Patrick, and Janet came forward, bows ready. Janet stopped and raised her arrow tip to aim it at Sir Ralph, while Patrick and Quentin trained their bolts on the men lying on the ground.

"Janet! Put that away!" Leslie shouted.

"If you move, I will put this arrow away in you, sir," she said. As she spoke, James walked between through the group.

"What are you waiting for? Get him!" Sir Ralph yelled at Sir Gawain and the other guard.

Isobel saw the guard glance at Gawain, then shook his head in refusal.

"God's bones!" Leslie snapped. "Gawain! Take care of them!"

Sir Gawain shoved back his chain mail hood, his dark hair whipping in the breeze. "I cannot do that, sir," he said, and circled his horse to ride toward the outlaws. The guard went with him. Sir Ralph snarled curses after them.

All the while, James moved closer, his stride long and sure, and the others came with him, their bows trained on Sir Ralph. Then Isobel saw her father standing at the edge of the path just as Sir Gawain and the other soldier halted their horses near him.

Ralph grabbed the hilt of his sword, the steel chiming as he pulled it free. Instantly an arrow sailed just past his ear to land in the earth beside his horse, which sidestepped. Patrick set another arrow in his bow as Leslie sheathed his sword slowly.

"What do you want?" he demanded. "Do you mean to rob us?"

"You do carry a treasure we want," James said. "Black Isobel of Aberlady." He stood on the path, gripping his upright, loaded bow. Isobel saw wariness and power in every line of his body, and saw a fierce, cool glint in his blue eyes. She wanted desperately to leap from her horse and run to him, but kept her seat, holding the hawk, suddenly uncertain. Surely he was furious with her for marrying Leslie.

"If you take her, you directly offend King Edward, who is waiting to welcome her," Sir Ralph growled. "And she is my wife now, as you know. So you have no right to claim her."

"I do not care about offending Edward of England—or you. I wish to speak with Lady Isobel," James said. Isobel frowned, watching, her heart quickening.

"She does not speak to brigands." Sir Ralph looked around as if hoping to see the return of his guards or the recovery of the men lying on the ground. "Step aside!" He urged his horse forward. "Come ahead, Isobel."

Patrick released another arrow. The bolt slammed into the ground in front of Sir Ralph's horse as it stepped back with a whinny. "Halt! The man wishes to speak with Lady Isobel," Patrick snarled.

Behind him, others emerged from the trees to stand guard over the fallen soldiers, some of whom began to stir. James came closer.

He moved toward Isobel's horse and looked up at her, his gaze keen, the hand wrapped around the upright bow white-knuckled. She held the hawk on her fist and gazed at him, calm as she could.

"Lady Isobel, tell me this," he said. "Will you choose safe passage through the forest"—his voice had such power, resonating in the air, in her very being—"or will you follow a different path with an outlaw?"

She caught her breath. "I would—"

"Enough!" Sir Ralph snapped. "The king awaits her. If you touch the prophetess, you will be hunted down by English soldiers. Isobel, if you leave me, these outlaws will die. I will see to it."

Uncertain, she glanced from him to James. On the glove, the hawk chittered, restless.

"Edward's men have hunted me before, and so have you." James dropped the bow and shouldered it. "Isobel, make your choice."

Yearning welled up inside of her, tugging between her and James. But she knew they would never be safe from Leslie and the English if she went with him. "I made a choice yesterday. You are free now because of that." *And I am trapped.*

"You have your answer. Clear the way!" Leslie took the reins of Isobel's horse and drew her along with him. "You will have safe passage and she has made her choice. Be gone!"

James snatched the bridle of Isobel's horse. "My lady, are you eager to see the English king?"

"I am not. This is much against my will."

"Then you must be in need of a rescue," he drawled.

"I am," she said breathlessly.

He yanked out his dagger and sliced through the taut reins that Ralph held. Then he shoved her horse aside and squared his stance in the path, raising his bow again.

Circling her horse, one hand on the reins and the other engaged with the agitated hawk, she halted at the edge of the path, watching anxiously. Her father stepped toward her then, and Sir Gawain walked his horse toward her, both men flanking her.

Sir Ralph grabbed the hilt of his sword again to draw it free. But in one swift, powerful motion, James loosed his bow to strike the man under the arm, the blow unseating him. He slammed to the ground with a loud grunt, the arrow clattering away, having done little damage.

Isobel quailed to see the dark fury in James's expression as he strode toward Ralph, who lay on his back awkwardly attempting to pull his long, heavy sword from its scabbard—until James flicked the blade deftly with his bow and sent it spinning. Ralph rolled to scramble away, but James hauled him to his feet by a handful of the black surcoat.

"Do not go anywhere just yet," he said. "I have some questions for you." He shoved him forward as Leslie stumbled, then set his back against a tree, and jammed the long side of his bow under the shorter man's chin to pin him back against the trunk. "Did you touch her?" he demanded.

"She is my wife," Leslie gasped.

"Did—you—touch—her?" James repeated in a growl.

Ralph blinked rapidly without answer, and James tightened the press of the bow against the man's throat, continuing to growl questions toward him.

Turning, Isobel gestured to ask her father's help to dismount from the horse. Standing, the hawk securely on her fist, she lifted the hem of her blue silk gown and crossed the path toward the tree. Janet fell into step with her, bow half-raised as they approached the tree together.

"James," Isobel said. "He did not touch me." Close enough to the truth, and she did not want more bloodshed on her account. Sir Ralph nodded rapidly, his face red.

"Isobel, stand back," James said, without looking at her. "Tell me this," he said to his captive. "Were you part of a conspiracy to betray William Wallace?"

"Menteith and others," Leslie gasped. "I did not know all of them. They planned it. Wallace stepped beyond his position. His rebellion interfered with Scottish nobles trying to seek peace with England. 'Twas decided he should be—stopped. We only wanted peace with England."

"Peace?" James snarled. "You wanted land and wealth, so you destroyed the greatest voice for freedom in Scotland. Then you went after me with a vile rumor."

"Not true, not true," the man gasped.

"Of course it is true. Because you wanted to ensure your

claim to Wildshaw—taken from me and handed to you by Edward."

Isobel placed her hand over her mouth. On her fist, the hawk beat his wings and squawked.

Sir Ralph narrowed his eyes. "I have it, and now the woman you want is lady of Wildshaw as my wife. And that pleases me well," he rasped out, though his eyes glittered.

James stared, breath heaving. Isobel could see the tension in him soaring. But suddenly he stepped back, pulled the bow away, and landed a violent blow to Ralph's jaw, dropping him to his knees with a retching groan.

James turned away from him, his face dark with anger. "Quentin," he growled, "make her a widow if you want. I will not sully my hands with that foul bastard any further."

Ralph uttered a roar and leaped after James, dragging on his legs, pulling both men to the ground. Standing close by, Isobel stumbled back, and saw the flash of a dagger emerge and plunge toward James's back. She screamed out a warning—

The hawk bated furiously, pulling upward with such strength that Isobel was thrown off balance, falling to her knees in a tangle of blue silk, gloved hand smacking against the earth. The movement loosened the jesses, and the goshawk tore away in a flurry of wings.

He veered and rose into the air, shrieking. Isobel got to her feet, watching the vanishing hawk, gasping with fright and panic. Only a few feet away, James and Ralph wrestled with the dagger, while Quentin, Patrick, and Janet stepped forward with bows ready should they separate.

Ralph Leslie snatched the blade and tried to bring it to James's throat but Lindsay had a deadly grip on his wrist. They twisted and turned until James reared back to slam his head against Sir Ralph's brow so that the man fell back, knife tumbling away.

James rose to his knees, stood, wiping his face. Isobel moved toward him, but screamed to see Leslie suddenly roll, snatched the dagger, and throw it point first at James's back.

Whirling to avoid the blade, James leaped forward—just as Leslie sank with a horrible cry, an arrow puncturing his chest. Isobel covered her mouth, unsure who had done it, while James dropped to his knees and bent over the fallen man.

"He is dead," he said flatly, shoving back his hair in exhaustion, standing again.

Overwhelmed, Isobel felt shaky and ill with panic. She looked around to see others gathering around the body, including her father with Father Hugh, who looked gray and stricken. A few guards stepped forward and Sir Gawain turned to speak with them.

James turned toward Isobel. She sobbed out and rushed the few steps toward him. As the warm bliss of his arms surrounded her, she sobbed out again.

"Oh God, are you hurt?" she asked.

"Fine," he said. She sank against him in relief and anguish. "There, soft, you," he murmured.

"The hawk—" she began.

"I know," he whispered. "I know."

"James," she said, "who shot Ralph?"

He lifted his head to look at those gathering around Leslie's form, and she looked there too. Janet now fell to her knees beside the body, her bow clutched upright in her hand, the nocked arrow gone. She covered her face with one hand and bent as if crying.

Patrick knelt beside her and put an arm around her, pulling her close, his big, rough fingers gentling over her red hair.

"Dear God," Isobel breathed. "She saved your life."

"I owe her."

"We both owe her," Isobel said, lifting a trembling hand to his sweaty, beard-rasped cheek.

From overhead came a cry, and Isobel looked up to see a streak of gray and cream fly between two trees. "Gawain!" She pointed.

The goshawk sailed overhead like an angel, the underside of

his wings pale, his legs golden. He canted sideways and sliced between birches, keeling a long cry as he went.

"We must call him back to us," James said. "He could get those jesses caught in a tree."

Isobel stepped away from his arms, her glove still on her hand. She tugged it on securely and began to run after the hawk as the bird cut between the trees, vanishing, appearing again. Isobel ran, holding her skirts high as she sprinted. James pounded behind her, taking a different angle.

The hawk sailed through the treetops, darting in and out, a shining prince in the sunlight that caught the tips of his wings. He rowed the air, glided, rowed and glided again, rising high and then skimming low, effortless mastery in the air. She called out, holding up her arm. He dipped and wheeled in a circle, and she followed.

She heard James nearby, calling and whistling. He dashed between the trees, and Isobel looked up to realize she had lost sight of the bird. Standing still, breath heaving, she watched and waited.

Then she lifted her head to begin singing. Her voice rose and fell with the natural rhythms of the chant. Moments later, she heard *kee-kee-kee-keer*—and ran toward it.

Off to the side, the melody rose through the trees again as James took up the chant this time, singing the plainsong in his mellow voice, letting it rise and flow in a tranquil current, a serene veil of sound. Isobel ran toward him.

Above, the goshawk wheeled and glided to a high treetop. Isobel ran, skimming through the forest, skirts billowing, veil lost somewhere, hair loose and flying. For a moment, she felt the exquisite freedom of her own flight—away from Leslie and the threats of the past, and toward James.

He waited. She slowed, went toward him. When he pointed, she looked up. The goshawk sat on the pinnacle of a tall tree, the sun striking silver off his wings. Drawing a breath, James began the chant again, an arc of floating sound. The hawk dipped his head and began to preen.

"He might not come to us," she said softly. "He might decide for freedom."

James looked up. "I cannot blame the lad for that. But he's jessed. We will have to get him back. Lift your arm, Isobel."

She did, and waited. The goshawk ignored her. James took her hand in his and began to sing; she joined him in a blend of voices.

Then the hawk lifted his wings and streamed downward on an angle, calling as he came, as if to join the song. He fluttered to the outstretched glove easily, as if nothing much had happened. Isobel laughed softly.

"He came back!" She smiled through tears. "He saw us as one master."

James wrapped the jesses securely around her fingers. Then he reached into the leather pouch at her waist to find a bit of food for the bird. While the goshawk bit at his reward, James smiled down at her. "I think he recognized two masters," he murmured, "with one heart between them."

He lowered his head to give her a lingering kiss, then wrapped an arm around her to nestle her close. The hawk perched on her fist and blinked at them as James slanted his mouth over hers. Then he drew back to sift back a stray lock of her hair.

"Keep good hold of that hawk, love," he said.

"I will," she answered, smiling.

"The wind is gentle today. Never let a hawk go on a soft downwind. 'Tis a sure way to lose a valuable bird."

"You never told me that before," she said.

"Ah, well." He turned with her to walk toward the others. "There is much left to teach you."

"I have learned a good deal about hawks already."

"You have. We both have," he murmured. "But there is more I want to show you, my love. So much more. And we will find the time now, aye?"

"Oh, aye, my love," she whispered.

$$\text{—◆··• •··◆—}$$

Epilogue

J AMES STRIPPED OUT of his breeches and dove into the water, cleaving the still surface with a soft splash. The chill hit him like a shock, and he rose, gasped for air, and dipped again, gliding through the water. His muscles warmed as he went, his powerful strokes creating wavelets.

He swirled at the far end, kicked out and turned back, glad of the warmer water at that end, where he had piled hot stones. He surged upward to stand chest high, sluicing his hair back.

Isobel stood at the side of the pool, watching him. Torchlight flooded its amber glow over her tall, slender figure, clad in a simple silk shift. She smiled.

"They are all sleeping by now," she said. "Quentin, Patrick, Janet, Sir Gawain—and Gawain the gos, too. We talked so long after you left us that I thought you might be gone when I got down here."

He swirled the water with his hand and beckoned. "I would wait for you forever, lass. Come in."

She tilted her head. "We have visitors to our high crag very soon after our marriage, husband. I was hoping we might be alone longer. Though I love them all dearly," she added.

"We have been wed a month—and we have matters that need attention. Quentin and Patrick, and Gawain of Avenel too— who is proving a fine ally—brought some interesting news."

"I know." She looked down and trailed a toe in the water. "I was glad to hear their news too. Janet said Alice and Eustace are getting on quite well, did you know? She says they giggle like bairns. Janet thinks it is wonderful. Even Ragnell likes Eustace."

He laughed. "A very good sign. Alice has been lonesome a long while. What of your father?"

"He went with Henry Rose and Geordie to Aberlady to look over the damage. My father wants to rebuild, but he must consult with the Guardians of the Realm about that. They may ask him to wait for fear of another English attack. If so, he wants to join your band of rogues."

"He would be welcome now that he is regaining his health. To be honest, years may pass before John or I can hold our own castles again. Wildshaw is still garrisoned, but Sir Gawain and I have a plan. We mean to take it to Robert Bruce, who is gathering forces to help win back Scottish castles."

"'Twill be yours soon enough, I think. I feel it is so."

"Do you now? Come in, lass."

"Quentin said more and more local men are talking of joining you. That may gather enough men one day to take Wildshaw back."

"I intend that to happen. I will request a meeting with Robert Bruce soon." He splashed a wavelet toward her. "Come in the water, lass."

She smiled. "Quentin said Father Hugh left to make a pilgrimage to Dunfermline, and on to Saint Andrews."

"I know. Father Hugh may go down to Canterbury and then on to Saint James at Compostela. He feels a deep need to cleanse his soul of the pride that he thinks caused his son's ambition and downfall."

Isobel dropped down to sit on the edge of the pool, drawing up her hem and swirling her bare legs in the water. "'Tis warm at this end. It may be cold where you are."

He surged toward her, dipping down to submerge his chest and shoulders in the water. "Come find out what it is like near me," he said.

"Do you know that Janet still feels the burden of killing Ralph?" She watched the rippling surface of the pool as she spoke. "I did what I could to help comfort her."

"She did what any of us might have done. But she must find peace with the matter."

"Patrick asked her to wed him, did you know?"

"That does not surprise me." He splashed water toward her.

"She refused. Though she loves Patrick, she likes her freedom. She needs time to think."

"Aye, well," he said, "some of us take time to decide who to wed. And some of us know from the first moment." When she cast him a glance, he smiled.

"Did you know from the first moment?" she asked.

"I knew my heart had been breached that first evening," he said softly. "But it took me a while to accept defeat."

"Naught could ever defeat you, brigand." She kicked a little water toward him. He came closer. "I know Quentin and Patrick saw your friend John Blair in Dunfermline, and they said he has urgent news for you. Will you leave soon?"

"I must," he answered somberly. "I want to show him the letter from the bishop concerning Wallace and Bruce. I want John to deliver the letter to Bruce himself, with a note that includes the words of the prophetess of Aberlady. That message will give him hope, I think. She predicted he would be king of Scotland soon, and eventually save Scotland from English domination."

"Did she? Then do tell him. James—Quentin said you have another matter in Dunfermline."

He sighed. The summons from John Blair involved brief mention of a clandestine task that made visiting the abbey imperative. "There is something I must do."

"Can I ask—" She hesitated. "I care what you care about, whatever is important to you."

James sighed. He could share this with so very few—just those who had to know, those he absolutely trusted. But he knew she was one of them. "We—John Blair and Quentin and I—have something we must do together to—honor Will Wallace yet. There is no one else to see it done. We hope to give him peace at last. Beside his mother," he murmured.

"You," she said then. "The pilgrim I saw in a vision, standing beside a tree."

"Aye." He spoke to the water's gleaming surface. To himself, his soul.

She watched him. "Will you find peace for yourself then?"

"Someday." He smiled ruefully, shaking his head to dispel the burden for now. Sinking down as if to wash it away, he rose and pushed water toward Isobel to ripple about her slender legs. "Come find out how peaceful I feel," he teased.

She shook her head. "You come out. I am cold."

"Let me warm you." He surged forward and reached up to take her waist, pulling her into the water with a deep splash. She gasped, her shift floating around her like a cloud. He grasped it and pulled it off in one easy motion, while she lifted her arms to assist him.

Draping her arms around his neck, she curved her body into his, and he leaned with it. Against his chest, her breasts felt divinely soft, and her body fitted to his like glove to hand.

"I did not want to come in. The reflections in the water and the sound of the spring could bring on a vision."

"You do not want another vision?" He brushed his lips over her cheek.

"Not just now," she answered.

"If you had a vision," he said, "I would kiss the darkness from your eyes."

"Would you?" She sought his mouth in a sweet kiss, then another.

Enfolding her in his arms, sinking down with her, he floated back a bit, covering her mouth with his in a kiss that stirred deep through his body, a salve for his soul as well. She wrapped her legs around his waist, the water lapping in warm currents about them.

"Jamie," she whispered. "I want you to find peace now that the threat is over."

"Over? Not for a long while. You yourself predicted that, seeing what the rest of us may not." He framed her face in his hands, her wet hair streaming down to pool like midnight around them. Her eyes were wide and beautiful, opalescent as moonlight. He kissed her eyelids, her brow, drew back to look at her. "Part of me may never find true peace, with one deed weighing on my heart. I may never forgive myself for that. But I am thankful each day for what you have brought to me."

"I know something is yet unresolved in your heart. I understand that. But here in this paradise, we can always find sanctuary."

"My love." He kissed her again, then set his hands on her hips, drawing her against him under the water. He wanted to surround her, immerse in her, soul and body. He kissed her again, so that she arched against him and mewed a little, the sound making his body surge. His hands drifted along to support her more fully. "We will always find peace together, wherever we are. Now, my love—"

"Now, my love," she breathed against his lips. "Now and always."

Requiem

THE HAWTHORN TREE stood in a gentle dawn rain, its leaves turned upward to catch the moisture. A man in a pilgrim's cloak strode toward the abbey church, pulling up his hood against the rain as he crossed the grass along the north side of the church. Tranquil plainsong floated out from within the abbey, where monks sang to welcome the hour of prime in rain and candlelight.

A few people stood in the arched shadow of the church entrance. Friends all, waiting for him. He treasured their faith and support, but this task he had to do alone.

A plain wooden box sat on the grassy mound beneath the hawthorn tree. James knelt on the damp grass, bowed his head, and folded his hands in prayer. Then he set to his task. The box was modest in size, nailed shut, latched in iron and fitted with an iron cross. Its sad contents were the broken earthly remnants of a brilliant and courageous man.

Rain beat a quiet rhythm on the wood as James brushed the drops away. Over several weeks, Quentin and Patrick had traveled in four directions to search out and reclaim the mournful remains of a great leader. Gathering the sun-bleached bones in the box, they brought it at last to Dunfermline Abbey, where some of Scotland's kings, queens, saints, leaders, and citizens had been laid to rest over the centuries. Under the tree, a single secret grave lay hidden. A cloth covered a new gap in the earth.

Murmuring another prayer to honor his friend, James stood,

removed the cloth to reveal the cavity, and lifted the box to set it deep in the earth. Then he reached up to pull a few sprigs from the hawthorn tree, scattering them over the box before he took up a spade to fill the hole. When that was done, he patted torn grassy sods back into place, fitting them so that the grass would grow together to hide the two graves.

He glanced at the friends who watched and waited and prayed, then finished his task. A prophetess had once spoken of the laird of the wind, the pilgrim who had a penance of the heart. Today, each prayer he said, each shovelful of earth he lifted, was part of that penance, acts of humility and love, and a request for forgiveness.

He owed William Wallace that much and more. The rest of the debt might take an eternity to repay. But for now, perhaps he could find an elusive peace.

Standing back, he bowed his head. *"Requiem aeternum dona eis, Domine,"* he whispered. *"Requiescat in pace,* my friend." He turned away.

She walked toward him then, gliding over the damp grass like a sylph, like an angel. Her eyes were beautiful in the rainy half-light, filled with a love offered without question. Her gentle spirit had given him the sense of redemption that had finally freed him. He would always be grateful to her for that.

The goshawk on her glove chirred and fluttered his wings, and she lifted her fist to cast him off. He flew the short distance to the hawthorn tree, where he settled to wait out the rain.

As Isobel moved closer, James held out his hand.

Author's Note

At Dunfermline Abbey, a hawthorn tree grows in a small graveyard on the north side of the church. Longstanding tradition says William Wallace's mother is secretly buried under the tree. But a lesser-known tradition claims that Wallace himself may be buried beside his mother, although no archaeological investigation has been made. The legend is enough; Wallace is a hero in Dunfermline.

According to local legend, the Benedictine monk John Blair, along with a friend, collected Wallace's remains from the four towns where they had been put on display. They placed them in a secret grave near the abbey, possibly beneath the same thorn tree where Wallace's mother lay.

John Blair, Wallace's confessor and a rebel fighter himself, retired to Dunfermline Abbey after Wallace's death to write a chronicle of his friend's life. The Latin manuscript was apparently sent to Pope Boniface, but has been lost to history. Supposedly, the fifteenth-century poet Blind Harry had seen a copy, using Blair's chronicle when he wrote his well-known life of Wallace.

Whether or not the legend of the grave is true, I could not resist exploring its fictional potential. I am grateful to Bert MacEwen of Abbot House in Dunfermline for telling me about the legend. At the time, we stood looking at the hawthorn tree, which was in spring bloom: a beautiful old tree in a peaceful spot.

The hawking techniques described in this novel are, for the most part, authentic to the time period and taken from early treatises on hawking, such as *The Boke of St Albans* and *A Jewell for Gentrie*. I was fortunate to observe falconers and their birds, a tiercel goshawk and a red-tailed hawk, and to speak with falconers regarding modern and medieval techniques. The chance to spend an afternoon watching the behavior of a rambunctious goshawk in training was invaluable, and the high-strung temperament of Gawain the goshawk in the novel is based on that bird's hotheaded, keenly intelligent, fascinating mystery.

Prophets and prophetesses were held in awe and suspicion both in medieval times, and in Scotland particularly, they had the respect of commoner and king alike; the witch hunts of medieval Europe, for the most part, occurred outside of Scotland until the late sixteenth century. One of the best-known among medieval Scottish prophets is Thomas of Ercildoune, or Thomas the Rhymer, who died in 1298, yet predicted events that came about centuries later. Historical evidence indicates that Thomas of Ercildoune may have acted as a spy under Robert the Bruce. In upcoming novels, I explore Thomas the Rhymer's legacy in Robert Bruce's Scotland. Please look for *The Scottish Bride, The Forest Bride,* and *The Guardian's Bride*—where we also revisit James Lindsay, Isobel Seton, and friends.

One question touched on in the novel is the puzzle of who betrayed Wallace; the historical record, as so often happens, does not reveal the full truth. The possibility exists that Robert Bruce, Earl of Carrick, who became King of Scots months Wallace's death, may have known about it. However, factual evidence indicates that Bruce secretly supported Wallace. Experts in Scottish medieval history in the time of Bruce and Wallace, including G.W.S. Barrow, one of the foremost authorities on the Scottish Wars of Independence, suggest that there are far more likely candidates. The man most often suggested, based on extant documents, is Sir John Menteith, a Scottish noble who supported King Edward of England, as so many Scotsmen did, either willingly or forced to the choice to protect their own.

James Lindsay and Isobel Seton were created within the

stream of historical truth, shaped and defined by what did happen, as well as by what could have happened, long ago. I hope you enjoyed their story as an entertaining romantic adventure solidly based in fact. I am always careful in my research, and I respect established and reasonable historical fact (an instinct that comes from years of training in graduate school!). Yet I'm a storyteller too, so I happily let go of footnotes and facts to weave accuracy, authenticity, and fiction together in a framework of history and romance. I hope the seams are always neatly hidden.

Thank you for reading my stories!

Susan

About the Author

Susan King is the bestselling, award-winning author of (so far) 28 historical novels and novellas, a hefty nonfiction history, and dozens of magazine and web articles on education and the craft of writing. Her books, including mainstream historicals Lady Macbeth: A Novel and Queen Hereafter: A Novel of Margaret of Scotland, have been published by Penguin, Random House, HarperCollins, Kensington, ePublishingWorks, and Dragonblade. Praised for historical accuracy, lyrical writing, and storytelling quality, she is a USA Today bestselling author with numerous awards, nominations, and career achievement awards as well as starred reviews from Publisher's Weekly, Booklist, and Library Journal. Most of her books are set in Scotland ranging from the 11th to the 19th centuries.

Susan is a former university lecturer in art history, a private school teacher, and a founding member of one of the longest-running author blogs, "Word Wenches" (wordwenches.com). She holds a Bachelor's in studio art and English literature, a Master's in art history, and completed most of her Ph.D./ABD in medieval art history. Raised in Upstate New York, she lives in Maryland with her husband and three sons in an ever-growing family.

Website – www.susanfraserking.com

9 781963 585193